Twenty Thousand Leagues Under the Sea

A strange sea monster... faster than any ship, and impenetrable. Bullets and harpoons bounce off its surface. A sea monster, or an underwater vessel?

Through a series of exciting events, three men accidentally become passengers on the *Nautilus* and prisoners of the mysterious Captain Nemo. The strange commander has broken all ties with the civilized world and is determined to keep his deep sea travels a secret. Like it or not, the three men are taken on a fantastic voyage of discovery and adventure many miles below the ocean's surface.

Twenty Thousand Leagues Under the Sea is an amazing piece of literature. Amazing because at the time when it was written, the first submarine had not been constructed or conceived, and the undersea world not yet explored.

Twenty Thousand Leagues Under the Sea

Jules Verne

A WATERMILL CLASSIC

Contents

straight to the heart, and reaching the other
arm their missions a week

Desperby, if the monster ever had to do with

PART 1

Chapter 1
A Shifting Reef

The year 1866 was made notable by a series of bizarre events, a chain of mysterious phenomena which have never been explained, that I am sure no one has forgotten. Rumors of these strange occurrences excited the inhabitants of seaports, the world over, and excited the imaginations of the public throughout all the continents. But men who followed the sea by profession were more frightened and disturbed than anyone else. Merchants, owners of ships, captains of large vessels, tugboat skippers, and masters of sailing ships of Europe and America, naval officers of all countries, and, after them, the governments of the several states on both continents became intensely concerned with these reports.

For some time past, ships at sea had been meeting with "an enormous thing," a long, spindle-shaped object, which sometimes gave off a phosphorescent light, and was infinitely larger and faster than any whale ever seen.

The reports describing the apparition (as entered in various log-books) agreed in most respects as to the shape of this object or creature, the untiring speed with which it moved, its astonishing power of locomotion, and the peculiar life with which it seemed endowed. If it was a cetacean, it surpassed in size all those hitherto classified in science. Taking into consideration the average of observations made at different times,—rejecting those timid estimates which granted this object a length of only two hundred feet. Along with these exaggerated opinions which claimed it to be a mile wide and three miles long, we could fairly conclude that this mysterious creature greatly surpassed all dimensions recognized by the ichthyologists of the day. And it *did* exist, this was an undeniable fact, and, knowing that tendency of the human mind to believe in miracles, we can understand the excitement produced throughout the world by this seemingly supernatural apparition. To classify it as a fabulous being was impossible.

On the 20th of July, 1866, the steamer *Governor Higginson,* of the Calcutta and Burnach Steam Navigation Company, had met this moving mass five miles off the east coast of Australia. Captain Baker thought at first that he was confronted by an uncharted reef; he was preparing to take a bearing in order to determine its exact position, when two columns of water were projected by the inexplicable object and shot with a hissing noise a hundred and fifty feet up into the air. Now, unless the reef was subject to the intermittent eruption of a geyser the *Governor Higginson* had met neither more nor less than a hitherto unknown aquatic mammal, which threw up columns of water mixed with air and vapor from its blowholes.

Similar events were observed on the 23rd of July in the same year, in the Pacific Ocean, by the *Columbus,* of the West India and Pacific Steam Navigation Company. This extraordinary cetaceous creature could transport itself from one place to another with amazing velocity; as, in an interval of three days, the *Governor Higginson* and the *Columbus* had observed it at two different points of the chart, separated by a distance of more than seven hundred nautical leagues.

Fifteen days later, two thousand miles away, the *Helvetia* of the Compagnie-Nationale, and the *Shannon,* of the Royal Mail Steamship Company, sailing to windward in that portion of the Atlantic lying between the United States and Europe, sighted the monster in 42⁰ 15′ n. lat. and 60⁰ 35′ w. long. respectively. In these simultaneous observations, they thought they could estimate its minimum length at more than three hundred and fifty feet, as both *Shannon* and *Helvetia* were smaller than the mammal, and they measured three hundred feet over all.

Now even the largest whales, those which inhabit the sea round the Aleutian, Kulammak, and Umgullich islands, have never exceeded a length of sixty yards, if they attain that.

These reports came one after the other, along

with new observations taken on board the trans-atlantic liner *Pereire.* A collision had occurred between the *Etna,* of the Inman line, and the monster. An official statement issued by the officers of the French frigate *Normandie;* a very careful survey made by the staff of Commodore Fitz-James on board the *Lord Clyde.* All these greatly influenced public opinion. Light-minded people jested about the Phenomenon, but grave practical countries, such as England, America and Germany, treated the matter more seriously.

In every gathering place, the monster was the height of fashion. They sang of it in the cafes, made jokes about it in the papers, and plays about it in the theatres. The wildest kind of stories were told about it. There appeared in the papers, which ran out of copies, pictures of every gigantic and imaginary creature, from the white whale, the terrible "Moby Dick" of hyperborean regions, to the immense kraken whose tentacles, it was said, could entangle a ship of five hundred tons, and plunge it to the bottom of the ocean. Even legends of ancient times were revived, and the opinions of Aristotle and Pliny quoted, both of whom admitted the existence of these monsters; the Norwegian tales of Bishop Pontoppidan, the accounts of Paul Heggede, were circulated and, last of all, the reports of Mr. Harrington (whose faith no one could suspect), who affirmed that, being on board the *Castillan,* in 1857, he had seen this enormous serpent, which never until that time had frequented any seas but those of the ancient *"Constitutionnel."*

Then burst forth an interminable controversy between the credulous and the incredulous among the societies of savants and in scientific journals. "The question of the monster" inflamed all minds. Editors of scientific journals quareling with believers in the supernatural, spilled seas of ink during this memorable campaign, some even drawing blood; for, starting with the sea-serpent, they soon engaged in direct personalities.

For six months war was waged with various fortune in the leading articles of the Geographical Institution of Brazil, the Royal Academy of Science of Berlin, the British Association, the Smithsonian Institution of Washington, in the discussions of the "Indian Archipelago" of the Cosmos of the Abbe Moigno, in the Mittheilungen of Petermann, in the scientific chronicles of the great journals of France and other countries. The cheaper journals replied keenly and with inexhaustible zest. These satirical writers parodied a remark of Linnaeus, quoted by the adversaries of the monster, maintaining "that nature did not make fools," and adjured their contemporaries not to give the lie to nature, by admitting the existence of krakens, sea-serpents, "Moby Dicks," and other nightmares of delirious sailors. At length an article in a well-known satirical journal by a favorite contributor, the chief of the staff, settled the monster, like Hippolytus, giving it the death-blow amidst a universal burst of laughter. Wit had conquered science.

During the first months of the year 1867, the

question seemed buried, never to revive, when new facts were brought before the public. It was then no longer a scientific problem to be solved, but a real danger seriously to be avoided. The question took quite another shape. The monster became a small island, a rock, a reef, but a reef of indefinite and shifting proportions.

On the 5th of March, 1867, the *Moravian,* of the Montreal Ocean Company, finding herself during the night in 27⁰ 30 ' lat. and 72⁰ 15 ' long., struck on her starboard quarter a rock, marked in no chart for that part of the sea. Under the combined efforts of the wind and its four hundred horse power, the *Moravian* was going at the rate of thirteen knots. Had it not been for the unusual strength of the *Moravian* 's hull, she would have been broken by the shock and gone down with the 237 passengers she was bringing home from Canada.

The accident happened about five o'clock in the morning, as the day was breaking. The officers of the quarter-deck hurried to the afterpart of the vessel. They examined the sea with the most scrupulous attention. They saw nothing but a strong eddy about three cables' length distant, as if the surface had been violently agitated. The bearings of the place were taken exactly, and the *Moravian* continued its route without apparent damage. Had it struck on a submerged rock, or on an enormous wreck? They could not tell; but on examination of the ship's bottom when undergoing repairs, it was found that part of her keel was broken.

This occurrence, though grave in itself, might perhaps have been forgotten like many others, if, three weeks after, it had not been re-enacted under similar circumstances. But, thanks to the nationality of the victim of the second shock, thanks to the reputation of the company to which the vessel belonged, the circumstance became extensively circulated.

The 13th of April, 1867, the sea being beautiful, the breeze favorable, the *Scotia,* of the Cunard Company's line, found herself in 15^0 $12'$ long. and 45^0 $37'$ lat. She was going at the speed of thirteen knots and a half.

At seventeen minutes past four in the afternoon, whilst the passengers were assembled at lunch in the great saloon, a slight shock was felt on the hull of the *Scotia,* on her quarter, a little aft of the port paddle.

The *Scotia* had not struck, but she had been struck, and seemingly by something sharp and penetrating rather than blunt. The shock had been so slight that no one would have been alarmed, had it not been for the shouts of the carpenter's watch, who rushed onto the bridge, exclaiming, "We are sinking! We are sinking!" At first the passengers were much frightened, but Captain Anderson hastened to reassure them. The danger could not be imminent. The *Scotia,* divided into seven compartments by strong partitions, could brave with impunity any leak. Captain Anderson went down immediately into the hold. He found that the sea was pouring into the fifth compartment; and the rapidity of the influx indicated that the force of the water was considerable. Fortunately this compartment did not hold the boilers, or the fires would have been immediately extinguished. Captain Anderson ordered the engines to be stopped at once, and one of the men went down to ascertain the extent of the injury. Some minutes afterwards he discovered a large hole, two yards in diameter, in the ship's bottom. Such a leak could not be stopped; and the *Scotia,* her paddles half submerged, was obliged to continue her course. She was then three hundred miles from Cape Clear, and after three days' delay, which caused great uneasiness in Liverpool, she entered the basin of the Cunard Company.

The engineers visited the *Scotia,* which was in dry dock. They could scarcely believe what they saw; two yards and a half below water mark, there was a rent in the form of an almost perfect isosceles triangle. The broken place in the iron plates was so clearly defined, that it could not have been more neatly done by a punch. It was evident then, that the instrument producing the perforation was not of a common stamp; and after having been driven with prodigious strength, and piercing an iron plate 1 3/8 inches thick, had withdrawn itself by a retrograde motion truly inexplicable.

Such was the last event, which resulted in exciting once more the torrent of public opinion. From this moment all unlucky casualties which could not otherwise be accounted for were credited to the monster. Upon this hypothetical creature rested the responsibility for all these shipwrecks, which unfortunately were considerable; for of three thousand ships whose sinking or damage was annually recorded at Lloyds', the number regarded as totally lost, because there was no news of them at all, amounted to not less than two hundred.

Now, it was the "monster" who, justly or unjustly, was accused of causing their disappearance, and, thanks to it, communication between the different continents became more and more dangerous. The public demanded peremptorily that the seas should at any price be relieved from this formidable cetacean.

Chapter 2
Pro and Con

During the period when these events took place, I was on my way back from a scientific research in the Bad Lands of Nebraska, in the United States. In virtue of my office as Assistant Professor at the Museum of Natural History in Paris, the French Government had attached me to that expedition. After six months in Nebraska, I arrived in New York towards the end of March, laden with a precious collection. My departure for France was fixed for the first days in May. Meanwhile, I was occupying myself in classifying my mineralogical, botanical, and zoological riches, when the accident happened to the *Scotia*.

I was thoroughly acquainted with the subject which was the question of the day. How could I be otherwise? I had read and re-read all the American and European papers, without finding an explanation. This mystery intrigued me. Unable to form an opinion, I jumped from one extreme to the other. That there really was something could not be doubted, and the incredulous were invited to put their finger on the wound of the *Scotia*.

On my arrival at New York, the question was burning. The hypothesis of the floating island, and the inacessible sandbank, supported by minds little competent to form a judgment, had been abandoned. And, indeed, unless this shoal had an engine in its belly, how could it change its position with such astonishing rapidity?

For the same reason, the idea of a floating hull of an enormous wreck was given up.

There remained then only two possible solutions of the question, which created two distinct groups of partisans; on one side were those who held out for a monster of colossal strength; on the other, those who suggested a submarine vessel of enormous motive power.

But this last hypothesis, admissible though it was, could not stand up against inquiries made on both continents. That a private person should have such a machine at his command was not likely. Where, when, and how was it built? And how could its construction have been kept secret? Only a nation could conceivably possess such a destructive machine. In these disastrous times, when the ingenuity of man has multiplied the power of weapons of war, it was possible that, without the knowledge of others, a state might try to employ such a formidable engine. After the chassepots came the torpedoes, after the torpedoes the submarine rams, then—the reaction. At least, I hope so.

But the hypothesis of a war machine fell before the declarations of various Governments. As world interest was at stake, and transatlantic communications were being endangered, sincerity could not be doubted. Moreover, how concede that the construction of such a submarine had escaped the public eye? For a private person, to keep it secret would be very difficult, and for a state whose every act is under constant scrutiny by powerful rivals, certainly impossible.

Consequently after inquiries were made in England, France, Russia, Prussia, Spain, Italy, America, and even in Turkey, the hypothesis of a submarine monitor was definitely rejected.

Upon my arrival in New York several persons did me the honor of consulting me on the phenomenon. I had published in France a work in quarto, in two volumes, entitled, *Mysteries of the Depths of the Sea*. This book, highly approved in the learned world, made me known as a specialist in this rather obscure branch of Natural History. My views were asked. Insofar as I could claim no actual knowledge, I confined myself to a firm denial. But, soon being pushed to the wall, I was obliged to explain myself categorically. And so the "Honorable Pierre Aronnax, Professor of the Museum of Paris," was called upon by the *New York Herald* to express a definite opinion of some sort. I did something. I spoke, for want of power to hold my tongue. I discussed the question in all its forms, politically and scientifically; and I give here an extract from a scholarly article which I published in the number of the 30th of April. It ran as follows:-

"After examining one by one the different hypotheses and rejecting all suggestions, it becomes necessary to admit the existence of a marine animal of enormous power.

"The greatest depths of the ocean are entirely unknown to us. Soundings cannot reach them. What goes on in those remote depths—what beings live, twelve or fifteen miles beneath the surface of the waters—how they are constituted, we can scarcely conjecture. However, the solution of the problem submitted to me may modify the form of the dilemma. Either we do know all the varieties of beings which people our planet, or we do not. If we do not know them all—if Nature has still secrets in ichthyology from us, nothing is more reasonable than to admit the existence of fishes or cetaceans, or other kinds or even of new species, an organism formed to inhabit strata inaccessible to soundings, and which either an accident of some sort, an impulse or caprice if you like, has brought at long last to the upper level of the ocean.

"If, on the contrary, we do know all living kinds, we must necessarily seek for the animal in question amongst those marine beings already classed; and, in that case, I should be disposed to admit the existence of a gigantic narwhal.

"The common narwhal, or unicorn of the

sea, often attains a length of sixty feet. Increase its size five fold or tenfold, give it strength proportionate to its size, lengthen its destructive weapons, and you have the animal required. It will have the proportions determined by the officers of the *Shannon,* the instrument required by the perforation of the *Scotia,* and the power necessary to pierce the hull of the steamer.

"Indeed the narwhal is armed with a sort of ivory sword, a halberd, according to the expression of certain naturalists. The principal tusk has the hardness of steel. Some of these tusks have been found buried in the bodies of whales, which the unicorn always attacks with success. Others have been drawn out, not without trouble, from the bottoms of ships, which they have pierced through and through, as a gimlet pierces a barrel. The Museum of the Faculty of Medicine of Paris possesses one of these defensive weapons, two yards and a quarter in length, and fifteen inches in diameter at the base.

"Very well! Suppose this weapon to be ten times stronger, and the animal ten times more powerful; launch it at the rate of twenty miles an hour, and you obtain a shock capable of producing the catastrophe required. Until further information, therefore, I shall maintain it to be a sea-unicorn of colossal dimensions, armed, not with a halberd, but with a real spur, like the armored frigates, or rams of war, whose massiveness and motive power it must possess. Thus may this inexplicable phenomenon be explained, unless there be something over and above all that one has ever conjectured, seen, perceived, or experienced; which is still within the bounds of possibility.''

These last words were cowardly on my part; but, up to a certain point, I wished to shield my dignity as Professor, and not give too much cause for laughter to the Americans, who, when they laugh, laugh well. I reserved for myself a way of escape. Although I gave credence to the existence of the ''monster.'' My article was heatedly discussed, and caused a great stir; rallied round it were a number of partisans. The solution proposed gave, at least, full liberty to the imagination. The human mind delights in grandiose conceptions of supernatural beings. And the sea is their best medium, the only one in which these giants (beside which terrestrial animals, such as the elephant or rhinoceros are as nothing) can be produced or developed. These waters contain the largest known species of mammals, and perhaps may harbor molluscs of incomparable size, cetaceans frightening to contemplate, such as lobsters a hundred feet long, or crabs weighing 200 tons. And why not! Formerly, earthy animals of the same geological epoch—quadrupeds, animals with four hands, reptiles, birds—were built on an enormous scale. The Creator hurled them into a colossal world that, little by little, time has made smaller. Perhaps the sea, which never changes, still maintains in its fathomless depths, vast patterns of another eon, while life on earth is in a constant ferment of change. The sea easily could shelter the last representatives of these gigantic species, whose years are as centuries, their centuries as millenniums.

But I engage in theories which no longer can be regarded as tenable. A truce to these theories, which time has changed into terrible reality. At that time opinion had taken shape regarding the nature of the phenomenon, and the public accepted without demur the existence of a prodigious creature that bore nothing in common with the fabulous sea serpents of old.

But if many thought of this as a problem to be solved by scientists, others, more aggressive—particularly in America and England—insisted that the ocean be purged of this formidable beast, which threatened international commerce and travel.

The industrial and commercial papers treated the question chiefly from this point of view. The Shipping and Mercantile Gazette, the Lloyds' List, the packetboat, and the Maritime and Colonial Review, all papers devoted to insurance companies which threatened to raise their rates of premium, were unanimous on this point. Public opinion had been pronounced. The United States was first in the field; and in New York preparations were made for an expedition designed to pursue this narwhal. A frigate of great speed, the *Abraham Lincoln,* was put in commission as quickly as possible. The arsenals were opened to Commander Farragut, who hastened the arming of this frigate; but, as always happens, the moment it was decided to pursue the monster, the monster did not appear. For two months no one heard it spoken of. No ship met with it. It seemed as if this unicorn of the sea knew of the plots being woven around it. The plan had been so much talked of, even through the Atlantic cable, that jesters pretended that our tiny insect had stopped a telegram on its passage, and was making the most of it.

Thus, with the frigate fitted out for a long campaign, and provided with the most elaborate fishing apparatus, no one knew what course to chart. Impatience had grown apace, when, on the 2nd of July, it was learned that a steamer of the San Francisco Line on a voyage from California to Shanghai; had sighted the animal three weeks earlier in the North Pacific. The excitement caused by this news was intense. The ship was revictualed and well stocked with coal.

Three hours before the *Abraham Lincoln* left Brooklyn pier, I received a letter worded as follows:

> To M. Aronnax, Professor of the Museum of Paris, Fifth Avenue Hotel, New York. Sir,—If you will consent to join the Abraham Lincoln on this expedition, the Government of the United States will with pleasure see France represented in the enterprise. Commander Farragut has a cabin at your disposal.
>
> Very cordially yours,
> J.B. Hobson,
> Secretary of the Navy

Chapter 3
I Form My Resolution

Three seconds before the arrival of J. B. Hobson's letter, I had no more thought of pursuing the unicorn than of attempting the North Sea passage. Three seconds after reading the letter of the Honorable Secretary of the Navy, I felt that my true vocation, the sole end of my life, was to chase this disturbing monster, and purge it from the world.

But I had just returned from a fatiguing journey, I was weary and longed for rest. I wished for nothing so much as to look again on my country, my friends, my little dwelling by the Jardin des Plantes, my dear and precious collections. But no such consideration could hold me back! I forgot all—fatigue, friends, and collections—and without hesitation accepted the offer of the American Government.

"Besides," I thought, "all roads bring one back to Europe, and perhaps the monster will be kind enough to sweep me towards the coast of France. This worthy animal may allow itself to be caught in the seas of Europe (for my particular benefit) and I will not bring back less than half a yard of his ivory halberd to the Museum of Natural History." But in the meanwhile I must seek this narwhal in the north of the Pacific Ocean, which, for going back to France, was like taking the road to the antipodes.

"Conseil," I called, in an impatient voice.

Conseil was my servant, a true, devoted Flemish boy, who had accompanied me in all my travels. I liked him, and he returned the liking well. He was phlegmatic by nature, reliable on principle, enthusiastic from force of habit, evincing little disturbance at the various surprises of life; very quick with his hands, and apt at any service required of him; and, despite his name, never giving advice—even when asked for it.

From his contact with the scientists of our little world at the Botanical Garden, Conseil had acquired some knowledge. I had in him a specialist who was well up in the scientific classification of flora and fauna, able to cover with acrobatic agility the full range of branches, groups, classes, sub-classes, orders, families, genuses and sub-genuses of every variety of species. But there his science stopped. To classify was his life and he never learned anything further. Well trained in theory, but without practice, he was unable to distinguish, I believe, a sperm whale from a whale bone in a lady's corset. But, withal, what a brave and worthy lad.

Conseil had followed me for the last ten years wherever science had taken me. Never once did he complain of the length or fatigue of a journey, nor made any objection to packing his valise for any country whatsoever, no matter how distant, whether China or the Congo. Besides all this, his strong health defied all sickness; he had solid muscles, but no nerves; his courage went without saying. This young man was thirty years old, and his age to that of his master as fifteen to twenty. May I be excused for saying that I was forty years old?

"Conseil," I called again, beginning with feverish hands to make preparations for my departure.

Certainly I was sure of his devotion. As a rule, I never asked him if it was convenient for him to follow me in my travels; but this time the expedition might be prolonged, and the enterprise hazardous since we would be seeking out an animal capable of sinking a frigate as easily as a nutshell. There was matter for reflection even to the most imperturbable man in the world. What would Conseil say?

"Conseil," I called a third time.

Conseil appeared.

"Did you call, sir?"

"Yes, my lad; make preparations for me and yourself too. We leave in two hours."

"As you please, sir," replied Conseil serenely.

"Not an instant to lose. Place in my trunk all

articles necessary for traveling, coats, shirts, stockings—without counting, as many as you can, and make haste.''

"And your collections, sir?" observed Conseil.

"We will concern ourselves with them later."

"What! The Archiotherium, the hyracotherium, the oreodons, the cheropotamus, and the other skins?"

"The hotel will keep them."

"And your live Babiroussa, sir?"

"The management will feed it during our absence, I will give instruction to forward our menagerie to France."

"We are not returning to Paris, then?" said Conseil.

"Oh! Certainly," I answered, evasively, "by making a curve."

"Will the curve please you, sir?"

"Oh! It will be nothing; not quite so direct a road, that is all. We take our passage in the *Abraham Lincoln.*"

"As you think proper, sir," coolly replied Conseil.

"You see, my friend, it has to do with the sea monster—the famous narwhal. We are going to purge it from the seas. The author of a work in quarto in two volumes, on the *Mysteries of the Depths of the Seas* cannot forbear embarking with Commander Farragut. A glorious mission, but a dangerous one! We cannot tell where we may go; these animals can be very capricious. But we will go whether or no; we have got a captain who is pretty wide awake."

I opened a credit account for Babiroussa, and

Conseil following, I jumped into a cab. Our luggage was carried to the deck of the frigate immediately. I hurried on board and asked for Commander Farragut. One of the sailors conducted me to the poop, where I found myself in the presence of a good-looking officer, who held out his hand to me.

"Monsieur Pierre Aronnax?" said he.

"Himself," replied I: "Commander Farragut?"

"You are welcome, Professor; your cabin is ready for you." I bowed and asked to be conducted to the cabin destined for me.

The *Abraham Lincoln* had been well chosen and equipped for her new destination. She was a frigate of great speed, equipped with superheated boilers, which permitted her engines to maintain the utmost pressure. Under this the *Abraham Lincoln* attained the mean speed of nearly eighteen knots and a third an hour—a considerable speed, but, probably insufficient to bring this gigantic cetacean to bay.

The interior arrangements of the frigate equaled its fine nautical qualities. I was well pleased with my cabin, which was in the afterpart adjoining the gunroom.

"We shall be well off here," I said to Conseil.

"As well, by your honor's leave, as a hermit-crab in the shell of a whelk," said Conseil.

I left Conseil to stow our trunks away conveniently, and remounted the poop in order to survey the preparations for departure.

At that moment Commander Farragut was ordering cast loose the mast moorings which held the *Abraham Lincoln* to the pier of Brooklyn.

In a quarter of an hour, perhaps less, the frigate would have sailed without me. I should have missed this extraordinary, supernatural, and incredible expedition, the recital of which may well meet with some skepticism.

Commander Farragut was determined not to lose a day nor an hour in scouring the seas where the animal had been sighted. He sent for an engineer.

"Are we under steam?" asked he.

"Yes, sir," replied the engineer.

"Go ahead," cried Commander Farragut.

The quay of Brooklyn, and all that part of New York bordering on the East River, was crowded with spectators. Three cheers burst successively from five hundred thousand throats; thousands of handkerchiefs were raised above the heads of the solid mass of people, waving to the *Abraham Lincoln,* until she reached the waters of the Hudson, at the point of that elongated peninsula which forms the town of New York. Then the frigate following the coast of New Jersey along the right bank of the beautiful river, with its handsome country homes, passed between the forts, which saluted her with their heaviest guns. The *Abraham Lincoln* answered by hoisting the American colors three times, their thirty-nine stars shining resplendent from the mizzenpeak; then modifying her speed to take the narrow channel marked by buoys placed in the inner bay formed by Sandy Hook Point, coasted the long sandy beach, where some thousands of spectators gave her one final cheer. The escort of small boats and tenders still followed the frigate, and did not leave her until they came abreast of the lightship, whose two lights marked the entrance into New York Channel.

Six bells struck, the pilot climbed down into his boat, and rejoined the little schooner which was waiting under our lee, the fires were made up, the screw beat the waves more rapidly, the frigate skirted the low yellow coast of Long Island; and at eight bells, after having lost sight of the lights of Fire Island to the northwest, she ran at full steam on to the dark waters of the Atlantic.

Chapter 4
Ned Land

Captain Farragut was a good seaman, worthy of the frigate he commanded. His vessel and he were one. He was the soul of it. As to the cetacean there was no doubt in his mind, and he would not allow the existence of the animal to be disputed on board. He believed in it, as certain good women believe in the leviathan—by faith, not by reason. The monster existed and he had sworn to rid the seas of it. He was a kind of Knight of Rhodes, a second Dieudonne de Gozon, going to meet the serpent which laid the island waste. Either Captain Farragut would kill the narwhal, or the narwhal would kill the captain. There was no middle course.

The officers on board shared the opinion of their chief. They were forever chatting, discussing, and calculating the various chances of an encounter, watching closely the vast surface of the ocean. More than one took up voluntary quarters in the cross trees, who would have cursed such a berth under any other circumstances. As long as the sun drew its daily course, the rigging was crowded with sailors, whose feet were so burnt by the heat of the deck as to make it unbearable; still the *Abraham Lincoln* had not yet breasted the suspected waters of the Pacific. As to the ship's company, they desired nothing better than to meet the unicorn, harpoon it, hoist it on board, and dispatch it. They watched the sea with eager attention.

Besides, Captain Farragut had mentioned the sum of two thousand dollars, set aside for whoever should first sight the monster, were he cabin boy, common seaman, or officer.

I leave you to judge how eyes were used on board the *Abraham Lincoln*. As for me, I did not lag behind the others, and left to no one my share of daily observations. The frigate might have been called the Argus, for a hundred reasons. Only one amongst us, Conseil, seemed to show indifference to the question which so interested the rest of us, and to be out of step with the general enthusiasm on board.

I said that Captain Farragut had carefully provided his ship with every apparatus for catching the gigantic cetacean. No whaler had ever been better armed. We possessed every known engine, from the harpoon thrown by the hand to the barbed arrows of the blunderbuss, and the explosive balls of the duck-gun. On the forecastle lay the perfection of a breech loading gun, very thick at the breech, and very narrow in the bore, the model of which had been in the Exhibition of 1867. This precious weapon of American origin could easily throw a conical projectile of nine pounds to a mean distance of ten miles.

Thus the *Abraham Lincoln* wanted for no means of destruction; and, better still, she had on board Ned Land, the prince of harpooners.

Ned Land was a Canadian, with an uncommon quickness of hand, who knew no equal in his dangerous occupation. Skill, coolness, audacity, and cunning, he possessed to a high degree, and it must be a cunning whale or a singularly "cute" cachalot to escape the stroke of his harpoon.

Ned Land was about forty years of age, a tall man (more than six feet high) strongly built, grave and taciturn, occasionally violent, and very excitable when contradicted. His appearance attracted attention, but above all the boldness of his look, which gave a singular expression to his face.

Who calls himself Canadian calls himself French; and, little communicative as Ned Land was, I must admit that he took a certain liking for me. My nationality drew him to me, no doubt. It was a chance for him to talk, and for me to hear, that old language of Rabelais which is still in use in some Canadian provinces. The harpooner's family was originally from Quebec, and was already a tribe of hardy fishermen when this town belonged to France.

Little by little, Ned Land acquired a taste for chatting, and I loved to hear of his adventures in the polar seas. He told of his fishing, and his fights with natural poetry of expression; his recital took the form of an epic poem, and I seemed to be listening to a Canadian Homer singing the Iliad of the northern regions.

I portray this hardy companion as I really knew him. We are old friends now, united in that unchangeable friendship which is born and cemented amidst extreme dangers. Ah, brave Ned! I asked no more than to live a hundred years longer, that I may dwell the longer on your memory.

Now, what was Ned Land's opinion on the question of the marine monster? I must admit that he did not believe in the unicorn, and was the only one on board who did not share that universal conviction. He even avoided the subject, which I one day thought it my duty to urge upon him. One fine evening, the 30th of July—that is to say, three weeks after our departure—the frigate was abreast of Cape Blanc, thirty miles to leeward of the coast of Patagonia. We had crossed the Tropic of Capricorn, and the Straits of Magellan opened less than seven hundred miles to the south. Before eight days were past, the *Abraham Lincoln* would be ploughing the waters of the Pacific.

Seated on the poop, Ned Land and I were chatting of one thing and another as we looked at this mysterious sea, whose great depths had up to this time been inaccessible to the eye of man. I naturally led up the conversation to the giant unicorn, and examined the various chances of success or failure of the expedition. But seeing that Ned Land let me speak without saying much himself, I pressed him more closely.

"Well, Ned," said I, "is it possible that you are not convinced of the existence of the cetacean that we are following? Have you any special reason for being so incredulous?"

The harpooner looked at me fixedly for some moments before answering, struck his broad forehead with his hand (a habit of his), as if to collect himself, and said at last, "Perhaps I have, M. Aronnax."

"But, Ned, you, a whaler by profession, familiar with all the great mammalia—you, whose imagination might easily accept the hypothesis of enormous cetaceans, *you* should be the last to doubt under such circumstances!"

"That is just what deceives you, Professor," replied Ned. "That the uninitiate should believe in extraordinary comets traversing space, and in the existence of antediluvian monsters in the heart of the globe, may well be; but neither astronomer nor geologist believes in such chimeras. As a whaler I have followed many a cetacean, harpooned a great number, and killed some; but however strong or well-armed they have been, neither their tails nor their weapons would have been able to so much as scratch the iron plates of a steamer."

"But, Ned, they tell of ships which the teeth of the narwhal have pierced through and through."

"Wooden ships—possibly," replied the Canadian; "but I have never seen it done; and, until further proof, I deny that whales, cetaceans, or sea-unicorns, could ever produce the effect you describe."

"Well, Ned, I repeat it with a conviction born of the logic of facts. I believe in the existence of a mammal powerfully constituted, belonging to the branch of vertebrata, like the whales, the cachalots, or the dolphins, and a horn defended by great penetrating power."

"Hum!" said the harpooner, shaking his head with the air of a man who would not be convinced.

"Notice one thing, my worthy Canadian," I resumed. "If such an animal is in existence, if it inhabits the depths of the ocean, if it frequents the strata lying miles below the surface of the water, it must necessarily possess a constitution, the strength of which would defy all comparison."

"And why this powerful structure?" demanded Ned.

"Because it requires incalculable strength to keep one's self in these strata and resist their pressure. Listen to me. Let us say that the pressure of the atmosphere is represented by the weight of a column of water thirty-two feet high. Actually the column of water would be shorter, as we are speaking of sea water, the density of which is greater than that of fresh water. Very well, when you dive, Ned, as many times thirty-two feet of water as there are above you, so many times does your body bear a pressure equal to that of the atmosphere, that is to say,

15 lbs. for each square inch of its surface. It follows then, that at 320 feet, this pressure equals that of 10 atmospheres, of 100 atmospheres at 3200 feet, and of 1000 atmospheres at 32,000 feet, that is, about 6 miles; which is equivalent to saying that, if you could attain this depth in the ocean, each square three-eighths of an inch of the surface of your body would bear a pressure of 5000 lbs. Ah! my brave Ned, do you know how many square inches you have on the surface of your body?''

''I have no idea, M. Aronnax.''

''About 6500; and, as in reality the atmospheric pressure is about 15 lbs. to the square inch, your 6500 square inches bear at this moment a pressure of 97,500 lbs.''

''Without my perceiving it?''

''Without your perceiving it. And if you are not crushed by such a pressure, it is because the air penetrates the interior of your body with equal pressure. Hence perfect equilibrium between the interior pressure, which neutralize each other, and allows you to bear it without inconvenience. But in the water it is another thing.''

''Yes, I understand,'' replied Ned, becoming more attentive; ''because the water surrounds me, but does not penetrate.''

''Precisely, Ned; so that at 32 feet beneath the surface of the sea you would undergo a pressure of 97,500 lbs.; at 320 feet, ten times that pressure; at 3200 feet, a hundred times that pressure; lastly, at 32,000 feet, a thousand times that pressure would be 97,500,000 lbs.,—that is to say, that you would be flattened as if you had been drawn from the plates of a hydraulic machine!''

"The devil!'' exclaimed Ned.

"Very well, my worthy harpooner, if some vertebrate, several hundred yards long, and large in proportion, can maintain itself in such depths—of those whose surface is millions of square inches, that is, by tens of millions of pounds, we must estimate the pressure they undergo. Consider, then, what the resistance of their bony structures and the strength of their organisms must be to withstand such pressure!''

"Why!'' exclaimed Ned Land, "they must be made of iron plates eight inches thick, like the armored frigates.''

"As you say, Ned. And think what destruction such a mass would cause, if hurled with the speed of an express train against the hull of a vessel.''

"Yes surely—perhaps,'' replied the Canadian, shaken by these figures, but not yet willing to give in.

"Well, have I convinced you?''

"You have convinced me of one thing, sir, which is that, if such animals do exist at the bottom of the seas, they must necessarily be as strong as you say.''

"But if they do not exist, my obstinate harpooner, how do you explain the accident to the *Scotia?*''

"Maybe it was...'' said Ned hesitantly.

"Well then!''

"Because—it wasn't true!'' replied the Canadian reproducing unwittingly the celebrated response of Arago.

Chapter 5
At a Venture

The voyage of the *Abraham Lincoln* was marked for a long time by no special incident. But one thing happened which showed the wonderful dexterity of Ned Land, and proved what confidence we might place in him.

The 30th of June, the frigate spoke with some American whalers, from whom we learned that they knew nothing of the narwhal. But one of them, the captain of the *Monroe*, knowing that Ned Land had shipped on board the *Abraham Lincoln,* begged for his help in chasing a whale they had sighted. Captain Farragut desirous of seeing Ned Land at work, gave him permission to go on board the *Monroe*. And luck served our Canadian so well that, instead of one whale, he harpooned two with a double blow, striking one straight to the heart, and catching the other after some minutes' pursuit.

Decidedly, if the monster ever had to do with

Ned Land's harpoon, I would not bet in its favor.

The frigate skirted the southeast coast of America with great rapidity. The 3rd of July we were at the opening of the Straits of Magellan, level with Cape Vierges. But Captain Farragut would not take a tortuous passage, but doubled Cape Horn.

The ship's crew agreed with him. And certainly it was possible that they might meet the narwhal in this narrow pass. Many of the sailors affirmed that the monster could not pass there, "that he was too big for that!"

The 6th of July, about three o'clock in the afternoon, the *Abraham Lincoln,* at fifteen miles to the south, doubled the solitary island, this lost rock at the very end of the American continent, to which some Dutch sailors gave the name of their native town Cape Horn. The course was taken towards the northwest, and the next day the screw of the frigate was at last beating the waters of the Pacific.

"Keep your eyes open!" called out the sailors.

And they were opened widely. Both eyes and glasses, a little dazzled, it is true, by the prospect of two thousand dollars, had not an instant's repose. Day and night they watched the surface of the ocean, and even nyctalopes, people with eyes like cats, whose faculty of seeing in the darkness multiplies their chances a hundredfold, would have had enough to do to gain the prize.

I myself, for whom money had little charm, was not the least attentive on board. Giving but few minutes to my meals, but a few hours to sleep, indifferent both to rain or sunshine, I did not leave the poop of the vessel. Now leaning on the netting of the forecastle, now on the taffrail, I devoured with eagerness the soft foam which whitened the sea as far as the eye could reach; and how often have I joined in the excitement of the majority of the crew, when some capricious whale raised its black back above the waves! The poop of the vessel was crowded in a moment. The cabins poured forth a torrent of sailors and officers, each with heaving breast and anxious eye watching the course of the cetacean. I looked and looked, till I was nearly blind, whilst Conseil, always phlegmatic, kept repeating in a calm voice:

"If, sir, you did not squint so much, you would see better!"

But what vain excitement! The *Abraham Lincoln* checked its speed and made for the animal sighted, a simple whale, or common sperm whale, which soon disappeared amidst a storm of imprecations.

But the weather was good. The voyage was being accomplished under the most favorable auspices. It was then the bad season in Australia, the July of that zone corresponding to our January in Europe; but the sea was beautiful and easily scanned round a vast circumference.

The 20th of July, the Tropic of Capricorn was cut by 105⁰ of longitude, and the 27th of the same month we crossed the equator on the 110th meridian. This passed, the frigate took a more decided westerly direction, and scoured the central waters of the Pacific. Captain Farragut thought, and with reason, that it was better to remain in deep water, and keep clear of continents or islands, which the beast itself seemed to shun (doubtless because there was not enough water for him! suggested the greater part of the crew). The frigate passed at some distance from Marquesas and the Sandwich Islands, crossed the Tropic of Cancer, and made for the China Seas. We were at the arena of the last frolics of the monster; and to tell the truth, we no longer lived on board. Our hearts sounded fearfully, preparing themselves for future incurable aneurism. The entire ship's crew was undergoing a nervous excitation, of which I can give no notion; they could not eat, they could not sleep—twenty times a day, a misconception or an optical delusion of some sailor seated on the taffrail, would cause fearful sweats, and these emotions, twenty times repeated, kept us in a state of excitement so violent that a reaction was unavoidable.

And truly, reaction soon showed itself. For three months, during which a day seemed an age, the *Abraham Lincoln* churned all the waters of the Northern Pacific, running after whales, making sharp deviations from her course, veering suddenly from one tack to another, stopping suddenly, putting on steam, and backing ever and anon at the risk of deranging her machinery; and not one point of the Japanese or American coast was left unexplored.

The warmest partisans of the enterprise now became its most ardent detractors. Reaction mounted from the crew to the captain himself, and certainly, had it not been for resolute determination on the part of Captain Farragut, the frigate would have headed due southward. This useless search could not last much longer. The *Abraham Lincoln* had nothing to reproach herself with, she had done her best to succeed. Never had an American ship's crew shown more zeal or patience; its failure could not be charged to them—there was nothing but to return.

This was apparent to the captain. The sailors could not hide their discontent, and the service suffered. I will not say there was a mutiny on board, but after a reasonable period of obstinacy, Captain Farragut, as had Columbus, asked for three days' patience. If in three days the monster did not appear, the man at the helm should give three turns of the wheel, and the *Abraham Lincoln* would make for the European seas.

This promise was made on the 2nd of November. It had the effect of rallying the ship's crew. The ocean was watched with renewed attention. Each one wished for a last glance in which to sum up his remembrance. Glasses were used with feverish activity. It was a grand defiance given to the giant narwhal, and he could scarcely fail to answer the summons and "appear."

Two days passed, the steam was at half pressure; a thousand schemes had been tried to attract the attention and stimulate the apathy of the animal in case it should be met in those parts. Large quantities of bacon were trailed in the wake of the ship, to the great satisfaction (I must say) of the sharks. Small craft radiated in all directions round the *Abraham Lincoln* as she lay to, and did not leave a spot of the sea unexplored. But the night of the 4th of November arrived without the unveiling of this submarine mystery.

The next day, the 5th of November, at twelve the delay would (morally speaking) expire; after which, Captain Farragut, faithful to his promise, was to turn the course to the southeast and abandon forever the northern regions of the Pacific.

The frigate was then in 31^0 $15'$ north latitude and 136^0 $42'$ east longitude. The coast of Japan still remained less than two hundred miles to leeward. Night was approaching. They had just struck eight bells; large clouds veiled the face of the moon, then in its first quarter. The sea undulated peaceably under the stern of the vessel.

At that moment I was leaning forward on the starboard netting. Conseil, standing near me, was looking straight before him. The crew, perched in the ratlines, examined the horizon, which contracted and darkened by degrees. Officers with their night glasses scoured the growing darkness; sometimes the ocean sparkled under the rays of the moon, which darted between two clouds, then all trace of light was lost in the darkness.

In looking at Conseil, I could see he was undergoing a little of the general influence. At least I thought so. Perhaps for the first time his nerves vibrated to a sentiment of curiosity.

"Come, Conseil," said I. "This is the last chance of pocketing that two thousand dollars."

"May I be permitted to say, sir," replied

Conseil, "that I never reckoned on getting the prize; and, had the government of the Union offered a hundred thousand dollars, it would have been none the poorer."

"You are right, Conseil. It is a foolish affair after all, and one upon which we entered too lightly. What time lost, what useless excitement. We should have been back in France six months ago."

"In your little room, sir," replied Conseil, "and in your museum, sir, and I should have already classified all your fossils, sir. And the Babiroussa would have been installed in its cage in the Jardin des Plantes, and have drawn all the curious people of the capital!"

"As you say, Conseil. I fancy we will run a fair chance of being laughed at for our pains."

"That's tolerably certain," replied Conseil, quietly; "I think they will make fun of you, sir. And, must I say it?"

"Go on, my good friend."

"Well, sir, you will only get your deserts."

"Indeed!"

"When one has the honor of being a savant as you are, sir, one should not expose one's self to—"

Conseil had no time to finish his compliment. In the midst of general silence a voice had just been heard. It was the voice of Ned Land shouting—

"Look out there! the very thing we are looking for—on our weather beam!"

Chapter 6
At Full Steam

At this cry the whole ship's crew hurried towards the harpooner—commander, officers, masters, sailors, cabin boys; even the engineers left their engines, and the stokers their furnaces.

The order to stop had been given, and the frigate now moved only on her own momentum. The darkness was profound, and however good the Canadian's eyes were, I asked myself how he had been able to see, and what it was that he could have seen. My heart pounded as if it would break. But Ned Land was not mistaken, and soon we all preceived the object he pointed out. At two cables' lengths from the *Abraham Lincoln*, on the starboard quarter, the sea appeared to be brilliantly illuminated. It was not merely a phosphorescent glow. The monster, having reared up several fathoms from the water, projected that very intense and wholly inexplicable light described in the report of several captains. This magnificent irradiation must have been produced by an agent of great *shining* power. The amazing light traced on the sea an immense elongated oval, its center a burning focus, whose insupportable brilliancy faded by successive degrees.

"It is only an agglomeration of phosphoric particles," cried one of the officers.

"No, sir, certainly not," I replied. "Never did pholades or salpae produce such a powerful light. That brightness is of an essentially electrical nature. Besides, see, see! It moves; it is moving forwards, backwards; it is rushing upon us!"

A general cry rose from the frigate.

"Silence!" said the captain; "up with the helm, reverse the engines."

The steam was shut off, and the *Abraham Lincoln,* beating to port, described a semicircle.

"Right the helm, full speed ahead," cried the captain.

These orders were executed, and the frigate moved rapidly away from the still brilliant burning light. At least, so I thought. But even as she tried to sheer off, the supernatural animal aproached with a velocity double our own.

We gasped for breath. Stupefaction more than fear held us mute and motionless. The animal gained on us, sporting with the waves. It circled the frigate, which was then making fourteen knots, and enveloped it with sheets of electricity like luminous dust. Then it rushed away, a distance of two or three miles, leaving a phosphorescent track, like those plumes of steam that the express trains leave behind them.

All at once from the dark line of the horizon whither it retired to gain its momentum, the monster rushed with incredible rapidity towards the *Abraham Lincoln*, abruptly stopped about twenty feet from our hull, and faded away—suddenly, and as if the source of its brilliant emanation had become exhausted. Then it reappeared on the other side of the vessel, as if it had turned and slid under the hull. Any moment a collision might have occurred, which would have been fatal to us. Moreover, I was astonished by the maneuvers of the frigate. She fled and did not attack. She was pursued, she who was the pursuer. I looked keenly at Captain Farragut. His face ordinarily so impassive wore an expression of inexpressible astonishment.

"Mr. Aronnax," he told me, "I do not know with what formidable being I have to deal, and I will not imprudently risk my frigate in the midst of this darkness. Besides, how attack this unknown thing, how defend one's self from it? Wait for daylight, and our role will be reversed."

"You have no further doubt, captain, of the nature of the animal?"

"No, sir, it is evidently a gigantic narwhal, and an electric one, at that."

"Perhaps," added I, "one can only approach it with a gymnotus or a torpedo."

"Undoubtedly," replied the captain, "if it possesses such dreadful power, it is the most terrible animal that ever came from the hand of the Creator. That is why, sir, I must be on my guard."

The crew were on their feet all night. No one thought of sleep. The *Abraham Lincoln*, not being able to maintain such velocity, had moderated its speed, and sailed at half speed. For its part, the narwhal, imitating the frigate, let the waves rock it at will, and seemed prepared to linger at the scene of the conflict. Towards midnight, however, it disappeared, or, to use a more appropriate term, it "died out" like a large glow-worm. Had it fled? One could only fear, not hope. But at seven minutes to one o'clock in the morning a deafening roar was heard, like that produced by a body of water rushing with great violence.

The captain, Ned Land, and I were then on the poop, eagerly peering through the profound darkness.

"Ned Land," asked the commander, "you have often heard the roaring of whales?"

"Often, sir, but never such whales the sight of which would bring me in two thousand dollars. If I can only approach within four harpoon lengths of it!"

"But to approach it," said the commander, "I must put a whale boat at your disposal."

"Certainly, sir."

"That will be risking the lives of my men."

"And mine too," said the harpooner simply.

Towards two o'clock in the morning, the dazzling light reappeared, no less intense, about five miles to windward of the *Abraham Lincoln*. Notwithstanding the distance, and the sound of wind and sea, one heard distinctly the great strokes of the animal's tail, and even its panting breath. It seemed that, at the moment when the enormous narwhal had arisen to take breath at the surface of the water, the air was dragged into its lungs, like the steam in the vast cylinders of a machine of two thousand horsepower.

"Hum!" thought I, "a whale with the strength of a cavalry regiment would be a pretty whale."

We were on the alert till daylight, and prepared for combat. The fishing implements were laid along the hammock nettings. The second lieutenant loaded the blunderbusses, which could throw harpoons to a distance of a mile, and long duck-guns, whose explosive bullets could inflict mortal wounds on even the most terrible of animals. Ned Land contented himself with sharpening his harpoon—a terrible weapon in his hands.

At six o'clock day began to break; and with the first glimmer of dawn, the electric light of the narwhal disappeared. At seven o'clock the day was well advanced, but a very thick morning fog obscured the horizon, and the best spyglasses could not pierce it. All of us felt disappointment and anger.

I climbed the mizzenmast. Some officers were already perched on the mast heads. At eight o'clock the fog lay heavily on the waves, but its thick clouds rose little by little. The horizon grew wider and clearer at the same time. Suddenly, just as on the day before, Ned Land's voice was heard:

"The thing itself on the port quarter!" cried the harpooner.

Every eye turned towards the point indicated. There, a mile and a half from the frigate, a long blackish body emerged a yard above the waves. Its tail, violently agitated, roiled the waters like a great wind. Never did a caudal appendage beat the sea with such violence. An immense track, of a dazzling whiteness, marked the passage of the animal, describing a long curve.

The frigate now sailed toward the cetacean. I examined it thoroughly.

The reports of the *Shannon* and of the *Helvetia* had somewhat exaggerated its size; I estimated its length at no more than two hundred and fifty feet. As to its dimensions, I could only conjecture them to be admirably proportioned. While I watched this huge creature, two jets of steam and water were ejected from its vents, and rose to the height of one hundred twenty feet; thus I ascertained its method of breathing. I concluded definitely that it belonged to the vertebrate branch, class mammalia.

The crew waited impatiently for their captain's orders. The latter, after having observed the animal attentively, called the engineer. The engineer ran to him.

"Sir," said the commander, "you have steam up?"

"Yes, sir," answered the engineer.

"Well, make up your fires and put on all steam."

Three hurrahs greeted this order. The time for the encounter had arrived. A few moments later, the two funnels of the frigate vomited torrents of black smoke, and the bridge quaked under the trembling of the boilers.

The *Abraham Lincoln,* propelled by her powerful screw, went straight at the animal. The latter allowed it to come within half a cable's length; then, as if disdaining to dive, took a little turn, and stopped a short distance away.

This kind of pursuit lasted nearly three-quarters of an hour, without the frigate gaining two yards on the cetacean. It became quite evident that at this rate we should never come up with it.

"Well, Mr. Land," asked the captain, "do you advise me to put the boats out to sea?"

"No, sir," replied Ned Land; "because we shall not take that beast easily."

"What shall we do then?"

"Put on more steam if you can, sir. With your leave, I mean to post myself under the bowsprit, and if we get within harpooning distance, I shall throw my harpoon."

"Go, Ned," said the captain. "Engineer, put on more pressure."

Ned Land repaired to his post. The fires were built up, the screw was revolving forty-three times each minute, and the steam was pouring out of the valves. We heaved the log, and calculated that the *Abraham Lincoln* was going at the rate of 18½ miles an hour.

But the accursed animal swam too at the rate of 18½ miles.

For an entire hour, the frigate kept up this speed, without gaining six feet on the narwhal. It was a humiliating experience for one of the fastest ships in the American navy. A stubborn anger seized the crew; the sailors shouted abuse at the monster, which, as before, disdained to answer them; the captain no longer contented himself with twisting his beard—he gnawed it.

The engineer was again called.

"You have turned on full steam?"

"Yes, sir," replied the engineer.

But still the speed of the *Abraham Lincoln* increased. Its masts trembled down to their stepping holes, and the clouds of smoke could hardly find their way out of the narrow funnels.

They heaved the log a second time.

"Well?" asked the captain of the man at the wheel.

"Nineteen miles and three-tenths, sir."

"Clap on more steam."

The engineer obeyed. The manometer showed ten degrees. But the cetacean grew warm itself, perhaps, for without seeming effort it made 19 3/10 miles.

What a pursuit! No, I cannot describe the emotion that vibrated through me. Ned Land kept his post, harpoon in his hand. Several times the animal let us gain upon it.—"We shall catch it! We shall catch it!" cried the Canadian. But just as he was to strike, the cetacean slipped away with a speed that could not be estimated at less than thirty miles an hour, and even when we reached our maximum of speed, the animal bullied the frigate, going round and round it. A cry of fury broke from every man!

At noon we were no further advanced than at eight o'clock in the morning.

The captain then decided to take more direct means.

"Ah!" said he, "that animal goes faster than the *Abraham Lincoln*. Very well! we will see whether it can escape these conical bullets. Send your men to the forecastle, sir."

The forecastle gun was immediately loaded and slewed round. But the shot passed some feet above the cetacean, which was now half a mile away.

"Another more to the right," cried the commander, "and five dollars to whomever will hit that infernal beast."

An old gunner with a gray beard—I can see him now—with steady eye and grave face, took his place at the gun and took careful aim. The gun's loud report was mingled with the cheers of the crew.

The gunner's aim was true; the bullet hit the animal, but not fatally, and sliding off the rounded surface, was lost in two miles depth of sea.

The chase began again, and the captain leaning towards me, said—

"I will pursue that beast till my frigate blows up."

"Yes," answered I, "and you will be quite right to do so."

I longed for the beast to exhaust itself, and wished that it were not insensible to fatigue like a steam engine! But it was of no use. Hours passed, and the animal showed no signs of exhaustion.

In praise of the *Abraham Lincoln*, it must be said that she struggled on indefatigably. I cannot reckon the distance she made at less than three hundred miles during this unlucky day, November the 6th. But night came on, and blotted out the rough ocean.

Now I thought our expedition was at an end, and that we should never again see the extraordinary animal. I was mistaken. At ten minutes to eleven in the evening, the electric light reappeared three miles to windward of the frigate, as bright, as intense as on the preceding night.

The narwhal seemed motionless; perhaps tired with its day's work, it slept letting itself float with the undulation of the waves. Now appeared the chance for which the captain waited, and on which he determined to act.

He gave his orders. The *Abraham Lincoln* kept up half steam, and advanced cautiously so as not to awake the adversary. It is no rare thing to meet in the middle of the ocean whales so sound asleep that they can be successfully attacked, and Ned Land had harpooned more than one during its sleep. The Canadian went to take his place under the bowsprit.

The frigate approached noiselessly, following the animal's wake, and stopped at two cables' lengths from the beast. No one breathed; a deep silence reigned on the bridge. We were not a hundred feet from the burning focus, the light of which increased and dazzled our eyes.

At this moment, leaning on the forecastle bulwark, I saw below me Ned Land grappling the martingale in one hand, brandishing his terrible harpoon in the other, scarcely twenty feet from the motionless animal. Suddenly his arm straightened, and the harpoon was thrown; I heard the sonorous stroke of the weapon, which seemed to have struck a hard body. The electric light went out suddenly, and two enormous waterpouts broke over the bridge of the frigate, rushing like a torrent from stem to stern, overthrowing men, and breaking the lashing of the spars. A fearful shock followed, and, thrown over the rail without having time to stop myself, I fell into the sea.

Chapter 7
An Unknown Species of Whale

This unexpected fall so stunned me that I have no clear recollection of my sensations at the time. I was at first drawn down to a depth of about twenty feet. I am a good swimmer (though without pretending to rival Byron or Edgar Allan Poe, who were masters of the art), and in that plunge I did not lose my presence of mind. Two vigorous strokes brought me to the surface of the water. My first concern was to look for the frigate. Had the crew seen me disappear? Had the *Abraham Lincoln* veered round? Would the captain put out a boat? Might I hope to be saved?

The darkness was intense. I caught a glimpse of a black mass disappearing in the east, its beacon lights dying out in the distance. It was the frigate! I was lost.

"Help! Help!" I shouted, swimming after the *Abraham Lincoln* in desperation.

My clothes encumbered me; they seemed glued to my body, and paralyzed my movements.

I was sinking! I was suffocating!

"Help!"

This was my last cry. My mouth filled with water, I struggled against being drawn down the abyss. Suddenly my clothes were seized by a strong hand, and I felt myself drawn up to the surface of the sea; and I heard, yes, I heard these words pronounced in my ear—

"If master would be so good as to lean on my shoulder, master would swim with much greater ease."

I seized with one hand my faithful Conseil's arm.

"Is it you?" said I, "you?"

"Myself," answered Conseil; "and waiting master's orders."

"That shock threw you as well as me into the sea?"

"No; but being in my master's service, I followed him."

The worthy fellow thought that was but natural.

"And the frigate?" I asked.

"The frigate?" replied Conseil, turning on his back; "I think that master had better not count too much on her."

"You think so?"

"I say that, because at the time I threw myself into the sea, I heard the men at the wheel say, "The screw and the rudder are broken.""

"Broken?"

"Yes, broken by the monster's teeth. It seemed to be the only injury the *Abraham Lincoln* sustained. But it is bad luck for us—she no longer answers her helm."

"Then we are lost!"

"Perhaps so," calmly answered Conseil. "However, we have still several hours before us, and one can accomplish much in a few hours."

Conseil's imperturbable calmness gave me strength. I swam more vigorously; but, hindered by my clothes, which stuck to me like a leaden weight, I found great difficulty in bearing up. Conseil saw this.

"Will master let me make a slit?" said he; and slipping an open knife under my clothes, he ripped them from top to bottom very skillfully. Then he cleverly slipped them off me, while I swam for both of us.

I did the same for Conseil, and we continued to swim side by side.

Nevertheless, our situation was no less terrible. Perhaps our disappearance had not been noticed; and even if it had, the frigate could not tack, being without its helm. Conseil argued on this supposition, and laid his plans accordingly. This phlegmatic boy was perfectly self-possessed. We decided that, as our only chance of rescue was being picked up by the *Abraham Lincoln's* boats, we must try to wait for them as long as possible, I resolved to husband our strength, so that both should not be exhausted at the same time; and this is how we managed: while one of us lay on his back, quite still, with arms crossed, and legs stretched out, the other would swim and push his comrade. These turns did not last more than ten minutes each; and relieving each other thus, we could swim on for some hours, perhaps till daybreak. Poor chance!

But hope is so firmly rooted in the heart of man! Moreover, there were two of us. Indeed I declare (though it may seem improbable) even if I sought to destroy all hope—if I had wished to despair, I could not.

The collision of the frigate with the cetacean had occurred about eleven o'clock the evening before. I reckoned then we should have eight hours to swim before sunrise, an operation quite practicable if we continued to relieve each other. The sea being very calm, was in our favor. Sometimes I tried to see through the intense darkness that was dispelled only briefly by the phosphorescence caused by our movements. I watched the luminous waves that broke over my hand, whose mirror-like surface was spotted with silvery rings. One might have thought that we were in a bath of quicksilver.

Near one o'clock in the morning, I was seized with dreadful fatigue. My limbs stiffened under the strain of violent cramp. Conseil was obliged to hold me up, and now our preservation devolved on him alone. I heard the poor boy pant; his breathing became short and hurried. I knew that he could not keep up such exertions much longer.

"Leave me! Leave me!" I said to him.

"Leave my master? Never!" replied he. "I would drown first."

Just then the moon appeared through the fringes of a thick cloud that the wind was driving to the east. The surface of the sea glittered with its rays. This kindly light reanimated us. My cramps were relieved. I looked at all the points of the horizon. I saw the frigate! She was five miles from us, and merely a dark mass, hardly discernible. But no boats!

I would have cried out. But what good would it have done at such a distance! Besides my swollen lips could utter no sounds. Conseil could articulate a few words, and I heard him repeat at intervals: "Help! Help!"

Our movements were suspended for an instant; we listened. It might be only a singing in the ear, but it seemed to me as if a cry had answered the cry from Conseil.

"Did you hear?" I murmured.

"Yes! yes!"

And Conseil gave one more despairing call.

This time there was no mistake! A human voice responded to ours! Was it the voice of another unfortunate creature, abandoned in the middle of the ocean, some other victim of the shock sustained by the vessel? Or was it rather a boat from the frigate, that was hailing us in the darkness?

Conseil made a last effort, and leaning on my shoulder, while I struck out in a despairing effort, he raised himself half out of the water, then fell back exhausted.

"What did you see?"

"I saw"—murmured he; "I saw—but do not talk—reserve all your strength!"

What had he seen? Then, I know not why, the thought of the monster came into my head for the first time! But that voice? The time is past for Jonahs to take refuge in whales' bellies! Now Conseil was towing me again. He raised his head occasionally, looked before us, and uttered a cry of recognition, which was responded to by a voice that came nearer and nearer. I could scarcely hear it. My strength was failing; my fingers stiffened; my hand afforded me support no longer; my mouth, convulsively opening, filled with saltwater. Cold crept over me. I raised my head for the last time, then I sank.

At this moment a hard body struck me. I clung to it; then I felt that I was being drawn up, that I was brought to the surface of the water, that my chest collapsed:—I fainted.

It is certain that I soon revived, thanks to the vigorous rubbings that I received. I half opened my eyes.

"Conseil!" I murmured.

"Does master call me?" asked Conseil.

Just then, by the waning light of the moon, which was sinking down to the horizon, I saw a face which was not Conseil's, but which I immediately recognized.

"Ned!" I cried.

"The same, sir, who is seeking his prize!" replied the Canadian.

"Were you thrown into the sea by the shock of the frigate?"

"Yes, Professor; but more fortunate than you, I was able to find a footing almost directly upon a floating island."

"An island?"

"Or, more correctly speaking, on our gigantic narwhal."

"Explain yourself, Ned!"

"Only I soon found out why my harpoon had not entered its skin and was only blunted."

"Why, Ned, why?"

"Because, Professor, that beast is made of sheet iron."

The Canadian's last words produced a sudden revolution in my brain. I wriggled myself quickly to the top of the being, or object, half out of the water, which served us for a refuge. I kicked it. It was evidently a hard impenetrable body, and not the soft substance that forms the bodies of the great marine mammalia. But this hard body might be a bony carapace, like that of the antediluvian animals; and I should be free to class this monster among amphibious reptiles, such as tortoises or alligators.

Well, no! The blackish back that supported me was smooth, polished, without scales. The blow produced a metallic sound; and incredible though it may be, it seemed, I might say, as if it was made of riveted plates.

There was no doubt about it! This monster, this natural phenomenon that had puzzled the learned world, staggered the mind and tricked the imagination of seamen of both hemispheres, was, it must be owned, a still more astonishing phenomenon, inasmuch as it was simply a human construction.

We had no time to lose in reflection, however. We were lying upon the back of some sort of submarine boat, which appeared (as far as I could judge) to resemble a huge fish of steel. Ned Land's mind was made up on this point. Conseil and I could only agree with him.

Just then a bubbling began at the back of this strange thing (which was evidently propelled by a screw), and it began to move. We had only time to seize hold of the upper part, which rose about seven feet out of the water; happily its speed was not great.

"As long as it sails horizontally," muttered Ned Land, "I do not mind; but if it takes a fancy to dive, I would not give two straws for my life."

The Canadian might have said still less. It had become essential to communicate with the beings, of whatever sort they might be, who were enclosed inside the machine. I searched all over the outside for an aperture, a panel or a man-hole, to use a technical expression; but the lines of the iron rivets, solidly driven into the joints of the iron plates, were clear and uniform. Besides, the moon disappeared and left us in total darkness.

Somehow, this long night passed. Clouded recollection prevents my describing the impressions it made. I can only recall clearly one circumstance. During some lull of the wind and sea noises, I fancied several times I heard vague sounds, a sort of fugitive harmony produced by distant words of command. What then was the mystery of this submarine craft, of which the whole world vainly sought an explanation? What kind of beings existed in this strange boat? What mechanical agent caused its prodigious speed?

Daybreak appeared. The morning mists surrounded us, but soon cleared off. I was about to examine the hull, which formed on deck a kind of horizontal platform, when I felt it gradually sinking.

"Oh! confound it!" cried Ned Land, kicking

the resounding plate; "open you inhospitable rascals!"

Happily the sinking movement ceased. Suddenly a noise, like heavy machinery being violently pushed, came from the interior of the boat. An iron plate was moved, a man showed himself, uttered an odd cry, and vanished immediately.

A few minutes later, eight strong men, with masked faces, appeared without a sound, seized us, and dragged us down into their formidable machine.

Chapter 8
Mobilis in Mobili

This brutal abduction was accomplished with the rapidity of lightning. My companions and I were not given time to look around us. I know not what they suffered on being introduced into this floating prison; but for my part a chill froze my skin. With whom had we to deal? Probably some new sort of pirates, who exploited the sea in their own way.

Hardly had the narrow panel closed upon me, when I was enveloped in profound darkness. My eyes, accustomed to the light outside, could distinguish nothing. I felt my naked feet cling to the rungs of an iron ladder. Ned

Land and Conseil, firmly held by our captors, followed me. At the bottom of the ladder, a door opened, and was closed behind us immediately with a loud noise. We were alone. Where, I could not say, could not even imagine. All was black, and such a dense black that, after some minutes, my eyes still were not able to discern even the faintest glimmer.

Meanwhile, Ned Land, furious at these proceedings, gave vent to his indignation.

"Confound it!" cried he, "here are people who almost match the Scotch for hospitality. They only just miss being cannibals. I shall not be surprised if they are, but I declare that they shall not eat me without my protesting."

"Calm yourself, friend Ned, calm yourself," replied Conseil quietly. "Do not cry out before you are hurt. We are not quite done for yet."

"Not quite," sharply replied the Canadian, "but pretty close to it. Things look black. Happily, I still have my bowie-knife and do not need light to use it. The first of these pirates who lays a hand on me—"

"Do not excite yourself, Ned," I said to the harpooner, "and do not compromise us by useless violence. Who knows that they will not listen to us? Let us rather try to find out where we are."

I groped about. In five steps I came to an iron wall, made of plates bolted together. Turning back I struck against a wooden table, near which were ranged several stools. The floor-boards of our prison were concealed under a thick mat of phormium, which deadened the noise of one's feet. The bare walls revealed no trace of window or door. Conseil, going round the reverse way, met me, and we went back to the middle of the cabin, which measured about twenty feet by ten. As to its height, even Ned Land, in spite of his own great size, could not measure it.

Half an hour passed without change in our situation, when the utter darkness gave way to the most dazzling light. Our prison was suddenly illuminated, flooded with a brilliant substance so strong that at first I could not bear it. In its whiteness and intensity I recognized that electric light which had played round what we thought to be a narwhal like a magnificent display of phosphorescence. After shutting my eyes involuntarily, I opened them and saw that this luminous agent came from a half globe, unpolished, in the ceiling of the cabin.

"At last one can see," cried Ned Land, who, knife in hand, stood on the defensive.

"Yes," said I; "but we are still in the dark about ourselves.

The sudden lighting of the cabin enabled me to examine it minutely. It contained only a table and five stools. The invisible door might be hermetically sealed. No noise could be heard. All seemed dead in the interior of this boat. Was it moving? Was it afloat on the surface of the ocean, or submerged in its depths? I could not tell. I hoped that the men of this vessel would not delay in showing themselves.

I was not wrong, a noise of bolts was heard, the door opened, and two men appeared.

One was short, very muscular, broad-shouldered, with robust limbs, large head, abundant black hair, thick moustache, a quick penetrating look and the vivacity which characterizes the population of southern France.

The second stranger merits a more detailed description. A disciple of Gratiolet or Engel would have read his face like an open book. I made out his prevailing qualities directly:—self-confidence,—because his head was well set on his shoulders, and his large black eyes looked around with quiet assurance; calmness,—for his pale skin showed the serenity of his blood; energy,—evinced by the rapid contraction of his lofty brows; and above all courage,—for his deep breathing denoted a great, vital expansiveness.

Whether this person was thirty-five or fifty years of age, I could not say. He was tall, had a large forehead, straight nose, a clearly cut mouth, beautiful teeth, and finely tapered hands, all indicative of a noble yet passionate soul. This man was certainly the most admirable specimen I had ever looked upon.

Particularly notable were his eyes, set far apart and able to take in nearly a quarter of the horizon at once.

This faculty—(I verified it later)—gave him a range of vision far superior to Ned Land's. When this stranger fixed upon an object his eyebrows met, his large eyelids tightened so as to contract the range of his vision. What a glance! It appeared to magnify objects made small by distance, to pierce those sheets of water so opaque to our eyes, to penetrate one's soul, read the very depths of the sea.

The two strangers, wearing caps made from the fur of the sea otter, and shod with sea boots of seal's skin, were dressed in clothes of a special material, which allowed great freedom of movement. The taller of the two, evidently the commander of the vessel, examined us with great attention, without saying a word: then turning to his companion, talked with him in an unknown tongue. It was a sonorous, harmonious, and flexible dialect, the vowels seeming to admit of very varied accentuation.

The other replied by a shake of the head, and added two or three perfectly incomprehensible words. Then he seemed to question me by a look.

I replied in French that I did not know his language; but he seemed not to understand me, and I felt at a loss.

"If master were to tell our story," said Conseil, "perhaps these gentlemen may understand some words."

So I began to recount our adventures, articulating each syllable clearly, and not omitting a single detail. I told them our names and positions, introducing in person Professor Aronnax, his servant Conseil, and master Ned Land, the harpooner.

The man with the gentle calm eyes listened to me quietly, even politely, and with extreme attention; but nothing in his countenance indicated that he had understood my story. When I finished, he said not a word. There remained one resource, to speak English. Perhaps they would know this almost universal language. I knew it, as well as German, sufficiently to read fluently, but not to speak it correctly. But, we must try to make ourselves understood.

"It is your turn," I said to the harpooner; "pull out from your bag the best English ever spoken by an Anglo-Saxon, and try to succeed better than I."

Ned not only retold our story, he complained violently of our imprisonment which contravened the right of man; demanded to know under what law we were held, invoked *habeas corpus;* threatened our captors with dire punishment, and finally showed with most expressive gestures that we were dying of hunger.

To his great disgust, the harpooner did not seem to have made himself more intelligible than I had. Our visitors did not turn a hair. They evidently understood neither the language of Arago nor of Faraday.

Very much embarrassed after having vainly exhausted our philological resources, I knew not what to try next, when Conseil said, "If master will permit me, I will relate it in German."

But in spite of the elegant phrases and good accent of the narrator, the German language had no success. At last non-plussed, I tried to remember my earliest lessons, and to narrate our adventures in Latin, but with no better luck. This last attempt being of no avail, the two strangers exchanged some words in their unknown language, and retired.

The door shut.

"It is an infamous shame," cried Ned Land, who broke out for the twentieth time; "we speak to those rogues in French, English, German and Latin, and not one of them has the politeness to answer!"

"Calm yourself," I said to the impetuous Ned, "anger will do no good."

"But do you not see, Professor," replied our irascible companion, "that we shall absolutely die of hunger in this iron cage?"

"Come, now," said Conseil, philosophically; "we can hold out some time yet."

"My friends," I said, "we must not despair. We have been worse off than this. Do me the favor of waiting a little before forming an opinion concerning the commander and crew of this boat."

"My opinion is formed," replied Ned Land, sharply. "They are rascals."

"Good! And from what country?"

"From the land of rogues!"

"My brave Ned, that country is not clearly indicated on any map of the world; but I admit that the nationality of the two strangers is hard to determine. Neither English, French, nor German, that is quite certain. However, I am inclined to think that the commander and his companion were born in low latitudes. There is southern blood in them. But I cannot determine from their appearance whether they are Spaniards, Turks, Arabians, or Indians. As to their language, it is quite incomprehensible."

"There is the disadvantage of not knowing all languages," said Conseil, "or the disadvantage of not having one universal language."

As he said these words, the door opened. A steward entered. He brought us clothes, coats and trousers, made of a stuff I did not know. I hastened to dress myself, and my companions followed suit. Meanwhile, the steward—dumb, perhaps deaf—had arranged the table, and laid three plates.

"This is something like," said Conseil.

"Bah," said the rancorous harpooner, "what do you suppose they eat here? Tortoise liver, filleted shark, and beefsteaks from sea-dogs."

"We shall see," said Conseil.

The dishes, each with a silver cover, were placed on the table, and we took our places. Undoubtedly we had to do with civilized people, and had it not been for the electric light which flooded us, I could have fancied I was in the dining room of the Adelphi Hotel at Liverpool, or at the Grand Hotel in Paris. I must say, however, that there was neither bread nor wine. The water was fresh and clear, but it was water, and did not suit Ned Land's taste. Amongst the dishes which were brought to us, I recognized several fish delicately dressed; but others, although their taste was excellent, I could not recognize, neither could I tell to what kingdom they belonged, whether animal or vegetable. As to the dinner service, it was elegant, and in perfect taste. Each utensil, spoon, fork, knife, plate, had a monogram engraved on it, with a motto above, of which this is an exact facsimile:

MOBILIS IN MOBILI
N.

Moving in the moving element! The device applied accurately to this submarine vessel. The letter N probably was the initial of the name of the enigmatical person, who commanded at the bottom of the sea.

Ned and Conseil did not reflect much. They devoured the food, and I did likewise. I was, besides, somewhat reassured as to our fate; it seemed evident that our hosts would not let us die of want.

However, everything has an end, even the hunger of people who have not eaten for fifteen hours. Our appetites satisfied, we felt overcome with sleepiness.

"Faith! I shall sleep well," said Conseil.

"So shall I," replied Ned Land.

My two companions stretched themselves on the cabin carpet, and were soon sound asleep. For my part, too many thoughts crowded my brain; too many insoluble questions pressed upon me; too many fancies kept my eyes half open. Where were we? What strange power carried us on? I felt—or rather fancied I felt—the machine sinking down to the lowest beds of the sea. Dreadful nightmares beset me; I saw in these mysterious harbors a whole world of unknown animals, amongst which this submarine boat seemed to be of the same kind, living, moving, and formidable as they. Then my brain grew calmer, my imagination wandered into vague unconsciousness, and I soon fell into a deep sleep.

Chapter 9
Ned Land's Temper

How many hours we slept I do not know; but
our sleep must have been long, for it rested us
completely from our fatigues. I woke first. My
companions had not moved, and were still
stretched in their corner.

Without moving from my hard couch, I
discovered that my brain felt freed, my mind
clear. I then began an examination of our cell.
Nothing was changed inside. The prison was
still a prison—the prisoners, prisoners.
However, the steward, during our sleep, had
cleared the table. Nothing promised a change in
our situation, and I wondered whether we
would remain forever in this cage. I breathed
with difficulty. The heavy air seemed to oppress
my lungs. Although the cell was large, we had
evidently consumed a great part of the oxygen
that it contained. Indeed, each man consumes,
in one hour, the oxygen contained in more than

176 pints of air, and this air charged (as then) with a nearly equal quantity of carbonic acid, becomes unbreathable.

It was urgently necessary to renew the atmosphere of our prison, and no doubt that of the whole submarine boat. That gave rise to a question in my mind. How would the commander of this floating dwelling-place proceed? Would he obtain air by chemical means, getting by heat the oxygen contained in chlorate of potash, and in absorbing carbonic acid by caustic potash? Or, as a more convenient, economical, and consequently more profitable alternative, would he prefer to rise and take air at the surface of the water, like a cetacean, and so renew for twenty-four hours the atmospheric provision?

In fact, I was already obliged to increase my breathing in order to eke out of this cell the little oxygen it contained, when suddenly I was refreshed by a current of air, pure and salt-laden. It was an invigorating sea breeze, charged with iodine. I opened my mouth wide, and saturated my lungs with fresh air.

At the same time I felt the boat rolling slightly but unmistakably. The ironplated monster had evidently just risen to the surface of the ocean to breathe, after the fashion of whales. That was how I found out the manner of the boat's ventilations.

While I had inhaled this air freely, I sought the conduit-pipe, which conveyed to us this beneficial whiff, and I was not long in finding it. Above the door was a ventilator, through which volumes of fresh air renewed the impoverished atmosphere of the cell.

I was making these observations, when Ned and Conseil awoke almost at the same time, under the influence of this reviving air. They rubbed their eyes, stretched themselves, and were on their feet in an instant.

"Did master sleep well?" asked Conseil, with his usual politeness.

"Very well, my brave boy. And you, Mr. Land?"

"Soundly, Professor. I don't know if I am right or not; but there seems to be a sea breeze!"

A seaman could not be mistaken, and I told the Canadian all that had passed during his sleep.

"Good!" said he; "that accounts for those roarings we heard, when the supposed narwhal sighted the *Abraham Lincoln*."

"Quite so, Master Land; it was taking breath."

"Only, Mr. Aronnax, I have no idea what o'clock it is, unless it is dinner-time."

"Dinner-time! My good fellow? Say rather breakfast-time, for we certainly have begun another day."

"So," said Conseil, "you are suggesting that we have slept twenty-four hours?"

"That is my opinion."

"I will not contradict you," replied Ned Land. "But dinner or breakfast, the steward will be welcome whichever he brings."

"Maybe both," said Conseil.

"Right," responded the Canadian, "by my count they owe us two meals, and I intend to honor them both."

"Master Land, we must conform to the rules on board, and I suppose our appetites are in advance of the dinner hour."

"That is just like you, friend Conseil," said Ned, impatiently. "You are never out of temper, always calm; you would return thanks before grace, and die of hunger rather than complain!"

Ned continued to speak angrily of our hosts, even hinting that they might be cannibals, so that I extended his promise to hold his temper.

Time was getting on, and we were fearfully hungry; and this time the steward did not appear. It was rather too long to leave us, if they really had good intentions toward us. Ned Land, tormented by the cravings of hunger, got still more angry; and, notwithstanding his promise, I dreaded an explosion when he found himself with one of the crew.

For two hours more Ned Land's temper increased; he cried, he shouted, but in vain. The walls were deaf. There was no sound to be heard in the boat; all was still as death. It did not move, for I should have felt the trembling motion of the hull under the influence of the screw. Plunged in the depths of the waters, it no longer belonged to earth:—all this cheerless silence was dreadful.

I felt terrified. Conseil was calm, Ned Land roared.

Just then a noise was heard outside. Steps sounded on the metal flags. The locks were turned, the door opened, and the steward appeared.

Before I could rush forward to stop him, the Canadian had thrown this unfortunate down, and had him by the throat. The steward was choking under the grip of his powerful hand.

Conseil was already trying to unclasp the harpooner's hands from his half-suffocated victim, and I too was about to fly to the rescue, when suddenly I was nailed to the spot by hearing these words in French—

"Be quiet Master Land; and you Professor, will you be so good as to listen to me?"

Chapter 10
The Man of the Seas

It was the commander of the vessel who had spoken. At these words, Ned Land rose at once. The steward, nearly strangled, tottered out on a sign from his master; but such was the power of the commander on board, that not a gesture betrayed the resentment which this man must have felt towards the Canadian. Conseil, interested in spite of himself, and I stupefied, waited in silence while this scene played itself out.

The commander, leaning against a corner of the table with his arms folded, scanned us with profound attention. Did he hesitate to speak? Did he regret the words which he had just spoken in French? One might almost think so.

After some moments of silence, which not one of us dreamed of breaking—"Gentlemen" said he, in a calm and penetrating voice, "I speak French, English, German and Latin equally well. I could therefore have answered you at our first interview, but I wished to know you first, then to reflect. The story told by each of you entirely agreeing in the main points, convinced me of your identity. I know now that chance has brought before me M. Pierre Aronnax, Professor of Natural History at the Museum of Paris, entrusted with a scientific mission abroad; Conseil, his servant; and Ned Land, of Canadian origin, harpooner on board the frigate *Abraham Lincoln* of the navy of the United States of America."

I bowed with an air of assent. It was not a question that the commander had put to me. Therefore there was no answer to be made. This man expressed himself with perfect ease, without any accent. His sentences were well turned, his words clear, and his fluency of speech remarkable. Yet, I did not sense in him a fellow-countryman.

He continued the conversation in these terms:

"You have doubtless found sir, that I delayed long in paying you this second visit. The reason is that, your identity recognized, I wished to weigh seriously how to act towards you. I have hesitated much. Exceedingly annoying circumstances have brought you into the presence of a man who has broken all ties to humanity. You have come to trouble my existence."

"Unintentionally!" said I.

"Unintentionally?" replied the stranger, raising his voice a little; "was it unintentionally that the *Abraham Lincoln* pursued me all over the seas? Was it unintentionally that you took passage with that frigate? Was it unintentionally that your cannon balls rebounded off the plating of my vessel? Was it unintentionally that Mr. Ned Land struck me with his harpoon?"

I detected a restrained irritation in these words. But to these recriminations I had a very natural answer to make and I made it.

"Sir," said I, "no doubt you are ignorant of the discussions about you which have taken place in America and Europe. You do not know that divers accidents, caused by collisions with your submarine machine, have excited public feeling on the two continents. I omit the numerous hypotheses by which it has sought to explain the inexplicable phenomenon of which you alone possess the secret. But you must understand that, in pursuing you all over the high seas of the Pacific, the *Abraham Lincoln* believed itself to be chasing some powerful sea-monster, of which it was necessary to rid the ocean at any price."

A half-smile curled the lips of the commander: then, in a calmer tone—

"M. Arronnax," he replied, "dare you affirm that your frigate would not as soon have pursued and cannonaded a submarine as it would a monster?"

This question embarrassed me, for certainly

Captain Farragut might not have hesitated. He might have thought it as much his duty to destroy a machine of this kind, as he would a gigantic narwhal.

"You understand then, sir," continued the stranger, "that it is my right to treat you as enemies?"

I answered nothing and with good reason. For what good would it do to discuss such a proposition, when force could destroy the best arguments?

"I hesitated for some time," continued the commander. "Nothing has obliged me to show you hospitality. If I chose to separate from you, I should have no interest in seeing you again; I could place you upon the deck of this vessel which has served you as a refuge, sink beneath the waters, and forget that you ever existed. Would not that be my right?"

"It might be the right of a savage," I answered, "but not that of a civilized man."

"Professor," replied the commander quickly, "I am not what you call a civilized man! I have done with society entirely, for reasons which I alone have the right to weigh. I do not therefore obey its laws, and I ask you never to allude to them before me again!"

This was said plainly. A flash of anger and disdain kindled in the eyes of the stranger, and I glimpsed a terrible past in the life of this man. Not only had he put himself beyond the pale of human laws, but he had made himself independent of them, free in the strictest sense of the word, quite beyond their reach. Who then would dare to pursue him at the bottom of the sea, when, on its surface, he defied all efforts made against him? What vessel could resist the shock of his submarine monitor? What armor, however thick, could withstand the blows of his spur? No man could make him account for his actions; God, if he believed in one—his conscience, if he had one,—were the sole judges to whom he was answerable.

These reflections crossed my mind rapidly, whilst the strange personage was silent, absorbed, seemingly wrapped up in himself. I regarded him with fear mingled with interest, as doubtless, Oedipus had the Sphinx.

After rather a long silence, the commander resumed the conversation.

"I did hesitate," said he, "but I thought that my interest might be reconciled with that pity to which every human being has a right. You will remain on my vessel, since fate has cast you there. You will be free; and in exchange for this liberty, I shall impose only one condition. Your word of honor that you submit to it will suffice."

"Speak, sir," I answered. "I suppose this condition is one which a man of honor may accept?"

"Yes, sir; it is this. It is possible that certain events, unforeseen, may oblige me to confine you to your cabins for some hours or days, as the case may be. As I desire never to use violence, I expect from you, more than all the others, a complete obedience. In thus acting, I take all responsibility. I acquit you entirely, for I make it impossible for you to see what ought not to be seen. Do you accept this condition?"

Then things took place on board which were singular, and which ought not to be seen by people who were not beyond the pale of social laws. Amongst the surprises which the future was preparing for me, this might not be the least.

"We accept," I answered; "but I ask your permission, sir, to address one question to you—one only."

"Speak, sir."

"You said that we should be free on board."

"Entirely."

"I ask you, then, what you mean by this liberty?"

"Why, the liberty to go, to come, to see, to observe everything that happens here, except under rare circumstances—the liberty, in short, which my companions and I enjoy ourselves."

It was evident that we did not understand one another.

"Pardon me, sir," I resumed, "but this liberty is only what every prisoner has of pacing his prison. It cannot suffice us."

"It must, however."

"What! We must renounce ever again seeing our country, our friends or our relations?"

"Yes, sir, but to renounce that unbearable worldly yoke which men believe to be liberty, is perhaps not so painful as you think."

"Well," exclaimed Ned Land, "never will I give my word of honor not to try to escape."

"I did not ask you for your word of honor, Master Land," answered the commander coldly.

"Sir," I replied, beginning to get angry in spite of myself, "you abuse your position with us; it is cruelty."

"No, sir, it is clemency. You are my prisoners of war. I keep you—when I could, by a word, plunge you into the depths of the ocean. You attacked me. You came to discover a secret which no man in the world may penetrate—the secret of my whole existence. And you think that I am going to send you back to that world which must know me no more? Never! In retaining you, it is not you whom I protect—it is myself."

These words indicated a resolution taken on the part of the commander, against which no arguments would prevail.

"So, sir," I rejoined, "you merely give us the choice between life and death?"

"That is all."

"My friends," said I, "to such a question, there is no answer. But no word of honor binds us to the master of this vessel."

"None, sir," answered the Unknown.

Then in a gentler tone, he continued—

"Now, permit me to finish what I have to say to you. I know you, M. Aronnax. You and your companions will not perhaps, have so much to complain of in the chance which has bound you to my fate. You will find amongst the books which are my favorite study the work which you have published on the depths of the sea! I have read it often. You have carried your work as far as terrestrial science permitted you. But you do not know all—you have not seen all. Let me tell you then, Professor, that you will not regret the time passed on board my vessel. You are going to visit the land of marvels. Your mind will be in a state of constant amazement and stupefaction. You will not tire easily of the spectacle which will be offered endlessly to your vision. I shall go on another submarine tour of the world—who knows? perhaps my last—revisiting all the wonders at the bottom of the sea that I have gone over time and again, and you shall be my companion in learning. From this day forth you will enter into a new element, you will see what has been seen by no other man—I do not count myself and my crew—and our planet, thanks to me and my *Nautilus* will yield its last secrets up to you.''

I cannot deny it, these words of the commander had a great effect upon me. My weak point was touched; and I forgot, for a moment, that the contemplation of these sublime subjects was not worth the loss of liberty. Besides, I trusted to the future to decide this grave question. So I contented myself with saying—

''By what name shall I address you?''

''Sir,'' replied the commander, ''I am nothing to you but Captain Nemo; and you and your companions are to me only the passengers of the *Nautilus.*''

Captain Nemo called. A steward appeared. The captain gave him his orders in that strange language which I did not understand. Then turning towards the Canadian and Conseil—

''A meal awaits you in your cabin,'' said he. ''Be so good as to follow this man.''

''And now, M. Aronnax, our breakfast is

ready. Permit me to lead the way.''

"At your service, Captain.''

I followed Captain Nemo; and as soon as I had passed through the door, I found myself in a kind of passage lighted by electricity, similar to the waist of a ship. After we had proceeded a dozen yards, a second door was opened to me.

I then entered a dining room, decorated and funished in severe taste. High oaken sideboards, inlaid with ebony, stood at the two ends of the room, and upon their shelves glittered china, porcelain and glass of inestimable value. The silver on the table sparkled in the rays which the luminous ceiling shed around, while the glare was tempered and softened by exquisite paintings.

In the center of the room, a table was richly laid out. Captain Nemo indicated the place I was to occupy.

"Be seated,'' he said, "and eat as befits a man who must die of starvation.''

Breakfast consisted of a number of dishes, the contents of which were obviously furnished by the sea alone; and others of whose nature and provenance I was ignorant. I acknowledged that they were good, but they had a peculiar flavor, to which I easily became accustomed. These different aliments appeared to me to be rich in phosphorus, and I thought they too must have a marine origin.

Captain Nemo looked at me. I asked him no questions, but he guessed my thoughts, and answered of his own accord the questions which I was burning to address to him.

"The greater part of these dishes are

unknown to you," he said to me. "However, you may partake of them without fear. They are wholesome and nourishing. For a long time I have renounced the food of the earth, and am never ill now. My crew, who are healthy, are fed on the same food."

"So," said I, "all these edibles are the produce of the sea?"

"Yes, Professor, the sea supplies all my wants. Sometimes I cast my nets in tow, and I draw them in ready to break. Sometimes I hunt in the midst of this element, which appears to be inaccessible to man, and quarry the game which dwells in my submarine forests. My flocks, like those of Neptune's old shepherds, graze fearlessly in the immense prairies of the ocean. I have a vast property there, which I cultivate myself, and which is always sown by the hand of the Creator of all things."

"I can understand perfectly, sir, that your nets furnish excellent fish for your table; I can understand also that you hunt aquatic game in your submarine forests; but I cannot understand at all how a particle of meat, no matter how small, can figure in your bill of fare."

"This, which you believe to be meat, Professor, is nothing else than fillet of turtle. Here are also some dolphins' livers, which you take to be ragout of pork. My cook is a clever fellow, who excels in dressing the various products of the ocean. Taste all these dishes. Here is a preserve of holothuria, which a Malay would declare to be unrivaled in the world; here is a cream, the milk of which has been furnished by the cetacea, and the sugar by the great fucus of the North Sea; and lastly, permit me to offer you some preserve of anemones, which is equal to that of the most delicious fruits.''

I tasted more from curiosity than as a connoisseur, whilst Captain Nemo enchanted me with his extraordinary stories.

''You like the sea, Captain?''

''Yes; I love it! The sea is everything. It covers seven-tenths of the terrestrial globe. Its breath is pure and healthy. It is an immense desert where man is never lonely, for he feels life stirring on all sides. The sea is only the embodiment of a supernatural and wonderful existence. It is nothing but love and emotion; it is the 'Living Infinite,' as one of your poets has said. In fact, Professor, Nature manifests herself in it by all her three kingdoms; mineral, vegetable, and animal. The sea is a vast reservoir of Nature. The globe began with sea, so to speak; and who can say it will not end with it? Here is supreme tranquility. The sea does not belong to despots. Upon its surface men can still exercise unjust laws, fight, tear one another to pieces, and be carried away with terrestrial horrors. But at thirty feet below its level, their reign ceases, their influence is quenched, and their power disappears. Ah! sir, live—live in the bosom of the waters! Only there is independence! There I recognize no master! There I am free!''

Captain Nemo suddenly became silent in the midst of this enthusiasm, by which he was quite carried away. For a few moments he paced up and down, much agitated. Then he became calm, regained his accustomed coldness of expression, and turning towards me—

"Now, Professor," said he, "if you wish to go over the *Nautilus*, I am at your service."

Captain Nemo rose, I followed him. A double door situated at the back of the dining room opened, and I entered a room the equal in dimensions of that which I had just quitted.

It was a library. High pieces of furniture, of black violet ebony inlaid with brass, carried on their wide shelves a great number of uniformly bound books. They followed the shape of the room, terminating at the lower part in huge divans, covered with brown leather, which were curved, to afford the greatest comfort. Light movable desks, made to slide in and out at will, allowed one to rest one's book while reading. In the center stood an immense table, covered with pamphlets, amongst which were some newspapers, already old. Electric light flooded this harmonious ensemble. It shone from four unpolished globes half sunk in the scrolls of the ceiling. I looked with real admiration at this room, so ingeniously fitted out, and I could scarcely believe my eyes.

"Captain Nemo," said I to my host, who had just thrown himself on one of the divans, "this is a library which would do honor to more than one of the continental palaces, and I am absolutely astounded at the thought that it can follow you to the bottom of the seas."

"Where could you find greater solitude or silence, Professor?" replied Captain Nemo.

"Did your study in the Museum afford you such perfect quiet?"

"No, sir; and I must confess it a very poor one after seeing yours. You must have six or seven thousand volumes here."

"Twelve thousand, M. Aronnax. These are the only ties which bind me to the earth. But I had done with the world on the day my *Nautilus* plunged for the first time beneath the waters. That day I bought my last volumes, my last pamphlets, my last papers, and from that time would like to believe that men no longer think or write. These books, Professor, are at your service besides, and you may use them freely."

I thanked Captain Nemo and approached the shelves of the library. Works on science, morals, and literature abounded in every language; but I did not see one single work on political economy; that subject appeared to be strictly proscribed. Strange to say, all these books were carelessly arranged, in whatever language they were written; and this medley showed that the Captain of the *Nautilus* must have read indiscriminately, books which he took up by chance.

"Sir," said I to the Captain, "I thank you for having placed this library at my disposal. It contains treasures of science, and I shall profit by them."

"This room is not only a library," said Captain Nemo, "it is also a smoking room."

"A smoking room!" I cried. "Then one may smoke on board?"

"Certainly."

"Then, sir, I am forced to believe that you have kept up communications with Havana."

"Not at all," answered the Captain. "Accept this cigar, M. Aronnax; and though it does not come from Havana, you will be pleased with it, if you are a connoisseur."

I took the cigar which was offered me; its shape recalled those of London, but it seemed to be of gold leaves. I lighted it at a little brazier, which was supported upon an elegant bronze stem, and drew the first whiffs with the delight of a smoking lover, who has not smoked for two days.

"It is excellent," said I, "but it is not tobacco."

"No!" answered the Captain, "this tobacco comes neither from Havana nor from the East. It is a kind of seaweed, rich in nicotine, with which the sea provides me, although somewhat stingily."

At that moment Captain Nemo opened a door which stood opposite that by which I had entered the library, and I passed into an immense and splendidly lighted drawing room.

It was a vast four-sided room, thirty feet long, eighteen wide, and fifteen high. A luminous ceiling, decorated with light arabesques, shed a soft clear light over all the marvels accumulated in this museum. For it was in fact a museum, in which an intelligent and prodigal hand had gathered all the treasures of nature and art, with the artistic confusion which distinguishes a painter's studio.

Thirty paintings by Masters, uniformly framed, separated by bright drapery, or-

namented the walls, which were hung with
tapestry of severe design. I saw works of great
value, the larger part of which I had admired in
special collections of Europe, and in exhibitions
of paintings. Several schools of the old masters
were represented by a Madonna of Raphael, a
Virgin of Leonardo da Vinci, a nymph of Cor-
reggio, a woman of Titian, an Adoration of
Veronese, and Assumption of Murillo, a portrait of Holbein, a monk of Velasquez, a martyr
of Ribera, a fair of Rubens, two Flemish landscapes of Teniers, three little "genre" pictures
of Gerard Dow, Metsu, and Paul Potter, two
specimens of Gericault and Prudhon, and some
sea-pieces of Backhuysen and Vernet. Amongst
the works of modern painters were pictures with
the signatures of Delacroix, Ingres, Decamps,
Troyon, Meissonier, Daubigny, etc.; and some
admirable statues in marble and bronze, after
the finest antique models, stood upon pedestals
in the corners of this magnificent museum.
Amazement, as the Captain of the *Nautilus* had
predicted, had already begun to take possession
of me.

"Professor," said this strange man, "you
must excuse the unceremonious way in which I
receive you, and the disorder of this room."

"Sir," I answered, "without seeking to know
who you are, may I recognize in you an artist?"

"An amateur, nothing more, sir. I used to
love to collect these beautiful works created by
the hand of man. I sought them avidly and fer-
reted them out indefatigably, and I have been
able to bring together some objects of great
value. These are my last souvenirs of that world

which is dead to me. In my eyes, your modern artists are already old; they have two or three thousand years of existence; I confuse them in my mind. Masters have no age.''

"And these musicians?" said I, pointing out some works of Weber, Rossini, Mozart, Beethoven, Haydn, Meyerbeer, Herold, Wagner, Auber, Gounod and a number of others, scattered over a large model piano-organ which occupied one of the panels of the drawing room.

"These musicians," replied Captain Nemo, "are contemporaries of Orpheus; for in the memory of the dead all chronological differences are effaced; and I am dead, Professor; as much dead as those of your friends who sleep six feet under the earth!"

Captain Nemo was silent, and seemed lost in a profound reverie. I studied him with deep interest, analyzing in silence the strange expression on his countenance. Leaning on his elbow against an angle of a costly mosaic table, he no longer saw me—had forgotten my presence.

I did not disturb this reverie, and continued my observation of the curiosities which enriched this drawing room. Interposed among these works of art were works of nature.

Under elegant glass cases, fixed by copper rivets, were classed and labeled the most precious productions of the sea ever presented to the eye of a naturalist. My delight as a professor may be imagined.

The division containing the zoophytes presented the most curious speciments of the two groups of polypi and echinoderms. In the first group, the tubipores, were: gorgones arranged like a fan; soft sponges of Syria; ises of the Moluccas; pennatules; an admirable virgularia of the Norwegian seas; variegated unbellulairae; alcyonariae; a whole series of madrepores, which my master Milne Edwards has so cleverly classified, amongst which I remarked some wonderful flabellinae oculinae of the Island of Bourbon; the "Neptune's car" of the Antilles; superb varieties of corals—in short, every species of those curious polypi of which entire islands are formed, which will one day become continents. Of the echinoderms—remarkable for their coating of spines—asteri, sea-stars, pantacrinae, comatules, asterophons, echini, holothuri, etc., represented individually a complete collection of this group.

A somewhat nervous conchyliologist would surely have fainted before other more numerous cases, in which were classified the specimens of molluscs. It was a collection of inestimable value, which time fails me to describe minutely. Amongst these specimens I will quote from memory only—the elegant royal hammer-fish of the Indian Ocean, whose regular white spots stood out brightly on a red and brown ground; an imperial spondyle, bright-colored, bristling with spines, a rare specimen in the European museums (I estimated its value at not less than 1000 pounds); a common hammer-fish of the seas of New Holland, which is procured only with difficulty; exotic buccardia of Senegal; fragile white bivalve shells, which a breath might shatter like soap-bubbles; several varieties of the aspirgillum of Java; a kind of calcareous tube, edged with leafy folds, and much debated by amateurs; a whole series of trochi, some a greenish-yellow, found in the American seas, others a reddish-brown, native to Australian waters; others from the Gulf of Mexico, noted for their imbricated shell; stellari found in the Southern Seas; and last, the rarest of all, the magnificent spur of New Zealand; and every kind of delicate and fragile shell to which science has given the most charming names.

Apart, in separate compartments, were spread out chaplets of pearls of the greatest beauty, which reflected the electric light in little sparks of fire; pink pearls, torn from the pinnamarina of the Red Sea; green pearls of the haliotyde iris; yellow, blue and black pearls, the curious productions of the divers molluscs of every ocean, and certain mussels of the watercourses of the North; lastly, several specimens of inestimable value which had been gathered from the rarest pintadines. Some of these pearls were larger than a pigeon's egg, and were worth as much and more than that which the traveler Tavernier sold to the Shah of Persia for three millions, and surpassed the one in the possession of the Imaum of Muscat, which I believed to be unrivaled in the world.

Therefore, to estimate the value of this collection was simply impossible. Captain Nemo must have expended millions in the acquisition of these various specimens, and I was wondering what source he could have drawn from, to have been able thus to gratify his fancy for collecting, when I was interrupted by these words—

"You are examining my shells, Professor? Unquestionably they must be interesting to a naturalist; but for me they have a more special charm, for I collected them all with my own hand, and there is not a sea on the face of the globe which has escaped my researches."

"I can understand, Captain, the delight of wandering about in the midst of such riches. You are one of those who have collected their treasures themselves. No museum in Europe possesses such a collection of the fruits of the ocean. But if I exhaust all my admiration upon it, I shall have none left for the vessel which carries it. I do not wish to pry into your secrets; but I must confess that this *Nautilus* with the motive power it contains, the contrivances which enable it to be worked, the power which propels it, all excite my curiosity to the highest pitch. I see suspended on the walls of this room instruments of whose use I am ignorant."

"You will find these same instruments in my own room, Professor, where I shall enjoy explaining their use to you. But first come and inspect the cabin which is for your own use. You must see how you will be accommodated on board the *Nautilus*."

I followed Captain Nemo, who took me back into the ship's alleyway, through one of the doors which opened from each panel of the drawing room. He led me towards the bow, and there I found, not a cabin, but an elegant room, with a bed, dressing table, and other furnishings.

I could only thank my host.

"Your room adjoins mine," said he, opening a door, "and mine opens onto the saloon that we have just left."

I entered the Captain's room; it had an almost monastic aspect. A small iron bedstead, a desk, some toilet articles. No comforts, only the strictest necessities.

Captain Nemo pointed to a seat.

"Be so good as to sit down," he said. I seated myself, and he began thus:

Chapter 11
All by Electricity

"Sir," said Captain Nemo, indicating various objects that hung on the walls of his room, "here are the instruments required for the navigation of the *Nautilus*. Here, as in the saloon, I have them always under my eyes, and they tell me my exact position and direction in the ocean. Some are familiar to you, such as the thermometer, which gives the internal temperature of the *Nautilus;* the barometer, which indicates the weight of the air and foretells changes in the weather; the hygrometer, which measures the moisture in the atmosphere; the storm-glass, which contains a mixture that separates when a tempest is approaching; the compass, which guides my course; the sextant, which shows the latitude by the altitude of the sun; chronometers, by which I calculate the longitude; and glasses for day and night, which enable me to examine all points of the horizon, when the *Nautilus* rises to the surface of the waves.''

"Those are the usual nautical instruments," I replied, "and I know their use. But these others very likely answer the particular needs of the *Nautilus*. This dial with the movable needle is a manometer, is it not?''

"It is actually a manometer. When connected with the water, whose external pressure it indicates, it gives our depth at the same time.''

"And these other instruments, the use of which I cannot guess?''

"Here, Professor, I ought to give you some explanations. Will you be kind enough to listen to me?''

He was silent for a few moments, then he said—

"There is a powerful medium, obedient, rapid, available, adaptable to every use, that rules as master on board my vessel. Everything is done by means of it. It lights the ship, warms it, and is the soul of all my machineries. This is electricity.''

"Electricity?'' I cried in surprise.

"Yes, sir.''

"Nevertheless, Captain, you possess an extreme rapidity of movement, which does not agree with the ability of electricity. Until now, its dynamic power has been very limited, and able to produce only a small amount of strength."

"Professor," said Captain Nemo, "my electricity is not everybody's."

"You know the composition of seawater. In a thousand grams are found 96½ percent of water, and about 2⅔ percent of chloride of sodium; then, in a smaller quantity, chlorides of magnesium and of potassium, bromide of magnesium, sulphate of magnesia, sulphate and carbonate of lime. You see that there is a large proportion of it.

"It is this sodium that I extract from seawater, and from which I compose elements. Mixed with mercury it forms a compound that takes the place of zinc. Mercury never wears out. Only the salt is consumed, and the sea supplies it endlessly. And salt furnishes tovici, the electron motive power of zinc."

"But since you must use your electrical batteries to extract the salt, it seems that you must use more electricity to obtain the salt than the salt can produce."

"I do not use my battery; I use the heat from coal—coal of the sea."

"Then you can exploit the underwater mines?"

"Sir, you shall see me at work. I ask only that you have a little patience. Remember only this: I owe all to the ocean; it produces electricity, and electricity gives heat, light, motion, and, in a word, life to the *Nautilus.*"

"But not the air you breathe?"

"Oh! I could manufacture the air necessary

for my consumption, but it is unnecessary, because I go up to the surface whenever I wish. However, if electricity does not actually furnish air to breathe, it works at least the powerful pumps that accumulate the air and store it in special reservoirs, and which allows me to stay underwater as long as I wish."

"Captain, you seem to have discovered the true dynamic capabilities of electricity, which all men may find someday."

"I do not know that they will find it," Nemo replied coldly. "Be that as it may, you now know the first use I have made of this precious stuff. It is that which gives us light, more steadily, more evenly, than does the sun."

"Observe this clock; it is electrical, and goes with a regularity that defies the best chronometers. I have divided it into twenty-four hours, like the Italian clocks, because for me there is neither night nor day, sun or moon, but only that artificial light that I take with me to the bottom of the sea. Look! It is now ten o'clock in the morning."

"Exactly."

"Another application of electricity. This dial hanging in front of us indicates the speed of the *Nautilus*. An electric wire connects it with the screw of the ship's log, and the needle indicates actual progress of the machine. We are now going at the moderate speed of fifteen miles an hour."

"It is marvelous! And I see Captain, you are wise to make use of this medium that is destined to take the place of wind, water, and steam."

"We have not finished, M. Aronnax," said

Captain Nemo, rising; "if you will follow me, we will visit the stern of the *Nautilus.*"

I already knew the rear section part of this underwater boat, which was divided in the following way, going from the center to the stern: the dining saloon, five yards long, separated from the library by a watertight partition; the library, five yards long; the large drawing saloon ten yards long, separated from the Captain's cabin by a second watertight partition; Nemo's room, five yards in length; mine, two and a half yards; and lastly, a storage tank of air, seven and a half yards, that extended to the bows. In all, thirty-five yards long, or one hundred and five feet. The partitions had doors that were shut hermetically by means of india-rubber valves, and ensured the safety of the *Nautilus* in case of a leak.

I followed Captain Nemo through the narrow alleyway and came to the center of the boat. There a sort of shaft opened between two partitions. An iron ladder, fastened with an iron hook to the wall, led to the top of the shaft. I asked the Captain what the ladder was used for.

"It leads to the small boat," he said.

"What! Have you a boat?" I exclaimed in surprise.

"Of course; an excellent vessel, light and insubmersible, that serves either as a fishing or as a pleasure boat."

"But then, when you wish to embark, are you obliged to come to the surface of the water?"

"Not at all. This boat is attached to the upper part of the hull of the *Nautilus,* and fits in an indentation made for it. It is quite watertight, and held together by solid bolts. This ladder leads to a man-hole in the hull of the *Nautilus*, that corresponds with a similar hole in the side of the boat. Through this double-opening I get into the cabin of the small vessel. The men shut the entrance to the *Nautilus*, I shut the other by means of screw pressure. I undo the bolts, and the little boat goes up to the surface of the sea with prodigious rapidity. I then open the hatch of the bridge, kept carefully shut till then; I mast it, hoist my sail, or take my oars, and I'm off."

"But how do you get back on board?"

"I do not come back, M. Aronnax; the *Nautilus* comes to me."

"By your orders?"

"By my orders. An electric thread connects us. I telegraph to it, and that is enough."

"Really," I said astonished at these marvels, "nothing can be more simple."

Having passed the cage of the staircase that led to the half-deck, I saw a cabin six feet long, in which Conseil and Ned Land, enchanted with their repast, were devouring it with appetite. Then a door opened into a kitchen nine feet long, situated between the large storerooms. There electricity, stronger than gas itself, supplied all the heat. Wires leading under the stoves conveyed to metal plates, a heat which was evenly maintained and distributed. They also heated a distilling apparatus, which, by evaporation, furnished excellent drinking water. Near the kitchen was a bathroom, comfortably arranged with hot and cold water taps.

Beyond the kitchen was the main cabin for

the men, sixteen feet long. But the door was shut, and I could not see how it was fitted out, which might have given me an idea of the number of men employed on board the *Nautilus*.

At the end was a fourth partition that separated this cabin from the engine-room. A door opened, and I found myself in the compartment where Captain Nemo—certainly an engineer of the first order—had set up his locomotive machinery. This engine-room, clearly lighted, measured not less than sixty-five feet in length. It was divided into two parts; the first contained the materials for producing electricity, and the second the mechanism that turned the screw. I examined with an interest easy to understand the engine of the *Nautilus*.

"You see," said the Captain, "I use Bunsen's elements, not those of Ruhmkorff. His would not have been powerful enough. Bunsen's are fewer in number, but strong and large, which experience proves to be the best. The electricity produced passes to the stern, where it operates by electromagnets of great size, on a special system of levers and gears that transmit the movement to the axle of the screw. The screw has a diameter of nineteen feet, and a thread of twenty-three feet, and performs almost a hundred and twenty revolutions a second."

"And this gives you...?"

"A speed of fifty miles an hour."

There was a mystery here. How could electricity set the propeller in motion with such power! Where did this almost unlimited force originate?

"I have seen the *Nautilus* maneuver before the *Abraham Lincoln*," I said, "and I well know its speed. But speed is not enough. You must see where you are going; turn to the right, to the left; go up, go down. How do you attain the great depths, where you must find greatly increased resistance? How do you rise again to the surface of the ocean? All in all, how do you maintain yourself in this environment which delights you so? Am I asking too much?"

"Not at all Professor," replied the Captain, after a slight hesitation, "since you will never be able to leave this underwater ship. Come into the saloon, it is my usual office, and there you will learn all you want to know about the *Nautilus.*"

Chapter 12
Some Figures

A moment later, we were seated on a sofa in the saloon, cigars at our lips. The Captain handed me a diagram that showed the plan, outline, and height of the *Nautilus*. Then he began his description in these words:—

"Here, M. Aronnax, are the various dimensions of the ship where you are. It is an elongated cylinder with conical ends. It is very like a cigar in shape, a shape already adopted in

London in several constructions of the same sort. The length of this cylinder, from stern to stern, is exactly 232 feet, and its maximum breadth is twenty-six feet. It is not designed on the order of transatlantic steamers, but its lines are so long, and its curves so gradual that the water it displaces slips away easily and presents no obstacle to its passage. Two dimensions enable you to obtain by a simple calculation the surface and volume of the *Nautilus*. Its surface measures 6032 feet; and its volume about 1500 cubic yards—that is to say, when completely immersed it displaces 50,000 cubic feet of water, or weighs 1500 tons.

"When I made the plans for a ship to sail under the sea, I meant that nine-tenths should be submerged; consequently, it ought only to displace nine-tenths of its bulk—that is to say, only to weigh that number of tons. I ought not, therefore to have exceeded that weight, constructing it on the aforesaid dimensions.

"The *Nautilus* is composed of two hulls, one inside, the other outside, joined by T-shaped irons, which give it great strength. Indeed, owing to this cellular arrangement it resists like a block as if it were solid. Its sides cannot yield; it holds together of itself, and not because of the closeness of its rivets; and the homogeneity of its construction, due to the perfect union of the materials, enables it to challenge the roughest seas.

"These two hulls are composed of steel plates, whose density is from 7/10 to 8/10 that of water. The first is not less than two inches and a half thick, and weighs 394 tons. The second envelope, the keel twenty inches high and ten thick, itself weighs sixty-two tons. The engine, the ballast, the several accessories and apparatus appendages, the partitions and bulkheads, weigh 961.62 tons. Do you follow all this?''

''I do.''

''Then when the *Nautilus* is afloat under these circumstances, one-tenth is out of the water. Now, if I make reservoirs of a size equal to this tenth, or capable of holding 150 tons, and I fill them with water, the boat, weighing then 1507 tons, will be completely immersed. That is what would happen, Professor. These reservoirs are in the lower parts of the *Nautilus*. I turn on taps and they fill, and the vessel sinks that had just been level with the surface.''

''Well, Captain, now we come to the real difficulty. I can understand your rising to the surface; but diving below the surface, does not your submarine encounter a pressure, and consequently undergo an upward thrust of just about fifteen pounds per square inch?''

''Just, so, sir.''

''Then, unless you quite fill the *Nautilus*, I do not see how you can draw it down to those depths.''

''Professor, you must not confuse statics with dynamics, or you will be exposed to grave errors. There is very little labor spent in attaining the lower regions of the ocean, for all bodies have a tendency to sink. When I wanted to find out the necessary increase of weight to sink the

Nautilus, I had only to calculate the reduction of volume that seawater acquires according to the depth."

"That is evident."

"Now, if water is not absolutely incompressible, at least it compresses very little. Indeed, after the most recent calculations this reduction is only .000436 of an atmosphere for each thirty feet of depth. If we want to sink 3000 feet, I should keep account of the reduction of bulk under a pressure equal to that of a column of water of a thousand feet. The calculation is easily verified. Now, I have supplementary reservoirs capable of holding a hundred tons. Therefore, I can sink to a considerable depth. When I wish to rise to the level of the sea, I only let off the water, and empty all the reservoirs if I want the *Nautilus* to emerge from the tenth part of her total capacity."

I had nothing to oppose to these reasonings.

"I admit your calculations, Captain," I replied. "I should be wrong to dispute them since daily experience confirms them; but I foresee a real difficulty in the way."

"What, sir?"

"When you are 1000 feet deep, the walls of the *Nautilus* bear a pressure of 100 atmospheres. If then, just now you were to empty the supplementary reservoirs, to lighten the vessel, and to go up to the atmospheres, which is 1500 pounds per square inch. From that a power—"

"That electricity alone can give," the Captain hastened to say. "I repeat, sir, that the dynamic ability of my engines is almost infinite. The pumps of the *Nautilus* have a prodigious force, as you must have observed when their jets of water descended like a torrent upon the *Abraham Lincoln*. Besides, I use my supplementary reservoirs to attain a depth of only 750 to 1000 fathoms, in order to spare my machines. When the fancy takes me to visit the depths of the ocean five or six miles below the surface, I make use of slower but not less infallible means.''

''What are they, Captain?''

''That leads naturally to my telling you how the *Nautilus* is operated.''

''I am impatient to learn.''

''To steer this ship to starboard or port, to progress, that is, along a horizontal plane, I use an ordinary rudder fixed to the back of the sternpost, and only a wheel and some tackle to move it. But I can also make the *Nautilus* rise and sink, and sink and rise in vertical plane by means of two inclined planes fastened to its sides, at the center of the water line movable planes that can take any direction, and that are worked from the inside by powerful levers. If the planes are kept parallel with the ship, it moves horizontally. If they are slanted, the *Nautilus*, under the thrust of the screw, either sinks diagonally or rises diagonally as it suits me. If I wish to rise more quickly to the surface, I ship the screw, and the pressure of the water causes the *Nautilus* to rise vertically, as a balloon filled with hydrogen rises in the air.''

''Bravo, Captain! I salute you, but how can the steersman follow the course you give him, when he is underwater?''

''The steersman is placed in a glass cage that

is projected from the highest part of the hull of the *Nautilus*, and strengthened with lenticular glasses.''

''These glasses are capable of resisting such pressure?''

''Perfectly. Crystal which breaks at a light blow is, nevertheless, capable of offering considerable resistance. While fishing by electric light in 1864 in the North Sea, we saw glass plates less than a third of an inch thick resist a pressure of sixteen atmospheres. The glass that I use is at least thirty times thicker.''

''True, yet if one is to see, the light must chase away the shadows. In the midst of all that water, how can the steersman see?''

''In the back of his cage is placed a powerful electric reflector, whose rays light up the sea for a distance of half a mile.''

''Ah! bravo, bravo, Captain! That explains the phosphorescence of the supposed narwhal that puzzled all the scholars. Now, please tell me of the collision between the *Nautilus* and the *Scotia*, which caused so much excitement; was it deliberate or an accident?''

''Quite accidental, sir. I was sailing only one fathom below the surface of the water, when the shock came. It had no bad result.''

''None, sir. But now about your encounter with the *Abraham Lincoln*?''

''Professor, I am angry with myself over one of the best vessels in the brave American navy; but they attacked me, and I was forced to defend myself. I contented myself, however, with putting the frigate out of commission; she will not have any difficulty in getting repaired at the next port.''

"Ah, Commander!" I said with feeling, "your *Nautilus* is certainly a marvelous ship."

"Yes, Professor; and I love it as if it were my own flesh and blood. If the dangers of the ocean threaten one of your vessels, a man's first thought is of the depths below. On the *Nautilus* men's hearts never fail them. No warping to fear, for the double hull has the strength of iron; no rigging to roll up or tangle; no sails for the wind to carry away; no boilers to burst; no fire to fear, for the vessel is made of metal, not of wood; no worry about running out of coal; electricity is the only energy used; no collision to fear, for it sails alone in deep water; no tempest to brave, for below the water, it finds absolute tranquility. There, sir! That is the vessel of perfection! And if it is true that the engineer has more confidence in the vessel than the builder, and the builder than the captain himself, you understand the trust I repose in my *Nautilus;* for I am at once captain, builder, and engineer.''

"But how could you construct this wonderful *Nautilus* in secret?''

"Each separate portion, M. Aronnax, was brought from different parts of the globe. The keel was forged at Creusot, the shaft of the screw at Penn & Co.'s, London, the iron plates of the hull at Laird's of Liverpool, the screw itself at Scott's of Glasgow. The reservoirs were made by Cail & Co. at Paris, the engine by Krupp in Prussia, its beak in Motala's workshop in Sweden, its mathematical instruments by Hart Brothers, of New York, and so on; and each of these people had my orders under different names."

"But these parts had to be put together and arranged?"

"Professor, I had set up my workshops upon a desert island in the ocean. There, I and my workmen, the brave men that I instructed and educated, put together our *Nautilus*. Then, when the work was finished, all trace of our proceedings on this island was destroyed by fire."

"Then the cost of this vessel is great?"

"M. Arronax, an iron vessel costs 45 pounds per ton. Now the *Nautilus* weighed 1500. It came therefore to 67,500 pounds, and 80,000 pounds more for fitting it up, and about 200,000 pounds with the works of art and the collections it contains."

"One last question, Captain Nemo."

"Ask it, Professor."

"You are rich?"

"Immensely rich, sir. I could, without missing it, pay the national debt of France."

I stared at the bizarre personage who spoke thus. Was he abusing my credulity? The future would teach me.

Chapter 13
The Black River

The portion of the earth covered by water is estimated at upwards of eighty millions of acres. This fluid mass comprises two-billion-two-hundred-and-fifty-millions of cubic miles, forming a spherical body of a diameter of sixty leagues, the weight of which would be three quintillions of tons. To comprehend the meaning of these figures, it is necessary to observe that a quintillion is to a billion as a billion is to a unit; in other words, there are as many billions in a quintillion as there are units in a billion. This mass of fluid is equal to about the quantity of water which would be discharged by all the rivers of the earth in forty thousand years.

During the geological epochs, the igneous period succeeded the aqueous. The ocean originally covered the earth. Then by degrees, in the silurian period, the tops of mountains began to appear, islands emerged, were flooded, reappeared, became settled, formed continents, till at length the earth became geographically arranged, as we see in the present day. The solid had wrested from the liquid thirty-seven-million-six-hundred-and-fifty-seven square miles, equal to twelve-billion-nine-hundred-and-sixty-millions of acres.

The shape of the continents allows us to divide the waters into five great portions: the Arctic or Frozen Ocean, the Antarctic or Frozen Ocean, the Indian, the Atlantic, and the Pacific Oceans.

The Pacific Ocean extends from north to south between the two polar circles, and from east to west between Asia and America, over an extent of 145 degrees of longitude. It is the quietest of seas; its currents are broad and slow, it has moderate tides, and abundant rain. Such was the ocean that I was destined first to traverse under the strangest of circumstances.

"Sir," said Captain Nemo, "we will, if you please, take our bearings and fix the starting point of this voyage. It is a quarter to twelve, I will go up again to the surface."

The Captain pressed an electric clock three times. The pumps began to drive the water from the tanks; the needle of the manometer showed by changing pressure the ascent of the *Nautilus,* then it stopped.

"We have arrived," said the Captain.

I went to the central staircase which opened onto the half-deck, clambered up the iron steps, and through the open hatches to the upper part of the *Nautilus*.

The half-deck was only three feet out of water. The front and rear ends of the *Nautilus* gave it that Spindle-shape which caused it accurately to be compared to a cigar. I noticed that its iron plates, slightly overlaying each other, resembled the shell which clothes the bodies of our large terrestrial reptiles. This made clear how natural it was, in spite of the best binoculars, that this ship should have been taken for a marine animal.

Towards the middle of the half-deck, the small boat, half buried in the hull of the vessel, formed a slight bulge. Fore and aft rose two cages of medium height with inclined sides, partly enclosed by thick lenticular glass, one meant for the steersman who guided the *Nautilus,* the other containing a brilliant electric lantern to give light on the way.

The sea was beautiful, the sky pure. The lone ship scarcely felt the broad waves. A light breeze from the east rippled the surface of the waters. The horizon, free from fog, made observation easy. Nothing was in sight. Not a rock, not an island, nor the *Abraham Lincoln.*

Captain Nemo, by the help of his sextant, took the altitude of the sun, which also gives the latitude. He waited for some moments till its disc touched the horizon. Whilst taking his observations not a muscle moved, the instrument could not have been more motionless in a hand of marble.

"Twelve o'clock, sir," said he. "When you like—"

I cast a look upon the sea, and descended to the saloon.

"And now, sir, I leave you to your studies," added the Captain. "Our course is E.N.E, our depth is twenty-six fathoms. Today, November 8th at noon, begins our voyage of exploration. Here are maps on a large scale by which you may follow it. The saloon is at your disposal, and with your permission I will retire." Captain Nemo bowed, and I remained alone, lost in thoughts all bearing on the commander of the *Nautilus,* his origins and the remarkable wealth he laid claim to.

For a whole hour was I deep in these reflections, seeking to pierce this mystery so interesting to me. Then my eyes fell upon the vast planisphere spread upon the table, and I placed my finger on the very spot where the given latitude and longitude crossed.

Like the continents, the sea has its large rivers. They are special currents recognized by their temperature and their color. The most remarkable of these is called the Gulf Stream. Science has decided on the globe, the direction of five principal currents: one in the North Atlantic, a second in the South, a third in the North Pacific, a fourth in the South, and a fifth in the Southern Indian Ocean. It is even probable that a sixth current existed at one time or another in the Northern Indian Ocean, when the Caspian and the Aral seas formed one and the same sheet of water.

One of these currents, the Kuro-Sivo of Japan, known to us as the Black River, flowed through the spot now indicated on the planisphere. Beginning at the Gulf of Bengal, where it is warmed by the perpendicular rays of a tropical sun, the Black River crosses the Straits of Malacca, passes along the coast of Asia, and turns into the North Pacific toward the Aleutian Islands, carrying with it trunks of camphor-trees and other tropical growths, and edging the waves of the ocean with the pure indigo of its warm water. It was this current that the *Nautilus* would follow. I traced it with my eye; saw it lose itself in the vastness of the Pacific, and felt myself moving with it, when Ned Land and Conseil appeared at the door of the saloon.

My two brave companions stood petrified at the sight of the wonders spread before them.

"Where are we, where are we?" exclaimed the Canadian. "In the museum at Quebec?"

"My friends," I answered, "you are not in Canada, but on board the *Nautilus,* fifty yards below the level of the sea."

"M. Aronnax," said Ned Land, "can you tell me how many men there are on board? Ten, twenty, fifty, a hundred?"

"I cannot answer you, Mr. Land. It is better to abandon for the present any idea of seizing the *Nautilus* or escaping from it. This ship is a masterpiece of modern construction, and I should be sorry not to have seen it. Many people would accept gladly the situation forced upon us, if only to exist amongst such wonders. So be quiet and let us try to watch what goes on around us."

"Watch!" exclaimed the harpooner. "We can see nothing in this iron prison! We are walking—we are sailing—blindly."

Ned Land had scarcely pronounced these

words when suddenly all was darkness. The luminous ceiling disappeared, and so rapidly that it was painful to my eyes.

We remained where we were, not knowing what surprise awaited us, whether pleasant or otherwise. We heard a sliding noise, as if panels were being moved in the sides of the *Nautilus*.

"It is the end of the end!" said Ned Land.

Suddenly light broke at each side of the saloon, through two oblong openings. The mass of water outside appeared, vividly lit up by the electric gleam. Only two crystal plates separated us from the sea. At first I trembled, fearing that those frail partitions might break, but strong bands of copper bound them, giving them an almost infinite power of resistance.

The sea was distinctly visible for a full mile all round the *Nautilus*. What a spectacle! What pen could describe it? Who could paint the effects of the light through those transparent sheets of water, and the softness of the successive gradua-tions from the lower to the superior strata of the ocean?

We know the transparency of the sea, and that it is far more clear than water which rises from earth. The mineral and organic substances which it holds in suspension heighten its transparency. In certain parts of the ocean at the Antilles, through seventy-five fathoms of water, can be seen a bed of sand with surprising clarity. The power of the solar rays seems to penetrate to a depth of one hundred and fifty fathoms. But in the depth where the *Nautilus* now traveled, the brightness seemed to come from the water itself. It was no longer luminous water, but liquid light.

On either side a window opened into this strange and wonderful world. The darkness of the saloon intensified the brightness, and we looked out as if this pure crystal had been the glass of an immense aquarium.

"You wished to see, friend Ned; well, you see now."

"Curious! Curious!" muttered the Canadian, who, forgetting his ill-temper, seemed overcome by irresistible fascination.

"One would come further to revel in such a sight!"

"Ah!" I thought to myself, "now I understand the life of this man; he has made an imaginary world apart for himself, where he treasures all his greatest wonders."

For two entire hours, the *Nautilus* was escorted by an aquatic army. They rivaled each other in beauty, brightness, and speed; but while she leaped and played, I was able to distinguish the green labre; the banded mullet, marked by a double line of black; the round-tailed goby, of a white color, with violet spots on the back; the Japanese scombrus, a beautiful mackerel of those seas, with a blue body and silvery head; the brilliant azurors, whose name alone defies description; some banded spares, with variegated fins of blue and yellow; some aclostones, the woodcocks of the seas, some specimens of which attain a yard in length; Japanese salamanders, spider lampreys, serpents six feet long, with eyes small and lively, and a huge mouth bristling with teeth; along with many other species.

Enthralled, we kept calling out to each other. Ned would name a fish, and Conseil would classify them. I was in ecstasies with the vivacity of their movements, and the beauty of their forms. Never had I thought it would be given me to surprise these animals, alive and at liberty, in their natural element. I cannot mention all of the different ones which passed before my dazzled eyes, all the varieties of the seas of China and Japan. They were more numerous than the birds of the air, attracted, no doubt, by the brilliant focus of the electric light.

Without warning, there was light again in the saloon, the iron panels closed again, and the enchanting vision vanished. But for a long time, I continued to dream on till my eyes fell on the instruments hanging on the partition. The compass still showed the course to be E.N.E., the manometer indicated a pressure of five atmospheres, equivalent to the depth of twenty-five fathoms, and the electric log showed a speed of fifteen miles an hour. I expected Captain Nemo, but he did not come back. The clock now marked the hour of five.

Ned Land and Conseil returned to their cabin, and I to my chamber. My dinner was already there. It was composed of turtle soup made of the most delicate hawkbills, of a sur-mullet served with puff paste (the liver of which, prepared by itself, was most delicious), and fillets of the emperor holocanthus, the savor of which seemed to me superior even to salmon.

I passed the evening reading, writing, and thinking. Then sleep overpowered me, and I stretched myself on my couch of zostera, and slept profoundly, whilst the *Nautilus* glided through the current of the Black River.

Chapter 14
A Note of Invitation

The next day was the 9th of November. I awoke after a long sleep of twelve hours. Conseil came, according to custom, to know "how I had passed the night," and to offer his services. He had left his friend the Canadian sleeping like a man who had never done anything else all his life. I let the worthy fellow chatter as he pleased, without troubling to answer him. I was preoccupied with thoughts of the Captain and wondering why he had left us alone to view his underwater paradise.

I hoped to see Nemo today, so as soon as I was dressed I went into the saloon. It was deserted.

I plunged into the study of the conchilogical treasures hidden behind the glasses. I reveled also in great herbals filled with the rarest marine plants, which, although dehydrated, retained their lovely colors. Amongst these precious hydrophytes I remarked some vorticellae, pavonariae, delicate ceramies with scarlet tints, some fan-shaped agari, and some natabuli-like flat mushrooms, which at one time used to be classed as zoophytes; in short, a perfect series of algae.

The whole day passed without my being honored by a visit from Captain Nemo. The panels of the saloon did not open. Perhaps they did not wish us to tire of these beautiful things.

The course of the *Nautilus* was E.N.E., her speed twelve knots, her depth between twenty-five and thirty fathoms below the surface.

The next day, the 10th of November, we spent again in solitude. I did not see any of the ship's crew; Ned and Conseil passed the greater part of the day with me. They were astonished at the inexplicable absence of the Captain. Was this man ill? Had he altered his intentions with regard to us?

However, as Conseil said, we enjoyed perfect liberty, we were deliciously and abundantly fed. Our host kept to his terms of the agreement. Indeed, the singularity of our fate held such wonderful compensation for us, that we had no right, as yet, to complain of it.

That day, I commenced the journal of these adventures, which has enabled me to relate them with the most scrupulous exactitude and minute detail. I wrote it on paper made from the zostera marina.

Early in the morning on the 11th of November, fresh air spreading through the interior of the *Nautilus* told me that we had come to the surface of the ocean to renew our supply of oxygen. I directed my steps to the central staircase, and mounted to the half-deck.

It was six o'clock, the weather was cloudy, the sea gray but calm. Scarcely a billow. Would I find Captain Nemo on deck? I found no one but the steersman imprisoned in his glass cage. Seated upon the projection formed by the hull of the pinnace, I inhaled the salt breeze with delight.

By degrees the fog disappeared under the action of the sun's rays, and the radiant orb rose from behind the eastern horizon. The sea flamed under its glance like a train of gunpowder. The scattered clouds were colored with lively tints of beautiful shades; and numerous "mare's tails," betokened wind that day. But what was wind to this *Nautilus* which tempests could not frighten!

I was admiring this joyous rising of the sun, so happy, so filled with life, when I heard steps approaching the deck. I was prepared to salute Captain Nemo, but it was his assistant, or executive officer (whom I had already seen on the Captain's first visit) who appeared. He crossed the deck apparently not seeing me. With a powerful glass to his eye he scanned every point of the horizon with great attention. His examination completed, he approached the panel and pronounced a sentence in exactly the following terms. I have remembered it, for every morning I heard it repeated, exactly the same way and under the same conditions. It was worded thus—

"Nautron respoc lorni virch."

What it meant, I had no idea.

After saying these words, the man descended. I thought that perhaps the *Nautilus* was about to return to its submarine navigation, so I regained the panel and returned to my chamber.

Five days sped thus, without any change in our situation. Every morning I mounted the platform. The same phrase was pronounced by the same individual. But Captain Nemo did not appear.

I had made up my mind that I should never see him again, when, on the 16th of November, on returning to my room with Ned and Conseil, I found upon my table a note addressed to me. I opened it impatiently. It was written in a bold, clear hand, the characters rather pointed, recalling German type. The note was worded as follows:

"16th of November, 1867.
To Professor Aronnax, on board the *Nautilus*.

"Captain Nemo invites Professor Aronnax to a hunting-party, to take place tomorrow morning in the forests of the island of Crespo. He hopes that nothing will prevent the Professor from being present, and will see him with pleasure together with his companions.

"Captain Nemo, Commander of the
Nautilus."

"A hunt!" exclaimed Ned.

"And in the forests of the island of Crespo!" added Conseil.

"Then our gentleman is going to step on terra firma?" asked Ned Land.

"That seems to be clearly indicated," said I, scanning the letter once more.

"Of course we must accept," said the Canadian. "Once on dry ground again, we will know what to do. I, for one, will not regret the chance to eat a piece of fresh venison."

Without seeking to reconcile the contradiction between Captain Nemo's manifest aversion to islands and continents, and his invitation to hunt in a forest, I merely said, "Let us first see where the island of Crespo is."

Consulting the planisphere, at 32° 40′ north lat., and 157° 50′ west long., I found a small island discovered in 1801 by Captain Crespo, and marked on the ancient Spanish maps as Rocca de la Plata, which means "The Silver Rock." We were now about eighteen hundred miles from our starting point, and the course of the *Nautilus*, a little changed, was bringing us back towards the southeast.

I showed my companions this little rock isolated in the midst of the North Pacific.

"Even if Captain Nemo does go on dry ground occasionally," I said, "at least he chooses desert islands."

Ned Land merely shrugged his shoulders, and Conseil and he went away.

After supper, which was served by the silent and impassive steward, I went to bed, not without some apprehension.

Awakening the next morning the 17th of November, I felt that the *Nautilus* was perfectly still. I dressed quickly and went to the saloon.

Captain Nemo was there, waiting for me. He rose, bowed, and asked if it was convenient for me to accompany him. As he made no allusion to his absence for the last eight days, I did not mention it either, and simply answered that my companions and myself were ready to follow him.

We went to the dining room, where breakfast was served.

"M. Aronnax," said the Captain, "pray share my breakfast without ceremony; we will chat as we eat. For though I promised you a walk in the forest, I cannot guarantee finding restaurants there. So breakfast as a man who most likely will not have his dinner till very late."

I did honor to the repast. It was composed of several kinds of fish, and slices of holothuridae (excellent zoophytes), and different sorts of seaweed. Our drink was pure water, to which the Captain added a few drops of a fermented liquor, extracted by the Kamschatcha method from a seaweed known under the name of *Rhodomenia palmata*. Captain Nemo ate for a few moments without saying anything further, then he began—

"Sir, when I proposed to you that we hunt in my forest of Crespo, you no doubt thought it strange that I would set foot on dry land. You may think my proposal even stranger when I tell you that the forest of Crespo is underwater."

"But Captain, believe me—"

"Be kind enough to listen, and you will learn whether it is possible to hunt in a forest under the sea."

116

"I listen."

"You know as well as I do, Professor, that man can live underwater, provided he carries with him a sufficient supply of breathable air. In building a submarine, the workman is clad in waterproof clothings, his head is in a metal helmet, and he receives air from above by means of forcing pumps and regulators."

"That is a diving apparatus," said I.

"Just so, but under these conditions the man is not free to move about. He is attached to the pump which sends him air, through the india-rubber tube. If we were obliged to be held thus to the *Nautilus* we would not go far."

"And the means of getting free?" I asked.

"It is to use the Rouquayrol-Denayrouge apparatus, invented by two of your own countrymen, which I have brought to perfection for my own use, and which allows you to explore these new physiological conditions, without damage to any organ. It consists of a reservoir of thick plates, in which I store the air under a pressure of fifty atmospheres. This reservoir is fixed on the back with braces, like a soldier's knapsack. Its upper part forms a box in which the air is kept by means of a bellows, and therefore cannot escape except at its normal pressure. In the Rouquayrol apparatus such as we use, two india-rubber pipes lead from this box and join a sort of tent, enclosing the nose and mouth; one pipe is to admit fresh air, the other to let out the foul, and the tongue closes one or the other pipe, according to the wants of the user. But in encountering great pressures at the bottom of the sea, I was obliged to enclose my head, like that of a diver, in a copper helmet; and the two pipes, inspirator and expirator, open into this helmet.''

"Quite clear, Captain Nemo; but the air that you carry with you must soon be used up. When it contains only fifteen percent of oxygen, it is no longer fit to breathe.''

"Right! but I told you, M. Aronnax, that the pumps of the *Nautilus* allow me to store air under considerable pressure. Therefore, the reservoir of the apparatus can furnish breathable air for nine or ten hours.''

"I have no further objections to make,'' I answered. "I will ask you only one thing, Captain—how are you able to light your way at the bottom of the sea?''

"With the Ruhmkorff apparatus, M. Aronnax. Part is carried on the back, the other fastened to the waist. It is composed of a Bunsen battery, which I do not operate with bichromate of potash, but with sodium. A wire collects the elctricity generated, and directs it towards an especially made lantern. In this lantern is a spiral glass containing a small quantity of carbonic gas. When the apparatus is at work this gas becomes luminous, giving out a continuous white light. Thus I can both breathe and see.''

"Captain Nemo, to all my objections you make such overwhelming answers, that I dare no longer doubt. But if I must agree to the Rouquayrol and Ruhmkorff apparatus, I must be allowed some reservations with regard to the gun I am to carry.''

"But it is not a gun for powder,'' answered the Captain.

"Then it is an air-gun."

"Of course! How would you have me manufacture gunpowder on board my ship without saltpeter, sulphur or charcoal?"

"Besides," I added, "to fire underwater, which is eight hundred and fifty-five times denser than the air, we would have to overcome very considerable resistance."

"That would present no difficulty. According to Fulton there are guns perfected in England by Philip Coles and Burley, in France by Furcy, and in Italy by Landi with a particular system of closing, which can fire underwater. But, having no powder, I use instead air under great pressure, which the pumps of the *Nautilus* furnish abundantly."

"But this air must be quickly used up?"

"Well, have I not my Rouquayrol reservoir, which can furnish air at need? A tap is all that is required. Besides, M. Aronnax, you must see for yourself that, during our underwater hunt, we can spend little air and few balls."

"But it seems to me that in the midst of this fluid, which is so very dense compared with the air above, shots could not go far, nor easily prove mortal."

"Sir, on the contrary, with this gun every blow is mortal. And however lightly the animal is touched, it falls as if struck by a thunderbolt."

"Why?"

"Because the balls shot from this gun are not ordinary ones, but little cases of glass (invented by Leniebroek, an Austrian chemist), of which I have a large supply. These glass cases are covered with a case of steel, and weighted with a pellet of lead. They are real Leyden bottles, into which electricity is forced at a very high tension. With the slightest shock they are discharged, and the animal, however strong it may be, falls dead. I must tell you that these cases are size number four, and that the charge for an ordinary gun would be ten.''

''I will argue no longer,'' I replied, rising from the table. ''There is nothing left for me to do but take my gun. I will follow wherever you go.''

Captain Nemo then led me aft. In passing Conseil's cabin, I called my two companions who joined me immediately. We then came to a cabin near the engine room, in which we were to change into our hunting clothes.

Chapter 15
A Walk on the Bottom of the Sea

This cabin was actually both arsenal and wardrobe of the *Nautilus*. A dozen diving outfits hung from the wall, awaiting our choice. Ned Land, on seeing them, showed clearly his reluctance to dress himself in one.

''But my worthy Ned, it turns out that the forests of the island of Crespo are at the bottom of the sea.''

"Splendid!" said the disappointed harpooner, who saw his dreams of fresh meat fade away. "And you M. Aronnax, are you going to put on those clothes?"

"There is no alternative, Master Ned."

"As you please, sir," replied the harpooner, shrugging his shoulders. "But as for me, unless I am forced, I will never get into one."

"No one will force you, Master Ned," said Captain Nemo.

"Is Conseil going to risk it?" asked Ned.

"I follow my master wherever he goes," replied Conseil.

At the Captain's call, two of the ship's crew came to help us into the heavy waterproof clothes, made of india-rubber without seam, and constructed expressly to resist considerable pressure. One would have thought them suits of armor, both firm and supple. There were trousers and coat, the bottom of the trousers being thick boots, weighted with heavy leaden soles. The material of the coat was reinforced by bands of copper, which crossed the chest, protecting it from the pressure of the water, yet leaving the lungs free to breathe. The sleeves ended in gloves, which in no way restrained the movement of the hands. There was a vast difference between these remarkable suits and the old cork breastplates, jackets, and other contrivances, which had been used formerly.

Captain Nemo and one of his companions (a sort of Hercules, possessed of great strength), Conseil and myself, were soon enveloped in the suits. There remained nothing more but to enclose our heads in the helmets. But first I asked the Captain's permission to examine the guns we were to carry.

One of the *Nautilus* men gave me a simple looking gun. The butt end, made of steel and hollow in the center, was rather large. It served as a reservoir for compressed air, which a valve, worked by a spring, allowed to escape into a metal tube. A box of projectiles, carried in a groove in the thickness of the butt end, contained about twenty of these electric balls, which were forced into the barrel of the gun by a spring. As soon as one shot was fired, another was ready.

"Captain Nemo," said I, "this weapon is perfect, and easily handled. I ask only to be allowed to try it. How shall we reach the bottom of the sea?"

"At this moment, Professor, the *Nautilus* is at five fathoms. We have nothing to do but to start."

"But how shall we get off?"

"You shall see."

Captain Nemo thrust his head into the helmet. Conseil and I did the same, not without hearing an ironical "Good sport!" from the Canadian. The upper part of our suits terminated in a copper collar, to which the metal helmet was screwed. Three holes, protected by thick glass, allowed us to see in all directions, simply by turning our heads. As soon as the helmet was in position, the Rouquayrol apparatus began to act. I found I could breathe with ease.

With the Ruhmkorff lamp hanging from my

belt, and the gun in my hand, I was ready to set out. But to speak the truth, imprisoned in these heavy garments, and glued to the deck by my leaden soles, it was impossible for me to take a step.

But this difficulty had been provided for. I felt myself being pushed into a little room adjoining the wardrobe-room. My companions followed, shoved along in the same way. I heard the watertight door, furnished with stopper valves, close upon us. We were wrapped in profound darkness.

After some minutes, a loud hissing could be heard. I felt cold mount from my feet to my chest. Evidently from some part of the vessel the water was allowed to enter our chamber. Soon the room was filled. A second door cut in the side of the *Nautilus* then opened. We saw a faint light. In another instant our feet trod the bottom of the sea.

And now, how can I recapture the impression left upon me by that walk under the waters? Words are impotent to describe such wonders! Captain Nemo walked in front. His companion followed some steps behind. Conseil and I remained near each other as if an exchange of words had been possible through our metallic cases. I no longer felt the weight of my clothing, or of my shoes, of my reservoir of air, or my thick helmet, inside of which my head rattled like an almond in its shell.

The light, which lit the soil thirty feet below the surface of the ocean, astonished me by its power. The solar rays traveled easily through the watery mass, and dissipated all color. I could distinguish objects clearly at a distance of a hundred and fifty yards. Beyond that the tints darkened into fine gradations of ultramarine and faded into vague obscurity. Truly this water which surrounded me seemed but another air, denser than the terrestrial atmosphere, but almost as transparent. Above, was the calm surface of the sea.

We were walking on fine even sand, not wrinkled, as on a flat shore, which retains the marks of the tides. This dazzling carpet became a reflector, returning the rays of the sun with wonderful intensity, which accounted for the brilliance that penetrated every atom of liquid. Shall I be believed when I say that, at the depth of thirty feet I could see as if I was in broad daylight?

For a quarter of an hour I trod this sand, sown with the impalpable dust of shells. The hull of the *Nautilus,* resembling a long shoal, disappeared by degrees. But should darkness overtake us in the water, its strong lantern would help to guide us back on board.

Soon, I recognized many magnificent rocks, hung with a tapestry of zoophytes of the most beautiful kind, and I was fascinated by the extraordinary effect of my surroundings.

It was now ten in the morning. The sun struck the surface of the waves at a slightly oblique angle. At the touch of its rays, separated by refraction as through a prism—flowers, rocks, plants, shells and polypi were shaded at the edges with all solar colors. It was marvelous, a feast for the eyes, this fantastic arrangement of color—a perfect kaleidoscope of green, yellow, orange, violet, indigo, red and blue. In a word, the whole palette of an ardent colorist! I longed to communicate to Conseil the lively sensations which were mounting to my brain, and to rival him in expressions of admirations. For aught I knew, Captain Nemo and his companion might be able to exchange thoughts by means of signs previously agreed upon. But for want of better, I talked to myself. I declaimed in the copper box, covering my head, thereby expending more air in vain words than was perhaps expedient.

Various kinds of isis, clusters of pure tuft-coral, prickly fungi, and anemones, formed a brilliant garden of flowers, enameled with porphitae, decked with collarettes of blue tentacles, sea-stars studding the sandy bottom, together with asterophtons like fine lace embroidered by the hands of naiads, whose festoons waved in the gentle undulations caused by our movements. It was a real grief to me to crush under my feet the brilliant specimens of molluscs which strewed the ground by thousands—hammer-heads, donaciae, (veritable bounding shells), staircases, and red helmet-shells, angel-wings, and many others produced by this inexhaustible ocean. But we were forced to walk, so we went on. Above our heads waved shoals of physalides, tentacles floating in their train, medusae whose umbrellas of opal or pink-rose, escalloped with a band of blue, sheltered us from the rays of the sun and fiery pelagiae, which, in darkness, would have strewn our path with phosphorescent light.

All these wonders I saw in the space of a quarter of a mile, scarcely stopping, and always following Captain Nemo, who beckoned me on by signs. Soon the nature of the soil changed from sand to a bed of slimy mud called "ooze" by the Americans, a substance composed of equal parts of silicious and calcareous shells. Then we passed over a meadow made of seaweed. Its growth was luxuriant, dense and soft under the foot. It rivaled the softest carpet woven by the hand of man. But whilst verdure was spread out at our feet, our heads were not neglected. A light network of marine plants, of that inexhaustible family of seaweeds of which more than two thousand kinds are known, grew on the surface of the water. I saw long ribbons of fucus floating, some globular, others tuberous; Laurenciae and cladostephi of the most delicate foliage; and a few rhodomeniae palmatae, which resemble the fan of a cactus. I noticed that the green plants kept nearer to the top of the sea, whilst the red were at a lower depth, leaving to the black or brown hydrophytes the task of forming gardens and flower beds at the bottom of the ocean.

We had left the *Nautilus* about an hour and a half ago. I knew by the perpendicularity of the sun's rays, which were no longer refracted, that it was nearly noon. The magical colors disappeared by degrees. The shades of emerald and sapphire faded away. The sound of our steps upon the ocean floor was surprisingly loud. Here the slightest noise was transmitted far more quickly than on the earth. Indeed, water is a better conductor of sound than air, in the ratio of four to one. Now, the ground sloped abruptly downwards; the light took on a uniform hue. We had reached a depth of one hundred and five yards and twenty inches, at a pressure of six atmospheres. But my clothing prevented my feeling any discomfort. I felt only a slight difficulty in moving my fingers. I moved through the water so easily that I experienced none of the fatigue I would have on land.

I could still see the rays of the sun, though faintly. The reddish glow of twilight, which lingers between day and night, had taken their place. But we could still see well enough; it was not yet necessary to resort to the Ruhmkorff apparatus. Captain Nemo stopped. He waited until I caught up with him, and then pointed to some dark, bulky masses, which loomed in the shadows, not far away.

"It is the forest of the island of Crespo," I thought;—and I was not mistaken.

Chapter 16
A Submarine Forest

We had arrived at last on the borders of this forest, surely one of the finest in Captain Nemo's immense domains. He looked upon it as his own, and considered he had the same right over it as had the first men, in the first days of the world. And, indeed, who could have disputed him for possession of this underwater estate? What other pioneer would come, hatchet in hand, to clear away these dark woods?

The forest was composed of very tall shrubs. The moment we penetrated under its vast arcades, I was struck by the singular way their branches grew, one I had never seen before.

None of the seaweeds seen before, which carpeted the ground, nor the branches which extended from the trees, was broken or bent, nor did they stretch out horizontally. All reached up to the surface of the ocean. Not a filament, not a ribbon, however thin, but kept as straight as a rod of iron. The fuci and llianas grew in rigid perpendicular lines, due to the density of the element in which they lived. When I bent them over with my hand, they immediately resumed their former position. Truly, here was the reign of the vertical!

I soon accustomed myself to this fantastic arrangement, as well as to the comparative darkness which now surrounded us. The soil of the forest was covered with sharp stones, difficult to avoid. The submarine flora struck me as being of great variety, more so than in the arctic or even tropical zones, where these growths are less numerous. But for a while I confused the genera, taking zoophytes for hydrophytes, animals for plants. Who would not have made such mistakes? The fauna and the flora are closely allied in this submarine world.

These plants are self-propagating, and the water supplies all their needs. Instead of leaves, most shot forth blades of unusual shapes, all within a scale of colors—pink, carmine, green, olive, fawn, and brown. I saw (but not dried up, as were our specimens on the *Nautilus*) pavonari spread like a fan, as if to catch the breeze; scarlet ceramies, whose laminaries extended their edible shoots of fern-shaped nereocysti, which grow to a height of fifteen feet; clusters of acetabuli, whose stems increase in size as they grow upwards; and many other marine plants, all devoid of flowers!

"Curious anomaly, fantastic element!" once said an ingenious naturalist, "in which the animal kingdom blossoms, and the vegetable does not!''

Beneath the great shrubs (as large as our familiar trees in the temperate zone), were massed actual bushes of living flowers, thick hedges of submarine animal life; zoophytes, on which blossomed zebrameandrines, with crooked grooves, yellow caryophylliae; and, to complete the allusion, fish-flies flew from branch to branch like a swarm of hummingbirds, whilst yellow lepisacomthi, with bristling jaws, dactylopteri, and monocentrides rose at our feet like a flight of snipes.

After about an hour Captain Nemo gave the signal to halt. I, for my part, was not sorry, and we all stretched out under an arbor of alariae, whose long thin blades stood up like arrows.

This short rest seemed delicious to me. There was nothing wanting but the charm of conversation; but since it was impossible to speak or to answer, I only put my great copper head next to conseil's. I saw the worthy fellow's eyes glistening with delight, and to show his satisfaction, he shook himself in his breastplate of air in the most comical way in the world.

After four hours of this walking I was surprised not to find myself dreadfully hungry. How to account for this state of the stomach I could not tell. But instead I felt an uncontrollable desire to sleep, which happens to all divers. Soon my eyes closed behind the thick glasses, and I fell into a heavy slumber. Captain Nemo and his robust companion set us the example.

How long I remained lost in sleep, I cannot

judge. When I woke, the sun seemed sinking towards the horizon. Captain Nemo already had risen, and I was beginning to stretch my limbs, when an unexpected apparition brought me briskly to my feet.

A few steps away, a monstrous sea-spider, about thirty-eight inches high, was watching me with squinting eyes, ready to spring upon me. Though my diver's suit was thick enough to protect me from the bite of this animal, I could not help shuddering with horror. Conseil and the sailor of the *Nautilus* awoke just as Captain Nemo struck the hideous crustacean, and knocked it over with the butt end of his gun. I saw its horrible claws, as the monster writhed in terrible convulsions. This incident reminded me that other fearsome animals might haunt these dark depths, against whose attacks my diving suit would not protect me. I had never thought of it before, but I now resolved to be upon my guard. Indeed, I had supposed that this halt would mark the end of our walk. But I was mistaken, for, instead of returning to the *Nautilus*, Captain Nemo continued his bold excursion. The ground was still descending. Its angle seemed to be growing steeper, and to be leading us to ever greater depths. It must have been about three o'clock when we reached a narrow valley, situated between high perpendicular walls, and about seventy-five fathoms deep. Thanks to the excellence of our equipment, we were now forty-five fathoms below the usual limit which nature has permitted man in his submarine excursions.

I say seventy-five fathoms, though I had no

instrument by which to judge the distance. But I knew that even in the clearest waters the solar rays could penetrate no further. And accordingly the darkness deepened. At ten paces not an object was visible. I was groping my way, when suddenly I saw a brilliant white light. Captain Nemo had just put his electric apparatus into use, his companion did the same, and Conseil and I followed their example. By turning a screw I established the connection between the wire and the spiral glass. The sea, lit by our four lanterns, was illuminated for a radius of thirty-six yards.

Captain Nemo still plunged on into the dark depths of the forest, whose trees now were getting scarcer at every step. I noticed that vegetable life disappeared sooner than animal life. The medusae had already abandoned the arid soil, from which a great number of animals, zoophytes, articulata, molluscs, and fishes still obtained sustenance.

As we walked, I thought the light of our Ruhmkorff apparatus could not fail to draw some inhabitant from its dark couch. But if they did approach us, they at least kept at a respectful distance from the hunters. Several times I saw Captain Nemo stop, put his gun to his shoulder, and after a few moments drop it and walk on. At last, after about four hours, this marvelous excursion came to an end. A wall of superb rocks rose before us in an imposing mass, an enormous steep granite shore, with many little caves, but no slope that could be climbed readily. It was the base of the island of

Crespo. It was the earth! Captain Nemo stopped suddenly. A gesture from him brought us all to a halt, and however much I wanted to scale the wall, I was obliged to stop. Here ended Captain Nemo's domains. And he would not go beyond them. Further on was a portion of the globe he might not tread upon.

We turned back, Captain Nemo at the head of his little band, directing our course without hesitation. I thought we were taking a different road to return to the *Nautilus*. The new way was very steep, and consequently very painful. We approached the surface of the sea quite rapidly, but not so fast as to lessen the pressure too quickly, which might have produced serious disorder in our bodies, and brought on internal lesions, so often fatal to divers. Very soon light reappeared and grew. The sun was low on the horizon and the refraction edged everything with a spectral halo. At a depth of ten yards and a half, we walked amidst a shoal of little fishes of all kinds, more numerous than the birds of the air, and more fleet. But we had met no aquatic game worthy of a shot, when I saw the Captain shoulder his gun quickly, and follow a moving object into the undergrowth. He fired. I heard a hissing sound, and an animal fell stunned, a distance away from us. We hastened to where it lay. It was a magnificent sea-otter, an enhydrus, the only exclusively marine quadruped. It was five feet long, and must have been very valuable. Its pelt, chestnut-brown on top and silvery underneath, would have made one of those beautiful furs so sought after in the

Russian and Chinese markets. The smoothness and luster of its coat certainly would fetch 80 pounds. I admired this curious mammal, with its rounded head, ornamented by short ears, round eyes and white whiskers like those of a cat, webbed feet and nails, and tufted tail. A precious animal, hunted and tracked by fishermen, the sea-otter has become very rare. It has taken refuge chiefly in the northern parts of the Pacific, which probably has saved it from extinction.

Captain Nemo's companion threw the beast over his shoulder, and we continued our journey. For an hour a plain of sand lay stretched before us. Sometimes it rose to within two yards and some inches of the surface of the water. I then saw our image clearly reflected, but pictured inversely, and above us appeared an identical group reflecting our movements and our actions. They were like us in every detail, except that they walked with their heads downward and their feet in the air.

Another effect I observed was the passage of thick clouds which formed and vanished rapidly. But on reflection I realized that these seeming clouds were due to reflections of clumps of reeds among which we walked. Their broken tops made fleecy foam on the water. We also saw the shadows of large birds passing above our heads, whose rapid flight I could follow on the surface of the sea.

Very shortly, I was witness to one of the finest gunshots which ever made the nerves of a hunter thrill. A large bird of great breadth of wing approached, clearly visible, and hovered over us. Captain Nemo's companion shouldered his gun and fired, when it was only a few yards above the waves. The creature fell stunned, and the force of its fall brought it within the reach of the dexterous hunter's grasp. It was an albatross of the finest kind.

Our march was barely interrupted by this incident. For two hours we followed these sandy plains, then came fields of algae very disagreeable to cross. Candidly, I felt that I could do no more when I saw a glimmer of light, which, half a mile away, broke the darkness of the waters. It was the lantern of the *Nautilus*. Before twenty minutes were past we should be on board, and I should be able to breathe with ease again for it seemed that the air supplied by my reservoir was becoming deficient in oxygen. But I did not reckon on an accidental encounter, which delayed our arrival for some time.

I had fallen some steps behind, when I saw Captain Nemo hurrying towards me. With his strong hand he bent me to the ground, his companion doing the same to Conseil. At first I knew not what to think of this sudden attack, but I was soon reassured by seeing the Captain lie down beside me, and stay perfectly still.

I was stretched on the ground, just under shelter of a bush of algae, when raising my head, I saw two enormous shapes casting phosphorescent gleams crashing through the water.

My blood froze in my veins as I recognized two formidable sharks—a pair of tintoreas, terrible creatures, with enormous tails and dull glassy eyes, the phosphorescent matter ejected from holes around the muzzle. Monstrous brutes! They would crush a man to bits in their iron jaws. I did not know whether Conseil stopped to classify them. For my part, I observed their silver bellies and their huge mouths bristling with teeth, from a very unscientific point of view, and more as a possible victim than as a naturalist.

Happily the voracious creatures have poor vision. They passed without seeing us, brushing us with their brownish fins, and we escaped by a miracle from a danger certainly greater than meeting a tiger head-on in the jungle. Half an hour later, guided by the electric light, we reached the *Nautilus*. The outside door had been left open, and Captain Nemo closed it as soon as we had entered the first chamber. He then pressed a knob. I heard the pumps working in the bowels of the vessel, I felt the water sinking away from me, and in a few moments the chamber was entirely empty. The inside door then opened, and we entered the cabin.

There we were helped out of our diving suits, not without some trouble. We were fairly worn out from want of food and sleep, and air to breathe. I returned to my room, filled with great wonder at this amazing expedition at the bottom of the sea.

Chapter 17
Four Thousand Leagues Under the Pacific

The next morning, the 18th of November, I had quite recovered from my fatigues of the day before. I went up onto the half-deck, just as the second lieutenant was uttering his daily speech.

I was admiring the magnificent view of the ocean when Captain Nemo appeared. He did not seem to be aware of my presence, and began a series of astronomical observations. When he had finished, he went and leant on the cage of the watch-light, and gazed abstractedly on the ocean. In the meantime, a number of the sailors of the *Nautilus,* all strong and healthy men, had come up onto the deck. They came to draw up the nets that had been laid during the night. These sailors were evidently of different nations, although the European type was recognizable in all. I noted some unmistakable Irishmen, Frenchmen, some Slavs, and a Greek. They were polite. Only among themselves did they use that odd language, the origin of which I could not guess, neither could I question them.

The nets were hauled in. They were a large kind of "chaluts," like those used on the Normandy coasts, great pockets kept open by the waves and by a chain running through the narrow meshes. These pockets, pulled by iron poles, swept through the water, and gathered everything in their way. That day they brought up curious specimens from those productive coasts—fishing-frogs that, from their comical movements, have acquired the name of buffoons; black commersons, equipped with antennae; trigger-fish, encircled with red bands; orthragorisci, with very subtle venom; some olive-colored lampreys; macrorhynci, covered with silvery scales; trichiuri, the elctric power of which is equal to that of the gymnotus and crampfish; scaly notoperi, with transverse brown bands; greenish cod; several varieties of gobies, etc.; also some larger fish; a caranx with a prominent head a yard long; several fine bonitos, streaked with blue and silver; and three splendid tunnies, which, in spite of the swiftness of their motion, had not escaped the net.

I reckoned that the haul had brought in more than nine hundred weight of fish. It was a fine haul, but not to be wondered at. The nets are let down for several hours, and are able to enclose in their meshes an infinite variety. We had no lack of excellent food, and with the speed of the *Nautilus* and the attraction of the electric light, we could always renew our supply. The catch was immediately lowered through the panel to the steward's room, part to be eaten fresh, and others pickled.

The fishing ended, the tanks of air renewed, I thought that the *Nautilus* was about to continue its submarine course. I was preparing to return to my room, when, without further preamble, the Captain turned to me, saying—

"Professor, is not this ocean gifted with real life? It has its tempers and its gentle moods. Yesterday it slept as we did, and now it has awakened after a quiet night. Look!" he continued, "it wakes under the caresses of the sun. It is going to renew its diurnal existence. It is an interesting study to watch the play of its organization. It has a pulse, arteries, spasms; and I agree with the learned Maury, who discovered in it a circulation as real as the circulation of blood in animals.

"Yes, the ocean has indeed circulation, and to promote it, the Creator has caused things to multiply in it—caloric, salt, and animalculae."

When Captain Nemo spoke thus, he seemed altogether transformed, and aroused an extraordinary emotion in me.

"Also," he added, "true life is there. I can imagine the foundation of nautical towns, clusters of submarine houses, which, like the *Nautilus,* would ascend every morning to breathe at the surface of the water—free towns, independent cities. Yet who knows whether some despot—"

Captain Nemo finished his sentence with a violent gesture, then, addressing me as if to chase away some sorrowful thought—

"M. Aronnax," he asked, "do you know the

depth of the ocean?"

"I only know, Captain, what the principal soundings have taught us."

"Could you tell me them, so that I can use them to my purpose?"

"These are some," I replied, "that I remember. If I am not mistaken, a depth of 8000 yards has been found in the North Atlantic, and 2500 yards in the Mediterranean. The most remarkable soundings have been made in the South Atlantic, near the 35th parallel, and they measure 12,000 yards, 14,000 yards, and 15,000 yards. To sum up, it is reckoned that if the bottom of the sea were leveled, its mean depth would be about one and three-quarter leagues."

"Well, Professor," replied the Captain, "we shall show you better than that, I hope. As to the mean depth of this part of the Pacific, I tell you it is only 4000 yards."

Having said this, Captain Nemo went towards the panel, and disappeared down the ladder. I followed him, and went into the large saloon. The screw was immediately put in motion, and the log showed twenty miles an hour.

During the days and weeks that passed, Captain Nemo was very sparing with his visits. I saw him seldom. The lieutenant pricked the ship's course regularly on the chart, so I could always tell exactly the route of the *Nautilus*.

Nearly every day, for some time, the panels of the saloon were opened, and we never tired of penetrating the mysteries of the submarine world.

The general direction of the *Nautilus* was

southeast, and it maintained a depth of between 100 and 150 yards. One day, however, I do not know why, being drawn diagonally by means of the inclined planes, it touched the bed of the sea. The thermometer indicated a temperature of 4.25 (cent.); a temperature that at this depth seemed common to all latitudes.

At three o'clock in the morning of the 26th of November, the *Nautilus* crossed the Tropic of Cancer at 172^0 longitude. On the 27th instant it sighted the Sandwich Islands, where Cook died, February 14, 1779. We had traveled 4860 leagues from our starting-point. In the morning, when I went on deck, I saw, two miles to windward, Hawaii, largest of the seven islands that form the group. I saw clearly the cultivated lands and the several mountain chains that run parallel with the coast and the volcanoes that overtop Mouna-Rea, rising 5000 yards above the level of the sea. Besides other things the nets brought up, were several flabellariae and graceful polypi, that are peculiar to that part of the ocean. The direction of the *Nautilus* was still to the southeast. It crossed the equator December 1, in 142^0 longitude; and on the 4th of the same month, after traveling rapidly and without anything particular occurring, we sighted the Marquesas group. I saw three miles off, at 8^0 57' latitude south, and 139^0 32' west longitude, Martin's peak in Nouka-Hiva, the largest of this group, that belongs to France. I saw only the wooded mountains against the horizon, because Captain Nemo did not wish to bring the ship to the wind. There the nets brought up beautiful specimens of fish;

choryphenes, with azure fins and tails like gold, the flesh of which is unrivaled; Hologymnoses, which have few scales, and are of exquisite flavor; ostorhyncs, with bony jaws, and yellow-tinged thasards, as good as bonitos; all fish that would be of use to us. After leaving these charming French protectorates, from the 4th to the 11th of December the *Nautilus* sailed about 2,000 miles. This voyage was remarkable for the meeting with an immense shoal of calmars, near neighbors to the cuttle. The French fishermen call them *hornets;* they belong to the cephalopod class, and to the dibranchial family, that includes the cuttles and the argonauts. These animals were particularly favored by students of antiquity, and they furnished numerous metaphors to the popular orators, as well as excellent dishes for the tables of the rich citizens, if one can believe Athenaeus, a Greek doctor, who lived before Galen. It was during the night of the 9th or 10th of December that the *Nautilus* came across this shoal of molluscs, that are peculiarly nocturnal. One could count them by millions. They emigrate from the temperate to the warmer zones, following the track of herrings and sardines. We watched them through the thick crystal panes, swimming down the wind with great rapidity, moving by means of their locomotive tube, pursuing fish and molluscs, eating the little ones, eaten by the big ones, and tossing about in indescribable confusion the ten arms that nature has placed on their heads like a crest of pneumatic serpents. The *Nautilus,* in spite of its speed, was delayed for several hours in the midst of these animals, and its nets brought in an enormous quantity, among which I recognized the nine species that D'Orbigny classed for the Pacific. One saw, during that voyage, that the sea is prodigal with the most wonderful sights. They were in endless variety. The scene changed continually for the pleasure of our eyes, and we were called upon not only to contemplate the works of the Creator in the environment of the liquid element, but to study the most unyielding mysteries of the ocean.

During the daytime of the 11th of December, I was busy reading in the large saloon. Ned Land and Conseil watched the luminous water through the half-open panels. The *Nautilus* was stationary. While its reservoirs were filled, it stayed at a depth of 1000 yards, an area in which large fish were seldom seen.

I was then reading a charming book by Jean Macé, "The Slaves of the Stomach," and I was learning some valuable lessons from it, when Conseil interrupted me.

"Will master come here for a moment?" he said, in a curious voice.

"What is the matter, Conseil?"

"I want master to look."

I rose, went and leaned on my elbows before the panes and looked.

In the full electric light, an enormous black mass, quite still, was suspended in the midst of the waters. I watched it attentively seeking to find out the nature of this gigantic cetacean. But a sudden thought crossed my mind. "A vessel!" I said half aloud.

"Yes," replied the Canadian, "a disabled

ship that has sunk on end.''

Ned Land was right; we were close to a vessel whose tattered shrouds still hung from their ropes. The hull seemed to be in good order, and the shipwreck to have occurred not more than a few hours ago. Three stumps of masts, broken off about two feet above the bridge, showed that the vessel had had to sacrifice its rigging. But, listing to one side it had filled with water, and was heeling over even more to port. Lost under the waves, the ship was a sad spectacle; but sadder still was the sight of her bridge, where some corpses, bound with ropes still lay. I counted five—four men, one of whom had been standing at the helm, and a woman by the poop, holding an infant in her arms. She was quite young. I could distinguish her features, which the water had not disfigured, by the brilliant light from the *Nautilus*. In one despairing effort, she had raised her infant above her head, poor little thing! whose arms encircled its mother's neck. The attitude of the four sailors was frightful, distorted as they were by convulsive movements, made evidently in a last effort to free themselves from the cords that bound them to the vessel. The steersman alone, calm, with a grave face, his gray hair glued to his forehead, and his hand clutching the wheel of the helm, seemed even then to be guiding the three broken masts through the depths of the ocean.

What a scene! We were dumb; our hearts beat fast before this shipwreck, taken as it were from life, and photographed in its last moments. And I saw already, coming towards it with hungry eyes, enormous sharks, attracted by the human flesh.

However, the *Nautilus,* turning, went round the submerged vessel, and in one instant I read on the stern—*The Florida Sunderland.*

Chapter 18
Vanikoro

This terrible spectacle was the forerunner of the series of maritime catastrophes that the *Nautilus* was destined to meet with. Whenever we sailed through more frequented waters, we often saw the gulls of shipwrecked vessels that were rotting in the water, and deeper down, cannons, bullets, anchors, chains, and a thousand other iron materials eaten up by rust. However, on the 11th of December, we sighted the Pomoton Islands, the old "dangerous group" of Bougainville, that extend over a space of 500 leagues at E.S.E., to W.N.W., from the Island Ducie to that of Lazareff. This archipelago covers an area of 370 square leagues, and it is formed of sixty groups of islands, among which the Gambier group is notable. These are coral islands, over which France holds sway. Built slowly but continuously by the daily work of polypi, this new island will be joined to the neighboring groups, and a fifth continent will stretch from New Zealand and New Caledonia, and from thence to the Marquesas.

One day, when I was suggesting this theory to Captain Nemo, he replied coldly—

"The earth does not want new continents, but new men."

Chance had conducted the *Nautilus* towards the Island of Clermont-Tonnerre, one of the most curious of the group, discovered in 1822 by Captain Bell of the *Minerva*. I now could study the madreporal system, which has produced these islands.

Madrepores (which must not be mistaken for corals) are covered with a calcareous crust, and the difference in its structure has induced M. Milne Edwards, my worthy master, to class them into five sections. The animalculae that the marine polypus secretes live by millions at the bottom of their cells. Their calcareous deposits grow into rocks, reefs, and islands large and small. Here they form a broken ring surrounding a little inland lake. Elsewhere, they construct barrier reefs like those on the coasts of New Caledonia and the various Pomoton islands. In still other places such as Reunion and Maurice, they built irregular high, straight walls, rising from deep water.

Some cable-lengths off the shores of the Island of Clermont I admired the gigantic work accomplished by these microscopial artisans. These walls are the work of those particular madrepores known as milleporas, porites, and astraeas. These polypi are found particularly in the rough waters, near the surface. And so they begin their construction at the top and work down! They bury themselves by degrees with the debris of the secretions that support them. Such, at least, was Darwin's theory, who thus explains the formation of the *atolls*, a theory superior (to my mind) to that which claims that the foundation of the madreporical constructions are mountains or volcanoes, whose summits are submerged below sea level.

I could observe closely these curious walls, for they were more than 300 yards high, and our electric lanterns lighted up this calcareous matter brilliantly. Conseil asked me how long it took for these colossal barriers to be built. I astonished him greatly by telling him that learned men reckoned that they grew an eighth of an inch in a hundred years.

Towards evening Clermont-Tonnerre was lost in the distance, and the route of the *Nautilus* was noticeably changed. After crossing the Tropic of Capricorn at 135° longitude, it sailed W.N.W., making again for the tropical zone. Although the summer sun was very strong, we did not suffer from heat, for at fifteen or twenty fathoms deep, the temperature did not change more than ten to twelve degrees.

On December 15, we passed to the east the bewitching Society Islands and lovely Tahiti, queen of the Pacific. Some miles to the windward, I saw the summits of her mountains. The waters surrounding these islands furnished our table with excellent fish, mackerel, bonitos and albacores, and some varieties of a sea-serpent called munirophis.

On the 25th of December the *Nautilus* sailed

into the midst of the New Hebrides, discovered by Quiros in 1606, explored by Bougainville in 1768, and to which Cook gave their present name in 1773. They are composed principally of nine large islands, that are grouped over 120 leagues N.N.S. to S.S.W., between 15^0 and 2^0 south latitude, and 164^0 and 168^0 longitude. We passed quite close to the island of Aurou; at noon it looked like a mass of green trees, dominated by a peak of great height.

That day being the Feast of the Nativity, Ned Land seemed unhappy that we did not celebrate "Christmas," the family holiday of which Protestants are so fond. I had not seen Captain Nemo for a week, when on the morning of the 27th, he came into the large saloon, seeming as usual, as if he had seen me only five minutes before. I was busily tracing the route of the *Nautilus* on the planisphere, when the Captain came up to me, put his finger on a spot on the chart and said this single word—

"Vanikoro."

The effect was magical! It was the name of the islands where the expedition of La Perouse had been lost! I leaped to my feet.

"The *Nautilus* has brought us to Vanikoro?" I asked.

"Yes, Professor," said the Captain.

"And I can visit the celebrated island where the *Boussole* and the *Astrolabe* were broken up?"

"If you like, Professor."

"When shall we be there?"

"We are there now."

Followed by Captain Nemo, I went up on deck and eagerly scanned the horizon.

To the N.E. emerged two volcanic islands of unequal size, surrounded by a coral reef that measured forty miles in circumference. We were close to Vanikoro which Dumont d'Urville named Island of the Quest, and exactly facing the little harbor of Vanou, situated in 16° 4′ south latitude, and 164° 38′ east longitude. The earth seemed covered with verdure from the shore to the inland heights that were crowned by Mount Kapogo nearly 3,000 feet high. The *Nautilus,* having passed through a strait in the outer belt of rocks, found itself among breakers where the sea was from thirty to forty fathoms deep. Under the verdant shade of some mangroves I perceived some savages who showed alarm, as the black shape of our vessel came toward them. The *Nautilus* must look to them, I thought, like a great sea-serpent.

Just then Captain Nemo asked me what I knew about the shipwreck of La Perouse's party.

"Only what everyone knows, Captain," I replied.

"And could you tell me what everyone knows about it?" he inquired ironically.

"Easily."

I told him briefly all that was revealed in the last works of Dumont d'Urville.

La Perouse, and his lieutenant Captain de Langle, were sent by Louis XVI, in 1785, on a voyage of circumnavigation. They embarked in the corvettes *Boussole* and *Astrolabe,* neither of which was again heard of. In 1791, the French government, anxious as to the fate of these two ships, manned two large merchantmen, the

Recherche and the *Esperance,* which left Brest September 28th under the command of Bruni d'Entrecasteaux.

Two months later, they were told by a man called Bowen, who commanded the *Albemarle,* that debris of shipwrecked vessels had been seen on the coasts of New Georgia. But d'Entrecasteaux, uncertain of the accuracy of this information, directed his course towards the Admiralty Isles, described in a report from Captain Hunter as the place where La Perouse was wrecked.

They sought in vain. The *Esperance* and the *Recherche* passed by Vanikoro without stopping, and in fact, this voyage was most disastrous, as it cost the life of d'Entrecasteaux, two of his lieutenants, and several of his crew.

In 1824, Captain Dillon, a shrewd old Pacific sailor, was the first to find unmistakable traces of the wrecks. On the 15th day of May, his vessel, the *St. Patrick,* sailed near Tikopia, one of the New Hebrides. There, an East Indian sailor came alongside in a canoe, and sold him a silver sword, with an engraved hilt. The man alleged that six years earlier, during a stay at Vanikoro, he had met two Europeans, who had been shipwrecked there some years before.

Dillon guessed that these were survivors of La Perouse's expedition. He tried to land on Vanikoro, where, according to the sailor, he would find much debris of the wreck, but winds and tide prevented him.

Dillon returned to Calcutta. There he interested the Asiatic Society and the Indian Company in his discovery. A vessel, to which was given the name of the *Recherche,* was put at his disposal, and he set out, January 23, 1827, accompanied by a French agent.

The *Recherche,* after touching at several points in the Pacific, dropped anchor near Vanikoro, July 7, 1827, in the harbor of Vanou where we were now.

There, the crew collected numerous relics of the wreck—iron utensils, anchors, pulley-strops, swivel-guns, and 18 lb. shot, fragments of astronomical instruments, a piece of crownwork, and a bronze clock, bearing this inscription—*"Bazin m'a fait,"* which was the mark of the foundry of the arsenal at Brest. There could be no further doubt.

Dillon, to complete his investigation, stayed in this sinister place till October. Then he left Vanikoro, and put into Calcutta, April 7, 1828. Soon afterwards, he returned to France, where he was warmly welcomed by Charles X. Dumont d'Urville, commander of a ship called *Astrolabe,* after La Perouse's vessel, learned from a whaler that some medals and a cross of St. Louis had been found in the hands of savages on Louisiade and New Caledonia. Knowing nothing of Dillon's voyage, Dumont d'Urville set out, and put into Hobart Town two months after Dillon had left Vanikoro. There he learned the results of Dillon's inquiries, and found that a certain James Hobbs, second lieutenant of the *Union* of Calcutta, after landing on an island situated 8^0 $18'$ south latitude, and 156^0 $30'$ east longitude, had seen some iron bars and red cloth being used by the natives of these parts. Dumont d' Urville, much perplexed, and not knowing how far to credit conflicting reports in the sensation-seeking newspapers, tried to follow in the tracks of Dillon.

On the 10th of February, 1828, the *Astrolabe* stopped at Tikopia, and Dumont d'Urville took on as guide and interpreter a deserter he found on the island. He proceeded to Vanikoro, sighted it on the 12th inst., lay among the reefs until the 14th, and did not cast anchor within the barrier in the harbor of Vanou until the 20th.

On the 23rd, several officers went ashore and searched the island. They found some bits of wreckage here and there, but the natives engaged in denials and evasions, and refused to show them where the ships had foundered. This ambiguous conduct led the officers to believe that the natives had ill-treated the castaways; and indeed the natives seemed to fear that Dumont d'Urville had come to avenge La Perouse and his unfortunate crew.

However, on the 26th, appeased by some presents and assured that they had no reprisals to fear, they led Lieutenant Jacquireot to the scene of the wreck.

There, in three or four fathoms of water, between the reefs of Pacou and Vanou, lay anchors, cannons, pigs of lead and iron, embedded in the limy concretions. The *Astrolabe's* boats were sent to this place, and, not without difficulty their crews hauled up an anchor weighing 1800 lbs., a brass gun, some pigs of iron and two copper swivel-guns.

Dumont d'Urville learned from the natives that La Perouse, after losing both his vessels on the reefs of this island, had succeeded in building a smaller boat, only to disappear a second time. Where?—no one could tell.

Meanwhile, the French government, fearing that Dumont d'Urville was not aware of Dillon's voyage, dispatched to Vanikoro the sloop *Bayonnaise* which had been stationed on the west coast of America. The *Bayonnaise* cast her anchor before Vanikoro several months after the departure of the *Astrolabe*. The Captain found no new evidence but stated that the savages had respected the monument which had been erected in honor of La Perouse. That is the substance of what I told to Captain Nemo.

"So," he said, "no one knows where the third vessel that was constructed by the castaways on the island of Vanikoro perished?"

"No one knows."

Captain Nemo said nothing, but signaled for me to follow him into the large saloon. The *Nautilus* sank several yards below the waves, and the panels were opened.

I hastened to the window, and under the crustations of coral, covered with fungi, syphonules, alcyons, madrepores, through myriad shoals of beautiful fish—girelles, glyphisidri, pompherides, diacopes, and holocentres—I recognized many objects showing that a ship had sunk here, iron stirrups, anchors, cannons, bullets, capstan fittings, the stem of a ship, all now carpeted with living flowers. While I was looking on this desolate scene, Captain Nemo said in a sad voice—

"Commander La Perouse set out December 7,1785, with his vessels *La Boussole* and the

Astrolabe. He first cast anchor at Botany Bay, visited the Friendly Isles, New Caledonia, then sailed towards Santa Cruz, and put into Namouka, one of the Hapai group. There his vessels struck on the uncharted reefs of Vanikoro. The *Boussole*, which went first, ran aground on the southerly coast. The *Astrolabe* went to its assistance, and ran aground too. The first vessel was destroyed almost immediately. The second, stranded to the leeward, held out for several days. The natives made the castaways welcome. They set up quarters on the island, and built a smaller boat from the wreckage of the two large ones. Some sailors stayed willingly at Vanikoro; the others, weak and ill, set out with La Perouse. He sailed towards the Solomon Isles, and perished along with all hands on board, on the western coast of the chief island of the group, between Capes Deception and Satisfaction.''

''How do you know that?''

''By this, which I found on the spot where the last wreck took place.''

Captain Nemo showed me a tin box, stamped with the Arms of France, and badly corroded by the saltwater. He opened it, and I saw a bundle of papers, yellow but still readable.

They were the instructions of the naval minister to Commander La Perouse, annotated in the margin in Louis XVI's handwriting.

''Ah! it is a fine death for a sailor!'' said Captain Nemo, at last. ''A coral tomb makes a quiet grave; and I trust to heaven that I and my comrades will find no other.''

Chapter 19
Torres Straits

During the night of the 27th or 28th of December, the *Nautilus* left the shores of Vanikoro with great speed. Her course was southwesterly, and in three days she had covered the 750 leagues that separated La Perouse's group from the southeast point of Papua.

Early on the 1st of January, 1863, Conseil joined me on deck.

"Master, will you permit me to wish you a happy new year?"

"What! Conseil; exactly as if I were in Paris, in my study at the Botanical Gardens? Well, I accept your good wishes, and thank you for them. Only, what exactly do you mean by a 'happy new year,' under our circumstances? Do you mean a year that would bring an end to our imprisonment, or a year in which we continue on this strange voyage?"

"Really, I do not know how to answer, master. We are sure to see curious things, and in the last two months we never have had time to be bored. The latest marvel is always the most astonishing; and if we continue at this rate, I do not know how it will end. It is my opinion that we shall never again have such an opportunity. I think, then, with no offense to master, that a happy year would be one in which we could see everything."

On January 2, we made 11,340 miles or 5250 French leagues, since our starting point in the Japan Seas. Before the ship's bow now stretched the dangerous shores of the Coral Sea, along the northeast coast of Australia. Our vessel lay some miles from the redoubtable bank on which Cook's ships came within an inch of being lost June 10, 1770. The boat which carried Cook struck on a rock, and was saved from sinking by a piece of coral that was broken off by the shock, and lodged itself in the broken keel.

I had wished to visit this reef, 360 leagues long, against which the sea always broke with great violence and with a sound like thunder. But just then the inclined planes drew the *Nautilus* down to a great depth, and I had to content myself with viewing the different specimens of fish brought up by the nets. I remarked, among others, some germons, a species of mackerel as large as a tunney, with bluish sides, and striped with transverse bands of color that disappeared when the animal died.

These fish followed us in shoals, and furnished us with very delicate food. We took also a large number of giltheads, about one and a half inches long, tasting like dorys; and flying pyrapeds like submarine swallows, which, in dark nights, light first the air and then the water with their phosphorescent glow. Among the molluscs and zoophytes, I found in the meshes of the net several species of alcyonarians, echini, hammers, spurs, dials, cerites, and hyalleae. The flora were represented by beautiful floating seaweeds, laminariae, and macrocystes, impregnated with a gluey material that is exuded through their pores; and among which I gathered an admirable *Nemastoma Geliniarois,* that was classed among the natural curiosities of the museum.

Two days after crossing the Coral Sea, January 4, we sighted the Papuan coasts. On this occasion, Captain Nemo informed me that his intention was to enter the Indian Ocean through the Strait of Torres, but that was all he told me of his plans.

The Torres Straits are nearly thirty-four leagues wide; but they contain innumerable obstructions in islands, islets, breakers, and rocks, that make navigation almost impossible. So that Captain Nemo took all extreme precautions in passing through them. The *Nautilus* sailing on the surface went at a cautious pace. Her screw, like a cetacean's tail, beat the waves slowly.

Profiting by this, I and my two companions went up on to the deserted deck. Before us was the steerman's cage, and I expected that Captain Nemo was there directing the course of the *Nautilus*. I had before me the excellent charts of the Strait of Torres made by the hydrographical engineer Vincendon Dumoulin. These and Captain King's are the best for solving the intricacies of this strait, and I consulted them attentively. Round the *Nautilus* the sea dashed furiously. The waves moving rapidly in a cross current, broke savagely on the coral that showed itself here and there.

"This is a bad sea!" remarked Ned Land. "Detestable indeed, and one that does not suit such a ship as the *Nautilus*."

"This damn captain must be very sure of his course, for I see coral reefs that would tear his *Nautilus* into a thousand pieces, if it barely touched them."

Indeed the situation was dangerous, but the *Nautilus* seemed to slide like magic past these rocks. It did not follow the routes designated on the charts exactly, for these had proved fatal to Dumont d'Urville. It bore more northwards, edged past the Island of Murray, and veered again to the southwest towards Cumberland Passage. I thought we were going through, but turning northwest again the *Nautilus* passed among hundreds of islands and islets, towards the Island and to the Canal Mauvais.

I wondered if Captain Nemo, imprudent to the point of madness, would take his vessel into that pass where Dumont d'Urville's two corvettes struck; when swerving again, and cutting straight through to the west, he steered for the Island of Gilboa.

It was then three in the afternoon. The tide having been quite full, began to recede. The *Nautilus* approached Gilboa with its remarkable border of screw-pines, and stood off about two miles away from it. Suddenly a shock knocked me down. The *Nautilus* had grazed a rock, and remained motionless listing lightly to port side.

When I rose, Captain Nemo and his lieutenant were on the deck. They were examining the situation of the vessel, and exchanging words in their incomprehensible dialect. Two miles away on the starboard side, appeared Gilboa, stretching from north to west like an immense arm. Towards the south and east were coral reefs, left bare by the ebb. We had run aground, and in one of those seas where the tides are never high, which made floating of the *Nautilus* problematical. The vessel had not suffered, for her keel was solidly joined. But if she could neither glide off nor move under her own power, she ran the risk of remaining forever on these rocks, and Captain Nemo's submarine vessel would be done for.

I was reflecting thus, when the Captain, cool and calm, always master of himself, approached me.

"An accident?" I asked.

"No; an incident."

"But an incident that will oblige you perhaps to become an inhabitant of the earth from which you flee?"

Captain Nemo looked at me curiously, and made a negative gesture, as much as to say that nothing would force him to set foot on *terra firma* again. Then he said—

"M. Aronnax, the *Nautilus* is not lost; it will carry you still among the marvels of the ocean.

Our voyage is only begun, and I do not wish to be deprived so soon of the honor of your company."

"However, Captain Nemo," I replied, ignoring his ironical turn of phrase, "the *Nautilus* ran aground in open sea. Now the tides are not strong in the Pacific; and if you cannot lighten the *Nautilus*, I do not see how it will be launched again."

"The tides are not strong in the Pacific; you are right there, Professor. But in Torres Straits, one finds still a difference of a yard and a half between the level of high and low tide. Today is January 4, and in five days the moon will be full. Now, I shall be very much astonished if that satellite does not raise these masses of water sufficiently, and render me a service that I should be indebted for."

Having said this, Captain Nemo, followed by his lieutenant, went down again to the interior of the *Nautilus*. As to the vessel, it was as motionless as if the coralline polypi had already walled it up with their indestructible cement.

"Well, sir?" said Ned Land, who came up to me after the departure of the Captain.

"Well, friend Ned, we will wait patiently for the tide on the 9th instant; for it appears that the moon will have the goodness to take the *Nautilus* off this rock."

"Really?"

"Really."

"And this Captain is not going to cast anchor at all since the tide will suffice?" said Conseil, simply.

The Canadian looked at Conseil, then shrugged his shoulders.

"Sir, you may believe me when I tell you that this piece of iron will navigate neither on nor under the sea again; it is good for nothing but scrap. I think, therefore, that the time has come to part company with Captain Nemo."

"Friend Ned, I do not despair of this stout *Nautilus*, as you do. In four days we shall know what to expect from the Pacific tides. Besides, flight might be possible if we were in sight of the English or Provencal coasts; but the Papuan shores are quite another thing. It will be time enough to consider flight if the *Nautilus* cannot be floated again, which I would look upon as a grave event."

"But do they know, at least, how to find the lay of the land? There is an island; on that island there are trees; under those trees, earthly animals, bearers of steaks and roast beef in which I would willingly sink my teeth."

"In this, friend Ned is right," said Conseil, "and I agree with him. Could not master obtain permission from his friend Captain Nemo for us to go on land, if only so as not to lose the habit of treading on the solid parts of our planet?"

"I can ask him, but he will refuse."

"Will master risk it?" asked Conseil, "and we shall know how to rely upon the Captain's amiability."

To my surprise Captain Nemo gave me the permission I asked for, and he gave it very agreeably, without even exacting from me a promise to return to the vessel; but flight across

New Guinea might be very perilous, and I should not have counseled Ned Land to attempt it. Better to be a prisoner on board the *Nautilus* than to fall into the hands of the natives.

At eight o'clock, armed with guns and hatchets, we disembarked from the *Nautilus*. The sea was quite calm; a slight breeze blew on land. Conseil and I rowed. We sped along quickly, and Ned steered through the narrow passage between the breakers. The boat was handled well, and went easily.

Ned Land could not restrain his joy. He was like a prisoner who has escaped from confinement, and knew not that he must return.

"Meat!" he said again and again "we are going to eat meat; and what meat! Real game. I never said that fish is not good; we must not abuse it; but a piece of fresh venison, grilled on live coals, will agreeably vary our ordinary course."

"Gourmand!" said Conseil, "he makes my mouth water."

"It remains to be seen," I said, "if these forests are full of game, and if the game is not such as will hunt the hunter himself."

"Well said, M. Aronnax," replied the Canadian, whose teeth seemed sharpened like the edge of a hatchet; "but I will eat tiger—loin of tiger—if there is no other quadruped on this island."

"Friend Ned is uneasy about it," said Conseil.

"Whatever it may be," continued Ned Land, "any animal with four feet and no feathers, or having two feet and feathers, will be saluted by my first shot.''

"Very well! Master Land's imprudences are beginning.''

''Never fear, M. Aronnax,'' replied the Canadian; ''I do not need twenty-five minutes to offer you a dish of my sort.''

At half-past eight our little boat ran gently aground, on thick sand, after having happily passed the coral reef that surrounds the Island of Gilboa.

Chapter 20

A Few Days on Land

I was strongly moved by touching land. Ned Land tried the soil with his feet, as if to take possession of it. It was two months since we had become, according to Captain Nemo, ''passengers on board the *Nautilus*,'' although in reality prisoners of its commander.

In a few minutes we were a musket-shot away from the coast. The soil was almost entirely madreporical, but certain dried-up river beds strewn with debris of granite, showed that this island was of a primordial formation. The horizon was hidden behind a curtain of splendid forests. Enormous trees 200 feet high, were tied to each other by garlands of bindweed, true natural hammocks, rocked by a light breeze. Mimosa, ficuses, casuarinae, teks, hibisci, and palm-trees mingled together in profusion. Under the shelter of their green vault grew orchids, leguminous plants, and ferns.

Without noticing all these beautiful specimens of Papuan flora, the Canadian abandoned the agreeable for the useful. He discovered a cocoa-tree, beat down some of the fruit, broke them, and we drank the milk and ate the meat, with a satisfaction that protested against our usual meals on the *Nautilus*.

"Excellent!" said Ned Land.

"Exquisite!" replied Conseil.

"And I do not think," said the Canadian, "that he would object to our introducing a cargo of coconuts on board."

"I do not think he would, but he would not taste them."

"So much the worse for him," said Conseil.

"And so much the better for us," replied Ned Land. "There will be more for us."

"One word only, Master Land," I said to the harpooner, who was beginning to ravage another coconut tree. "Coconuts are good things, but before filling the canoe with them it would be wise to look around and see if the island does not produce other things no less useful. Fresh vegetables would be welcome on board the *Nautilus*."

"Master is right," replied Conseil; "and I propose to reserve three places in our vessel, one for fruits, one for vegetables, and the third for venison, of which I have not yet seen the smallest bite."

"Conseil, we must not despair," said the Canadian.

"Let us continue," I returned, "but stay on the lookout. While this island seems uninhabited, it might still contain some individuals who are not so fussy as we are about what constitutes game."

"Ho! ho!" said Ned Land, moving his jaws significantly.

"Well, Ned!" cried Conseil.

"My word!" returned the Canadian, "I begin to understand the charms of anthropophagy."

"Ned! Ned! what are you saying?" cried Conseil. "You cannibal! I should not feel safe with you, especially as I share your cabin. I might wake one day to find myself half devoured."

"Friend Conseil, I like you much, but not enough to eat you, unless I had to."

"I would trust you," replied Conseil. "But enough. We absolutely must bring down some game to satisfy this cannibal, or else one of these fine mornings, master will find only pieces of his servant to serve him."

While we were talking thus, we were going deeply under the dark arches of the forest, and for two hours we investigated it in all directions.

Chance rewarded our search for eatable vegetables; and one of the most useful growths of the tropical zones gave us a precious food that we lacked on board. This was the bread-fruit tree, which we found in profusion, called "rima" in seedless variety.

Ned Land knew these fruits well. He had eaten many, during his numerous voyages, and he knew how to prepare them. Moreover, the sight of them excited his appetite, and he could not contain himself for long.

"Master," he said, "I shall die if I do not taste a little of the paste from this bread-fruit tree."

"Taste it, friend Ned—taste it as you want. We are here to make experiments—make them."

"It won't take long," said the Canadian.

And armed with an electric deck light, he made a fire of dead wood, that crackled joyously. During this time, Conseil and I chose the best fruits. Some were not ripe enough, and their thick skin covered a white but rather fibrous pulp. Others, the greater number yellow and gelatinous, waited only to be picked.

These fruits enclosed no kernel. Conseil brought a dozen to Ned Land, who cut them in thick slices, and put them on the embers of his fire.

"You will see, sir, how good this bread is. More so when one has been deprived of it so long. It is not even bread," added he, "but a delicate pastry. You have eaten one, sir?"

"No, Ned."

"Very well, prepare yourself for a tasty morsel. If you do not come back for more, I am no longer the king of harpooners."

After some minutes, the fruit was completely roasted. The interior looked like a white pastry, a sort of soft crumb, the flavor of which was like that of an artichoke. It must be confessed this bread was excellent, and I ate of it with great relish.

"What time is it now?" asked the Canadian.

"Two o'clock at least," replied Conseil.

"How time flies on solid ground!" sighed Ned Land.

We returned through the forest, and completed our collection by raiding the cabbage-palms from the tops of the trees, little beans that I recognized as the "Abrou" of the Malays, and yams of a superior quality.

We also found many bananas, savory mangoes, and pineapples of unbelievable size.

We were loaded when we reached the boat. Ned Land still was not satisfied. But fate favored him. Just as we were about to push off, he perceived several Sago trees, a species of palm tree from twenty-five to thirty feet high. These trees, as valuable as the bread-fruit, justly are reckoned among the most useful fruits of Malaya.

Ned Land well knew what to do with the Sago tree. Taking his hatchet, he chopped down several and stripped away their bark, revealing the fibers, which can be mashed into a flour. This is the Sago which is the principal food of all the Melanesian people. It can be dried and stored away, thus we could bake bread aboard the *Nautilus*.

At last, at five o'clock in the evening, burdened with our riches, we left the shore, and half an hour later, hailed the *Nautilus*. No one appeared to greet us. The enormous iron-plated cylinder seemed deserted. The provisions placed on board, I descended to my cabin, and after supper slept soundly.

The next day, January 6, nothing had changed. There was not a sound nor a sign of life. The boat was in the same place where we had left it, and we resolved to return to the island. Ned Land hoped for better luck than on the day before with regard to the hunt, and wished to visit another part of the forest.

At dawn we set off. The boat, carried forward by waves that flowed to shore, reached the island in a few minutes.

We landed, and thinking that it was better to give in to the Canadian, we followed Ned Land, whose long legs threatened to outdistance us. He circled up the coast towards the west; then, fording some streams, he gained a high plain that was bordered by the splendid forests. Some kingfishers were rambling along the water-courses, but they would not let themselves be approached. Their circumspection proved to me that these birds knew what to expect from bipeds of our species, and I concluded that, if the island was not inhabited, at least human beings occasionally frequented it.

After crossing a rather wide prairie, we arrived at the edge of a little wood that was enlivened by the songs and flight of a large number of birds.

"These are only birds," said Conseil.

"But they are eatable," replied the harpooner.

"I do not agree with you, friend Ned, for I see only parrots there."

"Friend Conseil," said Ned, gravely, "the parrot is like pheasant to those who have nothing else."

"And," I added, "this bird, suitably prepared, is worth knife and fork."

Indeed, under the thick foliage of this wood, a world of chattering parrots of all colors were flying from branch to branch, only needing a careful education to speak the human language. There were also grave cockatoos, who seemed to meditate upon some philosophical problem, whilst brilliant red lories passed like banners carried by the breezes; papuans, with the finest azure colors, and in all a variety of winged things most charming to behold, but few eatable.

However, a bird peculiar to these lands, and which has never passed the limits of the Arrow and Papuan islands, was missing. Fortune was saving it for me.

After passing through a moderately thick copse, we reached a plain covered with bushes. I saw then those magnificent birds, the arrangement of whose long feathers obliges them to fly against the wind. Their undulating flight, graceful aerial curves, and the shading of their colors, attracted and charmed one's attention. I had no trouble in recognizing them.

"Birds of paradise!" I exclaimed.

The Malays, who carry on a great trade in these birds with the Chinese, have several means for taking them, that we could not employ. Sometimes they put snares at the top of high trees that the birds of paradise prefer to frequent. Sometimes they catch them with a viscous birdlime that paralyzes their movements. They even go so far as to poison the springs that the birds usually drink from. But we were obliged to fire at them on the wing, which gave us little chance to bring them down; and indeed, we vainly exhausted half of our ammunition.

About eleven o'clock in the morning, we had crossed the first range of mountains that form the center of the island, and we had killed nothing. Hunger drove us on. The hunters had relied on the fruits of the chase, and they were wrong. Happily Conseil, to his great surprise, made a double shot and secured breakfast. He brought down a white pigeon and a wood-pigeon, which, cleverly plucked and suspended from a skewer, were roasted over a hot fire of dead wood. Whilst these interesting birds were cooking, Ned prepared some bread-fruit.

The wood-pigeons were devoured to the bones, and declared excellent. Nutmeg, with which they are in the habit of stuffing their crops, flavors their flesh and renders it delicious eating.

"Now, Ned what do you lack?"

"Some four-footed game, M. Aronnax. All these pigeons are only side-dishes, and trifles; and until I have killed an animal with cutlets, I shall not be content."

"Nor I, Ned, if I do not catch a bird of paradise."

"Let us continue hunting," replied Conseil. "let us go towards the sea. We have arrived at the first declivities of the mountains, and I think we had better regain the forest region."

That was sensible advice, and was followed out. After walking for one hour, we reached a forest of Sago trees. Some inoffensive serpents glided away from us. The birds of paradise fled at our approach, and truly I despaired of getting near one, when Conseil, who was walking in front, suddenly bent down, uttered a triumphal cry, and came back to me bringing a magnificent specimen.

"Ah! bravo, Conseil!"

"Master is very good."

"No, my boy; you have done something remarkable, to take one of these birds alive and carry it in your hand."

"If master will examine it, he will see that I have not deserved great merit."

"Why, Conseil?"

"Because this bird is as drunk as a lord."

"Drunk!"

"Yes, sir; drunk with the nutmegs that it devoured under the nutmeg-tree, where I found it. See, friend Ned, see the awful effects of intemperance!"

"By Jove!" exclaimed the Canadian, "because I have drunk gin for two months, you must needs reproach me!"

However, I examined the curious bird. Conseil was right. The bird, drunk with the nutmeg juice, was quite powerless. It could not fly; it could hardly walk.

This bird belonged to the most beautiful of the eight species that have been classified in Papua and in the neighboring islands. It was a "great. emerald, the most rare kind." It measured three feet in length, its head comparatively small, the eyes near the opening of the beak. But, it displayed a superb combination of colors, having a yellow beak, brown feet and claws, pale brown wings with purple tips, pale yellow plumage on the head and at the back of the neck, brilliant emerald at the throat, chestnut on the breast and belly. The long plumes of its tail were exquisitely delicate, and they completed the whole of this marvelous bird, that the natives have named poetically "bird of the sun."

But if my wishes were gratified by acquiring the bird of paradise, the Canadian's were not yet. Fortunately, about two o'clock, he brought down a magnificent hog, the kind the natives call "bari-outang," and he was well received. Ned Land was very proud of his shot. The hog, hit by the electric ball, fell stone dead. The Canadian skinned and cleaned it properly, after having cut half-a-dozen thick chops designed to furnish us with a grilled repast that evening. Then, we resumed the hunt, which was to be marked by still more of Ned and Conseil's exploits.

Indeed, the two friends, beating the bushes, roused a herd of kangaroos, that fled, bounding along on their resilient feet. But these animals did not take flight so rapidly that the electric capsule could not stop their course.

"Ah, Professor!" cried Ned Land, carried away by the excitement of the hunt, "what excellent game this is; above all, cooked in a stew!

What a supply, for the *Nautilus!* two! three! five down! And to think we shall eat that flesh, and that the idiots on board shall not have a crumb!''

I think that, in the excess of his joy, the Canadian, if he had not talked so much, would have killed them all. But he contented himself with a single dozen of these interesting marsupials. These animals were small. They were a species of those ''kangaroo rabbits'' that live in the hollows of trees. They can run very fast, but they are moderately fat and make fairly good eating. We were very pleased with the results of the hunt. Ned proposed to return to this enchanting island the next day, for he wished to depopulate it of all its edible quadrupeds. But he reckoned without his host.

At six o'clock in the evening we had regained the shore where our boat was moored at the usual place. The *Nautilus,* like a long rock, emerged from the waves two miles from the beach. Ned Land, without delay, set about the important business of dinner. He knew all about good cooking. The ''bari-outang,'' grilled on the embers, soon scented the air with a delicious odor.

Indeed, the dinner was excellent. Two wood-pigeons completed this extraordinary menu. The pastry made from sago flour, bread-fruit, mangoes, half-a-dozen pineapples, and liquor fermented from coconut juice, filled us with pleasure. I even believe that the thinking of my worthy companions was not as clear as it might have been.

"Suppose we do not return to the *Nautilus* this evening?" said Conseil.

"Suppose we never return?" added Ned Land.

Just then a stone fell at our feet, and cut short the harpooner's proposition.

Chapter 21
Captain Nemo's Thunderbolt

We looked at the edge of the forest without rising, my hand stopped in the action of putting it to my mouth, Ned Land's completing its office.

"Stones do not fall from the sky," remarked Conseil, "or they would merit the name of meteorites."

A second stone, carefully aimed, that made a savory pigeon's leg fall from Conseil's hand, gave still more weight to his observation. We all three arose, shouldered our guns, and were ready to meet any attack.

"Are they apes?" cried Ned Land.

"Very nearly—they are savages."

"To the boat!" I said, hurrying to the sea.

It was indeed necessary to beat a retreat, for about twenty natives with bows and slings of arrows, appeared at the edge of a copse that masked the horizon to the right, hardly a hundred steps from us.

Our boat was moored about sixty feet away. The savages approached us, not running, but making threatening gestures. Stones and arrows fell thickly.

Ned Land did not wish to leave his provisions; and, in spite of his imminent danger, with his pig on one side, and his kangaroo on the other, he went tolerably fast. In two minutes we were on the shore. To load the boat with provisions and arms, to push it out to sea, and ship the oars, was the work of an instant. We had not gone two cable lengths, when a hundred savages, howling and gesticulating, entered the water up to their waists. I watched to see if their appearance would bring the sailors of the *Nautilus* on deck. But no. The great vessel seemed absolutely deserted.

Twenty minutes later we were on board. The panels were open. After making the boat fast, we went inside.

I descended to the large saloon, from whence I heard some music. Captain Nemo was there, bending over his organ, and plunged in ecstasy.

"Captain!"

He did not hear me.

"Captain!" I said again, touching his hand.

He shuddered, and turning round, said "Ah! it is you, Professor? Well, have you had a good hunt, have you botanized successfully?"

"Yes, Captain; but we have unfortunately raised a troop of bipeds, whose closeness troubles me."

"Savages."

"Savages!" he echoed, ironically. "So you are astonished, Professor, at having set foot on a strange land and finding savages? Savages! where are there not any? Besides, are they worse than others, these whom you call savages?''

''But, Captain—''

''How many have you counted?''

''A hundred at least.''

''M. Aronnax,'' replied Captain Nemo, placing his fingers on the organ stops, ''when all the natives of Papua are assembled on this shore, the *Nautilus* will have nothing to fear from their attacks.''

The Captain's fingers were running over the keys of the instrument, and I remarked that he touched only the black or minor keys, which gave to his melodies a wild Scottish character. Soon he had forgotten my presence, and had plunged into a reverie that I did not disturb. I went up again on the deck. Night had already fallen; for, in this low latitude, the sun sets rapidly and without twilight. I could only see the island indistinctly; but the numerous fires, lighted on the beach, showed that the natives did not contemplate leaving it. I was alone there for several hours, sometimes thinking of the natives—but without any dread, for the imperturbable confidence of the Captain was catching—sometimes forgetting them to admire the splendors of night in the tropics. My recollections went toward France, following those zodiacal stars that would shine there in some hours' time. The moon shone in the midst of the constellations of the zenith.

At length I went to bed, and the night slipped away without mischance, the islanders frightened no doubt at sight of the monster aground in their bay. The panels were open, and would have offered an easy access to the interior of the *Nautilus*.

At six o'clock in the morning of the 8th of January, I went up on deck. The dawn was breaking. The island soon showed itself through the melting fogs, first the shore, then the summits.

The natives were there, more numerous than on the day before—500 or 600 perhaps—some of them, profiting by the low tide, had come onto the reef, less than two cable lengths from the *Nautilus*. I distinguished them easily. They were true Papuans, with athletic figures, men of good blood, with broad high foreheads, prominent noses and white teeth. Their woolly hair, with a reddish tinge, showed on their bodies black and shining like those of Nubians. From the lobes of their ears, cut and distended, hung chaplets of bone. Most of these savages were naked. Amongst them, I remarked some women, wearing skirts of grass, from hips to knees. Some chiefs had ornamented their necks with necklaces of glass beads, red and white. Nearly all were armed with bows, arrows and shields, and carried on their shoulders a sort of net containing those round stones which they hurled from their slings with such skill. One of these chiefs, rather near to the *Nautilus*, examined it attentively. He was probably of high rank, for he was draped in a cape of banana leaves, notched round the edges, and set off with brilliant colors.

I could easily have struck down the native,

but I thought it was better to wait for truly hostile actions. Between Europeans and savages, it is proper for the Europeans to parry sharply, not to attack.

At low tide, the natives roamed about near the *Nautilus,* but were not troublesome; I heard them frequently repeat the word "Assai," and by their gestures I understood that they invited me to go on land, an invitation that I declined.

On that day, the boat did not push off, to the great displeasure of Master Land, who could not complete his provisions.

This adroit Canadian employed his time in preparing the vegetables and meat that he had brought off the island. As for the savages, they returned to the shore about eleven o'clock in the morning, as soon as the coral reefs began to disappear under the rising tide; but I saw that their numbers had increased considerably on the shore. Probably they came from the neighboring islands, or even from Papua. However, I had not seen a single native canoe. Having nothing better to do, I thought of dragging these beautiful limpid waters, under which I saw a profusion of shells, zoophytes, and marine plants. Moreover, this was the last day that the *Nautilus* would spend in these parts, if it were to float in the open sea tomorrow, according to Captain Nemo's promise.

I therefore called Conseil, who brought me a little light drag, very like those used in oyster fishery. Now to work! For two hours we fished unceasingly, but without bringing up any rarities, although the drag was filled with midas-ears, harps, melames, and particularly the most beautiful hammers I have ever seen. We also brought up some holothurias, pearl oysters, and a dozen little turtles, that were saved for the pantry.

Just when I least expected it, I put my hand on a wonder, I might say a natural deformity, very rarely met with. Conseil was dragging, and his net came up filled with divers ordinary shells, when, all at once, he saw me plunge my arm quickly into the net, draw out a shell, and heard me give the shout of the conchologist, that is to say, the most piercing cry that human throat can utter.

"What is the matter, sir?" he asked, in surprise, "has master been bitten?"

"No, my boy; but I would willingly have given my finger for my discovery."

"This shell," I said, holding up the object of my triumph.

"It is simply an olive porphyry, genus olive, order of the pectinibranchidae, class of gasteropods, sub-class of mollusca."

"Yes, Conseil; but instead of being rolled from right to left, this olive turns from left to right."

"Is it possible?"

"Yes, my boy; it is a left shell."

Shells are all right-handed with rare exceptions; and, when by chance their spiral is left, collectors are ready to pay their weight in gold.

Conseil and I were absorbed in the contemplation of our treasure, and I was promising myself to enrich the museum with it, when a stone thrown by a native, struck and broke the precious object in Conseil's hand. I uttered a cry of despair! Conseil took up his gun, and aimed at a savage who was poising his sling ten yards away. Before I could stop him, his shot broke the bracelet of amulets which encircled the arm of the savage.

"Conseil!" cried I; "Conseil!"

"Well, sir! do you not see that the cannibal has commenced the attack!"

"No shell is worth the life of a man," said I.

"Ah! the scoundrel!" cried Conseil: "I would rather he had broken my shoulder!"

Conseil was in earnest, but I was not of his opinion. However, we did not realize that the situation had changed some minutes earlier. A score of canoes now surrounded the *Nautilus*. Scooped out of the trunk of a tree, long, narrow, well adapted for speed, these canoes were balanced by means of a long bamboo pole, which floated on the water. They were managed by skillful half-naked paddlers and I watched their approach with some uneasiness. It was evident that these Papuans had already had dealings with Europeans, and knew their ships. But what could they make of this long iron cylinder anchored in the bay, without masts or chimney? Nothing good, for at first they kept at a respectful distance. However, finding it motionless, by degrees they took courage, and sought to familiarize themselves with it. Now, this familiarity was precisely what we had to avoid. Our arms, which were noiseless, could produce only a moderate effect on the savages, who have little respect for aught but blustering things. The thunderbolt without the sound of thunder would frighten man but little, though the danger lay in the lightning, and not in the noise.

At this moment the canoes neared the *Nautilus*, and a shower of arrows landed on her.

I went down to the saloon, but found no one there. I ventured to knock at the door to the Captain's room "Come in," was the answer.

I entered, and found Captain Nemo deep in algebraical calculations of X and other quantities.

"I am disturbing you," said I for the sake of courtesy.

"That is true, M. Aronnax," replied the Captain; "but I think you must have serious reasons for wishing to see me?"

"Very grave ones; the natives are surrounding us in their canoes, and in a few minutes we shall certainly be attacked by many hundreds of savages."

"Ah!" said Captain Nemo, quietly, "they have come with their canoes?"

"Yes, sir."

"Well, sir, we must close the hatches."

"Exactly, and I came to tell you—"

"Nothing can be more simple," said Captain Nemo. And pressing an electric button, he transmitted an order to the ship's crew.

"It is done, sir," said he, after some moments. "The pinnace is ready, and the hatches are closed. You do not fear, I imagine, that these gentlemen could stave in walls on which the balls of your frigate had no effect?"

"No, Captain; but a danger still exists."

"What is that, sir?"

"It is that at about this time tomorrow, we must open the hatches to renew the air of the *Nautilus*. Now, if when this happens the Papuans should be on deck, I do not see how you could prevent them from entering."

"Then, sir, you think they will board us?"

"I am certain of it."

"Well, sir, let them come. I see no reason for hindering them. After all, these Papuans are poor creatures, and I do not want my visit to the Island of Gueberoan to cost the life of a single one of these wretches."

Upon that I would have left, but Captain Nemo detained me, and asked me to sit down by him. He questioned me with interest about our excursions on shore, and our hunting; and seemed not to understand the craving for meat that possessed the Canadian. Then the conversation turned to various subjects, and without being more communicative, Captain Nemo seemed to be more amiable.

Amongst other things, we happened to speak of the situation of the *Nautilus*, run aground in exactly the same spot in this strait as where Dumont d'Urville was nearly lost. Apropos of this—

"This d'Urville was one of your great sailors," said the Captain, to me, "one of your most intelligent navigators, the Captain Cook of you Frenchmen. An unfortunate man of science, who having braved the icebergs of the south pole, the coral reefs of Oceania, the cannibals of the Pacific, had to perish miserably in a railway train! If this vital man reflected during the last moments of his life, what do you suppose must have been uppermost in his thoughts?''

Captain Nemo seemed moved, and his emotion gave me a better opinion of him. Then, chart in hand, we reviewed the travels of the French navigator, his voyage of circumnavigation, his being twice detained at the South Pole, leading to the discovery of Adelaide and Louis Philippe, and fixing the hydrographical bearings of the principal islands of Oceania.

''What your d'Urville has done on the surface of the seas,'' said Captain Nemo, ''I have done under them, and more easily, more completely than he. The *Astrolabe* and the *Zelia,* incessantly tossed about by the hurricanes, could not equal the *Nautilus,* quiet repository of labor that she is, truly motionless in the midst of the waters.''

''Tomorrow,'' added the Captain, rising, ''tomorrow at twenty minutes to three p.m. the *Nautilus* shall float, and leave the Strait of Torres uninjured.''

Having curtly pronounced these words, Captain Nemo bowed slightly. This was to dismiss me, and I went back to my room.

There I found Conseil, who wished to know the result of my interview with the Captain.

''My boy,'' I said ''when I seemed to believe that his *Nautilus* was threatened by natives of Papua, the Captain answered me very sarcastically. I have but one thing to say to you: Have confidence in him, and go to sleep in peace.''

''Have you no need of my services, sir?''

''No, my friend. What is Ned Land doing?''

"Excuse me, sir," answered Conseil, "but friend Ned is busy making a kangaroo-pie, which will be a marvel."

I remained alone, and went to bed, but slept poorly. I heard the noise of the savages, who stamped on the deck uttering deafening cries. The night passed thus, although without disturbing the ordinary repose of the crew, on whom the presence of these cannibals had no more effect than the soldiers of a masked battery care for the ants that crawl over its front.

At six in the morning I rose. The hatches had not been opened. The inner air was not renewed, but the reservoirs, filled ready for any emergency, were now resorted to, and discharged several cubic feet of oxygen into the exhausted atmosphere of the *Nautilus*.

I worked in my room till noon, without seeing Captain Nemo, even for an instant. On board no preparations for departure were visible.

I waited some time more, and then went into the large saloon. The clock marked half-past two. In ten minutes it would be high-tide; and, if Captain Nemo had not made a rash promise, the *Nautilus* would be immediately freed. If not, many months would pass ere she could leave her bed of coral.

However, some warning vibrations began to be felt in the vessel. I heard the keel grating against the rough calcareous bottom of the coral reef.

At five-and-twenty minutes to three, Captain Nemo appeared in the saloon.

"We are going to start," said he.

"Ah!" replied I.

"I have given orders to open the hatches."

"And the Papuans?"

"The Papuans?" answered Captain Nemo, slightly shrugging his shoulders.

"Will they not come inside the *Nautilus*?"

"How?"

"Only by leaping over the hatches you have opened."

"M. Aronnax," quietly answered Captain Nemo, "they will not enter the hatches of the *Nautilus* that way, even if they were open."

I looked at the Captain.

"You do not understand?" said he.

"Hardly."

"Well, come and see."

I directed my steps towards the central staircase. There Ned Land and Conseil were slyly watching some of the ship's crew, who were opening the hatches, while cries of rage and fearful howlings resounded outside.

The port lids were pulled down outside. Twenty horrible faces appeared. But as the first native placed his hand on the stair-rail, he seemed to be struck from behind by some invisible force, and fled, uttering the most fearful cries, and making the wildest contortions.

Ten of his companions followed him. They met with the same fate.

Conseil was in ecstasy. Ned Land carried away by his violent instincts, rushed onto the staircase. But the moment he seized the rail with both hands, he too was overthrown.

"I was hit by a thunderbolt," cried he, with an oath.

This explained all. It was no rail, but a

metallic cable, charged with electricity from the deck, communicating with the half-deck. Whoever touched it felt a powerful shock—and this shock would have been mortal, if Captain Nemo had discharged the full force of the current into the conductor. It might truly be said that between his assailants and himself he had stretched a network of electricity which none could pass with impunity.

Meanwhile, the exasperated Papuans had retreated, paralyzed with terror. While half laughing, we consoled and rubbed poor Ned Land, who swore like a madman.

But, at this moment, the *Nautilus*, raised by the last waves of the tide, quitted her coral bed exactly at the fortieth minute as fixed by the Captain. Her screw swept the waters slowly and majestically. Her speed increased gradually, and sailing on the surface of the ocean, she safely and soundly left the dangerous passes of the Straits of Torres.

Chapter 22
"Aegri Somnia"

The following day, January 10th, the *Nautilus* kept on her course between two seas, but with such speed that I could estimate it at no less than thirty-five miles an hour. The rapidity of her screw was such that I could neither follow nor count its revolutions. When I reflected that this marvelous electric agent, having provided motion, heat, and light to the *Nautilus*, also protected her from outward attack, and transformed her into an ark of safety, which no profane hand might touch without being thunderstricken, my admiration was unbounded, and extended to the engineer who had called it into existence from the structure.

Our course was directed to the west, and on January 11th, we rounded Cape Wessel, which, situated in 135⁰ longitude, and 10⁰ north latitude, forms the east point of the Gulf of Carpentaria. The reefs were as numerous, but more scattered, and marked on the chart with extreme precision. The *Nautilus* easily avoided the breakers of Money to port, and the Victoria reefs to starboard, moving at 130° longitude, and on the tenth parallel which we strictly followed.

On January 13th, Captain Nemo arrived in the Sea of Timor, and recognized the island of that name in 122° longitude.

From this point, the *Nautilus* inclined towards the southwest. Her head was set for the Indian Ocean. Where would the fancy of Captain Nemo carry us next? Would he return to the coast of Asia, or again to the shores of Europe? Improbable conjectures both, for a man who had fled from inhabited continents. Then, would he descend to the south? Was he going to round the Cape of Good Hope, then Cape Horn, and finally go as far as the antarctic pole? Would he come back at last to the Pacific, where his *Nautilus* could sail free and independently? Time would tell.

After having skirted the sands of Cartier, Hibernia, Seringapatam, and Scott, the last efforts of the solid against the liquid element, on January 14th, we lost sight of land altogether. The speed of the *Nautilus* was considerably abated, and capriciously she sometimes swam in the depths of the waters, sometimes floated on their surface.

During this period of the voyage, Captain Nemo made some interesting experiments on the varied temperature of the sea, in different beds. Under ordinary conditions, these observations are made by means of rather complicated instruments, and lead to somewhat doubtful results, as when by means of thermometrical sounding-leads, the glasses often breaking under the pressure of the water, or using an apparatus grounded on the variations of the resistance of metals to electric currents. Results so obtained could not be correctly calculated. But on the contrary, Captain Nemo went himself to test the temperature in the depths of the sea, and his thermometer, placed in communication with the different currents of water, gave him the sought-after degree immediately and accurately.

Thus, either by overloading her reservoirs, or descending obliquely by means of her inclined planes, the *Nautilus* successively attained depths of three, four, five, seven, nine, and ten thousand yards, and the definite result of this experience was to show, that the sea preserved an average temperature of four and a half degrees, at a depth of five thousand fathoms, under all latitudes.

On January 16th, the *Nautilus* seemed becalmed only a few yards beneath the surface of the waves. Her electric apparatus was inactive, and her motionless screw left her to drift at the mercy of the currents. I supposed that the crew was occupied with interior repairs, necessitated by the violent mechanical movements of the machine.

My companions and I then witnessed a curious spectacle. The hatches of the saloon were open, and as the beacon-light of the *Nautilus* was not in use a vague darkness reigned on the waters. I observed the state of the sea under these conditions, and the largest fish appeared to me no more than barely visible shadows, when the *Nautilus* burst suddenly into full light. I thought at first that the beacon had been re-lighted, and was casting its electric radiance into the surrounding liquid. I was mistaken, and after a rapid survey, perceived my error.

The *Nautilus* floated in the midst of a phosphorescent glow, which, in this darkness was quite dazzling. It was produced by myriads of luminous animalculae, whose brilliance increased as they glided over the metal hull of the vessel. I was surprised by flashes of light in the middle of these radiant areas, as though they had been rivers of lead melted in a furnace, or metallic masses brought to a white heat, so that by contrast, certain lighted portions cast a shadow in this fiery atmosphere, from which it seemed all shade must be banished. No; this was not the calm radiation of our usual lightning. There was unusual life and vigor; this was truly living light!

Actually it was an endless agglomeration of colored infusoria, of veritable globules of diaphanous jelly, each provided with a threadlike tentacle, and of which as many as twenty-five thousand have been counted in less than two cubic half-inches of water. Their light was augmented by the glimmering peculiar to medusae, starfish, aurelia, and other phosphorescent zoophytes, impregnated with the grease of the organic matter decomposed by the sea, and, perhaps, the mucus secreted by fish.

190

For several hours the *Nautilus* floated in these brilliant waves, and our admiration increased as we watched marine monsters disporting themselves like salamanders. I saw there, in the midst of this unburning fire, the swift and elegant porpoise (indefatigable clown of the ocean), and some swordfish, ten feet long, those prophetic heralds of the hurricane, whose formidable sword would now and then strike the glass of the saloon. Then appeared the smaller fish, the variegated balista, the leaping mackerel, wolf-thorntails, and a hundred others, which zebra-striped the luminous atmosphere as they swam. This dazzling spectacle was enchanting! Perhaps some atmospheric condition increased the intensity of this phenomenon. Perhaps some storm agitated the surface of the waves. But at this depth of some yards, the *Nautilus* was unmoved by its fury, and living peacefully in still water.

So we progressed, incessantly charmed by some new marvel. Conseil arranged and classed his zoophytes, his articulata, his molluscs and his fishes. The days passed rapidly, and I took no account of them. Ned, as was his habit, tried to vary the diet on board. Like snails, we were fixed to our shells, and I declare it is easy to lead a snail's life.

Thus, this life seemed easy and natural, and we thought no longer of the life we led on land. But something happened to remind us of the strangeness of our situation.

On the 18th of January, the *Nautilus* was in 105⁰ longitude and 15⁰ south latitude. The weather was threatening, the sea rough and rolling. There was a strong east wind. The barometer, which had been going down for some days, threatened a coming storm. I went up onto the after-deck just as the second lieutenant was measuring the horary angles, and as usual waited, till the daily phrase was said. But, on this day, it was exchanged for another phrase no less incomprehensible. Almost immediately, I saw Captain Nemo appear, with a glass, looking toward the horizon.

For some minutes he was motionless, never taking his eye from the point of observation. Then he lowered his glass, and exchanged a few words with his lieutenant. The latter seemed to be the victim of some emotion that he tried in vain to repress. Captain Nemo, having more command over himself, was cool. He too seemed to be making objections, to which the lieutenant replied by formal assurances. At least I so concluded from the difference in their tones and gestures. I, myself, had looked carefully in the direction indicated without seeing anything. The sky and water were lost in the clear line of the horizon.

However, Captain Nemo walked from one end of the after-deck to the other without looking at me, perhaps without seeing me. His step was firm, but less regular than usual. He sometimes crossed his arms, and observed the sea. What could he be looking for on that immense expanse?

The *Nautilus* was then some hundreds of miles from the nearest coast.

The lieutenant had taken up his glass, and examined the horizon steadfastly, going and coming, stamping his foot and showing rather more nervous agitation than his superior officer. However, this mystery needs must be solved, and before long; for, upon an order from Captain Nemo, the engine increased its propelling power, making the screw turn more rapidly.

Just then, the lieutenant drew the Captain's attention again. The latter stopped walking and directed his glass towards the place indicated. He looked long. I felt very puzzled, and descending to the drawing room, took out an excellent telescope that I generally used. Then, leaning on the edge of the watch-light that jutted out from the front of the after-deck, I set myself to look over the line of the sky and sea.

But my eye was no sooner applied to it, than the glass was quickly snatched out of my hands.

I turned round. Captain Nemo was before me, but I did not know him. His face was fransfigured. His eyes flashed angrily, his teeth were set; his body stiff, fists clenched and head sunk between his shoulders, betraying the violent agitation that pervaded his whole frame. He did not move. My glass, fallen from his hands, rolled at his feet.

Had I unwittingly provoked this fit of anger? Did this incomprehensible person imagine that I had discovered some forbidden secret? No; I was not the object of his hatred, for he was not looking at me, his eye was steadily fixed upon the impenetrable point of the horizon. At last Captain Nemo recovered himself. His agitation subsided. He addressed some words in a foreign language to his lieutenant, then turned to me. "M. Arronnax," he said, in rather an imperious tone, "I must require you to keep one of the conditions that bind you to me."

"What is it, Captain?"

"You must be confined with your companions, until I see fit to release you."

"You are my master," I replied, looking steadily at him. "But may I ask one question?"

"None, sir."

There was no use resisting this imperious command, it would have been useless. I went down to the cabin occupied by Ned Land and Conseil, and told them the Captain's determination. You may guess how this communication was received by the Canadian.

But there was no time for altercation. Four of the crew were waiting at the door, and conducted us to the cell where we had passed our first night on board the *Nautilus*.

Ned Land would have remonstrated, but the door was shut upon him.

"Will master tell me what this means?" asked Conseil.

I told my companions what had passed. They were as astonished as I, and equally at a loss as to how to explain it.

All the while I was absorbed in my own reflections, and could think of nothing but the strange fear depicted in the Captain's countenance. I was utterly unable to account for it, when my cogitations were disturbed by these words from Ned Land—

"Hallo! Breakfast is ready."

And indeed the table was laid. Evidently

Captain Nemo had given this order at the same time that he had increased the speed of the *Nautilus*.

"Will master permit me to make a recommendation?" asked Conseil.

"Yes, my boy."

"Well, it is that master breakfasts. It is prudent, for we do not know what may happen."

"You are right, Conseil."

"Unfortunately," said Ned Land, "they have given us only the ship's fare."

"Friend Ned," asked Conseil, "what would you have said if the breakfast had been entirely forgotten?"

This argument cut short the harpooner's recriminations.

We sat down to table. The meal finished in silence.

Just then, the luminous globe that lighted the cell went out, and left us in total darkness. Ned Land was soon asleep, and what astonished me more was that Conseil went off into a heavy sleep. I was wondering what could have caused his irresistible drowsiness, when I felt my brain becoming stupefied. In spite of my efforts to keep my eyes open, they would close. A painful suspicion seized me. Evidently soporific substances had been mixed with the food we had just taken. Imprisonment was not enough to conceal Captain Nemo's projects from us, sleep was also necessary.

I then heard the panels shut. The undulations of the sea which caused a slight rolling motion, ceased. Had the *Nautilus* quitted the surface of the ocean? Had it gone back to the motionless bed of water? I tried to resist sleep. It was impossible. My breathing grew shallow. I felt a mortal cold freeze my stiffened and half paralyzed limbs. My eyelids, like leaden caps, fell over my eyes. I could not raise them; a death-like sleep, full of visions, bereft me of my being. Then even the visions disappeared, and left me in complete insensibility.

Chapter 23
The Coral Kingdom

The next day, I awoke with my head singularly clear. To my great surprise I was in my own room. My companions had no doubt been reinstated to their cabin, without having perceived it any more than I. Of what had passed during the night they were surely as ignorant as I was, and to penetrate this mystery I could only reckon on future chances.

I then thought of quitting my room. Was I free again or a prisoner? Quite free. I opened the door, went to the half-deck, and up the central stairs. The panels, shut the evening before, were now open. I went onto the after-deck.

Ned Land and Conseil waited there for me. I questioned them; they knew nothing. Lost in a heavy sleep in which they had been totally unconscious, they had been astonished at finding themselves in their cabin.

As for the *Nautilus,* it seemed quiet and mysterious as ever. It floated on the surface of the waves at a moderate pace. Nothing seemed changed on board.

The second lieutenant then came onto the after-deck and gave the usual order below.

As for Captain Nemo, he did not appear.

Of the people on board, I only saw the impassive steward, who served me with his usual dumb regularity.

About two o'clock, I was in the drawing room, busied in arranging my notes, when the Captain opened the door. I bowed. He made a slight inclination in return, without speaking. I resumed my work, hoping that he would perhaps give some explanation of the events of the preceding night. He made none. I looked at him. He seemed fatigued; his heavy eyes had not been refreshed by sleep; his face looked very sorrowful. He walked to and fro, sat down and got up again, took up a random book, put it down, consulted his instruments without taking his habitual notes, and seemed restless and uneasy. At last, he came up to me, and said—

"Are you a doctor, M. Aronnax?"

I so little expected such a question, that I stared for some time at him without answering.

"Are you a doctor?" he repeated. "Several of your colleagues have studied medicine."

"Well," said I, "I am a doctor and have been resident surgeon to a hospital. I practiced several years before entering the museum."

"Very well, sir."

My answer had evidently satisfied the Captain. But not knowing what he would say next, I waited for other questions, reserving my answers according to circumstances.

"M. Aronnax, will you consent to prescribe for one of my men?" he asked.

"Is he ill?"

"Yes."

"I am ready to follow you."

"Come, then."

I confess that my heart beat strongly. I do not know why. I felt a certain connection between the illness of one of the crew and the events of the day before; and this mystery interested me at least as much as did the sick man.

Captain Nemo conducted me to the poop of the *Nautilus*, and took me into a cabin near the sailor's quarters.

There, on the bed, lay a man about forty years of age, with a resolute expression on his face, a true Anglo-Saxon type.

I leant over him. He was not just ill, he was wounded. His head, swathed in blood-soaked bandages, lay on a pillow. I undid the bandages, and the wounded man looked at me with his large eyes and showed no sign of pain as I did it. It was a horrible wound. The skull, shattered by some deadly weapon, exposed the much injured brain. Clots of blood had formed in the bruised and broken mass, like in color to the dregs of wine.

There was both confusion and suffusion of the brain. His breathing was slow and some spasmodic movements agitated the muscles of his face. I felt his pulse. It was intermittent. The extremities of the body were growing cold already, and I saw death must inevitably ensue.

After dressing the unfortunate man's wounds, I readjusted the bandages on his head, and turned to Captain Nemo.

"What caused this wound?" I asked.

"What does it matter?" he replied, evasively. "A shock broke one of the levers of the engine, which struck him. But your opinion as to his state?"

I hesitated before giving it.

"He will be dead in two hours."

"Can nothing save him?"

"Nothing."

Captain Nemo's hand contracted, and some tears glistened in his eyes, which I had thought incapable of shedding any.

For some moments I still watched the dying man, whose life ebbed slowly. His pallor increased under the electric light that was shed over his death-bed. I looked at his intelligent forehead, furrowed with premature wrinkles, produced probably by misfortune and sorrow. I yearned to learn the secret of his life from the last words that escaped his lips.

"You can go now, M. Aronnax," said the Captain.

I left him in the dying man's cabin, and returned to my room much affected by this scene. For the whole day, I was haunted by uncomfortable suspicions, and at night I slept badly. Between my broken dreams, I fancied I heard distant sighs like the notes of a funeral psalm. Were they the prayers for the dead, murmured in that language that I could not understand?

The next morning I went on the bridge. Captain Nemo was there before me. As soon as he perceived me he came to me.

"Professor, will it be convenient to you to make a submarine excursion today?"

"With my companions?" I asked.

"If they like."

"We obey your orders, Captain."

"Will you be so good then as to put on your corkjackets?"

It was not a question of dead or dying. I rejoined Ned Land and Conseil, and told them of Captain Nemo's proposition. Conseil hastened to accept it, and this time the Canadian seemed quite willing to follow our example.

It was eight o'clock in the morning. By half-past eight we were equipped for this new excursion, and provided with two contrivances for light and breathing. The double door was open. Accompanied by Captain Nemo, who was followed by a dozen of the crew, we set foot, at a depth of about thirty feet, on the solid bottom on which the *Nautilus* rested.

A slight declivity ended in an uneven bottom, at fifteen fathoms depth. This bottom differed completely from the one I had visited on my first excursion under the waters of the Pacific Ocean. Here, there was no fine sand, no submarine prairie, no sea-forest. I immediately recognized that marvelous region in which, on that day, the Captain did the honors for us. It was the coral kingdom. In the zoophyte branch and in the alcyon class I noticed the gorgoneae, isidiae, and the corollariae.

Light produced a thousand charming variations playing in the midst of the branches that were so vividly colored. I seemed to see the membraneous and cylindrical tubes tremble beneath the undulation of the waters. I was tempted to gather their fresh petals, ornamented with delicate tentacles, some just blown, the others budding, while small fish, swimming swiftly, touched them slightly, like flights of birds. But if my hand approached these living flowers, these animated sensitive plants, the whole colony took alarm. The white petals re-entered their red cases, the flowers faded as I looked, and the bush changed into a block of stony knobs.

Luck had thrown me right by the most precious specimens of this zoophyte. This coral was more valuable than any to be found in the Mediterranean, on the coasts of France, Italy, and Barbary. Its tints justified the poetical names of "Flower of Blood," and "Froth of Blood," that custom has given to its most beautiful productions. Coral is sold for 20 pounds per ounce; and in this place, the watery beds would make the fortunes of a company of coral-divers. This precious matter, often confused with other polypi, formed then the inextricable plots called "macciota," and on these I noticed several beautiful specimens of pink coral.

But, as we moved along, soon the bushes contracted, and the arborizations increased. Real petrified thickets, long joists of fantastic architecture, were disclosed to us. Captain Nemo moved himself under a dark gallery, where by a slight declivity we reached a depth of 100 yards. The light from our lamps sometimes produced magical effects, following the rough outlines of the natural arches, and pendants, set like jewels, that were tipped with points of fire. Between the coralline shrubs I noticed other polypi no less curious, melites and irises with articulated ramifications, also tufts of coral, some green, others red, like seaweed encrusted in calcareous salts, that naturalists, after long discussion, have definitely classed in the vegetable kingdom. But, to follow the remarks of a thoughtful man, "There is perhaps the real point where life rises darkly from the sleep of a stone, without quite detaching itself from the rough point of departure."

At last, after walking two hours, we had attained a depth of about 300 yards, that is to say, the extreme limit on which coral began to form. But there was no isolated bush, nor modest brushwood, at the bottom of lofty trees. It was an immense forest of large mineral vegetations, enormous petrified trees, united by garlands of elegant plumarias, sea-bindweed, all adorned with clouds and reflections. We passed freely under their high branches, lost in the shade of the waves, while at our feet, tubipores, mandrines, stars, fungi, and caryophyllidae formed a carpet of flowers sown with dazzling gems. What an indescribable spectacle!

Captain Nemo had stopped. I and my companions halted. Turning around, we saw his men forming a semicircle around their chief. Watching attentively, I observed that four of them carried on their shoulders an object of an oblong shape.

We occupied, in this place, the center of a

vast glade surrounded by the lofty foliage of the submarine forest. Our lamps threw over this place a sort of clear twilight that strangely elongated the shadows on the ground. At the end of the glade the darkness increased, and was relieved only by little sparks reflected by the points of coral.

Ned Land and Conseil were near me. We watched, and I sensed that I was going to witness a strange scene. On observing the ground, I saw that it was raised in certain places by slight protuberances encrusted with limy deposits, and laid out with a regularity that betrayed the hand of man.

In the midst of the glade, on a pedestal of rocks roughly piled up, stood a cross of coral, that extended long arms, such as one might have thought were made of petrified blood.

Upon a sign from Captain Nemo, one of the men advanced; and at some feet from the cross, he began to dig a hole with a pickaxe that he took from his belt. I understood all! This glade was a cemetery, this hole a tomb, this oblong object the body of the man who had died in the night! The Captain and his men had come to bury their companion in this general resting place, at the bottom of this inaccessible ocean!

The grave was being dug slowly. The fish fled on all sides while their retreat was being thus disturbed. I heard the strokes of the pickaxe, which sparkled when it hit upon some flint lost at the bottom of the waters. The hole was soon large and deep enough to receive the body. Then the bearers approached. The body, wrapped in a tissue of white byssus, was lowered into the damp grave. Captain Nemo, with his arms crossed on his breast, and all the friends of him who had loved them, knelt in prayer.

The grave was then filled in with the rubbish taken from the ground, which formed a slight mound. When this was done, Captain Nemo and his men rose. Then, approaching the grave, they knelt again, and all extended their hands in a sign of a last adieu. Then the funeral procession returned to the *Nautilus*, passing under arches of the forest, through the midst of thickets, along coral bushes, always on the ascent. At last the lights on board appeared, and their luminous track guided us to the *Nautilus*. By one o'clock we had returned.

As soon as I had changed my clothes, I went up to the after-deck, and, a prey to conflicting emotions, I sat down near the binnacle. Captain Nemo joined me. I rose and said to him—

"So just as I said he would, this man died in the night?"

"Yes, M. Aronnax."

"And he rests now, near his companions, in the coral cemetery?"

"Yes, forgotten by all others, but not by us. We dug the grave, and the polypi undertake to seal our dead for eternity." And burying his face quickly in his hands, he tried in vain to suppress a sob. Then he added—"Our peaceful cemetery is there, some hundred feet below the surface of the waves."

"Your dead sleep quietly, at least, Captain, out of the reach of sharks."

"Yes, sir, of sharks and *men*," gravely replied the Captain.

PART 2

Chapter 1
The Indian Ocean

We now come to the second part of our journey under the sea. The first ended with that moving scene in the coral cemetery, which left such a profound impression on my mind. Thus in the midst of this great sea, Captain Nemo's life unfolded before us even to his grave, which he had prepared in one of its deepest abysses. There, not a single one of the ocean's monsters could trouble the last sleep of the crew of the *Nautilus*, of those friends riveted to each other in death as in life. "Nor any man either," had added the Captain. Still evincing the same fierce implacable defiance towards human society!

I could no longer content myself with the hypothesis which satisfied Conseil.

That worthy persisted in seeing in the commander of the *Nautilus*, one of those unknown savants who answer mankind's indifference with contempt. For him, he was a misunderstood genius, who, tired of earth's deceptions, had taken refuge in this inaccessible medium, where he might follow his instincts freely. To my mind, this hypothesis explained but one side of Captain Nemo's character.

Indeed, the mystery of that last night, during which we had been chained in prison, the sleep, and the precaution so violently taken by the Captain of snatching from my eyes the glass I had raised to sweep the horizon, the mortal wound of the man, due to an inexplicable shock of the *Nautilus,* all put me on a new track. No; Captain Nemo was not satisfied with shunning man. His formidable apparatus not only suited his instinct for freedom, but, perhaps, also the design of I know not what terrible reprisals.

At this moment, nothing is clear to me. I catch only a glimpse of light in all the darkness, and I must confine myself to writing as events dictate.

That day, the 24th of January, 1868, at noon, the second officer came to take the position of the sun. I mounted the platform, lit a cigar, and watched the operation. It seemed to me that the man did not understand French. Several times I made remarks in a loud voice, which should have drawn from him some involuntary sign of attention, if he had understood them; but he remained undisturbed and dumb.

As he was taking observations with the sextant, one of the sailors of the *Nautilus* (the strong man who had accompanied us on our first submarine excursion to the Island of Crespo) came to clean the glasses of the lantern. I examined the fittings of the apparatus, the strength of which was increased a hundredfold by lenticular rings, placed similarly to those in a lighthouse, and which projected their brilliance in a horizontal plane. The electric lamp was put together in such a way as to yield its most powerful light. Indeed, it was produced in *vacuo* which insured both its steadiness and intensity. This vacuum economized the graphite points between which the luminous arc was developed—an important point of economy for Captain Nemo, who could not easily have replaced them. Under these conditions their waste was imperceptible. When the *Nautilus* was ready to continue its submarine journey, I went down to the saloon. The panels were closed, and the course marked due west.

We were furrowing the waters of the Indian Ocean, a vast liquid plain, with a surface of 1,200,000,000 acres, and whose waters are so clear and transparent, that leaning over them one would turn giddy. The *Nautilus* usually floated between fifty and a hundred fathoms deep. We went on so for some days. To anyone but myself who had a great love for the sea, the hours would have seemed long and monotonous. But the daily walks on the afterdeck, when I steeped myself in the reviving air of the ocean, the sight of the rich waters through the windows of the saloon, the books in the library, the compiling of my memoirs, took up all my time, and left me not a moment of boredom or weariness.

Some days we saw a great number of aquatic

birds, sea-mews or gulls. Some were cleverly killed, and when prepared in a certain way, made very acceptable water-game. Amongst large winged birds, carried a long distance from all lands, and resting upon the waves from the fatigue of their flight, I saw some magnificent albatrosses, uttering discordant cries like the braying of an ass, and birds belonging to the family of the longipennates. The family of the totipalmates was represented by the sea-swallows, which caught the fish from the surface, and by numerous phaetons, or lepturi; amongst others, the phaeton with red lines, as large as a pigeon, whose white plumage, tinted with pink, shows off to advantage the blackness of its wings.

As to the fish, they always provoked our admiration when we surprised the secrets of aquatic life through the open panels. I saw many kinds which I had never before had a chance of observing.

I note chiefly, ostracions peculiar to the Red Sea, the Indian Ocean, and that water which washes the coast of tropical America. These fishes, like the tortoise, the armadillo, the sea-hedgehog, and the crustacea, are protected by a breastplate which is neither chalky nor stony, but real bone. In some it takes the form of a solid triangle, in others of a solid quadrangle. Amongst the triangular I found some an inch and a half in length, with wholesome flesh and a delicious flavor. They are brown at the tail, and yellow at the fins, and I recommend their introduction into fresh water, to which a number of sea-fish easily accustom themselves. I would also mention quadrangular ostracions, having on their backs four large tubercles; some dotted over with white spots on the lower part of the body, and which may be tamed like birds; trigons provided with spikes formed by the lengthening of their bony shell, and which, from their strange gruntings, are called "sea-pigs"; also dromedaries with large humps in the shape of a cone, whose flesh is very tough and leathery.

I now borrow from the daily notes of Master Conseil. "Certain fish of the genus petrodon peculiar to those seas, with red backs and white chests, which are marked by three rows of longitudinal filaments; and some electrical, seven inches long, decked out in the liveliest colors. Then, as specimens of other kinds, some ovoides, resembling an egg of a dark brown color, marked with white bands, and without tails; diodons, real sea-porcupines, furnished with spikes, and capable of swelling in such a way as to look like cushions bristling with darts; hippocampi, common to every ocean; some pegasi with lengthened snouts, which their pectoral fins, being quite long and wing-shaped allow, if not to fly, at least to shoot into the air; pigeon spatulae, with tails covered with many rings of shell; macrongnathi with long jaws, an excellent fish, nine inches long, and bright with most agreeable colors; pale-colored calliomores, with rugged heads; and plenty of chaetodons, with long and tubular muzzles, which kill insects by shooting them, as from an air-gun, with a single drop of water. We may call these fly-catchers of the seas.

"In the eighty-ninth genus of fishes, classed by Lacepede, belonging to the second lower class of bony fish, characterized by opercules and bronchial membranes, I noted the scorpaena, the head of which is furnished with spikes, and which has but one dorsal fin. These creatures are covered, or are not, with little shells, according to the sub-class given us specimens of didactyles fourteen or fifteen inches in length, with yellow rays, and heads of a most fantastic appearance. As to the first sub-class, it gives several specimens of that singular-looking fish appropriately called a "sea-frog," with large head, sometimes pierced with holes, sometimes swollen with protuberances, bristling with spikes, and covered with tubercles; it has irregular and hideous horns; its body and tail are covered with callouses; its sting makes a dangerous wound; it is both repugnant and horrible to look at."

From the 21st to the 23rd of January the *Nautilus* went along at the rate of two hundred and forty miles, or twenty-two miles an hour. If we recognized so many different varieties of fish, it was because, attracted by the electric light, they tried to follow us. The greater part, however, were soon out-distanced by our speed, though some kept their place in the waters of the *Nautilus* for a time. The morning of the 24th, in 12⁰ 5 ' south latitude, and 94⁰ 33 ' longitude, we sighted Keeling Island, a madrepore formation, planted with magnificent cocoas, and which had been visited by Mr. Darwin and Captain Fitzroy. The *Nautilus* skirted the shores of this desert island for a short distance. Its nets brought up numerous specimens of polypi, and curious shells of mollusca. Some precious productions of the species of delphinulae enriched the treasures of Captain Nemo, to which I added an astraea punctifera, a kind of parasite polypus often found fixed to a shell. Soon Keeling Island disappeared from the horizon, and our course was directed to the northwest in the direction of the Indian Peninsula.

From Keeling Island our course was slower and more capricious, often taking us into great depths. Several times use was made of the inclined planes, which internal levers placed obliquely to the water-line. We went about two miles in that way, but without ever obtaining the greatest depths of the Indian Sea, which soundings of seven thousand fathoms have never reached. As to the temperature of the lower strata, the thermometer invariably indicated 4⁰ above zero. I only observed that, in the upper regions, the water was always colder in the high levels than at the surface of the sea.

On the 25th of January, the ocean was entirely deserted. The *Nautilus* spent the day on the surface, beating the waves with its powerful screw, and making them rebound to a great height. Who under such circumstances would not have taken it for a gigantic cetacean? I spent three quarters of this day on the deck. I watched the sea. Nothing on the horizon, till about four o'clock a steamer running west on our counter. Her masts were visible for an instant, but she could not see the *Nautilus*, being too low in the water. I guessed this steamboat belonged to the P.O. Company, which runs from Ceylon to

Sydney, touching at King George's Point and Melbourne.

At five o'clock in the evening, before that fleeting twilight which joins night to day in tropical zones, Conseil and I were astonished by a curious spectacle.

It was a shoal of argonauts traveling along on the surface of the ocean. We could count several hundreds. They belonged to the tubercle kind which are peculiar to the Indian seas.

These graceful molluscs moved backwards by means of their locomotive tube, through which they expelled the water already drawn in. Of their eight tentacles, six were elongated and stretched out floating on the water, whilst the other two, rolled up flat, were spread to the wind like a light sail. I saw their spiral-shaped and fluted shells, which Cuvier justly compares to an elegant shallop. Quite a boat indeed! It bears the creature which secretes it without its adhering to it.

"The argonaut is free to leave its shell," I told Conseil, "but it never does." "The same is true of Captain Nemo," was the judicious reply. "He should have called his boat the *Argonaut*."

For nearly an hour the *Nautilus* floated in the midst of this shoal of molluscs. Then I know not what sudden fright took them. But as if at a signal every sail was furled, the arms folded, the body drawn in, the shells turned over, changing their center of gravity, and the whole fleet disappeared under the waves. Never did the ships of a squadron maneuver with more unity.

At that moment night fell suddenly, and the

reeds, scarcely moved by the breeze, lay peaceably under the sides of the *Nautilus*.

The next day, 26th of January, we crossed the equator at the eighty-second meridian, and entered the northern hemisphere. During the day, a formidable troop of sharks accompanied us, terrible creatures, which multiply in these seas, and make them very dangerous. They were "cestracio philippi" sharks, with brown backs and whitish bellies, armed with eleven rows of teeth—eyed sharks—their throats marked with a large black spot surrounded with white like an eye. There were also some Isabella sharks, with rounded snouts marked with dark spots. These powerful creatures often hurled themselves at the windows of the saloon with such violence as to make us feel very nervous. At such times Ned Land was no longer master of himself. He wanted to go to the surface and harpoon the monsters, particularly some smooth-hound sharks, whose mouth is studded with teeth like a mosaic; and large tiger-sharks nearly six yards long, the last named of which seemed to excite him more particularly. But the *Nautilus*, accelerating her speed, easily left the swiftest of them behind.

The 27th of January, at the entrance of the vast Bay of Bengal, we met repeatedly a forbidding spectacle, dead bodies floating on the surface of the water. They were the dead of the Indian villages, carried by the Ganges to the level of the sea, and which the vultures, the only undertakers of the country, had not been able to devour. But the sharks would not fail to help them at their funereal work.

About seven o'clock in the evening, the *Nautilus*, half immersed, was sailing in a sea of milk. At first sight the ocean seemed lactified. Was it the effect of the lunar rays? No; for the moon, scarcely two days old, still half hidden under the horizon in the rays of the sun. The whole sky, though lit by the sidereal rays, seemed black by contrast with the whiteness of the waters.

Conseil could not believe his eyes, and questioned me as to the cause of this strange phenomenon. Happily I was able to answer him.

"It is called a milk sea," I explained, "a large area of white wavelets often to be seen on the coasts of Amboyna, and in these parts of the sea."

"But, sir," said Conseil, "can you tell me what causes such an effect for I do not suppose the water is really turned into milk?"

"No, my boy; and the whiteness which surprises you is caused only by the presence of myriads of infusoria, a sort of luminous little worm, gelatinous and without color, of the thickness of hair, and whose length is not more than 7/100 of an inch. These insects adhere to one another sometimes for several leagues."

"Several leagues!" exclaimed Conseil.

"Yes, my boy; and you need not try to compute the number of these infusoria. You will not be able; for, if I am not mistaken, ships have floated on these milk seas for more than forty miles."

Towards midnight the sea suddenly resumed its usual color; but behind us, to the visible limits of the horizon, the sky reflected the whitened waves, and for a long time seemed saturated with the gleaming waves of an aurora borealis.

Chapter 2
A Novel Proposal of Captain Nemo's

On the 28th of February, at noon when the *Nautilus* surfaced in 9⁰ 4' north latitude, about eight miles to westward, there was land in sight. The first thing I noticed was a range of mountains irregularly shaped and about two thousand feet high. On taking the bearings, I knew that we were nearing the island of Ceylon, that pearl which hangs from the lobe of the Indian Peninsula.

Captain Nemo and his lieutenant appeared and the Captain glanced at the map. Turning to me he said—

"The Island of Ceylon, noted for its pearl-fisheries. Would you care to visit one, M. Aronnax?"

"Indeed, Captain."

"That can easily be arranged. We can see the fisheries, but not the fishermen. The annual work has not yet begun, but that does not matter. I will give orders for the Gulf of Manaar, where we shall arrive during the night."

The Captain said something to his lieutenant, who immediately went out. Soon the *Nautilus* returned to her native element, and the manometer showed that she was about thirty feet deep.

"Well, sir," said Captain Nemo, "you and your companions shall visit the Bank of Manaar, and if by chance some fisherman should be there, we shall see him at work.

"That is fine, Captain!"

"By the by, M. Aronnax, you are not afraid of sharks?"

"Sharks!" I exclaimed.

It seemed an idle question.

"Well?" continued Captain Nemo.

"I must admit, Captain, that I have not yet learned very much about this species of fish."

"We are accustomed to them," replied Captain Nemo, "and in time you will be too. However, we shall be armed, and on the way, perhaps we can hunt the sharks. It is an interesting hunt. So, till tomorrow, sir, and early."

Having said this most casually, Captain Nemo left the saloon. If someone invited you to hunt bear in the mountains of Switzerland, you would say, "Very well! tomorrow we will go and hunt the bear." If you were asked to hunt lions in the plains of Atlas, or tigers in the Indian jungles, you would say, "Ah! it appears we are going to hunt tigers or lions." But if you were invited to hunt the shark in its natural element, you might think it over before accepting the invitation. As for myself, I passed my hand over my forehead, on which stood large drops of cold perspiration. "Let us reflect," said I, "and take our time. Hunting otters in submarine forests, as we did at the Island of Crespo, was one thing; but going back and forth at the bottom of the sea, where one is almost certain to meet sharks, is quite another thing! I know well that in certain countries, particularly in the Andaman Islands, the Negroes do not hesitate to attack them with a dagger in one hand and a running noose in the other. But I also know that few who confront these formidable beasts come back alive. Moreover, I am not a Negro, and if I were, I think in this case a little hesitation would not be misplaced. Why could not the Captain have asked me to track some inoffensive fox through a wood? Conseil will refuse, I thought, and I can excuse myself to the Captain. I was not so sure of Ned Land, for whom danger has an attraction."

At this moment, Conseil and the Canadian came in, looking quite composed, and even joyous. They knew not what awaited them.

"Faith, sir," said Ned Land, "your Captain Nemo—the devil take him!—has just made us a very pleasant offer."

"Ah!" said I, "you know?"

"If agreeable to you, sir," interrupted Conseil, "the commander of the *Nautilus* has invited us to visit the magnificent Ceylon fisheries tomorrow, in your company. He did it kindly, and behaved like a real gentleman."

"He said nothing more?"

"Nothing more, sir," said the Canadian, "except that he had already spoken to you of this little excursion.''

"It may be dangerous," I told them.

"Dangerous? A simple trip to a bed of oysters?''

Decidedly, Captain Nemo had not thought it worthwhile to mention sharks to my companions. I looked at them with a troubled eye, already seeing them lacking an arm or leg. Should I warn them? Probably, but I knew not how.

"Sir," said Conseil, "would you tell us something of the pearl-fishery?''

"As to the fishing itself," I asked, "or what may happen?''

"The fishing," replied the Canadian. "Before taking on something new, it is as well to know something about it."

"Very well; sit down, my friends, and I will tell you all I know.''

Ned and Conseil seated themselves on an ottoman, and the first thing the Canadian asked was—

"Sir, what is a pearl?''

"My worthy Ned," I answered, "to the poet, a pearl is a tear of the sea. To the Orientals, it is a drop of dew solidified. To the ladies, it is a jewel of an oval shape, and a transparent gleam, made of a nacreous substance, which they wear on their fingers, their necks, or their ears. For the chemist, it is a mixture of phosphate and carbonate of lime, with a little gelatine. And lastly, for naturalists, it is simply a morbid secretion of the organ that produces the nacres within certain bivalves."

"Branch of mollusca," said Conseil, "class

of acephali, order of testacea."

"Precisely so, my learned Conseil; and, amongst these testacea, the earshell, the tridacnae, the turbots—in a word, all those which secrete nacre; that is, the blue, bluish, violet, or white substance which lines the interior of their shells, are capable of producing pearls."

"Mussels, too?" asked the Canadian.

"Yes, mussels of certain waters in Scotland, Wales, Ireland, Saxony, Bohemia, and France."

"Good! In the future I shall pay attention," replied the Canadian.

"But," I continued, "the mollusc which is pre-eminent in secreting the pearl is that precious pintadine, the *pearl-oyster,* or *meleagrina margaritfera.* The pearl is only a solid, nacreous mass, globular in shape. It may adhere to the shell, or be buried in the flesh. But it always has a small hard body as a kernel, maybe a sterile egg, maybe a grain of sand, around which the nacreous material is laid in thin, concentric layers throughout several years."

"Are many pearls found in an oyster?" asked Conseil.

"Yes, my boy. Some pintadines are a jewel casket. One oyster has been reputed, though I allow myself to doubt it, to have contained no less than a hundred and fifty sharks."

"A hundred and fifty sharks!" exclaimed Ned Land.

"Did I say sharks?" said I, hurriedly. "I meant to say a hundred and fifty pearls. Sharks would not make sense."

"Certainly not," said Conseil; "but will you

tell us now by what means they extract these pearls?''

"They proceed in various ways. When they adhere to the shell, the fishermen often pull them off with pincers; but the most common way is to lay the pintadines on mats of the seaweed which covers the beds. In the open air, they die, and at the end of ten days they are in an advanced state of decomposition. They are then plunged into large tanks of seawater; then they are opened and washed. Now begins the double task of the sorters. First they separate those pearls called in the trade "the real money" from the "bastard" whites and "bastard" blacks, which are shipped in boxes of two hundred and fifty and three hundred pounds each. Then they take the parenchyma of the oyster, boil it, and pass it through a sieve in order to extract the very smallest pearls."

"The price of these pearls varies according to their size?" asked Conseil.

"Not only according to their size," I answered, "but also according to their shape, their water (that is, their color), and their orient; that is, that bright and variegated luster which makes them so charming to the eye. The most beautiful are called virgin pearls or paragons. They are formed alone in the tissue of the mollusc, are white, often opaque, but sometimes have the transparency of an opal. They are generally round or oval. The round are made into bracelets, the oval into pendants; and, being more precious, are sold singly. Those adhering to the shell of the oyster are more irregular in shape, and are sold by weight.

Lastly, in a lower order are classed those small pearls known under the name of seed-pearls; they are sold by quantity, and are especially used in embroidery for church ornaments."

"Have not some famous pearls been sold for a very high price?" asked Conseil.

"Yes, my boy. It is said that Caesar gave Servillia a pearl worth one hundred and twenty thousand francs."

"I even heard a story," said Ned Land, "of a lady of ancient times who drank pearls in vinegar."

"Cleopatra," replied Conseil.

"That must have been vile," exclaimed Ned.

"Detestable, friend Ned. But a little glass of vinegar that cost a million francs—that is a pretty price!"

"I am sorry I didn't marry that lady," said the Canadian, brandishing his fist.

"Ned Land, the husband of Cleopatra!" exclaimed Conseil.

"But I was going to be married," the Canadian said seriously. "And it was not my fault that the affair broke off. I had bought a pearl necklace for my fiancée, Kitty Tender, who then married another man. The necklace cost only a dollar and a half, so the pearls cannot have been examined carefully."

"My good Ned," I said, laughing, "those were artificial pearls, lined with oil of Orient."

"Ah, that essence of Orient, it must cost dear."

"So little as to be nothing. It has no value."

"Perhaps that is why Kitty Tender married another man," said Ned Land philosophically.

"Captain Nemo has the finest pearl I have ever seen," I told them. "It is worth millions."

"Yes, that magnificent jewel he wears under his vest."

"Perhaps," cried Ned, "we shall find its equal."

"Bah!" said Conseil. "What would we do with such a pearl aboard the *Nautilus*?"

"If we take a pearl worth millions back to Europe or America," I said, "it adds not only authenticity but a high price to the story of our adventures."

"But," said Conseil who always came back to the serious side of things, "is this pearl-fishery dangerous?"

"No," I answered, quickly; "particularly if certain precautions are taken."

"What does one risk in such a calling?" said Ned Land; "the swallowing of mouthfuls of seawater?"

"As you say, Ned. By the by," said I, trying to take Captain Nemo's careless tone, "are you afraid of sharks, brave Ned?"

"I!" replied the Canadian; "a harpooner by profession? It is my profession to make fun of them."

"But," said I, "it is not a question of fishing for them with an iron swivel, hoisting them into the vessel, cutting off their tails with a blow of a chopper, ripping them up, and throwing their hearts into the sea!"

"Then, it is a question of—"

"Precisely."

"In the water?"

"In the water."

"Faith, with a good harpoon! You know, sir, these sharks are ill-fashioned beasts. They must turn on their bellies in order to seize you, and in that time—"

Ned Land had a way of saying "seize," which sent shivers down my back.

"Well, and you, Conseil, what do you think of sharks?"

"Me!" said Conseil. "I will be frank, sir."

"So much the better," thought I.

"If you, sir, mean to face the sharks, I do not see why your faithful servant should not face them with you."

Chapter 3
A Pearl of Ten Millions

The next morning at four o'clock I was awakened by the steward, whom Captain Nemo had placed at my disposal. I rose hurriedly, dressed, and went into the saloon.

Captain Nemo was awaiting me.

"M. Aronnax," said he, "are you ready to start?"

"I am ready."

"Then, please follow me."

"And my companions, Captain?"

"They have been told, and are waiting."

"Are we not to put on our diver's suits?" I asked.

"Not yet, I have not allowed the *Nautilus* to come too near this coast, and we are some distance from the Manaar Bank; but the boat is ready, and will take us to the exact point of disembarkation, which will save us a long walk. It contains our diving apparatus, which we will put on when we begin our journey underwater."

Captain Nemo led me to the central ladder which led on to the deck. Ned and Conseil were already there, delighted at the prospect of our jaunt. Five sailors from the *Nautilus*, their oars poised, waited for us in the boat, which had been made fast against the side.

The night was still dark. Layers of clouds covered the sky, allowing only a few stars to be seen. I looked off where the land lay, and saw nothing but a dark line enclosing three parts of the horizon, from southwest to northwest. The *Nautilus*, having sailed up the western coast of Ceylon during the night, was now west of the bay, or rather gulf, formed by the mainland and the Island of Manaar. There, under the dark waters, stretched the pintadine beds, an inexhaustible field of pearls, more than twenty miles long.

Captain Nemo, Ned Land, Conseil, and I, took our places in the stern of the boat. The master went to the tiller. His four companions leaned on their oars, the painter was cast off, and we sheered away.

The boat went towards the south; the oarsmen did not hurry. I noticed that they took their powerful strokes at ten second intervals, as is done in the professional Navy. Whilst the craft forged ahead, droplets from the oars hit the dark depths of the waves crisply like spats of melted lead. A little billow gave a slight roll to the boat, and some samphire reeds flapped before it.

We were silent. What was Captain Nemo thinking of? Perhaps of the land he was approaching, and which he found too near for comfort, contrary to the Canadian's opinion, who thought it too far off. As to Conseil, he was merely there from curiosity.

About half-past five, the first tints on the horizon showed the upper line of coast more distinctly. Flat enough in the east, it rose a little to the south. It was still five miles away. The shore merged with the mist on the water. At six o'clock suddenly it was broad daylight, with that rapidity peculiar to tropical regions, which know neither dawn nor twilight. The sun's rays pierced the curtain of clouds piled up on the eastern horizon, and the radiant orb rose rapidly. I now saw land clearly with a few trees scattered here and there. The boat neared Manaar Island, and rounded it to the south. Captain Nemo rose from his seat and watched the sea.

At a sign from him the anchor was dropped, but the chain scarcely ran, for the water was little more than a yard deep, and this spot was one of the highest points in the bed of pintadines.

"Here we are, M. Aronnax," said Captain Nemo. "You see that enclosed bay? Here, in a month, will be gathered all the boats belonging to the owners of the pearl fisheries and these are the waters their divers will ransack so boldly. Fortunately, this bay is well situated for that kind of fishing. It is sheltered from the strongest winds; the sea is never very rough here, which makes it favorable for the diver's work. We will now put on our suits and begin our journey."

I did not answer, and while watching the waves with suspicion, began with the help of the sailors to put my heavy sea-dress. Captain Nemo and my companions were also dressing. None of the *Nautilus* men were to accompany us on this new excursion.

Soon we were enveloped to the throat in our india-rubber clothing; the breathing apparatus attached to our backs by braces. As to the Ruhmkorff lights there was no need for them. Before putting my head into the copper helmet, I had asked the question of the Captain.

"They would be useless," he replied. "We are going to no great depth, and the sun will light our way. Besides, it would not be prudent to carry the electric light in these waters; its brilliancy might attract some of the dangerous inhabitants of the coast most inopportunely."

As Captain Nemo pronounced these words, I turned to Conseil and Ned Land. But my two friends had already put on their helmets and they could neither hear nor answer.

One last question remained to ask of Captain Nemo.

"And our weapons," asked I; "our guns?"

"Guns? What for? Do not mountaineers attack the bear with a dagger in their hand, and is not steel surer than lead? Here is a strong blade, put it in your belt, and we shall go."

I looked at my companions. They were similarly armed and, more than that, Ned Land was brandishing an enormous harpoon, which he had put in the boat before leaving the *Nautilus*.

Following the Captain's example, I allowed myself to be dressed in the heavy copper helmet, and our tanks of air went into operation at once. An instant later we were landed, one after the other, in about two yards of water, upon smooth sand. Captain Nemo made a sign with his hand, and we followed him down a gentle slope till we went under the waves.

Around our feet, like coveys of snipe in a bog, rose shoals of fish, of the genus monoptera, which have no other fins but their tail. I recognized the Javanese, a real serpent two and a half feet long, of pale color underneath, which might easily be mistaken for a conger eel if it were not for the golden stripes on its side. In the genus stromateus, whose bodies are flat and oval, and carrying their dorsal fin like a scythese, I saw some of the most brilliant colors. Dried and pickled, this fish is known by the name of *Karawade*. Also, I saw tranquebars, of the genus apsiphoroides, whose bodies are covered with a shell-like armor made of eight longitudinal plates.

The rising sun lit up the mass of water more and more. The ground changed by degrees. The fine sand was followed by a perfect causeway of boulders, covered with a carpet of molluscs and zoophytes. Amongst these I noticed some plancenae, with thin shells, a kind of ostracion peculiar to the Red Sea and the Indian Ocean; some orange lucinae with rounded shells; rockfish three and a half feet long, which raised themselves under the waves like hands ready to grasp one. There were also panopyres, slightly phosphorescent; and lastly, oculines, like magnificent fans, forming one of the richest vegetations of these seas.

In the midst of these living plants, and under the arbors of the hydrophytes, were layers of clumsy articulates, particularly raninae, whose shell forms a slightly rounded triangle; and some horrible looking parthenopes.

At about seven o'clock we reached the oyster-beds, in which the pearl-oysters breed by the millions.

Captain Nemo gestured with his hand to the enormous heap of oysters. I could well understand that this was an inexhaustible mine of treasures, for nature's power to create goes far beyond man's capability of destruction. Ned Land, faithful to his instinct, hastened to fill his net with some of the finest specimens. But we could not linger. We had to follow the Captain, who seemed to follow paths known only to himself. The ground was rising noticeably, and sometimes, I could stretch my hand above the surface of the sea. Then the level of the ground would sink capriciously. Often we rounded high rocks carved into pyramids. In their dark cracks huge crustacea, perched upon their high claws like some war-machines, watched us with unblinking eyes and under our feet crawled various kinds of annelids.

At this moment there opened before us a large grotto, hollowed out of a picturesque heap of rocks, and thickly carpeted with submarine flora. At first it seemed very dark to me. The solar rays seemed to be gradually extinguished, until its vague transparency became no more than drowned light. Captain Nemo entered; we followed. My eyes soon accustomed themselves to this relative darkness. I could distinguish arches springing capriciously from natural pillars, standing squarely upon their granite base, like the heavy columns of Tuscan architecture. Why had our incomprehensible guide led us to this submarine crypt? I was soon to know. After descending a rather sharp incline, we were at the bottom of a kind of circular pit. There Captain Nemo stopped and with his hand indicated an object I had not yet seen. It was an oyster of extraordinary dimensions, a gigantic tridacne, a holy water-basin which could have held a whole lake, a bowl more than two and a half yards wide and thus larger than the one which was ornamenting the saloon of the *Nautilus*. I approached this extraordinary mollusc. It adhered by its byssus to a shelf of granite, and there, isolated, it had matured in the calm waters of the grotto. I estimated the weight of this tridacne at 600 pounds. Such an oyster would contain thirty pounds of meat; and one must have the stomach of a Gargantua to demolish a dozen such.

Captain Nemo was evidently acquainted with the existence of this bivalve, and seemed to have a particular motive in discovering the true condition of this tridacne. The shells were a little open. The Captain came near and put his dagger between them to prevent them from closing. Then he raised the membrane, with its fringed edges, which formed a cloak for the creature.

There, between the folds of the flesh, I saw a loose pearl, whose size equaled that of a coconut. Its globular shape, perfect clarity and admirable luster made it altogether a jewel of inestimable value. Carried away by my curiosity, I stretched out my hand to seize it, weigh it, handle it; but the Captain stopped me, made a sign of denial. He quickly withdrew his dagger, and the two shells immediately closed. I then understood Captain Nemo's intention. In leaving this pearl hidden in the mantle of the tridacne, he was allowing it to grow slowly. Each year the secretions of the mollusc would add new concentric layers.

Only he could find this grotto. Perhaps one day he would give this marvel to a museum, or, as is done in China, he could put a bit of glass or metal into the folds of the oyster and new accretions would begin. In any case, comparing this pearl to any I had seen, I thought it worth at least ten million francs as a wonder of nature, not as a jewel—since what woman's ear could support it?

Our visit to the opulent oyster was ended. Captain Nemo led us back to the shallow waters of the oyster beds. After ten minutes Captain Nemo stopped suddenly. I thought he had halted to retrace his steps. No; by a gesture he bade us crouch beside him in a deep fissure in the rock, while he pointed to one spot in the liquid mass, which I watched attentively.

About five yards from me a shadow appeared, and sank to the ground. The disquieting idea of sharks shot through my mind, but I was mistaken; and once again we did not have to deal with monsters of the deep.

It was a man, a living man, an Indian, a fisherman, a poor devil who, I suppose, had come to glean before the harvest. I could see the bottom of his canoe anchored some feet above his head. He dived and went up alternately. A stone held between his feet, helped him to descend, whilst a rope fastened him safely to his boat. This was all his equipment. Reaching the bottom at about five yards, he went on his knees and filled his bag with oysters picked up at random. Then he went up, emptied it, pulled up his stone, and once more began the operation which lasted thirty seconds.

The diver did not see us. The shadow of the rock hid us from sight. And how should this poor Indian ever dream that men, beings like himself, should be there under the water watching his movements, and observing every detail? He did not carry away more than ten oysters at each plunge, for he was obliged to pull them from the bank to which they adhered by means of their strong byssus. And how many of those oysters for which he risked his life had no pearl in them! I watched him closely, his actions were regular; and, for the space of half an hour, no danger appeared to threaten him.

I was beginning to accustom myself to the sight of this interesting fishing, when suddenly, while the Indian was on the bottom, I saw him make a gesture of terror, rise, and make a leap toward the surface.

I understood his dread. A gigantic shadow appeared just above the unfortunate diver. It was a shark of enormous size, advancing diagonally, his eyes on fire, and his jaws open. I was paralyzed with horror, and unable to move.

The voracious creature shot towards the Indian, who threw himself to one side to avoid the shark's fins; but not its tail, for it struck his chest, and stretched him on the ground.

In a few seconds the shark was back and, turning on his back, prepared to cut the Indian in two. Captain Nemo suddenly stood up, and, dagger in hand, walked straight to the shark, ready to fight the monster hand to hand. The very moment the shark was going to seize the unfortunate fisherman in his jaws, he saw his new adversary, and, turning over, made straight for Captain Nemo.

I can still see Captain Nemo's attitude. Bending almost double, he waited for the shark with admirable coolness, and when it rushed at him, threw himself to one side with wonderful agility, avoiding the shock and burying his dagger deep into its belly. But all was not over. A terrible combat ensued.

The shark let out a great sound. Blood rushed in torrents from its wound. The sea was dyed red, and I could distinguish nothing for some moments until, as in a flash of lightning, I saw the undaunted Captain hanging onto one of the creature's fins, struggling, hand to hand with the monster, dealing blow after blow at his enemy, yet still unable to give a decisive one.

The shark's struggles agitated the water with such fury that the rocking threatened to upset me.

I wanted to go to the Captain's assistance,

but, nailed to the spot with horror, I could not stir.

I watched with staring eye, I saw the changing phases of the battle. The Captain fell to the earth, knocked down by the enormous mass which bore upon him. The shark's jaws opened wide, like a pair of factory shears, and it would have been all over with the Captain; but, quick as thought, Ned Land hurled himself at the shark, harpoon in hand, and struck him with its terrible point.

The waves were impregnated with a mass of blood. They rocked under the shark's movements, which beat them with indescribable fury. Ned Land had not missed his aim. It was the monster's death rattle. Struck to the heart, it struggled in dreadful convulsions, the shock of which overthrew Conseil.

Now Ned Land freed the Captain, who, getting up unhurt, went straight to the Indian, quickly cut the cord which held him to the stone, took him in his arms, and, with a sharp blow of his heel, mounted to the surface. Saved by a miracle we all three followed in a few seconds, and went to the fisherman's boat.

Captain Nemo's first care was to revive the unfortunate man. I did not think he could succeed. The poor creature's immersion was not long; but the blow from the shark's tail might have been his death-blow.

Happily, under the Captain's and Conseil's energetic rubbing, consciousness returned by degrees. He opened his eyes. What was his surprise, even terror at seeing four great copper heads leaning over him! And, above all, what must he have thought when Captain Nemo, drawing a bag of pearls from the pocket of his suit, placed it in his hand! This munificent gift from the man of the waters to the poor Cingalese was accepted with a trembling hand. His wondering eyes showed that he knew not to what superhuman beings he owed both fortune and life.

At a sign from the Captain we returned to the oyster bed, and going back the way we came in about half an hour reached the anchor which secured the small boat of the *Nautilus*.

Once on board, with the help of the sailors, we got rid of our heavy copper helmets.

Captain Nemo's first word was to the Canadian.

"Thank you, Master Land," said he.

"It was in revenge, Captain," replied Ned Land. "I owed you that."

A pale smile glided across the Captain's lips, and that was all.

"To the *Nautilus*," said he.

The boat flew over the waves. Some minutes later, we met the floating corpse of the shark. By the black marking on the ends of its fins, I recognized the terrible melanopteron of the Indian Seas, as this species of shark is properly called. It was more than twenty-five feet long. Its enormous mouth occupied one-third of its body area. It was an adult, as could be told from the six rows of teeth placed in an isoceles triangle in its upper jaw.

Conseil looked at it with scientific interest, and I am sure that he placed it, and not without reason, in the cartilaginous class, of the Chondropterygian order, with fixed gills, of the selacian family, in the genus of the sharks.

Whilst I was contemplating this inert mass, a dozen of the voracious beasts appeared round the boat. Without noticing us, they threw themselves upon the dead body and fought with one another for the pieces.

At half-past eight we were again on board the *Nautilus*. There I reflected on the incidents which had taken place during our excursion to the Manaar Bank.

Two conclusions I must inevitably draw from it—one bearing upon the unparalleled courage of Captain Nemo, the other upon his self sacrifice for another human being, a representative of that race from which he fled beneath the sea. Whatever he might say, this strange man had not yet succeeded in entirely crushing his heart.

When I made this observation to him, he answered in a slightly agitated tone—

"That Indian, sir, is an inhabitant of an oppressed country; and I am still, and shall be, to my last breath, one with the oppressed."

Chapter 4
The Red Sea

In the course of the day of January 29th the island of Ceylon disappeared under the horizon, and the *Nautilus*, at a speed of twenty miles an hour, slid into the labyrinth of canals which separates the Maldives from the Laccadives. It passed the island of Kiltan, a land originally madreporic, discovered by Vasco da Gama in 1499, and one of the nineteen principal islands of the Laccadive Archipelago, situated between 10^0 and 14^0 30' north latitude, and 69^0 50' 12'' east longitude.

We had made 16,200 miles, or 7500 (French) leagues from our point of departure in the Japanese seas.

The next day (30th January), when the *Nautilus* surfaced, there was no land in sight. Its course was N.N.E., in the direction of the Sea of Oman, between Arabia and the Indian Peninsula, which serves as an entrance to the

Persian Gulf. It was evidently a dead end without any possible way out. Where was Captain Nemo taking us to? I could not tell. This did not satisfy the Canadian, who came that day to ask me where we were going.

"We are going where our Captain's fancy takes us, Master Ned."

"His fancy cannot take us far, then," said the Canadian. "The Persian Gulf is landlocked. If we go in, it will not be long before we are out again."

"Very well, then, we will come out again, Master Land; and if, after the Persian Gulf, the *Nautilus* would like to visit the Red Sea, the Straits of Bab-el-mandeb are there to give us entrance."

"I need not tell you, sir," said Ned Land, "that the Red Sea has no more outlet than the Gulf, passage through has not been completed of Suez and if it were, a boat as mysterious as ours would not risk itself in a canal with all its sluices. And again, the Red Sea is not the way to take us back to Europe."

"But I never said we were going back to Europe."

"What do you suppose, then?"

"I suppose that, after visiting the curious coasts of Arabia and Egypt, the *Nautilus* will go down the Indian Ocean again, perhaps cross the Channel of Mozambique, perhaps off the Mascarenhas, so as to gain the Cape of Good Hope."

"And once at the Cape of Good Hope?" asked the Canadian, with peculiar emphasis.

"Well, we shall penetrate into that part of the

Atlantic which we do not yet know. Ah! friend Ned, you are getting tired of this journey under the sea. You are surfeited with the constantly changing spectacle of submarine wonders. For my part, I shall be sorry to see the end of a voyage which it is given to so few men to make.''

Till the 3rd of February, the *Nautilus* scoured the Sea of Oman, at different speeds and depths. It seemed to sail at random, as if uncertain of its way, but we never crossed the Tropic of Cancer.

Leaving the Sea of Oman we sighted Muscat, one of the most important towns of the country. I admired its strange appearance, surrounded by black rocks against which its white houses and forts stood out. I glimpsed the rounded domes of its mosques, the elegant points of its minarets, its fresh and verdant terraces. But it was a brief vision! The *Nautilus* soon sank under the waves of that part of the sea.

For a distance of six miles, we passed along the Arabian coast of Mahrah and Hadramaut, its undulating line of mountains being occasionally relieved by some ancient ruin. The 5th of February we at last entered the Gulf of Aden, a perfect funnel leading into the neck of the Straits of Bab-el-mandeb, through which the Indian waters entered the Red Sea.

The 6th of February, the *Nautilus* floated in sight of Aden, which is perched upon a promontory, joined to the mainland, by a narrow isthmus. Aden is like a remote Gibraltar, the English having rebuilt its fortifications after they took possession in 1839. I caught a glimpse of the octagonal minarets of this town, which was at one time, according to the historian Edrisi, the richest and busiest trading center on the coast.

I certainly thought that Captain Nemo, having come so far, would back out again. But I was mistaken, for much to my surprise, he did no such thing.

The next day, the 7th of February, we entered the Straits of Bab-el-mandeb, which, in the Arab tongue, means "The gate of tears."

Twenty miles wide, it is only thirty-two miles in length. And for the *Nautilus*, going at full speed, the crossing was the work of scarcely an hour. But I saw nothing, not even the island of Perim, which the British Government has used to strengthen the position of Aden. There were too many English or French steamers on the way from Suez to Bombay, Calcutta, Melbourne, Bourbon, or Mauritius, ploughing this narrow passage, for the *Nautilus* to venture showing itself. So it sailed prudently underwater. At about noon, we were pushing through the waves of the Red Sea.

I would not even try to fathom the caprice which caused Captain Nemo to enter the Red Sea. But I quite approved. Our speed was lessened. Sometimes we stayed on the surface, sometimes the *Nautilus* submerged to avoid a vessel, and thus I was able to observe the upper and lower parts of this curious gulf, famed in Bible tales.

The 8th of February, from the first dawn of day, Mocha came in sight—now in ruins, with walls that would fall at the sound of a cannon and which shelter little more than a few verdant date trees. But it was once an important city, containing six public markets, and twenty-six mosques, and its walls, defended by fourteen forts, formed a girdle of two miles around.

The *Nautilus* then approached the African shore, where the depth of the sea was greater and the water clear as crystal. Through the open windows of the saloon we were allowed to contemplate beautiful bushes of brilliant coral, and large blocks of rocks clothed with a splendid fur of green algae and fuci. What an indescribable spectacle, and what a variety of scenery and landscapes along these reefs and volcanic islands which mark the Libyan coast! But where these growths appeared in all their beauty was at Tehama on the eastern coast, for there not only did this gorgeous display of zoophytes flourish beneath the sea, but they formed picturesque interlacings which unfolded themselves sixty feet above the surface, wilder but less highly colored than those whose freshness was kept up by the vital powers of the waters.

What charming hours I passed thus at the window of the saloon! What new specimens of submarine flora and fauna did I admire under the brightness of our electric lantern!

There grew sponges of all shapes, pediculated, foliated, globular, and digital. They certainly justified the names of baskets, cups, distaffs, elks'-horns, lions'-feet, peacocks'-tails, and Neptunes'-gloves, which have been given to them by fishermen, finer poets than the scholars.

Other zoophytes which multiply near sponges

consisted principally of medusae of a most elegant kind. The molluscs were represented by varieties of the calmar (which, according to Orbigny, are peculiar to the Red Sea); and reptiles by the virgata turtle, of the genus cheloniae, which is a wholesome and delicate food for our table.

The fish were abundant, and often remarkable. The following are those which the nets of the *Nautilus* frequently brought on board:

Rays of a red-brick color, with bodies marked with blue spots, easily recognizable by their double spikes; some superb caranxes, marked with seven transverse bands of jet-black, blue and yellow fins, and gold and silver scales; mullets with yellow heads; gobies, and a thousand other species.

The 9th of February, the *Nautilus* floated in the broadest part of the Red Sea, which stretches for ninety miles between Souakin, on the west coast, and Kiimfidah, on the east coast.

That day at noon, after the bearings were taken, Captain Nemo ascended to the deck where I happened to be, and I was determined not to let him leave without pressing him regarding his ulterior designs. As soon as he saw me he approached, and graciously offered me a cigar.

"Well, sir, does this Red Sea please you? Have you sufficiently observed the wonders it covers, its fishes, its zoophytes, its flower beds of sponges, and its forests of coral? Did you catch a glimpse of the towns on its borders?"

"Yes, Captain Nemo," I replied; "and the

Nautilus is wonderfully fitted for such a study. Ah! it is an intelligent ship!"

"Yes, sir, intelligent and invulnerable. It fears neither the terrible tempests of the Red Sea, nor its currents, nor its reefs."

"Certainly," said I, "this sea is described as one of the most dangerous in the time of the ancients, if I am not mistaken, its reputation was execrable."

"Execrable, M. Aronnax. The Greek and Latin historians do not speak favorably of it, and Strabo says it is very dangerous during the Etesian winds, and in the rainy season. The Arabian Edrisi portrays it under the name of the Gulf of Colzoum, and relates that vessels perished there in great numbers on the reefs and that no one would risk sailing there at night. It is, he states, a sea subject to fearful hurricanes, strewn with inhospitable islands, and which offers nothing good either on its surface or in its depths. Such, too, is the opinion of Arrian, Agatharcides, and Artemidorus."

"One may see," I replied, "that these historians never sailed on board the *Nautilus.*"

"Just so," replied the captain, smiling; "and in that respect most moderns are not more advanced than the ancients. It has taken many centuries to discover the mechanical power of steam. Who knows if, in another hundred years, we may not see a second *Nautilus*? Progress is slow, M. Aronnax."

"It is true," I answered. "Your boat is at least a century before its time, perhaps an era. What a misfortune that the secret of such an invention should die with its inventor!"

Captain Nemo did not reply. After some minutes' silence he continued—

"You were speaking of the opinions of ancient historians regarding the dangers of navigation in the Red Sea."

"It is true," said I. "But were not their views exaggerated?"

"Yes and no, M. Aronnax," replied Captain Nemo, who seemed to know the Red Sea to its bottom. "What presents no danger to a modern vessel, well rigged, strongly built, and master of its own course, thanks to obedient steam, offered all sorts of perils to the ancients. Picture to yourself those first navigators going to sea in ships made of planks sewn together with fibers of the palm tree, saturated with grease from the sea-dog, and covered with powdered resin! They had no instruments to take their bearings, and they knew scarcely anything. Under such conditions shipwrecks must have been numerous. But in our time, steamers running between Suez and the South Seas have nothing to fear from the fury of this gulf, in spite of contrary trade-winds. The captain and passengers do not prepare for their departure by offering propitiatory sacrifices: and, on their safe return, they no longer go to the nearest temple, ornamented with laurel wreaths and gold crowns, to thank the gods."

"You are right," said I. "Steam seems to have killed all gratitude in the hearts of sailors. But, Captain, since you seem to have made an especial study of this sea, can you tell me the origin of its name?"

"There are several explanations, M. Aronnax. Would you like to know the opinion of a fourteenth century storyteller?''

''Willingly.''

''This imaginative writer says that the name was given to it to commemorate the miraculous passage of the Israelites, when Pharaoh perished in the waves which closed over him at the command of Moses.''

''A poet's explanation, Captain Nemo,'' I replied; ''but I cannot content myself with it. I ask for your personal opinion.''

''Very well, M. Aronnax. I think that in this appellation, Red Sea, we must see a translation of the Hebrew word 'Edom'; and if the ancients gave it that name, it was on account of the particular color of its waters.''

''But up to this time I have seen nothing but transparent waves without any particular color.''

''Very likely! but as we go toward the bottom of the gulf, you will note this singular appearance. I remember seeing the Bay of Tor entirely red, like a sea of blood.''

''And you attribute this color to the presence of a microscopic seaweed?''

''Yes; it is a mucilaginous purple matter, produced by the restless plants called trichodesmia, which are so small that it takes 40,000 to occupy the space of a square .04 of an inch. Perhaps we shall see some when we get to Tor.''

''So, Captain Nemo, this is not the first time you have explored the Red Sea on board the *Nautilus*?''

''No, sir.''

''As you spoke a while ago of the passage of

the Israelites, and of the catastrophe to the Egyptians, I will ask whether you have met with evidence under the water of this great historical event?''

''No, sir; and for a very good reason.''

''What is it?''

''The spot is situated a little above the Isthmus of Suez, in the arm, where formerly was a deep estuary at a time when the Red Sea extended to the Salt Lakes. Now, whether their passage were miraculous or not, nevertheless, the Israelites crossed there to reach the Promised Land, and Pharaoh's army perished precisely on that spot; and I think that excavations made under that sand would unearth a large number of arms and tools of Egyptian origin.''

''Very likely,'' I replied; ''and for the archaeologists' sake let us hope that these excavations will be made sooner or later, after the construction of the Suez Canal, not that this canal will be very useful to a vessel like the *Nautilus*.''

''Very likely; but useful to the whole world,'' said Captain Nemo. ''The ancients well understood the value of communications between the Red Sea and the Mediterranean for their commercial affairs. But they did not think of digging a canal direct, and used the Nile as an intermediary. The canal which connected the Nile to the Red Sea was begun by Sesostris, if we may believe tradition. One thing is certain, in the year 615 before Jesus Christ, Necos undertook the construction of a canal fed by the waters of the Nile, to cross the plain of Egypt which faces Arabia. It took four days to go up this canal, and it was so wide that two triremes could go abreast. It was carried on by Darius, son of Hystaspes, and probably finished by Ptolemy II. Strabo saw it navigated; but the slope from the start near Bubastes down to the Red Sea was so slight that the canal was only navigable for a few months in the year when rain was plentiful. Nevertheless, this canal served all commerce until the age of Antoninus, when it was abandoned and blocked up with sand. Restored by order of the Caliph Omar, it was finally destroyed in 761 or 762 by Caliph Al-Mansor, who wished to prevent the arrival of provisions against him. During the expedition into Egypt, your General Bonaparte discovered traces of the works in the Desert of Suez; and surprised by the tide, he nearly drowned before regaining Hadjaroth, at the very place where Moses had encamped three thousand years before him.''

''Well, Captain, what the ancients dared not undertake, this junction between the two seas, which will shorten the road from Cadiz to India, M. Lesseps has succeeded in doing; and before long he will have changed Africa into an immense island.

''Yes, M. Arronax; you are right to be proud of your countryman. Such a man brings more honor to a nation than great captains. He began, like so many others, with vexations and rebuffs; but he has triumphed, for he has the genius of determination. And it is sad to think that this work which should have been international, and would have made any ruler illustrious, should have succeeded by the energy of one man. All honor to M. Lesseps!"

"Yes, honor to the great citizen!" I replied, surprised by the manner in which Captain Nemo had just spoken.

"Unfortunately," he continued, "I cannot take you through the Suez Canal. But you will be able to see the long jetty of Port Said after tomorrow, when we shall be in the Mediterranean."

"The Mediterranean!" I exclaimed.

"Yes, sir. Does that astonish you?"

"What astonishes me is to think that we shall be there the day after tomorrow."

"Indeed?"

"Yes, Captain, although by this time I ought to have taught myself to be surprised at nothing as long as I am on board your boat."

"But the cause of this surprise?"

"Well, it is the fearful speed you will have to demand of the *Nautilus*, if the day after tomorrow she is to be in the Mediterranean, having circled Africa, and rounded the Cape of Good Hope!"

"Who told you that she would circle Africa, and round the Cape of Good Hope, sir?"

"Well, unless the *Nautilus* sails on dry land, and passes above the isthmus—"

"Or beneath it, M. Aronnax."

"Beneath it?"

"Certainly," replied Captain Nemo, quietly. "A long time ago under this neck of land Nature created what man has this day made on its surface."

"What! such a passage exists?"

"Yes, a subterranean passage, which I have

named the Arabian Tunnel. It takes us beneath Suez, and opens into the Gulf of Pelusium."

"But this isthmus is composed of nothing but quicksands!"

"To a certain depth. But at only fifty-five yards begins a solid layer of rock."

"Did you discover this passage by chance?" I asked, more and more surprised.

"Chance and reasoning, sir; and by reasoning even more than by chance. Not only does this passage exist, but I have profited by it several times. Without that I should not have ventured this day into the blind alley of the Red Sea."

"Would it be indiscreet to ask how you discovered this tunnel?"

"Sir, there can be no secrets between men who can never leave each other."

I did not refer to his insinuation, but waited to hear his story.

"Sir, it was the simple reasoning of a naturalist that led me to discover this passage. I noticed that both in the Red Sea and in the Mediterranean there were many identical fishes—ophidia, fiatoles, girelles, and exocoeti. Certain of that fact, I asked myself was it possible that there was some communication between the two seas? If so, the subterranean current must necessarily run from the Red Sea to the Mediterranean, as a result of the difference between their levels. I caught a large number of fishes in the neighborhood of Suez. I passed a copper ring through their tails, and threw them back into the sea. Some months later, on the coast of Syria, I caught some of my fish ornamented with the ring. Thus the communication between the two was proved. I then sought for it with my *Nautilus*. I discovered it, ventured into it, and before long, sir, you too will have passed through my Arabian Tunnel!''

Chapter 5
The Arabian Tunnel

That same evening, in 20° 30' north latitude, the *Nautilus* floated on the surface of the sea. Approaching the Arabian coast I saw Djeddah, which was the banking house for Egypt, Syria, Turkey, and India, its buildings, vessels anchored at the quays, and others whose deeper draught obliged them to anchor in the roads. The sun, somewhat low on the horizon, struck full on the houses emphasizing their whiteness. Outside the town were huts made of wood or reeds where the Bedouins lived. Soon Djeddah was lost in the shadows of night and around the *Nautilus* the water had a slightly phosphorescent gleam.

The next day, the 10th of February, we sighted several ships running to windward. The *Nautilus* returned to submarine navigation. But at noon, when her bearings were taken, the sea was deserted, and she rose again to her waterline.

Accompanied by Ned and Conseil, I seated myself on deck. The coast on the eastern side looked like a mass printed faintly upon a damp fog.

We were leaning on the sides of the pinnace, talking of one thing and another, when Ned Land, stretching out his hand towards a spot on the sea, said—

"Do you see anything there, sir?"

"No, Ned," I replied; "but I have not your eyes, you know."

"Look well," said Ned, "there, on the starboard beam, about the height of the lantern! Do you not see a mass which seems to move?"

"Certainly," said I, after scrutiny. "I see something like a long body on top of the water."

"Another *Nautilus*?" asked Conseil.

"No, some sea beast," said Ned.

"Are there whales in the Mediterranean?" Conseil asked.

"Yes," I told him.

"It is not exactly a whale," said Ned.

Before long the black object was not more than a mile from us. It looked like a great sandbank deposited in the open sea. It was a gigantic dugong!

Ned Land looked eagerly. His eyes shone with greed of sight of the animal. His hand seemed ready to harpoon it. One would have thought he only waited to throw himself into the sea, and attack the dugong in its native element.

Captain Nemo appeared on deck. He saw the dugong and Ned Land crouching to spring.

"If you held a harpoon just now, Master Land, would it not burn your hand?"

"Just so, sir."

"And you would not mind being a fisherman again for a day and adding this cetacean to the list of those you have already killed?"

"I should not, sir."

"Well, you may try."

"Thank you, sir," said Ned Land, his eyes flaming.

"Only," continued the Captain, "for your own sake I advise you not to miss the creature."

"Is it dangerous to attack a dugong?" I asked, in spite of the Canadian's shrug of his shoulders.

"Yes," replied the Captain. "Sometimes the animal turns upon its assailants and overturns their boat. But for Master Land, this danger is not to be feared. His eye is prompt, his arm sure. I warned him against missing the dugong only because I know he does not like his game in little pieces."

"This animal is good to eat!" exclaimed Ned.

"Its meat is the finest, saved in Malaysia for kings."

At this moment seven men of the crew, silent and impassive as ever, came on deck. One carried a harpoon and a line similar to those employed in catching whales. The pinnace was lifted from the bridge, pulled from its socket, and let down into the sea. Six oarsmen took their seats, and the coxswain went to the tiller. Ned, Conseil, and I went to the back of the boat.

"You are not coming, Captain?" I asked.

"No, sir; but I wish you good sport."

The boat was put off, and propelled by six rowers, drew rapidly towards the dugong, which now floated about two miles from the *Nautilus*.

A few cables' length from the cetacean, we slackened speed, and the oars dipped noiselessly in the quiet waters. The harpoon used in whaling attached to a long cord, which the wounded creature draws after him and is held by a sailor at the other end. But this cord was no more than ten fathoms long, and the end was attached to a small barrel, which would float and show the course the dugong took under the water.

I stood, and carefully observed the Canadian's adversary. This dugong, which also bears the name halicore, closely resembled the manatee. Its oval body terminated in an extended tail, and its lateral fins in perfect fingers. Its difference from the manatee consisted in its upper jaw, which was armed with two long and pointed tusks.

This dugong, which Ned Land was preparing to attack, was of colossal dimensions; it was more than seven yards long. It did not move, and seemed to be sleeping on the waves, which might make it easier to capture.

The boat approached with six yards of the animal. The oars rested on the rowlocks. I half rose. Ned Land, body leaning back a little, brandished the harpoon in his experienced hand.

Suddenly a hissing noise was heard, and the dugong disappeared. The harpoon, although thrown with great force, had apparently struck only the water.

"A thousand curses!" exclaimed the Canadian, furiously. "I have missed it!"

"No," said I; "the creature is wounded—look at the blood; but your weapon had not stuck in his body."

"My harpoon! my harpoon!" cried Ned Land.

The sailors rowed on, and the coxswain made for the floating barrel. The harpoon regained, we followed in pursuit of the animal.

The latter now and then came to the surface to breathe. The wound had not weakened it, for it shot onwards with great rapidity.

The boat, rowed by strong arms, flew on its track. Several times it approached within a few yards, and the Canadian was ready with his harpoon, but the dugong made off each time with a sudden plunge, before Ned could strike.

Imagine the passion which excited impatient Ned Land! He hurled at the unfortunate creature the most violent expletives in the English tongue. For my part, I was only vexed to see the dugong escape all our attacks.

We pursued it without let-up for an hour, and I began to think we would never capture it, when the animal, possessed with the perverse idea of vengeance, of which he soon had cause to repent, turned upon the pinnace and prepared to attack his assailants.

This maneuver did not escape the Canadian. "Look out!" he cried.

The coxswain said some words in his outlandish tongue, doubtless warning the men to keep on their guard.

The dugong came within twenty feet of the boat, stopped, sniffed the air briskly with its large nostrils (which were not at the end, but in the upper part of its muzzle). Then, taking a leap, he hurled himself upon us.

The pinnace could not avoid the shock, and half overturned, shipping at least two tons of water, which had to be bailed out; but thanks to the coxswain, we caught the attack sideways, not head-on, so we were not capsized. While Ned Land, clinging to the bow, belabored the gigantic animal with blows from his harpoon, the creature buried its tusks in the gunwale, and lifted the whole boat out of the water, as a lion lifts a roebuck by the neck. We tumbled over one another, and I know not how the adventure would have ended if the Canadian, still enraged with the beast, had not struck it to the heart.

I heard its teeth grind on the iron plate, and the dugong disappeared, taking the harpoon with him. But the barrel soon returned to the surface, and shortly afterward the body of the animal appeared, lying on its back. The boat came up with it, took it in tow, and made straight for the *Nautilus*.

It required tackle of enormous strength to hoist the dugong onto the deck. It weighed 10,000 pounds.

The next day, February 11th, the larder of

the *Nautilus* was enriched by more delicate game. A flight of sea-swallows fell on the *Nautilus*. This bird was a species of the Sterna nilotica, peculiar to Egypt; its beak is black, the head gray and pointed, the eye surrounded by white spots, the back, wings, and tail of a grayish color, the belly and throat white, and claws red. We also took some dozen of Nile ducks, a wild bird of high flavor, its throat and upper part of the head being white with black spots.

About five o'clock in the evening we sighted to the north the Cape of Ras-Mohammed. This cape forms the extremity of Arabia Petraea, and lies between the Gulf of Suez and the Gulf of Acabah.

The *Nautilus* penetrated into the Straits of Jubal, which lead to the Gulf of Suez. I distinctly saw a high mountain, towering between the two gulfs of Ras-Mohammed. It was Mount Horeb, that same Sinai, on whose summit Moses saw God face to face.

At six o'clock the *Nautilus*, sometimes floating, sometimes immersed, passed Tor, at the end of the bay where the waters seemed tinted with red, an observation already made by Captain Nemo. Then night fell in the midst of a heavy silence, sometimes broken by the cries of pelicans and other night-birds, and the noise of the surf chafing against the rocks, or the sound of some far-off steamer beating the waters of the gulf with its paddles.

From eight to nine o'clock the *Nautilus* remained some fathoms under the water. According to my calculation we were very near

Suez. Through the window of the saloon I saw the rocky bottom vividly lit up by our electric lamp. It seemed to me that the straits were retreating farther and farther.

At a quarter-past nine, the vessel having returned to the surface, I mounted the deck. So impatient to pass through Captain Nemo's tunnel that I could not stay in one place, I thought to get a breath of fresh night-air.

Soon, in the darkness and the fog I saw a pale light glimmering about a mile away from us.

"A floating lighthouse!" said someone near me.

I turned and saw the Captain.

"It is the floating light of Suez," he continued. "It will not be long before we gain the entrance of the tunnel."

"The entrance cannot be easy?"

"No, sir; and for that reason I am to go into the steersman's cage and direct our course myself. And now if you will go below, M. Aronnax, the *Nautilus* is going to submerge, and will not return to the surface until we have passed through the Arabian Tunnel."

Captain Nemo led me towards the main ladder. Halfway down he opened a door, went through the upper alleyway, and arrived at the pilot's cage, which it may be remembered rose at the extreme end of the deck. It was a cabin measuring six feet square, very much like that occupied by the pilot on the steamboats of the Mississippi or Hudson. In the middle stood the steering wheel, which was connected to the rudder-chains, which ran to the back of the *Nautilus*. Four portholes, with lenticular glass set into grooves in the walls of the cabin, allowed the steersman to see in all directions.

The cabin was dark; but soon my eyes accustomed themselves to the obscurity, and I perceived the pilot. He was a strong man, his hands resting on the spokes of the wheel. Outside, the sea was vividly lit up by the lantern, which shed its rays from the back of the cabin to the other end of the deck.

"Now," said Captain Nemo, "let us try to make our passage."

Electric wires connected the pilot's cage with the engine room, and the Captain could communicate both the direction and speed simultaneously to his *Nautilus* from the cage. He pressed a metal knob, and at once the speed of the screw diminished.

I watched in silence the high straight wall of rock we were running by, a solid base of sandy mountain mass along the coast. We followed it thus for an hour, only a few yards off.

Captain Nemo did not take his eye from the compass hanging with its two concentric circles. At a slight gesture, the pilot instantly modified the course of the *Nautilus*.

I had placed myself at the port-scuttle, and could see some magnificent substructures of coral, zoophytes, seaweed, and fucus, stretching their enormous claws from fissures in the rock.

At a quarter past ten, the Captain himself took the helm. A large gallery, black and deep, opened before us. The *Nautilus* went boldly into it. A strange roaring was heard from all sides. It was the waters of the Red Sea, which the incline of the tunnel precipitated violently towards the

Mediterranean. The *Nautilus* went with the torrent, swift as an arrow, in spite of the efforts of the engine which, to offer more effective resistance, beat the waves with screw in reverse.

On the walls of the narrow passage I could see nothing but brilliant rays, straight lines, furrows of fire, traced by the great speed, under the brilliant electric light. My heart pounded.

At thirty-five minutes past ten, Captain Nemo left the helm; and, turning to me, said—

"The Mediterranean!"

In less than twenty minutes, the *Nautilus*, carried along by the torrent, had passed beneath the Isthmus of Suez.

Chapter 6
The Grecian Archipelago

The next day, the 12th of February, at dawn, the *Nautilus* rose to the surface. I hastened on deck. Three miles to the south the dim outline of Pelusium was to be seen. The tunnel had carried us from one sea to the other. About seven o'clock Ned and Conseil joined me.

"Well, Sir Naturalist," said the Canadian, in a slightly jovial tone, "is this the Mediterranean?"

"We are floating on its surface, friend Ned."

"What!" said Conseil, "this very morning!"

"Yes, this very morning. In only a few minutes we went through this solid isthmus."

"I do not believe it," replied the Canadian.

"Then you are wrong, Master Land," I continued. "That low coast which rounds off to the south is the coast of Egypt. And you, who have such good eyes, Ned, you can see the jetty of Port Said stretching into the sea."

The Canadian looked attentively.

"You are right, sir, and your Captain is a first-rate man. We are in the Mediterranean. Good! Now, if you please, let us talk of our own little affair, but so that no one hears us."

I saw what the Canadian wanted, and, I thought it better to let him talk as he wished. So we all three went and sat down near the lantern, where we were less exposed to the spray from the waves.

"Now, Ned, we listen. What have you to tell us?"

"What I have to tell you is very simple. We are in Europe; and before Captain Nemo's whims drag us to the bottom of the Polar Seas, or lead us into Oceania, I want to leave the *Nautilus*."

I wished in no way to interfere with the freedom of my companions, but I certainly felt no desire to leave Captain Nemo.

Thanks to him, and thanks to his ship, each day I was nearer the completion of my submarine studies. I was rewriting my book on the ocean depths in its very element. Should I ever again have such an opportunity to observe the wonders of the sea? No, certainly not! And I could not bring myself to abandon the *Nautilus* before my investigations were accomplished.

"Friend Ned, answer me honestly, are you tired of being on board? Are you sorry that destiny has thrown us into Captain Nemo's hands?"

The Canadian waited some moments before answering. Then folding his arms, he said:

"Honestly, I do not regret this journey under the seas. I shall always be glad to have done it. But now that it is finished, let us have done with it. That is my idea."

"It will come to an end, Ned."

"Where and when?"

"Where I do not know—when I cannot say. I suppose it will end when these seas have nothing more to teach us."

"Then what do you hope for?" demanded the Canadian.

"That circumstances may occur six months hence as well as now, by which we may and should profit."

"Oh!" said Ned Land, "and where shall we be in six months, if you please, Sir Naturalist?"

"Perhaps here; perhaps in China. You know the *Nautilus* is a rapid traveler. It goes through water as swallows through the air, or as an express train on the land. It does not fear traveled seas; who can say that it may not raise the coasts of France, England, or America, where flight may be attempted as easily as here."

"M. Aronnax," replied the Canadian, "your arguments are rotten at the foundation. You speak in the future, 'We shall be there! we shall be there!' I speak in the present, 'We are here, and we must take advantage of it.' "

Ned Land's logic pressed me hard, and I felt myself beaten on this ground. I could not think of an argument that would have value in my favor.

"Sir," continued Ned, "let us suppose an impossibility. If Captain Nemo should offer you your liberty today, would you accept it?"

"Friend Ned, this is my answer. My arguments do not stand up against yours. We cannot rely on Captain Nemo's goodwill. Common prudence forbids him to set us at liberty. On the other side, prudence bids us to take the first opportunity to leave the *Nautilus*."

"M. Aronnax, that is wisely said."

"Only one observation—just one. The effort must be serious, and our first attempt must succeed. If it fails we shall never find another, and Captain Nemo will never forgive us."

"All that is true," replied the Canadian. "But your observation applies to all attempts at flight, whether in two years' time, or in two days'. But the question is still this: If a favorable opportunity presents itself, it must be seized."

"Agreed! and now, Ned, what would you regard as a favorable opportunity?"

"A dark night that will bring the *Nautilus* within an easy distance from some European coast."

"And you would try to escape by swimming?"

"Yes, if we were near enough to the shore, and if the vessel were floating at that time. Not if the shore was far away, and the boat submerged."

"And in that case?"

"In that case, I should seek to make myself master of the pinnace. I know how it is operated. All we have to do is get inside. The bolts can reach the surface without even the pilot in the bows being aware of our flight."

"Very well, Ned, watch for the opportunity. But do not forget that a single mistake will ruin us."

"I will not forget it sir."

"And now, Ned, would you like to know what I think of your project?"

"Certainly, M. Aronnax."

"Well, I think—I do not say I hope—I think that this favorable opportunity will never present itself."

"Why not?"

"Because Captain Nemo cannot persuade himself that we have given up all hope of regaining our liberty, and he will be on his guard, above all within sight of the European coast."

"We shall see," replied Ned Land, shaking his head obstinately.

"And now, Ned Land," I added, "let us talk no more. Not another word on the subject. When you are ready, come and tell us, and we will follow you. I rely upon you entirely."

Thus ended the conversation that led to such grave results a little later. Remark that events seemed to confirm my prophecy, to the Canadian's despair. Was it true Captain Nemo distrusted us in these traveled waters? Or did he only wish to hide from the many ships, of all nations, which ploughed the Mediterranean? I could not tell; but we were often submerged and even oftener far from shore. Or, if the *Nautilus* did surface, there was nothing to be seen but the pilot's cage. Sometimes it descended to great depths; between the Greek Archipelago and Asia Minor, at more than a thousand fathoms, we still could not touch bottom.

Thus I knew we were near the island of Carpathos, one of the Sporades, only by Captain Nemo reciting these lines from Virgil:

"Est in Carpathio Neptuni gurgite vates,
            Caeruleus Proteus,"

as he indicated a spot on the planisphere.

It was indeed the ancient abode of Proteus, old shepherd of Neptune's flocks; between Rhodes and Crete, it is now called the Island of Scarpanto. I saw nothing of it but the granite base through the glass panels of the saloon.

The next day, the 14th of February, I planned to spend some hours in studying the fishes of the Archipelago. But for some reason or other, the panels remained hermetically sealed. Upon plotting the course of the *Nautilus* I found that we were headed towards Candia, the ancient Isle of Crete. At the time I embarked on the *Abraham Lincoln*, people of this island had revolted against the despotism of the Turks. I was completely ignorant of how the insurgents had fared since and Captain Nemo, lacking all land communications, would not be able to tell me.

When I found myself alone with him in the saloon that night I made no allusion to this event. He seemed taciturn and preoccupied. Contrary to his usual custom, he ordered both panels to be opened, and going from one to the other, observed the mass of waters attentively. I could not guess his purpose, so I employed my time in studying the fish passing before my eyes.

Amongst others, I remarked some gobies, mentioned by Aristotle, and commonly known by the name of sea-branches, which are most often found near the Delta of the Nile. Sea-bream played nearby. This is a type of sparus somewhat phosphorescent. Ranked by the ancient Egyptians amongst their sacred animals, its arrival in the waters of their river heralded a fertile overflow, and was celebrated with religious ceremonies. I also noticed some cheilines about nine inches long, this being a bony fish with transparent shell, whose livid color is mixed with red spots. They are great eaters of marine vegetation, which gives them an exquisite flavor. Cheilines were much sought after by the epicures of ancient Rome; stuffed with the delicate roe of the lamprey, peacocks' brains and tongues of the phenicopters, its flesh was that divine fish which Vitellius so admired.

Another inhabitant of these seas called my attention, and led my mind back to recollections of antiquity. This was the remora, that fastens onto the shark's belly. According to the ancients, this little fish, by hooking onto the ship's bottom, could bring it to a halt. By holding back Antony's ship during the battle of Actium, one is said to have helped Augustus gain the victory. On how little may hang the destiny of nations! I observed some fine anthiae, which belong to the order of lutjans, a fish held sacred by the Greeks, who attributed to them the power of chasing sea monsters away from waters they sailed. Their name means *flower*, and they justify their appellation by their graduated colors, shades comprising the whole gamut of red, from the paleness of the rose to the brightness of the ruby. I was lost in the fascination of these wonders of the sea, when I was stunned by an unexpected apparition.

In the midst of the waters a man appeared, a diver wearing a leathern purse at his belt. Not a dead body abandoned to the waves, this was a living man, swimming with a powerful stroke, rising occasionally to the surface for air.

I turned towards Captain Nemo, and in an agitated voice exclaimed—

"A man shipwrecked! He must be saved at any cost."

The Captain did not answer me, but came and leaned against the panel.

The man approached again, and with his face flattened against the glass, looked in at us.

To my utter amazement, Captain Nemo signaled to him. The diver waved back, rose immediately to the surface and did not appear again.

"Do not be distressed," said Captain Nemo. "That is Nicholas of Cape Matapan, nicknamed The Fish. He is well known throughout the Cyclades. A bold diver! Water is his element, and he lives in it more than on land, swimming from one island to another, even as far as Crete."

"You know him, Captain?"

"Why not, M. Aronnax?"

Saying which, Captain Nemo went towards a

piece of furniture, a sort of strong box, that stood near the left panel of the saloon. Beside it was a chest ringed with iron bands, a copper plate on its cover, engraved with the initial and the emblem of the *Nautilus*.

The Captain, without paying attention to me, opened the strong box. Inside were a great many ingots.

They were ingots of gold. From whence came all this precious metal, which represented an enormous sum? Where did the Captain find this gold? And what was he going to do with it?

I did not say one word. I looked. Captain Nemo took the ingots one by one, and placed them methodically in the chest, filling it entirely. I estimated the contents at more than 4000 lbs. of gold, that is to say nearly 5,000,000 francs.

The Captain fastened the chest securely and wrote an address on the lid in characters which resembled modern Greek.

This done, Captain Nemo pressed a button, which connected with the quarters of the crew. Four men appeared, and, not without difficulty, pushed the chest out of the saloon. I heard them hoisting it up the iron ladder by means of pulleys.

At that moment, Captain Nemo turned to me.

"And you were saying, sir?" said he.

"I was saying nothing, Captain."

"Then, sir, if you will allow me, I will wish you good-night."

I went to my cabin much troubled, as one may imagine. I vainly tried to sleep—I sought the connecting link between the apparition of the diver and the chest filled with gold. Soon I knew by the pitching and tossing that the *Nautilus* was leaving the depths and rising to the surface.

Then I heard steps upon the deck! and I could tell that the men were unfastening the pinnace and launching it upon the waves. It struck against the side of the *Nautilus*, then all noise ceased.

Two hours later the boat was hoisted on board, replaced in its socket, and the *Nautilus* again plunged under the waves.

So these millions had been transported to their address. At what point on the Continent? Who was Captain Nemo's correspondent?

The next day, I told Conseil and the Canadian the events of the night, which had excited my curiosity to the highest degree. My companions were not less astonished than myself.

"But where does he spend his gold?" asked Ned Land.

To that there was no possible answer. After breakfast I went to the saloon and set to work. I employed myself in arranging my notes, till five o'clock in the evening, when suddenly I felt a heat so great that I was obliged to take off my coat. It was strange, for we were not in the low latitudes; and even when we were, the *Nautilus* experienced little change of temperature underwater. I looked at the manometer; it showed a depth of sixty feet, where the heat of the atmosphere never penetrated.

I continued my work, but the temperature rose to such a degree as to be intolerable.

"Could there be fire on board?" I asked myself.

I was about to leave the saloon, when Captain Nemo entered. He approached the thermometer, consulted it, and turning to me, said—

"Forty-two degrees."

"I have noticed it, Captain," I replied. If it gets much hotter we cannot bear it."

"Oh sir, it will not get hotter if we do not wish."

"You can reduce it as you please, then?"

"No; but I can go further from the cauldron which produces it."

"It is outside then!"

"Certainly. We are floating on a current of boiling water."

"Is it possible!" I exclaimed.

"Look."

The panels opened, and I saw that the sea was entirely white. A sulphurous smoke was curling amid the waves, which boiled like water in a kettle. I placed my hand on one of the panes of glass, but the heat was so great that I quickly removed it.

"Where are we?" I asked.

"Near the island of Santorin, sir," replied the Captain, "in the channel which separates Nea Kamenni from Pali Kamenni. I wished to give you a sight of the curious spectacle of a volcanic eruption underwater."

"I thought," said I, "that the formation of these new islands was ended."

"Nothing is ever ended in the volcanic parts

of the sea," replied Captain Nemo. "The earth is always being disturbed by subterranean fires. In the nineteenth year of our era, according to Cassiodorus and Pliny, a new island called Theia, the goddess, arose in the very place where these islets recently have been formed. Theia sank under the waves, rose again in the year 69, and later sank again. The labors of Pluto have been suspended ever since, until on February 3rd, 1866, a new island emerged from the sulphurous vapor near Nea Kamenni, and sank again three days later. A week afterward, the island of Aphroessa appeared, creating a channel ten yards wide between Nea Kamenni and itself. I was in these seas when the phenomena occurred, and I was able to observe all the different phases. The island of Aphroessa, round in shape, measured 300 feet in diameter, and thirty feet in height. It was composed of black and vitreous lava, mixed with fragments of felspar. Later, on March 10th, a smaller island, called Reka, arose near Nea Kamenni. Since then, all three have joined together, forming one island."

"And the channel where we are at this moment?" I asked.

"Here it is," replied Captain Nemo, showing me a map of the Archipelago. "You see I have marked the new islands."

I returned to the window. The *Nautilus* was no longer moving, the heat was becoming unbearable. The sea had changed from white to red, owing to the presence of salts of iron. In spite of the ship's being hermetically sealed, an insufferable smell of sulphur filled the saloon, and I saw scarlet flames brighter than our electric lights. I was bathed in perspiration; I was strangling; I was being cooked.

"We can remain no longer in this boiling water," I said to the Captain.

"It would not be wise," replied the impassive Captain Nemo.

An order was given. The ship tacked about and left this cauldron that even the *Nautilus* could not brave with impunity. A quarter of an hour later we were on the surface breathing fresh air. The thought struck me that had Ned Land chosen this part of the sea for our flight, we never should have come out of this sea of fire alive.

The next day, February 16th, we departed these waters, which, between Rhodes and Alexandria, are about 1500 fathoms in depth, and, passing Cerigo in the distance, the *Nautilus* rounded Cape Matapan and left the Greek Archipelago.

Chapter 7
The Mediterranean in Forty-eight Hours

The Mediterranean, the bluest of blue seas, the "great" sea of the Hebrews; to the Greeks, "the" sea; to the Romans, "our" sea; bordered by orange-trees, aloes, cacti, and sea-pines; fragrant with the perfume of the myrtle girdled by rugged mountains, bathed in pure, transparent air, but constantly shaken by underground fires, it is a veritable battleground where Neptune and Pluto still dispute who shall rule the world!

Upon these shores, and on these waters, says Michelet, man is renewed by one of the most invigorating climates of the globe. But, beautiful as it was, I could only take a rapid glance at the sea, which covers two million square yards. Captain Nemo's personal knowledge was denied me, for this enigmatical person did not appear once during our passage. The *Nautilus* proceeded underwater at full speed. I estimated our course at about six hundred leagues, and it took us only forty-eight hours. Leaving the shores of Greece on the morning of the 16th of February, we had cleared the Straits of Gibraltar by sunrise on the 18th.

It was plain to me that the Mediterranean, surrounded by those countries which he wished to avoid, was distasteful to Captain Nemo. Those waves and those breezes brought back too many memories, if not too many regrets. Here he no longer had that independence of movement, that liberty of speed which he had in the open sea. He and his *Nautilus* felt cramped between the close shores of Africa and Europe.

Our speed was now twenty-five miles an hour. It goes without saying that Ned Land, to his great disgust, was obliged to renounce his intended flight. He could not launch the pinnace, while we moved at the rate of twelve or thirteen yards every second. To quit the *Nautilus* under such conditions would be as bad as jumping from a train going at full speed—imprudent to say the least. Besides, our vessel only rose to the surface at night to renew its stock of air. It was steered entirely by the compass and the log.

I saw no more of the interior of the Mediterranean than a traveler by express train sees of the landscape which flies before his eyes—only the distant horizon, not the nearer objects which pass like a flash of lightning.

Under the water, brightly lit up by the electric light, glided some of those lampreys, more than a yard long, which are common to almost every climate. Oxyrhynchi, a kind of ray five feet broad, with white belly and gray spotted back were spread out like a large shawl, carried along by the current. Other rays passed so quickly that I could not see if they deserved the name of eagle which was given to them by the ancient Greeks, or the titles of rat, toad, and bat, with which modern fishermen have loaded them. A few milander sharks, twelve feet long, and much feared by divers, shouldered quickly among them. Sea-foxes eight feet long, endowed with wonderful keenness of scent, appeared like large blue shadows. Dorades, some measuring seven and a half feet, showed themselves in their dress of blue and silver. The dorade is consecrated by Venus, its eyes are encased in a socket of gold. It is a precious species, friend of all waters, fresh or salt, an inhabitant of rivers, lakes, and oceans, living in all climates, and bearing all temperature; a race belonging to the geological era of the earth, which has preserved all the beauty of the world's earliest. Magnificent sturgeons, nine or ten yards long, creatures of great speed, striking the panes of glass with their strong tails, displayed their bluish backs with the small brown spots. They resemble sharks, but are not equal to them in strength, and are to be met with in all seas. But of all the diverse inhabitants of the Mediterranean, those I observed to the greatest advantage, when the *Nautilus* approached the surface, belonged to the sixty-third genus of bony fish. They were a kind of tunny, with bluish-black backs, and silvery breastplates, and their dorsal fins threw off sparks of gold. They are said to follow in the wake of vessels seeking refreshing shade from the fire of a tropical sky, and they did not belie the saying, for they accompanied the *Nautilus* as they did in former times the vessel of La Perouse. For many a long hour they struggled to keep up with our vessel. I never tired of admiring these creatures that were really built for speed—small heads, bodies sometimes over nine feet long, lithe and cigar-shaped, their pectoral fins and forked tail endowed with remarkable strength. They swam in a triangle-shaped formation, like flocks of certain birds, whose speed they equaled, and who were credited by the ancients with understanding geometry and strategy. But still they do not escape the Provencals, who esteem them as highly as do the inhabitants of the Propontis and of Italy. These precious, but blind and fool-hardy creatures, perish by the millions in the nets of the Marseillaise.

With regard to the species of fish common to the Atlantic and the Mediterranean, the giddy speed of the *Nautilus* prevented me from observing them with any degree of accuracy.

As to marine mammals, I thought, in passing the entrance to the Adriatic, that I saw two or three cachalots, with one dorsal fin, of the genus physetera, some dolphins of the genus globicephali, peculiar to the Mediterranean, the back part of the head being marked like a zebra with small stripes; also, a dozen of seals three yards long with white bellies and black hair, known by the name of monks, and which really have the air of a Dominican.

As to zoophytes, for a few moments I was able to admire a beautiful orange galeolaria, which had fastened itself to the port panel. It held on by a long filament, and was divided into an infinity of branches, terminating in the finest lace which could ever have been woven by the rivals of Arachne herself. Unfortunately, I could not capture this fine specimen. Doubtless no other Mediterranean zoophyte would have offered itself to my observation, if, on the night of the 16th, the *Nautilus* had not, unexpectedly, slackened its speed, under the following circumstances.

We were passing between Sicily and the coast of Tunis. In the narrow space between Cape Bon and the Straits of Messina, the bottom of the sea rose abruptly. There was a real, underwater hill; its top not more than nine fathoms deep, whilst on either side the depth was ninety fathoms.

The *Nautilus* had to maneuver very carefully to avoid this submarine barrier.

I showed Conseil, on the map of the Mediterranean, the spot occupied by this reef.

"But if you please, sir," observed Conseil, "it is like a real isthmus joining Europe to Africa."

"Yes, my boy, it extends to the Straits of Libya, and the soundings of Smith have proved that in former times the continents were joined between Cape Boco and Cape Furina."

"I can well believe it," said Conseil.

"I will add," I continued, "that a similar underwater hill lies between Gibraltar and Ceuta, which in geological times were the end of the Mediterranean."

"What if some volcanic burst should raise

these two barriers above the waves one day?"

"It is not probable, Conseil."

"Well, but allow me to finish, please, sir. If this phenomenon should take place, it will be troublesome for M. Lesseps, who has taken so much pains to cut through the isthmus of Suez."

"True; but I repeat, Conseil, this phenomenon will never happen. The violence of subterranean force is ever diminishing. Volcanoes, so plentiful in the first days of the world, gradually are being extinguished. The internal heat is lowered, the temperature of the inner strata of the earth is reduced by a perceptible quantity every century, to the detriment of our world, for heat is its life."

"But the sun?"

"The sun is not sufficient, Conseil. Can it give heat to a dead body?"

"Not that I know of."

"Well, my friend, this earth will one day be that cold corpse. It will become uninhabitable and uninhabited like the moon, which has long since lost all its vital heat."

"In how many centuries?"

"In some hundreds of thousands of years, my boy."

"Then," said Conseil, "we shall have time to finish our journey, that is, if Ned Land does not interfere with it."

And Conseil, reassured, returned to the study of the reef which the *Nautilus* was skirting at a moderate speed.

There, beneath the rocky and volcanic bottom, lay outspread a living flora of sponges and reddish cydippes, which emitted a slight phosphorescent light; beroes, commonly known by the name of sea-cucumbers; and walking comatulae more than a yard long, which stained with purple the water all around.

The *Nautilus*, having now passed the high reef in the Libyan Straits, returned to deep water and its accustomed speed. After that, no more molluscs, no more articulates, no more zoophytes; only a few large fish passing like shadows.

During the night of the 16th and 17th February, we had entered the second Mediterranean basin, 1450 fathoms at its greatest depth. The *Nautilus* descended to the bottom of the sea.

On the 18th of February, about three o'clock in the morning, we reached the entrance to the Straits of Gibraltar. Once there existed two currents here: an upper one, long known which brings the waters of the Atlantic into the basin of the Mediterranean; and a lower countercurrent, which science now has proven to exist. Indeed, the volume of water in the Mediterranean, constantly increased by water from the Atlantic, and from rivers flowing into it, each year would raise its level. The evaporation is not sufficient to maintain the equilibrium. As this does not happen, we must necessarily admit the existence of an undercurrent, which carries the surplus waters of the Mediterranean through the Straits of Gibraltar and empties them into the basin of the Atlantic. A fact indeed; and it was this counter-current by which the *Nautilus* profited. It advanced rapidly through the narrow pass. For one instant I caught a glimpse of the beautiful ruins of the temple of Hercules, drowned, according to Pliny, along with the low island which supported it. A few minutes later we were sailing on the Atlantic.

Chapter 8
Vigo Bay

The Atlantic! A vast expanse of water, covering twenty-five million square miles, nine thousand miles long, with a mean breadth of two thousand seven hundred miles. Important sea, almost ignored by the ancients, except perhaps the Carthaginians, those Dutchmen of long ago, who, in their trading voyages, explored the western coasts of Europe and Africa. Ocean whose shores, winding through many latitudes, embrace an immense perimeter, fed by some of the world's greatest rivers. The St. Lawrence, the Mississippi, the Amazon, the Plata, the Orinoco, the Niger, the Senegal, the Elbe, the Loire and the Rhine, all bring water to the Atlantic from the most civilized lands, as well as from the most savage. A magnificent plain of water, ploughed by the ships of every nation, shielded by the flags of every nation, and ending at last in those two terrible points dreaded by all mariners—Cape Horn and the Cape of Tempests!

The *Nautilus*, leaving the Straits of Gibraltar, had taken to the open sea. It returned to the surface and our daily walks on the deck were restored to us.

I went up at once, accompanied by Ned Land and Conseil. About twelve miles away, Cape St. Vincent, the southwestern point of the Spanish peninsula, was dimly to be seen. A strong southerly gale was blowing. The sea was heavy, and the *Nautilus* pitched and rolled. It was almost impossible to keep one's footing on the deck, which was pounded by the waves. So, after inhaling some mouthfuls of fresh air, we went below.

I returned to my room, Conseil to his cabin; but the Canadian, with a preoccupied air, followed me. Our rapid journey through the Mediterranean had not allowed him to put his project into execution, and he could not help showing his disappointment. When the door of my room was shut, he sat down and looked at me silently.

"Friend Ned," said I, "I understand you. But you cannot reproach yourself. To have attempted to leave the *Nautilus* under the circumstances would have been madness."

Ned Land did not answer. His tight lips and scowling brow indicated the strength of his obsession.

"Let us see," I continued. "We need not despair yet. We are going up the coast of Portugal. In France and England we can easily find refuge. Now, if the *Nautilus*, on leaving the

Straits of Gibraltar, had gone to the south, taking us towards regions where there are no continents, I should share your uneasiness. But we know now that Captain Nemo does not shun civilized seas, and before too long I think you can proceed in safety."

Ned Land still stared at me, but at length his lips parted, and he said, "It is for tonight."

I got up suddenly. I was, I admit, little prepared for this communication. I wanted to answer the Canadian, but words would not come.

"We agreed to wait for an opportunity," continued Ned Land, "and the opportunity has arrived. This night we shall be but a few miles from the Spanish coast. It will be dark. The wind is brisk. I have your word, M. Aronnax, and I rely upon you."

As I was still silent, the Canadian approached me.

"Tonight, at nine o'clock," said he. "I have warned Conseil. At that moment, Captain Nemo will be in his room, probably in bed. Neither the engineers nor the sailors will see us. Conseil and I will go to the main ladder and you, M. Aronnax, will wait in the library for my signal. The oars, the mast, and the sail, are in the small boat. I have even managed to put some provisions aboard. I have a wrench, to unfasten the bolts which fasten the boat to the hull of the *Nautilus*. So all is ready, for tonight."

"The sea is bad."

"True," replied the Canadian. "But we must risk it. Liberty is worth the price. Besides, the boat is strong, and a few miles, with a fair wind behind us, is no great difficulty. Who knows if tomorrow we may be a hundred leagues away. If luck favors us by ten or twelve o'clock we shall be on solid earth, or we shall be dead. Good-bye till tonight.''

With these words, the Canadian left, leaving me in a state of shock. I had imagined that, when the time came, I should have time to reflect and discuss the matter. My obstinate companion had given me no time; and, after all, what could I have said to him? Ned Land was perfectly right. When could we expect a better chance? Could I retract my word, and take upon myself the responsibility of compromising the future of my companions? Tomorrow Captain Nemo might take us a thousand miles from land.

At that moment a loud hissing told me that the air tanks were filling, and that the *Nautilus* was sinking under the Atlantic.

I passed a sad day torn between the desire to regain my freedom and the grief of abandoning the wonderful *Nautilus* and leaving my studies unfinished.

What fearful hours! Sometimes I saw myself and companions safely landed. Sometimes, in spite of my reason, I hoped that some unforeseen circumstances would prevent Ned Land's project from being carried out.

Twice I went to the saloon to consult the compass. I wished to see if the course of the *Nautilus* was taking us away from the shore. But no; the *Nautilus* continued in Portuguese waters.

I must therefore do my part, and prepare for flight. My luggage was not heavy. My notes weighed nothing.

As to Captain Nemo, I asked myself what he would think of our escape. What trouble, what ill might it cause him, and what might he do in case of discovery or failure? Certainly I had no cause to complain of him. On the contrary, never was hospitality freer than his. But I could not be taxed with ingratitude for taking leave. No oath bound us to him. It was on the force of circumstances he relied, and not upon our word, to hold us forever.

I had not seen the Captain in several days. Would chance bring us together before our departure? I wished it, and feared it at the same time. I listened for his footsteps in the next room, but heard nothing. I felt an unbearable tension. The day seemed eternal.

My dinner was served in my room as usual. I ate but little, I was too preoccupied. At seven o'clock I left the table. A hundred and twenty minutes still separated me from the moment in which I was to join Ned Land and Conseil. My agitation increased. My pulse pounded. I could not stay still. I walked back and forth, seeking to calm my troubled spirit. The prospect of failure in our rash enterprise was the least painful of my anxieties. But the thought of being found out before we could get away, of being brought before Captain Nemo, and finding him angered or, worse, hurt by my desertion, made my heart thump.

I wanted to see the saloon one last time. I went below to the museum where I had passed so many valuable and pleasant hours. I looked on all its riches, all its treasures, like a man on the eve of an eternal exile. These wonders of Nature, these masterpieces of art, upon which my life had been concentrated for so many days—I was about to abandon them forever! I longed to take a last look through the saloon windows into the waters of the Atlantic: but the panels were hermetically closed, and a wall of steel separated me from that ocean which I had not yet explored.

Going through the saloon, I came near the door, which opened at the angle into the Captain's room. To my great surprise, this door stood ajar. I drew back, involuntarily. If Captain Nemo should be there, he could see me. But, hearing no noise, I drew nearer. The room seemed deserted. I pushed open the door, and stepped inside. Only the same monastic severity of aspect.

I thought about the noble soul of Captain Nemo and wondered if I should ever solve his mysteries. Was he a champion of oppressed peoples, a liberator of the enslaved? Did he take part in the political and social struggles of our age?

Suddenly the clock struck eight. The first beat of the hammer on the bell roused me from my dreams. I trembled as if an invisible eye had penetrated into my most secret thoughts, and I hurried from the room.

In the saloon, my eye fell upon the compass. Our course was still north. The log indicated moderate speed, the manometer a depth of about sixty feet.

I returned to my room, dressed warmly—sea boots, an otterskin cap, a woolen great-coat lined with sealskin, I was ready, I was waiting. Only the vibration of the screw broke the deep silence which reigned on board. I could not imagine where Nemo might be. I listened attentively. Would a loud voice suddenly tell me that Ned Land had been taken by surprise? A mortal dread hung over me. I tried in vain to calm my fears.

A few minutes before nine, I put my ear to the Captain's door. No sound. I went back to the saloon, which was half in darkness, but deserted.

I opened the door to the library. The same light, the same solitude. I stood near the door leading to the main ladder, and waited for Ned Land's signal.

At that moment the vibration of the screw diminished perceptibly, then stopped dead. The silence now was broken only by the beating of my own heart. Suddenly I felt a slight shock; and I knew that the *Nautilus* had come to the bottom of the ocean. My anxiety intensified. The Canadian's signal did not come. I wanted to go to Ned Land and beg him to put off his attempt. I felt something strange in the atmosphere of the *Nautilus*.

The door of the large saloon opened, and Captain Nemo appeared. He saw me, and, without further preamble, began in an amiable tone of voice.

"Ah, sir! I have been looking for you. Do you know the history of Spain?"

Now, one might know the history of one's own country by heart; but in my state of mind I could not have uttered a word of it.

"Well," continued Captain Nemo, "you heard my question? Do you know the history of Spain?"

"Very poorly," I managed to answer.

"Well, many scholars are unfamiliar with it," said the Captain. "Come, sit down, and I will tell you a curious episode in this history. It will interest you, by the way, for it will answer a question which I think you have not been able to solve."

"I am listening, Captain," said I, not knowing where my instructor was leading to, and asking myself if this incident had a bearing on our attempted flight.

"Sir," said the Captain, "if you have no objection, we will go back to 1702. You must know that your king, Louis XIV, thinking that a show of strength was sufficient to bring the Pyrenees under his yoke, had imposed his grandson, the Duke of Anjou, on the Spaniards. This prince reigned more or less badly under the name of Philip V, and strong opposition to him grew up abroad. Indeed, the preceding year, the royal houses of Holland, Austria, and England, had concluded a treaty of alliance at The Hague, with the intention of plucking the crown of Spain from the head of Philip V, and placing it on that of an archduke to whom they prematurely gave the title of Charles III.

"Philip had to resist this coalition; but he was almost entirely lacking in either soldiers or sailors. However, money would not fail him, provided that galleons, laden with gold and silver from America, could enter their ports. And at about the end of the year a rich convoy was expected. France was escorting the convoy with a fleet of twenty-three vessels, commanded by Admiral Chateau-Renaud, for the warships of the coalition already were beating the Atlantic. This convoy was going to Cadiz, but the Admiral, hearing that an English fleet was cruising in those waters, resolved to make for a French port.

"The Spanish commanders of the convoy objected to this decision. They wanted to be taken to a Spanish port, if not to Cadiz, then to Vigo Bay, on the northwest coast of Spain, which was not blockaded.

"Admiral Chateau-Renaud was so weak as to obey this injunction, and the galleons entered Vigo Bay.

"Unfortunately, this was an open anchorage with no defenses at all. Therefore the galleons had to be unloaded quickly before the arrival of the English fleet. They would have succeeded had not a miserable question of rivalry suddenly arisen.

"You are following the chain of events?" asked Captain Nemo.

"Perfectly," said I, not yet knowing why I was getting this lesson in history.

"I will continue. This is what happened. The merchants of Cadiz had the privilege of receiving all goods coming from the West Indies. Now, to disembark these ingots of gold and silver at the port of Vigo, was depriving these merchants of their rights. They complained at Madrid, and obtained the consent of the weak-minded Philip for the convoy to remain in the anchorage of Vigo without unloading until the enemy had disappeared.

"But whilst this decision was being reached, on the 22nd of October, 1702, the English fleet arrived in Vigo Bay. Admiral Chateau-Renaud, in spite of inferior forces, fought bravely. But, seeing that the treasure must fall into the enemy's hands, he burnt and scuttled every galleon, all of which went to the bottom bearing their immense riches."

Captain Nemo stopped. I could not yet see why this history should interest me.

"Well?" I asked.

"Well, M. Aronnax," replied Captain Nemo, "we are now in Vigo Bay; and it rests with yourself whether you will penetrate its mysteries."

The Captain rose, telling me to follow him. I had had time to recover. I obeyed. The saloon was dark, but through the transparent glass the waves were sparkling.

For half a mile around the *Nautilus*, the waters seemed bathed in electric light. The sandy bottom was clean and bright. Some of the ship's crew in their diving suits were clearing away half rotten barrels and empty cases from the midst of the blackened wrecks. From these cases and barrels slipped ingots of gold and silver, cascades of piasters and jewels. The sand was heaped with them. Laden with their precious booty the men returned to the *Nautilus*, disposed of their burden, and went back to this inexhaustible fishery of gold and silver.

I understood now. This was the scene of the battle of the 22nd of October, 1702. Here on this very spot the galleons destined for King

Philip and the Spanish government had sunk. Here Captain Nemo came, according to his needs, to pack up those millions with which he burdened the *Nautilus*. It was for him and him alone that South America had given up her precious metals. He was heir direct, without anyone to share, in those treasures torn from the Incas by conquests of Hernando Cortez.

"Did you know, sir," he asked, smiling, "that the sea contained such riches?"

"I knew," I answered, "that gold sunk in these waters is estimated at two million tons."

"Doubtless; but to raise this gold by ordinary means the expense would be greater than the profit. Here, on the contrary, I have but to pick up what man has lost—and not only in Vigo Bay, but in a thousand other spots where shipwrecks have occurred and which are marked on my chart of the ocean's bottom. Can you understand now the extent of my wealth?"

"I understand, Captain. But allow me to tell you that in exploring Vigo Bay you soon will have a rival."

"Who?"

"A company has been formed which has received from the Spanish government the privilege of seeking these buried galleons. The shareholders are led on by the allure of an enormous bounty, for these rich shipwrecks are valued at five hundred millions."

"Five hundred millions they were," answered Captain Nemo, "but they are so no longer."

"Just so," said I; "and a warning to those shareholders would be an act of charity. But who knows if it would be well received? What gamblers usually regret above all is less the loss of their money, than of their foolish hopes. After all, I pity them less than the thousands of unfortunates who could benefit from the distribution of these riches, which will always be sterile."

I had no sooner expressed this sentiment, than I felt that I had wounded Captain Nemo.

"Sterile!" he exclaimed, with animation. "Do you think, sir, that these riches are lost because I gather them? Is it for myself alone, according to your idea, that I take the trouble to collect these treasures? Who told you that I did not make a good use of it? Do you think I am unaware that there are suffering people and oppressed races on this earth, unhappy creatures to be consoled, victims to be avenged? Do you not understand?"

Captain Nemo stopped, regretting perhaps that he had spoken so much. But I had long ago guessed that, whatever the motive which had driven him to seek his independence under the sea, it had left him still a man. His heart still beat for the sufferings of humanity, and his immense charity was for oppressed peoples as well as individuals. And I knew that those millions which were dispatched by Captain Nemo when the *Nautilus* was cruising in the waters of Crete, were destined to those who rebelled against Turkish cruelty and tyranny.

Chapter 9

A Vanished Continent

The next morning, the 19th of February, the Canadian came to my room. I expected this visit. He looked very disappointed.

"Well, sir?" said he.

"Well, Ned, fortune was against us yesterday."

"Yes, that Captain must needs stop exactly at the hour when we planned to leave his vessel."

"Yes, Ned, he had business at his banker's."

"His banker's!"

"Or rather his banking-house. By that I mean the ocean, where his riches are safer than in the coffers of the State."

I then related to the Canadian the incidents of the preceding night, hoping to dissuade him from abandoning the Captain. But my recital had no other effect than a forcefully expressed regret that Ned had not been able to tour the battlefield of Vigo on his own account.

"However," said he, "all is not ended. Only a single blow of the harpoon is lost. Another time we must succeed; and tonight, if necessary—"

"In what direction is the *Nautilus* going?" I asked.

"I do not know," replied Ned.

"Well, at noon we shall see the position."

The Canadian returned to Conseil. As soon as I was dressed, I went into the Saloon. The compass was not reassuring. The course of the *Nautilus* was S.S.W. We were turning our backs on Europe.

I waited with some impatience till the ship's position was marked on the chart. At about half-past eleven the tanks were emptied, and our vessel rose to the surface. I rushed on deck. Ned Land had preceded me. No more land in sight. Nothing but an immense sea. Some sails on the horizon, doubtless bound for San Roque in search of favorable winds for rounding the Cape of Good Hope. The sky was cloudy. A gale was building up. Ned raved, and tried to see through the cloudy horizon. He still hoped that behind all that fog stretched the land he so longed for.

At noon the sun came out for an instant. The lieutenant took a bearing from its altitude. Then the sea becoming rougher, we went below.

An hour later, upon consulting the chart, I saw the position of the *Nautilus* was marked at 16^0 $17'$ longitude, and 33^0 $22'$ latitude, 150 leagues from the nearest shore. There was no possibility of flight, and I leave you to imagine the rage of the Canadian, when I informed him of our situation.

For myself, I was not particularly sorry. I felt relieved of a burden which had oppressed me, and was able to return with some degree of calmness to my accustomed work.

That night, about eleven o'clock, I received a most unexpected visit from Captain Nemo. He asked me very graciously if I felt fatigued from my watch of the preceding night. I answered in the negative.

"Then, M. Aronnax, I propose a curious expedition."

"Propose, Captain, by all means!"

"You have hitherto visited the ocean depths by only day, in the sunlight. Would it suit you to see them in the darkness of night?"

"Certainly!"

"I warn you, the way will be tiring. We shall have far to walk, and must climb a mountain. The paths are rough."

"What you say, Captain, only heightens my curiosity; I am ready to follow you."

"Come then, sir, we will put on our diving suits."

Arrived at the dressing room, I saw that neither my companions nor any of the ship's crew were to follow us on this excursion. Captain Nemo had not even suggested my taking with me Ned or Conseil.

In a few moments we had put on our diving suits. The men placed the tanks of air on our backs, but no electric lamps were provided. I called this to the Captain's attention.

"They will be useless," he replied.

I thought I had not heard aright, but I could say no more, for the Captain's head had already disappeared into its metal case. I put on the rest of my gear. An iron-pointed stick was put in my hand, and soon we set foot on the bottom of the Atlantic, at a depth of 150 fathoms. Midnight was near. The waters were profoundly dark, but Captain Nemo pointed out in the distance a reddish glow, some kind of large light that must be shining brilliantly, about two miles from the *Nautilus*. What this fire might be, what could fuel it, why and how it lit up the waters, I could not guess. In any case, it did light our way, dimly, it is true, but I soon accustomed myself to the strange darkness, and I understood, under such circumstances, the uselessness of the Ruhmkorff apparatus.

As we went forward, I heard a kind of pattering above my head. The noise increased and became continuous. I soon understood the cause. It was raining hard up above. Instinctively the thought flashed across my mind that I should be wet through! At the bottom of the ocean! I could not help laughing at the notion. But, indeed, in the thick diving suit, one no longer is aware of the water, and one seems only to be in an atmosphere somewhat denser than that on earth.

After half an hour the ground became stony. Medusae, microscopic crustacea, and pennatules lit it slightly with their phosphorescent gleam. I caught a glimpse of pieces of stone covered with millions of zoophytes, and masses of seaweed. My feet often slipped upon this viscous carpet, and without my iron-tipped stick

I should have fallen more than once. Turning, I could see the lantern of the *Nautilus* beginning to pale in the distance.

But the rosy light which guided us grew brighter and lit up the distance. The presence of this fire underwater puzzled me in the highest degree. Was it some electric effulgence? Was I going towards a natural phenomenon as yet unknown to scholars of the world? Or even had the hand of man something to do with this conflagration? Had man fanned this flame? Was I to meet in these depths comrades and friends of Captain Nemo whom he was going to visit, and who, like him, led this strange existence? Should I find down there a whole colony of exiles, who, weary of the miseries of this earth, had sought and found independence in the ocean depths? These foolish and unreasonable ideas would not let me alone. In this state of mind, overexcited by the succession of wonders continually passing before my eyes, I should not have been surprised to find at the bottom of the sea one of those underwater cities of which Captain Nemo dreamed.

Our road grew lighter and lighter. The glimmer came from the top of a mountain about 800 feet high. But the light I saw was only reflected by the water. The true source of this light was the inexplicable fire beyond the mountain.

In the midst of the stony maze, which lay at the bottom of the Atlantic, Captain Nemo advanced without hesitation. He knew this hard road. I followed him with unshakable confidence. He seemed to me like one of the gods of the sea. As he walked ahead of me, I could not help admiring his tall stature, which was outlined in black on the luminous horizon.

It was one in the morning when we arrived at the first slopes of the mountain; but to climb to them we must go along the rough paths of a large wood.

Yes; a wood of dead trees, without leaves, without sap, trees turned to stone by the action of the water, which here and there were overtopped by gigantic pines. They were like coal in a mine, only standing up, holding by their roots to the broken soil. Their branches, like fine black paper cuttings, showed clearly against a watery ceiling. Picture to yourself a forest in the Hartz, clinging to the sides of the mountain, but a drowned forest. The paths were littered with seaweed and fucus, among which crawled a whole world of crustacea. I went along, climbing the rocks, striding over extended trunks, breaking the sea bind-weed, which hung from one tree to the next; and frightening the fishes, which flew from branch to branch. Pressing onward, I felt no fatigue. I followed my guide, who never tired. What a spectacle! How can I express it? How paint the aspect of those woods and rocks—their under parts dark and wild, the upper, colored with red tints, whose brightness was doubled by the reflecting powers of the water? We climbed over rocks, which fell behind us with the deep roar of an avalanche. To right and left long, dark galleries were hollowed out. Vast clearings opened up which seemed made by the hand of man; and I asked myself if some inhabitant of these submarine regions would not soon appear before me.

Captain Nemo was still climbing. I could linger, but I followed without fear. My stick was a great help. A false step would have been dangerous on the narrow paths that bordered the chasms. But I walked with firm step, without feeling any giddiness. Now I jumped a crevasse whose depth would have made me hesitate among the glaciers on land; now I ventured on the unsteady trunk of a tree, thrown across one abyss to the other side, without looking under my feet, having only eyes to admire the wild scenery of this region.

Monumental rocks, resting on irregularly cut bases, seemed to defy all laws of balance. From between their stony knees, trees sprang, like a jet under heavy pressure, and upheld others which upheld themselves. Natural towers, large sections of rock, cut to a point like the curtains on a bed, inclined at an angle which the laws of gravitation could never have tolerated in terrestrial regions.

Two hours after leaving the *Nautilus*, we had crossed the tree line, and a hundred feet above our heads rose the top of the mountain, casting a shadow over the brilliant light beyond. Some petrified shrubs grew here and there in grotesque shapes. Fishes rose under our feet like pheasants in tall grass. The massive rocks were broken by impenetrable fissures, deep caves and unfathomable holes, at the bottom of which formidable creatures could be heard moving. My blood curdled when I saw enormous antennae blocking my way, or a frightful claw closing with a bang in the shadow of some cavity. Millions of luminous spots shone brightly in the midst of the darkness. They were the eyes of giant crustacea crouched in their holes; huge lobsters setting themselves up like halberdiers, and moving their claws with the clicking sound of rifles; titanic crabs, poised like a cannon on its carriage; and frightful looking polyps, interweaving their tentacles like a living nest of serpents.

We had now arrived on the first plateau, where other surprises awaited me. Before us lay some picturesque ruins, which betrayed the hand of man, and not that of the Creator. There were vast heaps of stone, amongst which might be traced the dim and shadowy forms of castles and temples, clothed with a world of blossoming zoophytes. Instead of ivy, seaweed and fucus covered them with a thick green mantle. But what was this part of the world which had been swallowed by cataclysms? Who had arranged these rocks and stones like the tombs and monuments of prehistoric times? Where was I? Whither had Captain Nemo's fancy hurried me?

I would fain have asked him; not being able to, I stopped him—I seized his arm. But shaking his head, and pointing to the highest point of the mountain, he seemed to say—

"Come, come along; come higher!"

I followed, and in a few minutes I had climbed to the peak, which, for only a dozen yards, commanded the entire mass of rock.

I looked down the side we had just climbed. It was not more than seven or eight hundred feet down to the plain we came from; but on the other side, the mountain was more than twice that height. My eyes ranged far over a large space lit by a violent refulgence. In fact, this mountain was a volcano!

Fifty feet above the peak, in a shower of stones and scoriae, a large crater was vomiting forth torrents of lava which fell in a cascade of fire into the bottom of the ocean. Thus situated, this volcano lit the lower plain like an immense torch, even to the farthest limits of the horizon. I stated that the crater threw up lava, but no flames. Flames require the oxygen of the air to feed upon, and cannot be developed under water; but streams of lava, containing in themselves the elements of incandescence, can attain a white heat, fight vigorously against the liquid element, and turn it into steam on contact.

Rapid currents bearing all these gases in diffusion, and torrents of lava, slid to the bottom of the mountain like an eruption of Vesuvius over ancient Tuscany.

There, indeed, under my eyes, ruined, destroyed, lay a city—its roofs open to the sky, its temples fallen, its arches displaced, its columns lying on the ground in which one still could recognize the massive character of Tuscan architecture. Further on, were the remains of a gigantic aqueduct; here the high base of an acropolis, with the floating outlines of another Parthenon; there were traces of a quay, as if an ancient port had once existed here, on the borders of the ocean, only to disappear with its merchant vessels and its triremes of war. Further still, showed long lines of sunken walls and broad deserted streets—a perfect Pompeii sunk beneath the ocean. Such was the sight that Captain Nemo brought before my eyes!

Where was I? Where was I? I must know, at any cost. I tried to speak, but Captain Nemo stopped me by a gesture, and picking up a piece of chalk stone, went to a rock of black basalt, and traced the one word—

ATLANTIS.

What light shot through my mind! Atlantis, the ancient Meropis of Theopompus, the Atlantis of Plato, that continent denied by Origen, Jamblichus, d'Anville, Malte-Brun, and Humboldt, who placed its disappearance amongst the legendary tales admitted by Posidonius, Pliny, Ammianus, Marcellinus, Tertullian, Engel, Buffon, and d'Avezac. I had it there now before my eyes, displaying the unquestionable evidence of the catastrophe that overtook it. The region thus engulfed lay beyond Europe, Asia, and Libya, beyond the columns of Hercules, where lived those powerful people, the Atlantides, against whom the first wars of ancient Greece were waged.

Thus, led by the strangest destiny, I was treading under foot the mountains of this continent, touching with my hand those ruins a thousand generations old, built during the geological epochs. I was walking on the very spot where the contemporaries of the first man had walked.

Whilst I was trying to fix in my mind every detail of this magnificient landscape, Captain Nemo stood like a statue, as if petrified in silent ectasy, leaning on a mossy stone. Was he dreaming of those generations long since disappeared? Was he asking them the secret of human destiny? Was it here this strange man came to steep himself in historical recollections, and live again this ancient life—he who wanted no modern one? What would I not have given to know his thoughts, to share them, to understand them! We remained for an hour at this place, contemplating the vast plain under the light from the volcano which was sometimes wonderfully intense. The boiling heat inside the mountain caused shudders to run down its sides. Sounds were transmitted clearly through the water, and echoed back with majestic grandeur. Now the moon appeared through the mass of water and over our heads, shed her pale rays on the buried continent. It was but a gleam, but what an indescribable effect! The Captain rose, cast one last look on the immense plain, and gestured for me to follow him.

We went down the mountain rapidly, and once through the petrified forest, I saw the lantern of the *Nautilus* shining like a star. The Captain walked straight to it, and we got on board as the first moving light played on the surface of the ocean.

Chapter 10
The Submarine Coal Mines

The next day, the 20th of February, I awoke very late. The labors of the previous night had prolonged my sleep until eleven o'clock. I dressed quickly, and hastened to find the course the *Nautilus* was taking. The instruments showed the course to be still towards the south, at a speed of twenty miles an hour, and a depth of fifty fathoms.

The species of fishes here did not differ much from those already observed. There were rays of giant size, five yards long, and endowed with great muscular strength which enabled them to leap above the waves; sharks of many kinds, amongst others, a glaucus fifteen feet long, with triangular sharp teeth, and almost transparent brown sagrae, humantins, prism-shaped, and with a hide full of little tubes, sturgeons, resembling their relatives in the Mediterranean;

trumpet syngnathes, a foot and a half long, having grayish bladders, no teeth or tongue, and being supple as snakes.

Amongst bony fish, Conseil noticed some blackish makairas, about three yards long, armed at the upper jaw with a sharp sword, other bright colored creatures, known in the time of Aristotle by the name of the sea-dragon, which are dangerous to capture on account of the spikes on their back; also some coryphaenes, whose brown backs are marked with little blue stripes, and edged with a gold border; some beautiful dorades; and swordfish four-and-twenty feet long, swimming in troops, fierce animals, but herbivorous rather than carnivorous.

About four o'clock, the soil, commonly composed of a thick mud mixed with petrified wood, changed by degrees and became more stony, seeming strewn with conglomerate and pieces of basalt, with a sprinkling of lava and sulphurous obsidian. I thought that a mountainous region was succeeding the long plains; and accordingly, from certain motions of the *Nautilus*, I could tell that the southerly horizon was blocked by high walls which seemed to close all exit. Its height evidently exceeded the level of the ocean. It must be a continent, or at least an island—one of the Canaries, or the Cape Verde Islands. The bearings not having been taken yet, perhaps I was deliberately being kept in ignorance of our exact position. In any case, such a wall seemed to me to mark the limits of Atlantis, of which we had really seen so little.

Much longer should I have remained at the window, admiring the beauties of sea and sky, but the panels closed, just as the *Nautilus* reached the fort of this high perpendicular wall. What it would do now, I could not guess. I returned to my room; the ship was still. I laid myself down with the full intention of waking after a few hours sleep. But it was eight o'clock the next day when I entered the saloon. I looked at the manometer. It told me that the *Nautilus* was floating on the surface. Hearing steps on the deck I went to the panel. It was open; but, instead of broad daylight, as I expected, I was surrounded by profound darkness. Where were we? Was I mistaken? Was it still night? No; not a star was shining, and night has not that utter darkness.

I knew not what to think when a voice near me said—

"Is that you, Professor?"

"Ah! Captain," I answered, "where are we?"

"Underground, sir."

"Underground!" I exclaimed. "And the *Nautilus* floating still?"

"It always floats."

"But I do not understand."

"Wait a few minutes, our lantern will be lit, and if you like light places, you will be satisfied."

I stood on the deck and waited. The darkness was so complete that I could not even see Captain Nemo; but looking to the zenith, exactly above my head, I seemed to see an uncertain gleam, a kind of twilight through a circular hole. At this instant the lantern was lit, and its vividness dispelled the faint light. I closed my dazzled eyes for an instant, and then looked again. The *Nautilus* was stationary, floating on a lake near a mountain which formed a sort of quay. The lake was imprisoned by a circle of walls, measuring two miles in diameter and six in circumference. Its level (the manometer showed) could only be the same as the lake and the sea. The high walls, leaning forward on their base, grew into a vaulted roof shaped like an immense inverted funnel, the height being about five or six hundred yards. At the top was a circular orifice, through which I had caught the slight gleam of light, evidently daylight.

"Where are we?" I asked.

"In the very heart of an extinct volcano, the interior of which has been invaded by the sea, after some great convulsion of the earth. Whilst you were sleeping, Professor, the *Nautilus* penetrated to this lagoon through a natural channel which lets out about ten yards beneath the surface of the ocean. This is the harbor of refuge for the *Nautilus*, safe, commodious, and unknown, sheltered from all gales. Show me, if you can, on the coasts of any of your continents or islands, an anchorage which can give such perfect refuge from all storms."

"Certainly," I replied, "you are in safety here, Captain Nemo. Who could reach you in the heart of a volcano? But did I not see an opening at its summit?"

"Yes; its crater, formerly filled with lava,

vapor, and flames, and which now gives entrance to the life-giving air we breathe."

"But what is this volcanic mountain?"

"It is part of one of the numerous islands with which this sea is strewn—to vessels a simple reef—to us an immense cavern. Chance led me to discover it, and chance served me well."

"But of what use is this refuge, Captain? The *Nautilus* needs no port."

"No, sir; but it needs electricity to make it move, and the materials to make the electricity—sodium to feed the electrical elements, coal from which to get the sodium and a coal-mine to supply the coal. And exactly on this spot the sea covers entire forests embedded during the geological periods, which have turned into coal. For me they are an inexhaustible supply."

"Your men follow the trade of miners here, then, Captain?"

"Exactly so. These mines extend under the waves like those of Newcastle. Here, in their diving suits armed with shovels, my men extract the coal, so that I do not ask even that from the mines of the earth. When I burn this material in the manufacture of sodium, the smoke escaping from the crater of the mountain, gives it the appearance of a still active volcano."

"And we shall see your companions at work?"

"No; not this time at least; for I am in a hurry to continue our submarine tour of the earth. So I shall content myself with drawing on the reserve of sodium I already possess. The time allowed for loading is only one day; then we will continue our voyage. So if you wish to see the cavern, and tour the lagoon, you must take advantage of today, M. Aronnax.''

I thanked the Captain, and went to look for my companions, who had not yet left their cabin. I invited them to follow me without saying where we were. They came up on deck. Conseil, who was astonished at nothing, seemed to regard it as quite natural that he should wake under a mountain, after having fallen asleep under the ocean. But Ned Land thought only of trying to find a way of escape from the cavern. After breakfast, about ten o'clock, we went down to the mountain.

"Here we are, once more on land," said Conseil.

"I do not call this land," said the Canadian, "and besides, we are not on it, but beneath it.''

Between the mountain and the lake lay a sandy shore, which, at its greatest breadth measured five hundred feet. On this soil one might easily walk around the lake. But at the base of the high walls was stony ground, with volcanic blocks and enormous pumice stones lying about in picturesque heaps. All these had a covering of enamel, polished by the action of the subterranean fires, and shone resplendent in the light of our electric lantern. The mica dust from the shore rising under our feet, flew like a cloud of sparks. The ground began to rise, and we soon arrived at long circuitous slopes, or inclined planes, which took us higher by degrees. But we were obliged to walk carefully, because the surface was formed of conglomerates, bound by no cement, our feet flipping on the glassy trachyte, composed of crystal, felspar, and quartz.

The volcanic nature of this enormous excavation was confirmed on all sides, and I pointed it out to my companions.

"Picture to yourselves," said I, "what this crater must have been like when filled with boiling lava, and when the level of the incandescent liquid rose out of the orifice of the mountain, as though melting on top of a hot plate."

"I can picture it perfectly," said Conseil. "But, sir, will you tell me why the Great Architect has suspended operations, and how it is that the furnace is replaced by the quiet waters of the lake?"

"Most probably, Conseil, because some convulsion beneath the ocean produced that very opening which has served as a channel for the *Nautilus*. Then the waters of the Atlantic rushed into the interior of the mountain. There must have been a terrible struggle between the two elements, a struggle which ended in the victory of Neptune. But many ages have run out since then, and the submerged volcano is now a peaceful grotto."

"Very well," replied Ned Land. "I accept the explanation, sir; but, in our own interests, I regret that the opening of which you speak was not made above the level of the sea."

"But, friend Ned," said Conseil, "if the passage had not been under the sea, the *Nautilus* could not have gone through it."

We continued climbing. The path became more and more steep and narrow. There were deep excavations which we had to step over;

sliding rock had to be avoided. We got upon our knees and crawled along. But Conseil's dexterity and the Canadian's strength surmounted all obstacles. At a height of about thirty-one yards the nature of the ground changed without becoming any easier to walk on. Black basalt followed the conglomerate and trachyte, the first spread out in layers full of bubbles, the basalt forming regular prisms, arranged in a colonnade which supported the sides of the immense vault, an admirable specimen of natural architecture. Between the blocks of basalt wound long streams of lava, long since grown cold, encrusted with bituminous coal; and some parts were covered by large carpets of sulphur. A brighter day shone through the upper crater, shedding a faint glow over these geological distortions buried for all time in the heart of this dead volcano.

Our upward march was halted at a height of about two hundred and fifty feet. We were too close to the arch of the vaulted walls, and our climb became a circular walk. At the last level vegetable life began to struggle with the mineral. Some shrubs, and even some trees, grew from the fissures in the walls. I recognized some euphorbias, with the caustic sugar coming from them; heliotropes, quite incapable of justifying their name, sadly drooped their clusters of flowers, both their color and perfume half gone. Here and there some chrysanthemums grew timidly at the foot of an aloe with long sickly-looking leaves. But between the streams of lava, I saw some little violets still slightly perfumed, and I admit that I smelt them with delight. Perfume is the soul of the flower, and sea-flowers, those splendid hydrophytes, have no soul.

We had arrived at the foot of some sturdy dragon trees, which had pushed aside the rocks with their strong roots, when Ned Land exclaimed—

"Ah! sir, a hive! a hive!"

"A hive!" I replied, with a gesture of incredulity.

"Yes, a hive," repeated the Canadian, "and bees humming round it."

I approached, and was forced to believe my own eyes. There, in a hole bored in one of the dragon trees, were some thousands of these ingenious insects, so common to all the Canaries, whose produce is so much esteemed. Naturally enough, the Canadian wished to gather the honey, and I could not well oppose his wish. With a spark from his flint, he set fire to a pile of dry leaves, mixed with sulphur, and he began to smoke out the bees. The humming ceased by degrees, and eventually the hive yielded several pounds of the sweetest honey, with which Ned Land filled his haversack.

"When I have mixed this honey with the paste of the bread-fruit," said he, "I shall be able to offer you a succulent cake."

"Upon my word," said Conseil, "it will be gingerbread."

"Never mind the gingerbread," said I. "Let us continue our interesting walk."

At every turn of the path we were following, the lake appeared in all its length and breadth.

The lantern lit up the whole of its tranquil surface, which knew neither ripple nor wave. The *Nautilus* remained perfectly motionless. On the deck and on the mountain, the ship's crew were working, like black shadows clearly outlined against the luminous atmosphere. We were not going round the highest crest of the top layers of rock which upheld the roof. I then saw that bees were not the only representatives of the animal kingdom in this volcano. Birds of prey hovered here and there in the shadows, or fled from their nests at the top of the rocks. There were sparrow-hawks with white breasts, and kestrels, and down the slopes with their long legs scampered several fine fat bustards. I leave anyone to imagine the greed of the Canadian at the sight of this savory game, and his regret at having no gun. But he did his best to replace the bullets by stones, and after several fruitless attempts, he succeeded in bringing down a magnificent bird. To say that he risked his life twenty times before reaching it, is but the truth; but he managed so well, that the creature joined the honeycombs in his bag.

We now had to start down again, since we could climb no further. Above the crater seemed to gape like the mouth of a well. From this place the sky could be seen clearly and clouds, dispersed by the west wind, leaving their misty remnants behind them, at the summit—certain proof that these mountains were only moderately high, for the volcano itself did not rise more than eight hundred feet above sea level.

Half an hour after the Canadian's last exploit we had regained the inner shore. Here the flora were represented by large carpets of marine crystal, a little umbelliferous plant very good to pickle, which also bears the names of pierce-stone, and sea-fennel. Conseil gathered some bundles of it. As to the fauna, they might be counted in thousands of crustacea of all sorts, lobsters, crabs, palaemons, spider crabs, chameleon shrimps, and a large number of shells, rock-fish and limpets. Three quarters of an hour later, we had finished our circuitous walk, and were back on board. The crew had just finished loading the sodium, and the *Nautilus* could have left that instant. But Captain Nemo gave no order. Did he wish to wait until night, and go through the channel secretly? Perhaps so. Whatever his reason, the next day, the *Nautilus* left its port, and sailed for the open sea a few yards beneath the surface of the Atlantic.

Chapter 11
The Sargasso Sea

The course of the *Nautilus* never changed. All hope of returning to European waters had to be put aside for the time being. Captain Nemo kept his bow pointed south. Where was he taking us? I had no idea.

One day the *Nautilus* traveled through a singular part of the Atlantic Ocean. No one can be ignorant of the existence of that current of warm water, known as the Gulf Stream. After emerging from the channels near Florida, it turns upward toward Spitzbergen. But before entering the Gulf of Mexico at about the forty-fifth degree of latitude north this current divides into two arms. The principal one goes towards the coast of Ireland and Norway, whilst the second bends to the south near the longitudinal position of the Azores; then, touching the African shore, and describing a lengthened oval, it returns to the Antilles. This second arm—it is more like a necklace than an arm—goes all around that quiet, motionless part of the ocean called the Sargasso Sea. This is like a field in the middle of the Atlantic, an area filled with dense growths. It takes no less than three years for the current to pass round it.

This was the region where the *Nautilus* was now visiting, its surface like a meadow, a close carpet of seaweed, fucus, and tropical berries, so thick and so compact, that the stem of a vessel could hardly tear its way through it. And Captain Nemo, not wishing to entangle his screw in this herbaceous mass, kept some distance beneath the surface. The name Sargasso comes from the Spanish word "Sargazzo," which means kelp. This kelp, or varech, or berry-plant, is the principal ingredient of this extraordinary sea.

According to the learned Maury, author of *The Physical Geography of the Globe,* there is only one explanation for the gathering of all these hydrophytes in this strange place.

"It seems to me," he says, "to arise from an experiment familiar to everyone. Place in a vase some fragments of cork or, start the water in the vase moving in a circular direction. The scattered fragments of cork then will unite in a group in the center of the liquid, that is to say, in the least agitated part. In the phenomenon we now are considering, the Atlantic is the vase, the Gulf Stream the circular current and the Sargasso Sea the central point at which the floating bodies unite."

I share Maury's opinion, and I was able to study the phenomenon in its very midst, where vessels rarely penetrate. Above us floated articles of all kinds, heaped up among these brownish plants; trunks of trees torn from the Andes or the Rocky Mountains, and floated by the Amazon or the Mississippi; pieces of wreckage, remains of keels, or ships' bottoms, side planks stove in, and so weighted with shells and barnacles that they could never rise again And time one day will bear out another opinion of Maury's, that these substances, accumulating thus for ages, will turn into mineral through action of the water, and will then form inexhaustible mines of fuel—a precious reserve prepared by far-seeing Nature for the moment when men shall have exhausted the fuels of the continents.

In the midst of this unfathomable mass of plants and seaweed, I noticed some charming pink halcyons and actiniae, with their long tentacles trailing after them; medusae, green, red, and blue, and the great rhyostoms of Cuvies, which has a large umbrella bordered and festooned with violet.

We spent all day of the 22nd of February in the Sargasso Sea. For the nineteen days following, from the 23rd of February to the 12th of March, the *Nautilus* stayed in the middle of the Atlantic, carrying us at a steady speed of a hundred leagues in twenty-four hours. Captain Nemo obviously intended to complete his underwater tour of the world, and I imagined that he intended, after rounding Cape Horn, to return to the Australian seas of the Pacific. Ned Land had cause for fear. In the wide seas, void of islands, we could not attempt to leave the boat. Nor had we any means of opposing Captain Nemo's will. Our only course was to submit; but what we would gain neither by force nor cunning, I liked to think might be won by persuasion. This voyage ended, would he not consent to restore our liberty? Had he not said from the beginning, in the firmest manner, that the secret of his life demanded that he keep us prisoner on board the *Nautilus*? And would not my four months' silence appear to him a tacit acceptance of our situation? And would not a return to the subject raise suspicions which might be hurtful to our plans for escape?

During the nineteen days mentioned above, no incident occurred worth noting. I saw little of the Captain; he was at work. In the library I often found books left open, many concerned with Natural History. My work on ocean depths, conned over by him, was covered with marginal notes, often questioning my theories and systems; but the Captain contented himself with these comments on my work; it was very rare for him to discuss it with me. Sometimes I heard the melancholy tones of his organ; but only at night, in the midst of the deepest darkness, when the *Nautilus* slept upon the deserted ocean. During this part of our voyage we sailed for days at a time on the surface. The sea seemed abandoned. A few sailing-vessels, on the way to India, were making for the Cape of Good Hope. One day we were followed by the boats of a whaler, who, no doubt, took us for some enormous whale of great value; but Captain Nemo did not wish the worthy fellows to waste their time and effort so ended the chase by plunging under the water. Our journey continued until the 13th of March; that day the *Nautilus* was employed in taking soundings, which greatly interested me. We had then made about 13,000 leagues since our departure from the high seas of the Pacific. The bearings put us at 45° 37' south latitude, and 37° 53' west longitude. This was the water in which Captain Denham of the *Herald* sounded 7000 fathoms without reaching bottom. Here, too, Lieutenant Parker, of the American frigate *Congress*, could not touch bottom with 15,140 fathoms. Captain Nemo intended to seek the bottom along a diagonal maintained by means of the lateral planes which were at an angle of forty-five degrees to the waterline of the *Nautilus*. The screw was put to work at its maximum speed, its four blades beating the waves with tremendous force. Under this powerful impetus the hull of the *Nautilus* quivered like a violin string and sank evenly under the water.

At 7000 fathoms I saw some dark summits rising in the midst of the waters; but these peaks might belong to high mountains like the Himalayas or Mont Blanc, or even higher; and the depth of the abyss remained incalculable. The *Nautilus* descended still farther in spite of great pressure. I felt the steel plates tremble where their bolts were fastened. Its bars bent, its walls groaned; the windows of the saloon seemed to curve under the pressure of the waters. And this firm structure must have yielded, unless, as its Captain had said, the *Nautilus* had the resistance of a solid mass.

Skimming past great rocks, lost under water, I saw a few shells, some living serpulae and spinorbes, and some specimens of asteriads. But soon the last representative of animal life disappeared; and at a depth of more than three leagues, the *Nautilus* had passed beyond the limits of underwater existence, even as a balloon does when it rises higher than the air we can breathe. We had reached a depth of 16,000 yards (four leagues), and the sides of the *Nautilus* sustained a pressure of 1600 atmospheres, that is to say, 3200 pounds to each square two-fifths of an inch of its surface.

"What a situation to be in!" I exclaimed. "To travel over these deep regions where man has never gone! Look, Captain, look at these magnificent rocks, these uninhabited grottoes, these last spaces on earth where life is no longer possible! What unknown sights are here! Why must we be unable to preserve a remembrance of them?"

"Would you like to carry away more than the remembrance?" said Captain Nemo.

"What do you mean by those words?"

"I mean to say that nothing is easier than to take a photographic view of this region."

I had not time to express my surprise at this new proposition, when, at Captain Nemo's call, an instrument was brought into the saloon.

Lit up by our electric lights through the windows, which were opened wide, the watery mass was spread out in perfect clarity. Not a shadow, not a gradation, was to be seen under our artificial light. The *Nautilus* remained motionless, the force of its screw restrained by the slant of its planes: the instrument was aimed at the scenery of the ocean's depths, and in a few seconds we had obtained a perfect negative. I still have the positive, in which may be seen those primitive rocks, which have never looked upon the light of heaven; that granite which forms the very foundation of the world; those deep grottoes carven from the stony mass, with outlines so clear, and borders drawn in black, as if by the pencil of a Flemish artist. Beyond these a horizon of mountains, a lovely undulating line, giving perspective to the landscape. I cannot describe the effect of these glistening black, polished rocks, strangely shaped, without moss, without a mark, standing solidly on their carpet of sand, which sparkled under the jets of our electric light.

The operation completed, Captain Nemo said, "Let us go up; we must not abuse our position, nor expose the *Nautilus* too long to such great pressure."

"Go up again!" I exclaimed.

"Hold on firmly!"

I had not time to understand why the Captain cautioned me thus, when I was thrown forward onto the floor. At a signal from the Captain, the screw was shipped, and the blades lifted vertically. The *Nautilus* shot upward like a balloon filled with air, rising with stunning rapidity, and cutting the mass of water with loud hissing. Nothing was to be seen and in four minutes it had shot through the four leagues which separated it from the surface, and, emerging like a flying-fish, fell back, making the waves rise to a prodigious height.

Chapter 12
Cachalots and Whales

During the nights of the 13th and 14th of March the *Nautilus* returned to its southerly course. I fancied that, when on a level with Cape Horn, he would turn the helm westward, in order to churn the waters of the Pacific and thus complete the tour of the world. He did nothing of the kind, but continued on his way to the southern regions. Where was he going? To the pole? It was madness! I began to think that the captain's temerity justified Ned Land's fears. For some time the Canadian had not spoken to me of his escape plans. He was less communicative, almost silent. I could see that this lengthy imprisonment was weighing upon him, and I felt that rage was burning inside him. When he met the Captain, his eyes glowed with suppressed anger and I feared that his natural violence would lead him to some extreme. That day, the 14th of March, Conseil and he came to me in my room. I inquired the cause of their visit.

"To ask you a simple question, sir," replied the Canadian.

"Speak, Ned."

"How many men are there on board the *Nautilus*, do you think?"

"I cannot tell, my friend."

"I should say that its running does not require a large crew."

"Certainly, under existing conditions, ten men, at the most, ought to suffice."

"Well, why should there be any more?"

"Why?" I replied, looking fixedly at Ned Land, whose meaning was easy to guess. "Because if my surmises are correct, and if I have properly understood the Captain's way of life, the *Nautilus* is not only a vessel: it is also a refuge for those who, like its commander, have broken every tie with earth."

"Perhaps so," said Conseil. "But, in any case, the *Nautilus* can contain only a certain number of men. Could not you, sir, estimate their maximum?"

"How, Conseil?"

"By calculation; given the size of the vessel, which you know, sir, and consequently the quantity of air it contains; knowing also how much each man uses at a breath, and comparing these results with the fact that the *Nautilus* is obliged to surface every twenty-four hours."

Conseil had not finished the sentence before I saw what he was driving at.

"I understand," said I; "but that calculation, though simple enough, can give but a very uncertain result."

"Never mind," said Ned Land, urgently.

"Here it is, then," said I. "In one hour each man consumes the oxygen contained in twenty gallons of air; and in twenty-four, that contained in 480 gallons. We must, therefore, find how many times 480 gallons of air the *Nautilus* contains."

"Just so," said Conseil.

"Or," I continued, "the size of the *Nautilus* being 1500 tons; and one ton holding 200 gallons, it contains 300,000 gallons of air, which, divided by 480, gives a quotient of 625. Which means to say, strictly speaking, that the air contained in the *Nautilus* would suffice for 625 men for twenty-four hours."

"Six hundred and twenty-five!" repeated Ned.

"But remember, that all of us, passengers, sailors, and officers included, would not form a tenth part of that number."

"Still too many for three men," murmured Conseil.

The Canadian shook his head, passed his hand across his forehead, and left the room without answering.

"Will you allow me an observation, sir?" said Conseil. "Poor Ned is longing for everything he can't have. His past life haunts him; everything that we are forbidden he regrets. His head is full of memories. And we must understand him. What can he do here? Nothing; he is not learned like you, sir; and has not the same taste for the beauties of the sea that we have. He would risk everything to be able to go once more into a tavern in his own country."

Certainly the monotony on board must seem

intolerable to the Canadian, accustomed as he was to a life of liberty and activity. Events were rare which could rouse in him any show of spirit; but that day something happened which recalled the bright days of the harpooner. About eleven in the morning, being on the surface, the *Nautilus* fell in with a troop of whales—an encounter which did not astonish me, knowing that these creatures, hunted to the death, had taken refuge in high latitudes.

We were seated on the deck and the sea was quiet. The month of October in those latitudes gave us some lovely autumnal days. It was the Canadian—he could not be mistaken—who signaled a whale on the eastern horizon. Looking attentively one might see its black back rise and fall with the waves five miles from the *Nautilus*.

"Ah!" exclaimed Ned Land, "if I were on board a whaler now, such a meeting would give me pleasure. It is one of large size. See with what strength its blow-holes throw up columns of air and steam! Confound it, why am I bound to these steel plates?"

"What, Ned," said I, "you have not forgotten your dreams of fishing?"

"Can a whale-fisher ever forget his old trade, sir? Can he ever tire of the excitement of such a chase?"

"Have you never fished in these seas, Ned?"

"Never, sir; in the north only, and as much in Bering as in Davis Straits.

"Then the southern whale is still unknown to you. You have hunted the Greenland whale up to this time, and that would never risk passing through the warm waters of the equator. Whales are localized, according to their kinds, in certain seas which they never leave. If one of these went from Bering to Davis Straits, it must be simply because there is a passage from one sea to the other, either on the American or the Asiatic side."

"In any case, as I have never fished these seas, I do not know the kind of whale frequenting them."

"I have told you, Ned."

"A greater reason for making their acquaintance," said Conseil.

"Look! Look!" exclaimed the Canadian, "they approach; they aggravate me; they know that I cannot get at them!"

Ned stamped his feet. His hand trembled, as he grasped an imaginary harpoon.

"Are these cetacea as large as those of the northern seas?"

"Very nearly, Ned."

"Because I have seen large whales, sir, whales measuring a hundred feet. I have been told that those of Hullamoch and Umgallick, of the Aleutian Islands, are sometimes a hundred and fifty feet long."

"That seems to me exaggeration. These creatures are only balaenopterons, provided with dorsal fins; and, like the cachalots, are generally much smaller than the Greenland whale."

"Ah!" exclaimed the Canadian, whose eyes never left the ocean, "they are coming nearer;

they are in the same water as the *Nautilus*!"

Then returning to the conversation, he said—

"You spoke of the cachalot as a small creature. I have heard of gigantic ones. They are intelligent cetacea. It is said of some that they cover themselves with seaweed and fucus, and then are taken for islands. People encamp upon them, and settle there; light a fire—"

"And build houses," said Conseil.

"Yes, joker," said Ned Land. "And one fine day the creature plunges, carrying all the inhabitants to the bottom of the sea."

"Something like the travels of Sinbad the Sailor," I replied, laughing.

"Ah!" suddenly exclaimed Ned Land. "It is not just one whale. There are ten—there are twenty—a whole troop. And I not able to do anything! Tied, hand and foot!"

"But, friend Ned," said Conseil, "why not ask Captain Nemo's permission to chase them?"

Conseil had not finished his sentence when Ned Land lowered himself through the panel to seek the Captain. A few minutes afterwards the two appeared together on the deck.

Captain Nemo watched the troop of cetacea playing on the waters about a mile from the *Nautilus*.

"They are southern whales," said he. "There goes the fortune of a whole fleet of whalers."

"Well, sir," asked the Canadian, "can I not chase them, if only to remind me of my old trade of harpooner?"

"And to what purpose?" replied Captain Nemo; "only to destroy! We do nothing with whale-oil on board."

"But, sir," continued the Canadian, "in the Red Sea you allowed us to follow the dugong."

"Then it was to procure fresh meat for my crew. Here it would be killing for killing's sake. I know that is a privilege reserved for man, but I do not approve of such a murderous pastime. In destroying the southern whale (like the Greenland whale, an offensive creature), your traders are culpable, Master Land. They have already depopulated the whole of Baffin's Bay, and are annihilating a class of useful animals. Leave the unfortunate cetacea alone. They have plenty of natural enemies, cachalots, swordfish, and sawfish, without your troubling them."

The Captain was right. The barbarous and inconsiderate greed of these fishermen will one day cause the disappearance of the last whale in the ocean. Ned Land whistled "Yankee Doodle" between his teeth, thrust his hands into his pockets, and turned his back upon us. But Captain Nemo watched the troop of cetacea, and addressing me, said—

"I was right in saying that whales had natural enemies enough, without counting man. These will have plenty to do before long. Do you see, M. Aronnax, about eight miles to leeward, those blackish moving points?"

"Yes, Captain," I replied.

"Those are cachalots—terrible animals, which I have sometimes met in packs of two or three hundred. As to those, they are cruel, mischievous creatures; they would be right in exterminating them.''

The Canadian turned quickly at the last words.

''Well, Captain,'' said he, ''it is still time, in the interest of the whales.''

''It is wasteful to expose one's self, Professor. The *Nautilus* will disperse them. It is armed with a steel bow effective as Master Land's harpoon, I think.''

The Canadian did not put himself out enough to shrug his shoulders. Attack cetacea with the bow of a ship! Who had ever heard of such a thing?

''Wait, M. Aronnax,'' said Captain Nemo. ''We will show you something you have never yet seen. We have no pity for these ferocious creatures. They are nothing but mouth and teeth.''

Mouth and teeth! No one could better describe the macrocephalous cachalot, which is sometimes more than seventy-five feet long. Its enormous head takes up one-third of its entire body. Better armed than the whale, whose upper jaw is furnished only with whale bone, it is equipped with twenty-five large cylindrical tusks, about eight inches long and conical, each weighing two pounds. It is in the upper part of this enormous head, in great cavities divided by membranes, that is found from six to eight hundred pounds of that precious oil called spermaceti. Altogether the cachalot is a disagreeable creature, more tadpole than fish, according to Fredol's description. It is badly formed, the whole of its left side being (if we may say it) almost useless, and able to see only with its right eye. But the formidable pack was nearing us. They had seen the whales and were preparing to attack them. One could judge beforehand that the cachalots would be victorious, not only because they were better designed for attack than their inoffensive adversaries, but also because they could remain longer underwater without coming to the surface. There was only just time to go to the aid of the whales. The *Nautilus* dived. Conseil, Ned Land and I took our places before the window in the saloon, and Captain Nemo went to the pilot's cage to use the *Nautilus* as an engine of destruction.

Soon I felt the beatings of the screw quicken, and our speed increased. The battle between the cachalots and the whales had already begun when the *Nautilus* arrived. At first they showed no fear at the sight of this new monster joining in the conflict. But soon the cachalots had to guard against its blows. What a battle! The *Nautilus* was like the most formidable harpoon, brandished in the hand of its captain. It hurled itself against the fleshy mass, passing through from one part to the other, leaving behind it two quivering halves of an animal. It could not feel their blows upon its sides, nor yet the shocks inflicted by itself. One cachalot killed, it ran at the next, tacked on the spot that it might not miss its prey, going forwards and backwards, answering to its helm, plunging when the cetacean dived into the deep waters, coming up with it when the animal returned to the surface, striking it front or sideways, cutting or tearing in all directions, and at any pace, piercing it with its terrible spur. What carnage! What a noise on the surface of the waves! What sharp hissing, and that snorting peculiar to these enraged animals. In the midst of these waters, generally so peaceful, their tails made great waves. For one hour this wholesale massacre continued, from which the cachalots could not escape. Several times ten or twelve united tried to crush the *Nautilus* by their weight. From the window we could see their enormous mouths studded with tusks, and their terrifying eyes. Ned Land could not contain himself, he threatened and swore at them. We could feel them clinging to our vessel like dogs worrying a wild boar in a wood. But the *Nautilus*, working its screw, carried them here and there, down, or to the upper levels of the ocean, without feeling their enormous weight, nor the strain on the vessel. At length, the mass of cachalots broke up, the water became quiet, and I felt that we were rising to the surface. The panel opened, and we hurried onto the deck. The sea was covered with mutilated bodies. A big explosion could not have broken and torn this fleshy mass with more violence. We were floating amid gigantic bodies, bluish on the back and white underneath, covered with enormous protuberances. A few terrified cachalots were flying toward the horizon. The waves were dyed red for several miles, and the *Nautilus* floated in a sea of blood. Captain Nemo joined us.

"Well, Master Land?" said he.

"Well, sir," replied the Canadian, whose enthusiasm had somewhat calmed. "It is a terrible spectacle, certainly. But I am not a butcher. I am a hunter, and I call this a butchery."

"It is a massacre of mischievous creatures," replied the Captain; "and the *Nautilus* is not a butcher's knife."

"I like my harpoon better," said the Canadian.

"Everyone to his own," answered the Captain, looking steadily at Ned Land.

I feared Ned would commit some act of violence, which would end in sad consequences. But his anger was diverted by the sight of a whale which the *Nautilus* had just come up with. The creature had not quite escaped from the cachalot's teeth. I recognized the southern whale by its flat head, which is entirely black. Anatomically, it is distinguished from the white whale and the North Cape whale by the seven cervical vertebrae, and it has two ribs more than its relative. The unfortunate cetacean was lying on its side, riddled with holes from the bites, and quite dead. From its mutilated fin still hung a young whale which it had not been able to save from the massacre. The water flowed in and out of its open mouth murmuring like waves breaking on the shore. Captain Nemo steered close to the corpse of the creature. Two of his men climbed its side, and I saw, not without surprise, that they were drawing from its breasts all the milk which they contained, that is to say, about two or three tons. The Captain offered me a cup of the milk, which was still warm. I could not help showing my repugnance to the drink; but he assured me that it was excellent, and not to be distinguished from cow's milk. I tasted it, and was of his opinion. It was a useful store for us, for in the shape of salt butter or cheese it would form an agreeable variety from our ordinary food. From that day I noticed with uneasiness that Ned Land's ill-will towards Captain Nemo increased, and I resolved to watch the Canadian's actions closely.

Chapter 13
The Iceberg

The Nautilus was steadily pursuing its southerly course, following the fiftieth meridian with considerable speed. Did he wish to reach the pole? I did not think so, for every attempt to reach that point had hitherto failed. Again the season was far advanced, for in the antarctic regions, the 13th of March corresponds with the 13th of September of northern regions. On the 14th of March I saw floating ice in latitude 55°, merely pale chunks from twenty to twenty-five feet long, forming reefs over which the sea curled. The *Nautilus* remained on the surface. Ned Land, who had fished in the arctic seas, was familiar with its icebergs; but Conseil and I admired them for the first time. In the air near the southern horizon there stretched a band of dazzling white. English whalers have given it the name of "ice blink." However thick the clouds may be, it is always visible, and announces the presence of an ice pack or bank. Accordingly, larger blocks soon appeared, whose brilliancy changed with the caprices of the fog. Some of these masses showed green veins, as if long undulating lines had been traced with sulphate of copper; others resembled enormous amethysts with the light shining through them. Some reflected the light of day upon a thousand crystal facets. Others, shaded with vivid calcareous reflections, resembled a city of marble. The more we neared the south, the more these floating ice islands increased both in number and size.

At the sixtieth degree of latitude, every channel had disappeared. But seeking carefully, Captain Nemo soon found a narrow opening, through which he boldly slipped, knowing, however, that it would close behind him. Thus, guided by this clever hand, the *Nautilus* passed through all this ice with a precision which quite charmed Conseil: icebergs or mountains, icefields or smooth plains, drift ice or floating ice packs, or plains broken up, called *palchs* when they are circular, and streams when they are made up of long strips. The temperature was very low; the thermometer exposed to the air marked two or three degrees below zero, but we were warmly clad in fur, at the expense of the sea-bear and seal. The interior of the *Nautilus*, warmed evenly by its electric apparatus, defied the most intense cold. Besides, it would have been necessary only to go a few yards beneath the surface to find a more bearable temperature. Two months earlier we should have had perpetual daylight in these latitudes; but now we had nights three or four hours long, and by and by, there would be six months of darkness in these regions. On the 15th of March we were in the latitude of New Shetland and South Orkney. The Captain told me that formerly numerous tribes of seals inhabited them; but that English and American whalers, in their rage for destruction, massacred both old and young. Thus, where once there was life and activity, they had left silence and death.

About eight o'clock on the morning of the 16th of March, the *Nautilus*, following the fifty-fifth meridian, crossed the antarctic polar circle. Ice surrounded us on all sides, and shut off the horizon. But Captain Nemo found one opening after another. I cannot express my astonishment at the beauties of these new regions. The ice took most surprising forms. Here the grouping formed an oriental town, with innumerable mosques and minarets; there a fallen city thrown to earth, as it were, by some convulsion of nature. The whole aspect changed constantly under the oblique rays of the sun and sometimes was lost in the grayish fog amidst hurricanes of snow. Detonations and falls were heard on all sides, great overthrows of icebergs, which altered the whole landscape like a changing diorama. Often, seeing no way out, I thought we were prisoners. But instinct directing him at the slightest indication, Captain Nemo would discover a new pass. He was never mistaken when he saw the thin threads of bluish water trickling along the ice-fields; and I had no doubt that he had ventured among these antarctic seas before. On the 16th of March, however, the ice-fields finally blocked our way. It was not the ice itself, as yet, but vast fields hardened by the cold. But even this obstacle could not stop Captain Nemo. He hurled himself against it with frightful violence. The *Nautilus* entered the brittle mass like a wedge, and split it with frightful cracklings. It was the battering ram of the ancients hurled with infinite strength. The ice, thrown high in the air, fell around us, like hail. By its own power our vessel made a channel for itself. Sometimes, carried away by its own impetus, it lodged on the ice-field, crushing it with its weight. Sometimes we were buried beneath the ice-field, then broke through by a simple pitching movement, producing large rents in it. Violent gales assailed us at this time, accompanied by thick fogs, through which we could not see from one end of the deck to the other.

The wind blew sharply from all points of the compass, and the snow lay in such hard heaps that we had to break it with a pickaxe. The temperature was always at five degrees below zero. Every outer part of the *Nautilus* was covered with ice. A rigged vessel could never have worked its way here, for all the rigging would have been frozen into the ice. Only a vessel without sails, with electricity for its motive power, and needing no coal, could brave such high latitudes. At length, on the 18th of March, after many vain assaults, the *Nautilus* was blocked. This was no longer streams, packs, or ice-fields, but an interminable and immovable barrier, formed by mountains soldered together.

"An iceberg!" said the Canadian to me.

I knew that to Ned Land, as well as to all other navigators who had preceded us, this was the end. The sun appearing for an instant at noon, Captain Nemo took an observation, which gave our situation as at 51° 30' longitude and 67° 39' of south latitude. We had advanced one degree more in this antarctic region. Of the liquid surface of the sea there was no longer a glimpse. Under the spur of the *Nautilus* lay stretched a vast plain, piled with tumbled blocks of ice. Here and there were sharp points, and slender needles, rising to a height of 200 feet. Further on was a steep shore, hewn as if with an axe, and colored with grayish tints. Huge mirrors of ice reflected a few rays of sunshine, half drowned in the fog. And over this desolate face of Nature a stern silence reigned, scarcely broken by the flapping of wings of petrels and puffins. Everything was frozen—even the noise. The *Nautilus* was obliged to stop in its adventurous course. In spite of our efforts, in spite of the powerful means employed to break up the ice, the *Nautilus* remained immovable. Generally, when we can proceed no further, the way back is still open to us. But here, return was as impossible as advance, for every pass had closed behind us. During the few moments when we were stationary, we were likely to be frozen in, which did, indeed, happen about two o'clock in the afternoon. Fresh ice formed around the sides with astonishing rapidity. I was obliged to admit that Captain Nemo had been more than imprudent. I was on the deck at that moment. The Captain had been observing our situation for some time, when he said to me—

"Well, sir, what do you think of this?"

"I think that we are caught, Captain."

"So, M. Aronnax, you really think that the *Nautilus* cannot disengage itself?"

"With difficulty, Captain; for the season is already too far advanced for you to reckon on the breaking up of the ice."

"Ah! sir," said Captain Nemo, in an ironical tone, "you will always be the same. You see nothing but difficulties and obstacles. I affirm that not only can the *Nautilus* disengage itself, but also that it can go further still."

"Further to the south?" I asked, looking at the Captain.

"Yes, sir; it shall go to the pole."

"To the pole!" I exclaimed, unable to repress a gesture of incredulity.

"Yes," replied the Captain coldly, "to the antarctic pole—to that unknown point from whence springs every meridian of the globe. *You* know whether I can do as I please with the *Nautilus*!"

Yes, I knew that. I knew that this man was bold, even to rashness. But to conquer those obstacles which bristled round the south pole, rendering it even more inaccessible than the north, which had not yet been reached by the boldest navigators—was it not a mad enterprise, one which only a maniac would have conceived? It then came into my head to ask Captain Nemo if he had yet discovered that pole which had not been trodden by a human creature.

"No, sir," he replied; "but we will discover

it together. Where others have failed, I will not fail. I have never yet led my *Nautilus* so far into southern seas; but, I repeat, it shall go further yet."

"I can well believe you, Captain," said I, in a slightly ironical tone. "I believe you! Let us go ahead! There are no obstacles for us! Let us smash this iceberg! Let us blow it up; and if it resists, let us give the *Nautilus* wings to fly over it!"

"Over it!" I exclaimed, a sudden idea of the Captain's projects flashing upon my mind. I understood. The wonderful qualities of the *Nautilus* were going to serve us in this superhuman enterprise.

"I see we are beginning to understand one another, sir," said the Captain, half smiling. "You begin to see the possibility—I should say the success—of this attempt. That which is impossible for an ordinary vessel, is easy to the *Nautilus*. If a continent lies before the pole, it must stop before the continent; but if, on the contrary, the pole is washed by open sea, it will go even to the pole."

"Certainly," said I, carried away by the Captain's reasoning; "if the surface of the sea is solid ice, the lower depths are still free by the providential law which has placed the maximum of density of the waters of the ocean one degree higher than freezing point; and, if I am not mistaken, the portion of this iceberg which is above the water, compares as four to one with that which is below."

"Very, nearly, sir; for one foot of iceberg above the sea there are three below it. If these ice mountains are not more than 300 feet above the surface, they are not more than 900 beneath. And what are 900 feet to the *Nautilus*?"

"Nothing, sir."

"It could seek at even greater depths that uniform temperature of seawater, and there brave with impunity the thirty or forty degrees of surface cold."

"Just so, sir—just so," I replied, getting animated.

"The only difficulty," continued Captain Nemo, "is that of remaining down several days without renewing our tanks of air."

"Is that all? The *Nautilus* has vast reservoirs; we can fill them, and they will supply us with all the oxygen we want."

"Well thought of, M. Aronnax," replied the Captain, smiling. "But not wishing you to accuse me of rashness, I will first give you all my objections."

"Have you any more to make?"

"Only one. It is possible, if the sea exists at the south pole, that it may be covered; and, consequently, we shall be unable to come to the surface."

"True, sir! But do you forget that the *Nautilus* is armed with a powerful spur, and could we not send it diagonally against these fields of ice, which would split at the blow?"

"Ah! sir, you are full of ideas today."

"Besides, Captain," I added, enthusiastically, "why should we not find the sea open at the south pole as well as at the north? The frozen poles and the poles of the earth do not coincide, either in the southern or in the northern regions; and, until it is proved to the contrary, we may suppose either a continent or an ocean free from ice at these two points of the globe."

"I think so, too, M. Aronnax," replied Captain Nemo. "I only wish you to observe that, after having made so many objections to my project, you are now crushing me with arguments in its favor!"

The preparations for this audacious attempt now began. The powerful pumps of the *Nautilus* were working air into the reservoirs and storing it at high pressure. About four o'clock Captain Nemo announced the closing of the panels on the deck. I threw one last look at the massive iceberg which we were going to cross. The weather was clear, the atmosphere clear, the cold very great, being twelve degrees below zero; but the wind having gone down, this temperature was not so unbearable. About ten men climbed the sides of the *Nautilus*, armed with pickaxes to break the ice around the vessel, which was soon free. The operation was quickly performed, for the fresh ice was still very thin. We all went below. The usual reservoirs were filled with the newly liberated water, and the *Nautilus* soon descended. I had taken my place with Conseil in the saloon. Through the open window we could see the lower beds of the Southern Ocean. The thermometer went up, the needle of the compass trembled on the dial. At about 900 feet, as Captain Nemo had foreseen, we were floating beneath the rippling bottom of the iceberg. But the *Nautilus* went lower still—to the depth of four hundred fathoms. The temperature of the water at the surface showed twelve degrees, it was now only eleven; we had gained two. I need not say the temperature of the *Nautilus* was raised by its heating apparatus to a much higher degree; every maneuver was carried out with wonderful precision.

"We shall pass it, if you please, sir," said Conseil.

"I believe we shall," I said, in a tone of firm conviction.

In this open sea, the *Nautilus* had taken its course direct to the pole, without leaving the fifty-second meridian. From 67° 30' to 90°, twenty-two degrees and a half of latitude remained to travel; that is, about five hundred leagues. The *Nautilus* kept a mean speed of twenty-six miles an hour —the speed of an express train. If that was kept up, in forty hours we should reach the pole.

For part of the night the novelty of the situation kept us at the window. The sea was lit with the electric lantern; but it was deserted; fishes did not stay in these imprisoned waters. They only sought there a channel to take them from the Antarctic to the open, polar sea. Our pace was rapid. We could feel it by the quivering of the long steel body. About two in the morning, I took some hours' repose, and Conseil did the same. In crossing the alleyway I did not meet Captain Nemo. I supposed him to be in the pilot's cage. The next morning, the 19th of March, I took my post once more in the saloon. The electric log told me that the speed of the *Nautilus* had slackened. It was rising towards the surface; but prudently emptying its reservoirs very slowly. My heart beat fast. Were we going to emerge into the open polar air? No! A shock told me that the *Nautilus* had struck the bottom of an iceberg, still very thick, judging from the deadened sound. We had indeed "struck," to use a sea expression, but in an inverse sense, and a thousand feet down. This would mean three thousand feet of ice above us; one thousand being above the water-mark. The iceberg was higher than at its edges—not a very reassuring discovery. Several times that day the *Nautilus* tried again, and every time struck the ice which lay like a ceiling above it. Sometimes it met with but 900 yards, only 200 of which rose above the surface. But the iceberg was twice the height of where the *Nautilus* had gone underwater. I carefully noted the different depths, and thus obtained a submarine profile of the chain as we followed it underwater. No change had taken place that night in our situation. Still ice between four and five hundred yards in depth! It was diminishing, but still what a thickness between us and the surface of the ocean! It was now eight o'clock. According to daily custom on board the *Nautilus*, its air should have been renewed four hours ago. But I did not suffer much, although Captain Nemo had not begun to use his reserve of oxygen. My sleep was disturbed that night; hope and fear besieged me by turns: I rose several times. The groping of the *Nautilus* continued.

About three in the morning, I went to the saloon where I found that the lower surface of the iceberg was only about fifty feet deep. One hundred and fifty feet of ice separated us from the surface of the waters. The iceberg was by degrees becoming an ice-field, the mountain a plain. My eyes never left the manometer. We were still rising diagonally toward the surface, which sparkled in the electric light. The iceberg was stretching both above and below into lengthening slopes; mile after mile it was getting thinner. At length, at six in the morning of that memorable day, the 19th of March, the door of the saloon opened, and Captain Nemo appeared.

"The sea is open!" was all he said.

Chapter 14
The South Pole

I rushed on deck. Yes! the open sea, with but a few scattered pieces of ice and floating reefs—a long stretch of sea; a world of birds in the air, and myriads of fishes under the waters, which ranged from intense blue to olive green, according to the bottom. The thermometer marked three degrees centigrade above zero. It was like spring, shut up as we had been under the vast iceberg, whose long mass was dimly visible on our northern horizon.

"Are we at the pole?" I asked the Captain, with a beating heart.

"I do not know," he replied. "At noon I will take our bearings."

"But will the sun show himself through this fog?" said I, looking at the leaden sky.

"However little it shows, it will be enough," replied the Captain.

About ten miles south, a solitary island rose to a height of one hundred and four yards. We made for it, but carefully, for the sea might be strewn with reefs. One hour afterwards we had reached it, two hours later we had sailed around it. It measured four or five miles in circumference. A narrow channel separated it from a considerable stretch of land, perhaps a continent, for we could not see its limits. The existence of this land seemed to give some color to Maury's hypothesis. The ingenious American has remarked, that between the south pole and the sixtieth parallel, the sea is covered with floating ice of enormous size, which is never met with in the North Atlantic. From this fact he has drawn the conclusion that the antarctic circle encloses considerable continents, as icebergs cannot form in open sea, but only on the coasts. According to these calculations, the mass of ice surrounding the southern pole forms a vast cap, the circumference of which must be at least 2500 miles. But the *Nautilus*, for fear of running aground, had stopped about three cables' length from a strand over which reared a superb heap of rocks. The boat was launched. The Captain, two of his men bearing instruments, Conseil, and myself, were in it. It was ten in the morning. I had not seen Ned Land. Doubtless the Canadian did not wish to admit the presence of the south pole. A few strokes of our oar brought us to the sand, where we ran ashore. Conseil was going to jump on to the land, when I held him back.

"Sir," said I to Captain Nemo, "to you belongs the honor of first setting foot on this land."

"Yes, sir," said the Captain; "and if I do not hesitate to tread this south pole, it is because, up to this time, no human being has left a trace there."

Saying this he jumped lightly onto the sand. His heart beat with emotion. He climbed a rock, sloping to a little promontory, and there, with his arms crossed, mute and motionless, and with an eager look, he seemed to take possession of these southern regions. After five minutes passed in this ecstasy, he turned to us.

"When you like, sir."

I landed, followed by Conseil, leaving the two men in the boat. For a long way the soil was composed of a reddish, sandy stone, something like crushed brick, scoriae, streams of lava, and pumice stones. One could not mistake its volcanic origin. In some parts, slight curls of smoke emitted a sulphurous smell, proving that the internal fires had lost nothing of their expansive powers, though, having climbed a high acclivity, I could see no volcano for a radius of several miles. We know that in those antarctic countries, James Ross found two craters, the Erebus and Terror, in full activity, on the 167th meridian, latitude 77° 32'. The vegetation of this desolate continent seemed to me very limited. Some lichens of the species usnes melanoxantha lay upon the black rocks; some microscopic plants, rudimentary diatomas, a kind of cells, placed between two quartz shells; long purple and scarlet fucus, supported on little swimming bladders, which the breaking of the waves brought to shore. These constituted the meager flora of this region. The shore was strewn with molluscs, little mussels, limpets, smooth buccards in the shape of a heart, and particularly some clios, with oblong membraneous bodies, the heads formed of two rounded lobes. I also saw myriads of northern clios, one and a quarter inches long, of which a whale would swallow a whole world at a mouthful; and some charming pteropods, perfect sea-butterflies, playing in the water on the edges of the shore.

Amongst other zoophytes, there appeared some coral shrubs, of that kind which, according to James Ross, live in the antarctic seas at a depth of more than 1000 yards. Then there were little kingfishers, belonging to the species procellaria pelagica, as well as a large number of asteriads, peculiar to these climates, and many starfish. But where life abounded most was in the air. There, thousands of birds of all kinds fluttered and flew, deafening us with their cries. Others crowded the rocks, looking at us without fear, as we passed by, and pressing familiarly close to our feet. There were penguins, so agile in the water, that they have been mistaken for the rapid bonitos, heavy and awkward on the ground; they were a large assembly, sober in gesture, but extravagant in clamor, uttering harsh cries. Amongst the birds I noticed the chionis, of the long-legged family, as large as pigeons, white, with a short conical beak, the eye framed in a red circle. Conseil laid in a stock of them, for these winged creatures, properly prepared, make an agreeable meat. Giant albatrosses passed above which are justly called the vultures of the ocean; huge petrels, and damiers, a kind of small duck, the under part of whose body is black and white; then there were a whole series of petrels, some whitish, with brown-bordered wings, others blue, native to the antarctic seas, and so oily, as I told Conseil, that the inhabitants of the Ferroe Islands had nothing to do before lighting them, but to put a wick in.

"A little more," said Conseil, "and they would be perfect lamps! After all, we cannot expect Nature to have previously furnished them with wicks!"

About half a mile further on, the soil was riddled with ruffs' nests; it was a sort of breeding ground, from which many birds were issuing. Captain Nemo had some hundreds killed. They uttered a cry like the braying of an ass, were about the size of a goose, slate color on the body, white beneath, with a yellow line round their throats. They allowed themselves to be killed with a stone, never trying to escape. But the fog did not lift, and at eleven the sun had not yet shown itself. Its absence made me uneasy. Without it no observations were possible. How, then, could we decide whether we had reached the pole? When I rejoined Captain Nemo, I found him leaning on a piece of rock, silently watching the sky. He seemed impatient and vexed. But what was to be done? This rash and powerful man could not command the sun as he did the sea. Noon arrived without the orb of day showing itself for an instant. We could not even tell its position behind the curtain of fog; and soon the fog turned to snow.

"Till tomorrow," said the Captain, quietly, and we returned to the *Nautilus* amid these atmospheric disturbances.

The snowstorm continued till the next day. It was impossible to remain on deck. From the saloon, where I was taking notes of incidents happening during this expedition to the polar continent, I could hear the cries of petrels and albatrosses sporting in the midst of this violent storm. The *Nautilus* did not stay still, but skirted the coast, advancing ten miles more to the south in the half light left by the sun as it skimmed the horizon. The next day, the 20th of March, the snow had ceased. The cold was a little greater, the thermometer showing two degrees below zero. The fog was rising, and I hoped that our observations might be taken. Captain Nemo not having yet appeared, the boat took Conseil and myself to land. The soil was still of the same volcanic nature. Everywhere were traces of lava, scoriae, and basalt; but the crater which had vomited them I could not find. Here, as elsewhere, this continent was alive with myriads of birds. But their kingdom was now shared with large packs of sea-mammals, looking at us with their soft eyes. There were several kinds of seals, some stretched on the earth, some on flakes of ice, many going in and out of the sea. They did not flee at our approach, never having had anything to do with man; and I reckoned that there were provisions there for hundreds of vessels.

"Sir," said Conseil, "will you tell me the names of these creatures?"

"They are seals and walruses."

It was now eight in the morning. Four hours remained before the sun could be observed with advantage. I directed our steps towards a vast bay cut in the steep granite shore. There, I can aver that earth and ice were hidden by the vast numbers of sea-mammals covering them, and I involuntarily thought of old Proteus, the mythological shepherd who watched the immense flocks of Neptune. There were more seals than anything else, forming distinct groups, male and female, the father watching over his family, the mother suckling her little ones, some already strong enough to take a few steps. When they wished to go somewhere, they took little jumps, helped awkwardly enough by their imperfect fin which with their cousin the lamantin forms a perfect forearm. I should say that in the water, which is their element, their spines are flexible; their fur smooth and thick, and their feet are webbed; they swim admirably. When resting on the ground they take most graceful attitudes. Thus the ancients, observing their soft and expressive looks, which cannot be surpassed by the most beautiful look from a woman, their clear voluptuous eyes, their charming positions, and the poetry of their manners, metamorphosed them, the male into a triton and the female into a mermaid. I made Conseil notice the considerable development of the lobes of the brain in these interesting ceta-ceans. No mammal, except man, has such a quantity of cerebral matter. They are also capable of responding to a certain amount of training, are easily domesticated, and I think, with other naturalists, that, if properly taught, they would be of great service as fishing-dogs. The greater part of them slept on the rocks or on the sand. Amongst these seals, which have no external ears, I noticed several varieties of stenorhynchi about three yards long, with white coats, bulldog heads, teeth in both jaws, four in-cisors at the top and four at the bottom, and two large canines in the shape of the French lily-of-the-valley. Amongst them glided sea-elephants, a kind of seal, with short flexible trunks. The giants of this species measured twenty feet round, and ten yards and a half in length; they did not move as we approached.

"These creatures are not dangerous?" asked Conseil.

"No; not unless you attack them. When they have to defend their young, their rage is terri-ble, and it is not uncommon for them to break fishing-boats to pieces."

"They are quite right," said Conseil.

"I do not say they are not."

Two miles further on we were stopped by the promontory which shelters the bay from the southerly winds. Beyond it we heard loud bellowings such as a herd of cattle would utter.

"Good!" said Conseil; "a concert of bulls!"

"No; a concert of walruses!"

"They are fighting!"

"They are either fighting or playing."

We now began to make our way through the black rocks, with many unforeseen stumbles, over stones made slippery by the ice. More than once I rolled over to the detriment of my back. Conseil, more prudent or more steady, did not stumble, and helped me up, saying—

"If, sir, you would be so gracious as to take longer steps, you would preserve your equilibrium better."

Arrived at the upper ridge of the promontory, I saw a vast white plain covered with walruses. They were playing amongst themselves, and what we heard were bellowings of pleasure, not of anger.

As I passed near these curious animals, I could examine them leisurely, for they did not startle. Their hides were thick and rugged, of a yellowish tint, almost red; their hair was short and scant. Some of them were four and a quarter yards long. Quieter, and less timid than their cousins to the north, they did not, like them, place sentinels round the outskirts of their encampment. After looking over this city of walruses, I began to think of going back. It was eleven o'clock, and if Captain Nemo found the conditions favorable for observations, I wished to be present. We followed a narrow pathway going along the cliffside of the steep shore. At half-past eleven we reached the place where we landed. The boat had run aground, bringing the Captain. He was standing on a block of basalt, his instruments nearby, his eyes fixed on the northern horizon, near which the sun was describing a long curve. I took my place beside him, and waited without speaking. Noon arrived, and, as before, the sun did not come out. It was a blow. Observations were still lacking. If not done tomorrow, we must give up all idea of taking any. So was the 20th of March. Tomorrow, the 21st, would be the equinox; the sun would go down behind the horizon for six months, and the long polar night would begin. Since the September equinox it had come up from the northern horizon, rising by lengthened spirals until the 21st of December. At this date, the summer solstice of the polar regions, it had begun to descend; and tomorrow would shed its last rays upon them. I communicated my fears and observations to Captain Nemo.

"You are right, M. Aronnax," said he. "If tomorrow I cannot take the altitude of the sun, I shall not be able to do it for six months. But precisely because chance has led me into these seas on the 21st of March, my bearings will be easy to take, if at twelve we can see the sun."

"Why, Captain?"

"Because then the orb of day describes such protracted curves, that it is difficult to measure its height above the horizon exactly, and grave errors may be made with instruments."

"What will you do then?"

"I shall use only my chronometer," replied Captain Nemo. "If tomorrow, the 21st of March, the disc of the sun, allowing for refraction, is exactly divided by the northern horizon, it will show that I am at the south pole."

"Just so," said I. "But this statement is not mathematically correct, because the equinox does not necessarily begin at noon."

"Very likely, sir; but the error will not be over a hundred yards, and we do not ask for more. Till tomorrow then!"

Captain Nemo returned on board. Conseil and I remained to survey the shore, observing and studying until five o'clock. After dinner, I went to bed, not, however, without invoking, like the Indian, the favor of the radiant orb. The next day, the 21st of March, at five in the morning, I went on deck. I found Captain Nemo there.

"The weather is lightening a little," said he. "I have some hope. After breakfast we will go ashore, and choose a post for observation."

That point settled, I sought Ned Land. I wanted to take him with me. But the obstinate Canadian refused, and I saw that his taciturnity and his bad humor grew day by day. After all I did not regret his obstinacy under the circumstances. There were too many seals on shore, and we ought not to lay such temptations in this unreflecting hunter's way. Breakfast over, we went ashore. The *Nautilus* had gone some miles further during the night. It was a whole league from the coast, above which reared a sharp peak, about five hundred yards high. Along with me, the boat took Captain Nemo, two men of the crew, and the instruments, which consisted of a chronometer, a telescope, and a barometer. While crossing, I saw numerous whales belonging to the three kinds native to the southern seas: the English "right whale," which has no dorsal fin; the "humpback," or balaenopteron, with reeved chest, and large whitish fins which, in spite of its name, do not form wings; and the fin-back, of a yellowish brown, the liveliest of all the cetacea. This powerful creature can be heard a long way off when he emits columns of air and vapor, which rise to a great height and look like whirlwinds of smoke. These different mammals were disporting themselves in troops in the quiet waters; and I could see that this basin of the Antarctic pole served as a place of refuge to cetacea tracked too closely by the hunters. I also noticed long whitish lines of salpae, a gregarious kind of mollusc, and large medusae floating between the reeds.

At nine we landed. The sky was brightening, the clouds were flying to the south, and the fog seemed to be leaving the cold surface of the waters. Captain Nemo went towards the peak, which he doubtless meant to be his observatory. It was a difficult ascent over sharp lava and pumice stones, in an atmosphere often thick with a sulphurous smell from the smoking cracks. For a man unaccustomed to walking on land, the Captain climbed the steep slopes with an agility I never saw equaled, and which a hunter would have envied. We were two hours getting to the summit of this peak, which was half porphyry and half basalt. From thence we looked upon a vast sea, which, towards the north, distinctly traced its boundary line against the sky. At our feet lay fields of dazzling whiteness. Over our heads was a pale azure, free from fog. To the north the disc of the sun seemed like a ball of fire, already horned by the cutting of the horizon. In the distance lay the

Nautilus like a cetacean asleep on the water.

Behind us, to the south and east lay an immense country, a chaotic heap of rocks and ice, the limits of which were not visible. On arriving at the summit, Captain Nemo carefully took a bearing with the barometer, for he would have to consider that in taking his observations. At a quarter to twelve, the sun, seen only by reflection, looked like a golden disc shedding its last ray upon this deserted continent, and seas never yet ploughed by man. Captain Nemo, equipped with a lenticular glass, which, by means of a mirror, corrected the refraction, watched the orb sinking below the horizon by degrees, following a lengthened diagonal. I held the chronometer. My heart beat fast. If the disappearance of the half-disc of the sun coincided with twelve o'clock on the chronometer, we were at the pole itself.

"Twelve!" I exclaimed.

"The South Pole!" replied Captain Nemo, in a grave voice, handing me the glass, which showed the orb cut in exactly equal parts by the horizon.

I looked at the last rays crowning the peak, and the shadows mounting its slopes by degrees. At that moment Captain Nemo, resting his hand on my shoulder, said—

"I, Captain Nemo, on this 21st day of March, 1868, have reached the south pole on the ninetieth degree; and I take possession of this part of the globe, equal to one-sixth of the known continents."

"In whose name, Captain?"

"In my own, sir!"

Saying which, Captain Nemo unfurled a black banner, bearing an N in gold quartered on its bunting. Then turning towards the orb of day, whose last rays lapped the horizon of the sea, he exclaimed—

"Farewell, sun! Disappear, thou radiant orb! Rest beneath this open sea, and let a night of six months spread its shadows over my new domains!"

Chapter 15
Accident or Incident

The next day, the 22nd of March, at six in the morning, preparations for departure were begun. The last gleams of twilight were melting into night. The cold was intense; the constellations shone with wonderful brilliance. In the zenith glittered that wondrous Southern Cross—the polar star of Antarctic regions. The thermometer showed twelve degrees below zero, and when the wind freshened, it was most biting. Flakes of ice increased on the open water. The sea seemed everywhere alike. Numerous blackish patches spread on the surface, showing the formation of fresh ice. Evidently the southern basin, frozen during the six winter months, was completely inaccessible.

What became of the whales in that time? Doubtless they went beneath the icebergs, seeking more practicable seas. As to the seals and walruses, accustomed to living in a hard climate, they remained on these icy shores. These creatures instinctively break holes in the ice-fields, and keep them open. To these holes they come for breath, and when the birds, driven away by the cold, have emigrated to the north, these sea-mammals remain sole masters of the polar continent. But the reservoirs were filling with water, and the *Nautilus* was slowly descending. At 1000 feet deep it stopped; its screw churned the waves and it headed straight towards the north, at a speed of fifteen miles an hour. By night it was already floating under the immense body of the iceberg. At three in the morning I was awakened by a violent shock. I sat up in bed listening in the darkness, when I was precipitated to the middle of the room. The *Nautilus* had struck something and then rebounded violently. I groped along the partition, and by the staircase to the saloon, which was lit by the luminous ceiling. The furniture was turned over. Fortunately the windows were firmly set, and had held fast. The pictures on the starboard-side, no longer vertical, were clinging to the paper, whilst those of the portside were hanging at least a foot from the wall. The *Nautilus* was lying on its starboard side and perfectly motionless. I heard footsteps, and a babble of voices; but Captain Nemo did not appear. As I was leaving the saloon, Ned Land and Conseil entered.

"What is the matter?" said I, at once.

"I came to ask you, sir," replied Conseil.

"Confound it!" exclaimed the Canadian, "I know well enough! The *Nautilus* has struck something, and judging by the way she lies, I do not think she will right herself as she did the first time in Torres Straits."

"But," I asked, "has she at least come to the surface of the sea?"

"We do not know," said Conseil.

"It is easy to decide," I answered. I studied the manometer. To my great surprise it showed a depth of more than 180 fathoms. "What does that mean?" I exclaimed.

"We must ask Captain Nemo," said Conseil.

"But where shall we find him?" said Ned Land.

"Follow me," said I, to my companions.

We left the saloon. There was no one in the library. At the center staircase, by the berths of the ship's crew, there was no one. I thought that Captain Nemo must be in the pilot's cage. It was best to wait. We all returned to the saloon. For twenty minutes we waited thus, listening for the slightest noise which might be made on board the *Nautilus*, when Captain Nemo entered. He seemed not to see us. His face, generally so impassive, showed signs of uneasiness. He watched the compass silently, then the manometer; and going to the planisphere, placed his finger on a spot representing the southern seas. I would not interrupt him; but some minutes later, when he turned towards me, I said, using one of his own expressions in the Torres Straits—

"An incident, Captain?"

"No, sir; an accident this time."

"Serious?"

"Perhaps."

"Is the danger immediate?"

"No."

"The *Nautilus* has stranded?"

"Yes."

"And this has happened—how?"

"By a caprice of nature, not because of man's ignorance. Not a mistake has been made in maneuvering. But we cannot prevent equilibrium from producing its effects. We may brave human laws, but we cannot resist natural ones."

Captain Nemo had chosen a strange moment for uttering this philosophical reflection. On the whole, his answer helped me little.

"May I know sir, the cause of this accident?"

"An enormous block of ice, a whole mountain, has turned over," he replied. "When icebergs are undermined at their base by warmer water or reiterated shocks, their center of gravity rises, and the whole thing turns over. This is what has happened; one of these, as it tumbled, struck the *Nautilus*, then, gliding under its hull, raised it with irresistible force, bringing it into climes which are less thick, where it is now lying on its side."

"But can we not get the *Nautilus* off by emptying its reservoirs, that it may regain its equilibrium?"

"That, sir, is being done at this moment. You can hear the pump working. Look at the needle of the manometer; it shows that the *Nautilus* is rising, but the block of ice is rising with it; and, until some obstacle stops its ascending motion, our position will not be altered."

Indeed, the *Nautilus* still held the same position to starboard; doubtless it would right itself when the block stopped. But at that moment who knew if we might not be frightfully crushed between the two glassy surfaces? I reflected on all the consequences of our position.

Captain Nemo never took his eyes off the manometer. Since the fall of the iceberg, the *Nautilus* had risen about a hundred and fifty feet, but it still remained at the same angle to the perpendicular. Suddenly a slight movement was felt in the hold. Evidently it was righting a little. Things hanging in the saloon were sensibly returning to their normal position. The partitions were nearing upright. No one spoke. With beating hearts we watched and felt the straightening. The boards became horizontal under our feet. Ten minutes passed.

"At last we have righted!" I exclaimed.

"Yes," said Captain Nemo, going to the door of the saloon.

"But are we floating?" I asked.

"Certainly," he replied; "since the reservoirs are not empty; and, when empty, the *Nautilus* must rise to the surface of the sea."

We were in open sea; but at a distance of about ten yards, on either side of the *Nautilus*, rose a dazzling wall of ice—above and beneath the same wall. Above, because the lower surface of the iceberg stretched over us like an immense ceiling. Beneath, because the overturned block, having slid by degrees, had found a resting place on the lateral walls, which kept it in that position. The *Nautilus* was actually imprisoned in a perfect tunnel of ice more than twenty yards wide filled with quiet water. It was easy to get out of it by going either forward or backward, and then make a free passage under the iceberg, some hundreds of yards deeper. The luminous ceiling had been extinguished, but the saloon was still resplendent with intense light. It was the powerful reflection from the glass partition sent violently back to the sheets of the lantern. I cannot describe the effect of the electric rays upon the great blocks so capriciously shaded; upon every angle, every ridge, every facet was thrown a different light, according to the nature of the veins running through the ice. The effect was of a dazzling mine of gems, particularly of sapphires, their blue rays crossing with the green of the emerald. Here and there were opal shades of wonderful softness, running through bright spots like diamonds of fire, the brilliancy of which the eye could not bear. The power of the lantern seemed increased a hundredfold, like a lamp through the lenticular plates of a first-class lighthouse.

"How beautiful! How beautiful!" cried Conseil.

"Yes," I said, "it is a wonderful sight. Is it not, Ned?"

"Yes, confound it! Yes," answered Ned Land. "It is superb! I am mad at being obliged to admit it. No one has ever seen anything like it; but the sight may cost us dear. And if I must say all, I think we are seeing here things which God never intended man to see."

Ned was right, it was too beautiful. Suddenly a cry from Conseil made me turn.

"What is it?" I said.

"Shut your eyes, sir! Do not look, sir!" Saying which, Conseil clapped his hands over his eyes.

"But what is the matter, my boy?"

"I am dazzled, blinded."

My eyes turned involuntarily towards the glass, but could not bear the fire which seemed to devour them. I understood what had happened. The *Nautilus* had put on full speed. All the quiet luster of the ice-walls was at once changed into flashes of lightning. The fire from the myriads of diamonds was blinding. It required some time to put our eyes to rights. At last the hands were taken down.

"Faith, I should never have believed it," said Conseil.

It was five in the morning; and at that moment a shock was felt at the bows of the *Nautilus*. I knew that its bow had struck a block of ice. It must have taken a wrong maneuver, for this submarine tunnel, obstructed by blocks of ice, was not very easy to navigate. I thought that Captain Nemo, by changing his course, would go round these obstacles or else follow the windings of the tunnel. In any case, the road before us could not be entirely closed. But, contrary to my expectations, the *Nautilus* took a decided retrograde motion.

"We are going backwards?" said Conseil.

"Yes," I replied. "This end of the tunnel must have no exit."

"And then?"

"Then," said I, "the going is easy. We must return again, and go out at the southern opening. That is all."

In speaking thus, I wished to appear more confident than I really was. But the retrograde motion of the *Nautilus* was increasing; and it carried us at great speed.

"It will be a hindrance," said Ned.

"What does it matter, some hours more or less, provided we get out at last!"

For a short time I walked from the saloon to the library. My companions were silent. I soon threw myself on an ottoman, and took a book, which I ran my eyes over mechanically. A quarter of an hour later Conseil, approaching me, said, "Is what you are reading very interesting sir?"

"Very interesting!" I replied.

"I should think so, sir. It is your own book you are reading."

"My book?"

And indeed I was holding in my hand the work on the "Great Submarine Depths." I did not even dream of it. I closed the book, and returned to my walk. Ned and Conseil rose to go.

"Stay here, my friends," said I, detaining them. "Let us remain together until we are out of this impasse."

"As you please sir," Conseil replied.

Some hours passed. I often looked at the instruments hanging from the partition. The manometer showed that the *Nautilus* kept at a constant depth of more than three hundred yards, the compass still pointed to the south; the log indicated a speed of twenty miles an hour which, in such cramped space, was very great. But Captain Nemo knew that he could not hasten too much, and that the minutes were worth ages to us. At twenty-five minutes past eight a second shock took place, this time from behind. I turned pale. My companions were close by my side. I seized Conseil's hand. Our looks expressed our feelings better than words. At this moment the Captain entered the saloon. I went up to him.

"Our course is barred southward?" I asked.

"Yes, sir. The iceberg has shifted, and closed every outlet."

"We are locked in, then?"

"Yes."

Chapter 16
Want of Air

Thus, around the *Nautilus*, above and below, was an impenetrable wall of ice. We were prisoners of the iceberg. I watched the Captain. His face had resumed its habitual imperturbability. He crossed his arms. The *Nautilus* was motionless.

"Gentlemen," he said, calmly, "there are two ways of dying in the circumstances in which we are placed." (This inexplicable person had the air of a mathematical professor lecturing to his pupils.) "The first is by being crushed; the second is to die of suffocation. I do not speak of the possibility of dying of hunger, for the supply of provisions in the *Nautilus* will certainly last longer than we shall. Let us then calculate our chances."

"As to suffocation, Captain," I replied, "that is not to be feared, because our reservoirs are full."

"Quite so; but they will only yield two days' supply of air. Now, for thirty-six hours we have been hidden under the water, and already the heavy atmosphere of the *Nautilus* requires renewal. In forty-eight hours our reserve will be exhausted."

"Well, Captain, can we be saved before forty-eight hours?"

"We will attempt it, at least, by piercing the wall that surrounds us."

"On which side?"

"Sound will tell us. I am going to run the *Nautilus* aground on the lower bank, and my men will attack the iceberg on the side that is least thick."

Captain Nemo went out. A hissing noise told me that water was entering the reservoirs. The *Nautilus* sank slowly, and rested on the ice at a depth of 350 yards, the depth at which the lower bank was immersed.

"My friends," I said, "our situation is serious, but I rely on your courage and energy."

"Sir," replied the Canadian, "I am ready to do anything for the general safety."

"Good! Ned," and I held out my hand to the Canadian.

"I will add," he continued, "that being as handy with the pickaxe as with the harpoon, if I can be useful to the Captain, he can command my services."

"He will not refuse your help. Come, Ned!"

I led him to the room where the crew of the *Nautilus* were putting on their cork-jackets. I told the Captain of Ned's proposal, which he accepted. The Canadian put on his diving suit and was ready as soon as his companions. When Ned was dressed, I re-entered the drawing room, where the panes of glass were open and standing near Conseil, I examined the layers that supported the *Nautilus*. Some instants after, we saw a dozen of the crew set foot on the bank of ice, and among them Ned Land, easily known by his stature. Captain Nemo was with them. Before proceeding to dig the walls, he took soundings, to be sure of working in the right direction. Long sounding lines were sunk in the side walls, but after fifteen yards they were again stopped by the thick wall. It was useless to attack it on the ceiling-like surface, since the iceberg itself measured more than 400 yards in height. Captain Nemo then sounded the lower surface. There ten yards of wall separated us from the water, so great was the thickness of the ice-field. It was necessary, therefore, to cut from it a piece equal in extent to the waterline of the *Nautilus*.

There were about 6000 cubic yards to move, so as to dig a hole by which we could descend to the ice-field. The work was begun immediately, and carried on with indefatigable energy. Instead of digging round the *Nautilus*, which would have involved greater difficulty, Captain Nemo had an immense trench made at eight yards from the port quarter. Then the men set to work simultaneously with their screws, on several points of its circumference. Presently the pickaxe attacked this compact matter vigorously, and large blocks were detached from the mass. By a curious effect of specific gravity, these blocks, lighter than water, fled, so to speak, to the vault of the tunnel, that increased in thickness at the top as it diminished at the base. But that mattered little, so long as the lower part grew thinner. After two hours' hard work, Ned Land came in exhausted. He and his comrades were replaced by new workers, whom Conseil and I joined. The second lieutenant of the *Nautilus* superintended us. The water seemed dreadfully cold, but I soon got warm handling the pickaxe. My movements were free, although they were made under a pressure of thirty atmospheres. When I came inside, after working two hours, for some food and rest, I found a perceptible difference between the pure fluid with which the Rouquayrol engine supplied me, and the atmosphere of the *Nautilus*, already charged with carbonic acid. The air had not been renewed for forty-eight hours, and its refreshing qualities were considerably diminished. However, after a lapse of twelve hours, we raised a block of ice only one yard thick, on the designated surface, which was about 6000 cubic yards! Reckoning that it took twelve hours to accomplish this much, it would take five nights and four days to bring this enterprise to a satisfactory conclusion. Five nights and four days! And we had air enough for only two days in the reservoirs? "Without taking into account," said Ned, "that even if we get out of this infernal prison, we shall still be locked under the iceberg closed off from all possible connection with the air." True enough! Who could then foresee the minimum of time necessary for our deliverance? We might be suffocated before the *Nautilus* could regain the surface of the waves. Was it destined to perish in this ice-tomb, with all those it enclosed? The situation was terrible. But everyone looked the danger in the face, and each was determined to do his duty to the last.

As I expected, during the night another block a yard square was carried away, and depressed still further the immense hollow. But in the morning, dressed in my cork-jacket, I went through the slushy mass at a temperature of six or seven degrees below zero, and I remarked that the side walls were gradually closing. The beds of water farthest from the ditch, that were not warmed by the men's body heat, showed a tendency to freeze solid. In the presence of this new and imminent danger, what would happen to our chances of safety? How could we halt the freezing that would burst the walls of the *Nautilus* as if they were made of glass?

I did not tell my companions of this new danger. What was the good of dampening the energy they displayed in the difficult struggle to escape? But when I went on board again, I told Captain Nemo of this grave complication.

"I know it," he said, in that calm tone which could counteract the most terrible apprehensions. "It is one more danger, but I see no way of escaping it. The only chance of safety is to be quicker than the freezing. We must be beforehand about it, that is all."

For several hours I used my pickaxe vigorously. The work strengthened me. Besides, to work was to leave the *Nautilus*, and breathe the pure air from the reservoirs, supplied by our apparatus. Towards evening the trench was dug one yard deeper. When I returned on board, I was nearly suffocated by the carbonic acid with which the air was filled—ah! If we had only the chemical means to get rid of this harmful gas. We had plenty of oxygen; all this water contained a considerable quantity, and by melting it with our powerful batteries, we would restore the life-giving fluid. But what good would that accomplish, since the carbonic acid produced by our respiration had invaded every part of the vessel? To absorb it, it would be necessary to fill jars with caustic potash, and shake them incessantly. Now this substance was lacking on board and nothing could replace it. That evening Captain Nemo ought to open the taps of his reservoirs, and let some pure air into the *Nautilus*. Without this precaution, we could not get rid of the feeling of suffocation. The next day, March 26th, I resumed my miner's work by attacking the fifth yard. The side walls and the lower surface of the iceberg had thickened visibly. It was evident that they would meet before the *Nautilus* was able to disengage itself. Despair seized me for an instant, my pickaxe nearly fell from my hands.

What was the use of digging if I was to be suffocated, crushed by water that was turning into stone?—a punishment that the ferocity of savages could not have invented! Just then Captain Nemo passed near me. I touched his hand and showed him the walls of our prison. The wall to port had advanced to less than four yards from the hull of the *Nautilus*. The Captain understood me, and signed to me to follow him. We went on board. I took off my cork-jacket, and accompanied him to the saloon.

"M. Aronnax, we must attempt a desperate remedy, or we shall be sealed up in this solidified water as in cement."

"Yes; but what is to be done?"

"Ah! if my *Nautilus* were strong enough to bear this pressure without being crushed!"

"Sir?" I asked, not catching the Captain's idea.

"Do you not understand," he replied, "that this congealing water can help us? Do you not see that, as it solidifies, it could burst through this field of ice that imprisons us, as, when water freezes, it bursts the hardest stones? Do you not perceive that it could be an agent of rescue instead of destruction?"

"Yes, Captain, perhaps. But whatever much resistance to being crushed the *Nautilus* possesses, it could not sustain this terrible pressure, and would be flattened like an iron plate."

"I know it, sir. Therefore we must not reckon on the aid of nature, but on our own exertions. We must stop this solidification. Not only will the side walls be pressed together; but there is not ten feet of water before or behind the *Nautilus*. The congealing gains on us from all sides."

"How long will the air in the reservoirs enable us to breathe on board?"

The Captain looked in my face. "After tomorrow they will be empty!"

A cold sweat came over me. However, should I have been astonished at the answer? For five days we had lived on our air reserves. And what was left of the fresh air must be kept for the workers. Even now, as I write, my recollection is still so vivid, that an involuntary terror seizes me, and my lungs feel depressed air. Meanwhile Captain Nemo reflected silently, and evidently an idea struck him; but he seemed to reject it. At last, these words escaped his lips—

"Boiling water!" he muttered.

"Boiling water?" I cried.

"Yes, sir. We are enclosed in a space that is relatively confined. Would not jets of boiling water, constantly forced by the pumps, raise the temperature and halt the congealing?"

"Let us try it," I said, resolutely.

"Let us try, Professor."

The thermometer outside stood at seven degrees. Captain Nemo took me to the galley, where stood the large distillery that supplied drinkable water by evaporation. These were filled with water, and all the electric heat from the batteries was forced through the coils bathed in water. In a few minutes this water reached a hundred degrees. It was directed towards the pumps, while fresh water replaced it in proportion. The heat developed by the batteries was such that even cold water taken from the sea, after merely going through the distillery, came boiling into the barrels of the pump. The injection was begun, and three hours later the thermometer showed six degrees below zero outside. One degree had been gained. Two hours later the thermometer showed only four degrees. "We shall succeed," I said to the Captain, after watching anxiously for the result of the operation.

"I think," he answered, "that we shall not be crushed. We need not fear suffocation any longer."

During the night the temperature of the water rose to one degree below zero. The injections could not bring it higher. But as the seawater cannot congeal at less than two degrees, I no longer feared the dangers of solidification.

The next day, March 27th, six yards of ice had been removed, only four yards remaining to be cleared away. There was forty-eight hours' work. The air inside the *Nautilus* could not be renewed, and this day would make it worse. A feeling of intolerable heaviness oppressed me. Towards three o'clock in the afternoon this anguish increased to a violent degree. Yawns almost dislocated my jaws. My lungs panted after oxygen and the air became more and more rarefied. A mental torpor seized me. I lay powerless, almost unconscious. My brave Conseil, though exhibiting the same symptoms and suffering in the same manner, never left me. He took my hand and encouraged me, and I heard him murmur, "Oh, if I could only not breathe, so as to leave more air for my master!"

Tears came into my eyes on hearing him speak thus. If the situation was so unbearable to everyone inside the ship, we should hasten joyously to put on our cork-jackets and take our turn to work. Pickaxes rang on the frozen icebeds. Our arms ached, skin tore off our hands. But what were these labors, what did the wounds matter? The air of life came to our lungs! we breathed! we breathed!

All this time, no one prolonged his turn beyond the prescribed time. His task accomplished, each one handed his panting companions the breathing apparatus that kept him alive. Captain Nemo set the example of submitting to this severe discipline. When his turn came, he gave up his tank to another, and returned to the vitiated air on board, calm, unflinching, unmurmuring.

On that day the usual work was accomplished with more vigor than ever. Only two yards remained to be raised on all the surface. Two yards only separated us from the open sea. But the reservoirs were nearly emptied of air. The little that remained must be kept for the workers; not a particle for inside the *Nautilus*. When I went back on board, I became half suffocated. What a night! I know not how to describe it. The next day my breathing was oppressed. Dizziness accompanied the pain in my head, and made me like a drunken man. My companions showed the same symptoms. Some members of the crew breathed with a death rattle.

On that day, the sixth of our imprisonment, Captain Nemo, finding the pickaxes too slow, resolved to crush the ice-bed that still separated us from the water. This man's coolness and energy never forsook him. He subdued his physical pains by moral strength.

He ordered the vessel lightened, that is to say, raised from the ice-bed by changing the specific gravity. When it was floating the men towed it into place over the immense trench designed to follow the waterline. Then filling his reservoirs of water, he went below and shut himself in the watertight compartment.

All the crew then came on board, and the double door was shut. The *Nautilus* then rested on a bed of ice less than one yard thick, which by the sounding leads had been perforated in a thousand places. The taps of the reservoir were then opened, and a hundred cubic yards of water was let in, increasing the weight of the *Nautilus* by 1800 tons. We waited, we listened, forgetting our suffering in hope. Our lives depended on this last chance. Notwithstanding the buzzing in my head, I soon heard a humming sound under the hull of the *Nautilus*. The ice cracked with a strange noise, like a tearing paper, and the *Nautilus* dropped.

"We are off!" murmured Conseil in my ear.

I could not answer him. I seized his hand, and pressed it convulsively. All of a sudden, under the weight of its frightful overcharge, the *Nautilus* shot under the water like a bullet, as if falling into a void. Then all the electric power was applied to the pumps, that soon began to force water out of the reservoirs. After a few minutes, our fall was halted. Soon the manometer indicated an ascending movement. The screw, going at full speed, made the iron hull tremble to its very bolts, sweeping us toward the north. But if we had to sail under the iceberg another day before reaching open sea, we would all be dead.

Stretched upon a divan in the library, I was almost gone. My faculties were suspended. I neither saw nor heard. All notion of time had gone from my mind. My muscles could not contract. I do not know how many hours passed thus, but I became aware of an agony that was overwhelming me. I felt that I was dying. Suddenly I revived. Some breaths of air penetrated my lungs. Had we risen to the surface? Were we free of the iceberg? No; Ned and Conseil, my two brave friends, were sacrificing themselves to save me. Some air still remained at the bottom of one tank. Instead of using it, they had saved it for me, and while they were being suffocated, they gave me life drop by drop. I wanted to push the thing away, they held my hands, and for a few moments I breathed freely. I looked at the clock; it was eleven in the morning. It should be the 28th of March. The *Nautilus* was going at a frightful pace, forty miles an hour. It literally tore through the water. Where was Captain Nemo? Had he succumbed? Were his companions dead with him? The manometer indicated that we were not more than twenty feet from the surface. A mere shell of ice separated us from the air, could we not break it? Perhaps. At least, the *Nautilus* was going to try. I felt the ship take an oblique position, lowering its stern, and raising the bow. One introduction of water had been enough to alter its equilibrium. Then, impelled by its powerful screw, it attacked the ice-field from below with the force of a great battering ram. It broke through, bit by bit, pulling back and then putting on full speed against the ice-field which shattered; and at last, with one supreme effort, forced itself out upon the icy surface that cracked beneath its weight. The panel was opened—one could say ripped off—and the fresh air came pouring into every part of the *Nautilus*.

Chapter 17

From Cape Horn to the Amazon

How I got on deck, I have no idea; perhaps the Canadian carried me there. But I breathed, I inhaled the life-giving air. My two companions were almost drunk on it. Starving men hardly dare to eat the first simple food offered to them. We, on the contrary, felt no need to restrain ourselves. We could draw the air freely into our lungs, and it was the breeze, the breeze alone, that filled us with voluptuous delight.

"Ah!" said Conseil, "how delightful this oxygen is! Master need not fear to breathe it. There is enough for everybody."

Ned Land did not speak, but he opened his jaws wide enough to frighten a shark. Our strength soon returned, and when I looked round me, I saw we were alone on deck. Except for the Captain, the crew of the *Nautilus* were satisfied with the air that circulated below; none of them had come to drink in the open air.

The first words I spoke were words of

gratitude and thankfulness to my two companions. Ned and Conseil had saved my life during the last two hours of this long agony. All my gratitude could not repay such devotion.

"My friends," said I, "we are bound one to the other forever, and I am under infinite obligations to you."

"Which I shall take advantage of," exclaimed the Canadian.

"What do you mean?" said Conseil.

"I mean that I shall take you with me when I leave this infernal *Nautilus*.

"Well," said Conseil, "after all this, are we going in the right direction?"

"Yes," I replied, "for we are following the sun, and here the sun is in the north."

"No doubt," said Ned Land. "But it remains to be seen whether Nemo will bring the ship into the Pacific or the Atlantic Ocean, that is, into seas that are traveled, or deserted."

I could not answer that question, and I feared that Captain Nemo would rather take us to that vast ocean that touches the coasts of Asia and America at the same time. He would thus complete this underwater tour of the world, and return to those waters where the *Nautilus* could sail freely. We ought, before long, to settle this important point.

The *Nautilus* was going fast. The polar circle was soon crossed and the course set for Cape Horn. We passed the cape March 31st, at seven o'clock in the evening. Then all our sufferings were forgotten. The remembrance of that imprisonment in the ice was effaced from our minds. We thought only of the future. Captain Nemo did not appear again either in the saloon or on the deck. The point shown each day on the planisphere, and marked by the lieutenant, showed me the exact direction of the *Nautilus*. Now, it was evident, to my great satisfaction, that we were going back to the north by way of the Atlantic. The next day, April 1st, when the *Nautilus* ascended to the surface, some minutes before noon, we sighted land to the west. It was Tierra del Fuego, which the first navigators named thus from seeing the quantity of smoke that rose from the natives' huts. The coast seemed low to me, but in the distance rose high mountains. I even thought I had a glimpse of Mount Sarmiento, that rises 2070 yards above the level of the sea, with a very sharp summit, which, depending on whether it is misty or clear, is a sign of wet or fine weather. At this moment, the peak was clearly defined against the sky. The *Nautilus*, diving again under the water, approached the coast, which was only some few miles off.

From the windows in the saloon I saw long seaweeds, and gigantic fuci, and varech with their sharp polished filaments—of which the open polar sea contains so many specimens. They measured about 300 yards in length—real cables, thicker than one's thumb. Having great strength, they are often used as ropes by vessels. Another weed known as kelp, with leaves four feet long, buried in the coral concretions, waved at the bottom. It served as nest and food for myriads of crustacea and molluscs, crabs and cuttle-fish. There seals and otters had splendid repasts, eating the flesh of fish along with sea-vegetables, according to the English fashion. Over this fertile and luxuriant ground the *Nautilus* passed with great speed. Towards evening, it approached the Falkland group, the rough summits of which I recognized the following day. The depth of the sea was moderate. On deck, our nets brought in beautiful specimens of seaweed, and particularly a certain fucus, the roots of which were filled with the best mussels in the world. Geese and ducks landed by dozens on the deck, and soon took their places in the pantry. With regard to fish, I observed especially specimens of the goby species, some two feet long, white and yellow spots all over. I admired also numerous medusae, and the finest of the sort, the crysaora, peculiar to the sea about the Falkland Isles. I should have liked to preserve some specimens of these delicate zoophytes; but they are like clouds, shadows, apparitions, that evaporate when out of their native element.

When the last heights of the Falklands had disappeared from the horizon, the *Nautilus* dived to between twenty and twenty-five yards, and followed the South American shoreline. Captain Nemo did not appear. Until the 3rd of April we did not leave the shores of Patagonia, sometimes underwater, sometimes at the surface. The *Nautilus* passed the large estuary at the mouth of the River Plata, and on the 4th of April, was fifty-six miles off Uruguay. We had now covered sixteen-thousand leagues since our embarkation in the seas of Japan. About eleven o'clock in the morning the Tropic of Capricorn was crossed on the thirty-seventh meridian, and we passed Cape Frio standing well out to sea. Captain Nemo, to Ned Land's great displeasure, did not like the neighborhood of the inhabited coasts of Brazil, for we went at a giddy speed. Not a fish, nor a bird of the swiftest kind could follow us, and the natural wonders of these seas escaped my observation.

This speed was kept up for several days, and in the evening of the 9th of April we sighted Cape San Roque, the most westerly point of South America. But then the *Nautilus* swerved again, and sought the lowest depth of an underwater valley that extends from this cape to Sierra Leone on the African coast. This valley bifurcates to the parallel of the Antilles, and ends at the north in an enormous depression 9000 yards deep. Here, the geological basin of the ocean forms, as far as the Lesser Antilles, a steep cliff three and a half miles high and at the parallel of the Cape Verde Islands, another wall no less considerable, that encloses the sunken continent of Atlantis. The bottom of this immense valley is dotted with mountains, that give to these submarine places a picturesque aspect. I speak, in part, from the manuscript charts that were in the library of the *Nautilus*—charts evidently made by Captain Nemo's hand, from his personal observations. For two days the deep, deserted waters were visited by means of the inclined planes. But, on the 11th of April, the *Nautilus* rose suddenly, and land was sighted near the opening of the Amazon River, a vast estuary, the mouth of which is so wide that it freshens the seawater for a distance of several leagues.

The equator was crossed. Twenty miles to the west were the Guianas, a French territory, on which we could have found an easy refuge. But a stiff breeze was blowing, and the angry waves would not have allowed a small boat to face them. Ned Land understood that, no doubt, for he spoke not a word about it. For my part, I made no allusion to his schemes of flight, for I would not urge him to make an attempt that must inevitably fail. I passed the time pleasantly in interesting studies. During the days of April 11th and 12th, the *Nautilus* did not leave the surface of the sea, and the net brought in a marvelous haul of zoophytes, fish and reptiles. Some zoophytes had been fished up in the meshes of the nets. They were for the most part beautiful phyctallines, belonging to the actinidian family, and among other species the phyctalis protexta, peculiar to that part of the ocean, with a little cylindrical trunk, ornamented with vertical lines, speckled with red dots, crowning a marvelous blossoming of tentacles. As to the molluscs, they consisted of some I had already observed—turritellas, olive porphyras, with regular lines intercrossed, with red spots standing out plainly against the flesh; odd pteroceras, like petrified scorpions; translucid hyaleas, argonauts, cuttle-fish (excellent eating), and certain species of calmars that naturalists of antiquity have classed amongst the flying-fish, and that serve principally for bait for cod-fishing. I had now an opportunity of studying several species of fish on these shores. Amongst the cartilaginous ones, "petromyzons-pricka," a sort of eel, fifteen inches long, with a greenish head, violet fins, gray-blue back, brown belly, silvered and sown with bright spots, the pupil of the eye encircled with gold—a curious animal, that the current of the Amazon had drawn to the sea, for they inhabit fresh waters—tubular streaks, with pointed snouts, and a long loose tail, armed with a long jagged sting; little sharks, a yard long, gray and whitish skin, and several rows of teeth, bent back, that are generally known by the name of pantouffles; vespertillios, a kind of red isosceles triangle, half a yard long, to which pectorals are attached by fleshy prolongations that make them look like bats, but that their horny appendage, situated near the nostrils, has given them the name of sea-unicorns; lastly, some species of balistae, the curassavian, whose spots were of brilliant gold color, and the caspriscus of clear violet, and with varying shades like a pigeon's throat.

I end here this catalogue, which is somewhat dry perhaps, but very exact, with a series of bony fish that I observed in passing belonging to the apteronotes, and whose snout is white as snow, the body of a beautiful black, marked with a very long loose fleshy strip, odontognathes, armed with spikes; sardines, nine inches long, glittering with a bright silver light; a species of mackerel provided with two anal fins; centronotes of a blackish tint, that are fished for with torches, long fish, two yards in length, with fat flesh, white and firm, which, when they are fresh, taste like eel, and when dry, like smoked salmon; labres, half red, covered with scales only at the bottom of the dorsal and anal fins; chrysoptera, on which gold and silver blend their brightness with that of the ruby and topaz; golden-tailed spares, the flesh of which is extremely delicate, and whose phosphorescent properties betray them in the midst of the waters; orange-colored spares with long tongues; maigres, with gold caudal fins, dark thorntails, anableps of Surinam, etc.

Notwithstanding this "et cetera," I must not omit to mention fish that Conseil will long remember, and with good reason. One of our nets had hauled up a sort of very flat rayfish, which, with the tail cut off, formed a perfect disc, and weighed twenty ounces. It was white underneath, red above, with large round spots of dark blue encircled with black, very glossy skin, terminating in a bilobed fin. Laid out on the platform, it struggled, tried to turn itself by convulsive movements, and made so many efforts, that one last turn nearly sent it into the sea. But Conseil, not wishing to let the fish go, rushed to it, and, before I could prevent him, had seized it with both hands. In a moment he was overthrown, his legs in the air, and half his body paralyzed, crying—

"Oh! Master, master! Come to me!"

The Canadian and I lifted him up, and rubbed his arms till he became conscious. The unfortunate Conseil had attacked a cramp-fish of the most dangerous kind, the cumana. This odd animal, a conductor of electricity like water, strikes fish at several yards' distance, so great is the power of its electric organ, the two principal surfaces of which do not measure less than twenty-seven square feet.

The next day, April 12th, the *Nautilus* approached a Dutch island near the mouth of the Maroni. There several groups of sea-cows herded together. They were manatees, that, like the dugong and the stellera, belong to the sirenaian order. These beautiful animals, peaceable and inoffensive, from eighteen to twenty-one feet in length, weigh at least sixteen hundredweight. I told Ned Land and Conseil that provident nature had assigned an important role to these mammalia. Indeed, they, like the seals, are designed to graze on the submarine prairies, and thus destroy the accumulation of weed that obstructs the tropical rivers.

"And do you know," I added, "what has been the result since men have almost entirely annihiliated this useful race? The putrefied weeds have poisoned the air, and the poisoned air causes yellow fever, that desolates these beautiful countries. Enormous vegetations are multiplied under the warm seas, and the evil is irresistibly spread from the mouth of the River Plata to Florida. If we are to believe Toussenel, this plague is nothing to what it would be if the seas were cleared of whales and seals. Then, infested with poulps, medusae, and cuttle-fish, they would become immense centers of infection, since their waves would not possess these vast stomachs that God had charged to digest the surface of the seas."

However, without disputing these theories, the crew of the *Nautilus* took possession of half a dozen manatees. They provisioned the larders with excellent flesh, superior to beef and veal. This sport was not interesting. The manatees allowed themselves to be shot without defending themselves. Several thousand pounds of meat were stored up on board to be dried. On this day, a successful haul of fish increased the stores of the *Nautilus*, so full of game were these seas. They were echeneides belonging to the third family of the malacopterygiens. Their flattened discs were composed of transverse movable cartilaginous plates, by which the animal was enabled to create a vacuum, and so to adhere to any object like a cupping-glass. The remora that I had observed in the Mediterranean belongs to this species. But the one of which we are speaking was the echeneis osterchara, peculiar to this sea.

The fishing over, the *Nautilus* neared the coast. A number of sea turtles were sleeping on the surface of the water. It is difficult to capture these valuable reptiles, for the least noise awakens them, and their solid shell is proof against the harpoon. But the echeneis effects their capture with extraordinary precision and certainty. The enemies are, indeed, a living fishhook, which would make the fortune of an inexperienced fisherman. The crew of the *Nautilus* tied a ring to the tail of these fish, large enough not to encumber their movements, and to this ring a long cord, lashed to the ship's side by the other end. The echeneids, thrown into the sea, directly began their game, and attached themselves to the armor of the turtles. Their tenacity was such, that they were torn apart rather than let go their hold. The men hauled them on board, and with them the turtles to which they adhered. They took also several cacouannes a yard long, which weighed 400 lbs. Their carapace is covered with large bony plates, thin, transparent, brown, with white and yellow spots and fetch a good price in the market. Besides, they were excellent from the edible point of view, as well as the fresh turtles which brought to a close our stay on the shores of the Amazon, and by nightfall the *Nautilus* had regained the high seas.

Chapter 18
The Poulps

For several days the *Nautilus* sailed off the American coast. Evidently it did not wish to risk the tides of the Gulf of Mexico, or of the seas of the Antilles. April 16th, we sighted Martinique and Guadaloupe from a distance of about thirty miles. I saw their tall peaks for only an instant. The Canadian, who counted on carrying out his schemes in the Gulf, either by landing or by hailing one of the numerous boats that go from one island to another, was quite disheartened. Flight would have been quite practicable, if Ned Land had been able to take possession of the small boat without the Captain's knowledge.

But in the open sea it could not be thought of. The Canadian, Conseil, and I, had a long conversation on this subject. For six months we had been prisoners on board the *Nautilus*. We had traveled 17,000 leagues; and, as Ned Land said, there was no reason why it should not come to an end. We could hope for nothing from the Captain of the *Nautilus*, only from ourselves. Besides, for some time past Nemo had become graver, more retiring, less sociable. He seemed to shun me. I met him rarely. Formerly, he was pleased to explain the submarine marvels to me. Now, he left me to my studies, and came no more to the saloon. What change had come over him? For what reason? For my part, I did not wish to have buried with me my curious and novel studies. I now had the ability to write a true book about the sea. Sooner or later, I wished it to see daylight.

Then again, in the water by the Antilles, ten yards below the surface of the waters, through open panels, what interesting growths I had to enter on my daily notes! There were, among other zoophytes, those known under the name of physalia pelagica, a sort of large oblong bladder, with mother-of-pearl rays, holding out their membranes to the wind, and letting their blue tentacles float like threads of silk; charming medusae to the eye, real nettles to the touch, that distill a corrosive fluid. There were also annelids, a yard and a half long, furnished with a pink horn, and with 1700 locomotive organs, that wind through the waters, and throw out in passing all the light of the solar spectrum. There were, in the fish category, some Malabar rays, enormous gristly things, ten feet long, weighing 600 pounds, the pectoral fin triangular in the midst of a slightly humped back, the eyes fixed in the extremities of the face, beyond the head, and which floated like weft, and looked sometimes like an opaque shutter on our glass window. There were American balistae, which nature has only dressed in black and white; gobies, with yellow fins and prominent jaw; mackerel sixteen feet long, with short-pointed teeth, covered with small scales, belonging to the albacore species. Then, in swarms, appeared gray mullet. Covered with stripes of gold from head to tail, beating their resplendent fins, they are like masterpieces of jewelry, and were consecrated formerly to Diana. They were destroyed by rich Romans, and a proverb says of them, "whoever takes them does not eat them." Lastly, pomacanthe dorees, ornamented with emerald bands, dressed in velvet and silk, passed before our eyes like Veronese lords; spurred spari passed with their pectoral fins; clupanodons fifteen inches long, surrounded by their phosphorescent light; mullet beat the sea with their large jagged tails; red vendaces seemed to mow the waves with their showy pectoral fins; and silvery selenes, worthy of their name, rose on the horizon of the waters like so many moons. April 20th, we had risen to a mean height of 1500 yards. The land nearest us then was the archipelago of the Bahamas. There rose high, underwater cliffs covered with large weeds, giant laminariae and fuci, a perfect trellis of hydrophytes worthy of a Titan world. It was about eleven o'clock when Ned Land drew my attention to a severe stinging which was inflicted by the large seaweeds.

"Well," I said, "these are proper caverns for poulps, and I should not be astonished to see some of these monsters."

"What!" said Conseil, "cuttle-fish, of the cephalopod class?"

"No," I said, "poulps of huge dimensions."

"I will never believe that such animals exist," said Ned.

"Well," said Conseil, with the most serious air in the world, "I remember perfectly having seen a large vessel drawn under the waves by a cephalopod's arm."

"You saw that?" said the Canadian.

"Yes, Ned."

"With your own eyes?"

"With my own eyes."

"Where, pray, might that be?"

"At St. Malo," answered Conseil.

"In the port?" said Ned, ironically.

"No; in a church," replied Conseil.

"In a church!" cried the Canadian.

"Yes, friend Ned. In a picture representing the poulp in question."

"Good!" said Ned Land, bursting out laughing.

"He is quite right," I said. "I have heard of this picture. But the subject represented is taken from a legend, and you know what to think of legends in the matter of natural history. Besides, when it is a question of monsters, the imagination is apt to run wild. Not only is it supposed that these poulps can draw down vessels, but a certain Olaus Magnus speaks of a cephalopod a mile long, that is more like an island than an animal. It is also said that the Bishop of Nidros was building an altar on an immense rock. Mass finished, the rock began to walk, and returned to the sea. The rock was a poulp. Another bishop, Pontoppidan, speaks also of a poulp on which a regiment of cavalry could maneuver. Lastly, the ancient naturalists speak of monsters whose mouths were like gulfs, and which were too large to pass through the Straits of Gibraltar.''

"But how much is true of these stories?'' asked Conseil.

"Nothing, my friends—or least what passed the limit of truth and becomes a legend. Nevertheless, there must be some food for the imagination of storytellers. One cannot deny that poulps and cuttle-fish of a large species exist, inferior, however, to the cetaceans. Aristotle has said that the dimensions of a cuttle-fish were five cubits, or nine feet two inches. Our fishermen frequently see some that are more than four feet long. Some skeletons of poulps are preserved in the museums of Trieste and Montpellier, that measure two yards in length. Besides, according to the calculations of some naturalists, one of these animals, only six feet long, would have tentacles twenty-seven feet long. That would suffice to make a formidable monster.''

"Do they fish for them in these days?'' asked Ned.

"If they do not fish for them, sailors at least see them. One of my friends, Captain Paul Bos of Havre, has often affirmed that he met one of these monsters, of colossal dimensions, in the Indian seas. But the most astonishing event, and one which does not permit denial of the existence of these gigantic animals, happened some years ago, in 1861.''

''What is the event?'' asked Ned Land.

''In 1861, to the northeast of Teneriffe, very nearly in the same latitude we are in now, the crew of the dispatch-boat *Alector* perceived a monstrous cuttle-fish swimming in the waters. Captain Bouguer went near to the animal, and attacked it with harpoons and guns, without much success, for balls and harpoons glided over the slippery back. After several fruitless attempts, the crew tried to pass a slip-knot round the mollusc. The noose slipped as far as the caudal fins, and there stopped. They tried to haul it on board, but its weight was so great that the cord separated the tail from the body, and, deprived of this ornament, he disappeared under the water.''

''Indeed! is that a fact?''

''An indisputable fact, my good Ned. They proposed to name this poulp 'Bouguer's cuttle-fish.' ''

''What length was it?'' asked the Canadian.

''Did it not measure about six yards?'' said Conseil, who, posted at the window, was examining again the irregular windings of the cliff.

''Precisely,'' I replied.

''Its head,'' rejoined Conseil, ''was it not crowned with eight tentacles, that beat the water like a nest of serpents?''

''Precisely.''

"Had not its eyes, placed at the back of its head, considerable development?"

"Yes, Conseil."

"And was not its mouth like a parrot's beak?"

"Exactly, Conseil."

"Very well! no offense to master," he replied, quietly; "if this is not Bouguer's cuttle-fish, it is, at least, one of its brothers."

I looked at Conseil. Ned hurried to the window.

"What a horrible beast!" he cried.

I looked in my turn, and could not repress a gesture of disgust. Before my eyes was a horrible monster, worthy to figure in the legends of the marvelous. It was an immense cuttle-fish, eight yards long. It swam crossways in the direction of the *Nautilus* with great speed, watching us with its enormous staring green eyes. Its eight arms, or rather feet, fixed to its head, that have given the name of cephalopod to these animals, were twice as long as its body, and were twisted like the furies' hair. One could see the 250 air-holes on the inner side of the tentacles. The monster's mouth, a horned beak like a parrot's, opened and shut vertically. Its tongue, a horned substance furnished with several rows of pointed teeth, came out quivering from this veritable pair of shears. What a freak of nature, a bird's beak on a mollusc! Its spindle-like body formed a fleshy mass that might weigh 4000 to 5000 lbs. Its color changed very quickly according to some irritation of the animal, going from livid gray to reddish brown. What angered this mollusc? No doubt the presence of the *Nautilus*, more formidable than itself, and on which its suckers or its jaws had no hold. Yet, what monsters these poulps are! What vitality the Creator has given them! What vigor in their movements! And they possess three hearts! Chance had brought us to view this cuttle-fish, and I did not wish to lose the opportunity of carefully studying this specimen of cephalopods. I overcame the horror that filled me; and, taking a pencil, began to draw it.

"Perhaps this is the same which the *Alector* saw," said Conseil.

"No," replied the Canadian, "for this is whole, and the other had lost its tail."

"The arms and tails of these animals are reformed by reintegration. In seven years, the tail of Bouguer's cuttle-fish has no doubt had time to grow."

By this time other poulps appeared at the port light. I counted seven. They formed a procession following the *Nautilus*, and I heard their beaks gnashing against the iron hull. I continued my work. These monsters kept formation with such precision, that they hardly seemed to move. Suddenly the *Nautilus* stopped. A shock made it tremble in every plate.

"Have we struck anything?" I asked.

"In any case," replied the Canadian, "we shall be free, for we are floating."

The *Nautilus* was floating, no doubt, but it did not move. A minute passed. Captain Nemo, followed by his lieutenant, entered the drawing room. I had not seen him for some time. He seemed dull. Without noticing or speaking to us, he went to the panel, looked at the poulps, and said something to his lieutenant. The latter went out. Soon the panels were shut. The ceiling was lighted. I went towards the Captain.

"A curious collection of poulps?" I said.

"Yes, indeed, Mr. Naturalist," he replied, "and we are going to fight them, man to beast."

I looked at him. I thought I had not heard aright.

"Man to beast?" I repeated.

"Yes, sir. The screw is stopped. I think that the horny jaws of one of the cuttle-fish is entangled in the blades. That is what prevents our moving."

"What are you going to do?"

"Rise to the surface, and slaughter this vermin."

"A difficult enterprise."

"Yes, indeed. The electric bullets are powerless against the soft flesh, which does not offer resistance enough to make them go off. But we shall attack them with the hatchet."

"And the harpoon, sir," said the Canadian, "if you do not refuse my help."

"I will accept it, Master Land."

"We will follow you," I said, and following Captain Nemo, we went towards the main ladder.

There, about ten men with boarding hatchets were ready for the attack. Conseil and I took hatchets. Ned Land seized a harpoon. The *Nautilus* had risen to the surface. One of the sailors, posted on the top ladder-step, unscrewed the bolts of the panels. But hardly were the screws loosed, when the panel was pulled with great violence, evidently drawn by the suckers of a poulp's arm. Immediately one of these arms slid like a serpent down the opening, and twenty others were above. With one blow of the axe, Captain Nemo cut this formidable tentacle, that slid wriggling down the ladder. Just as we were pressing one on the other to reach the deck, two other arms, lashing in the air, came down on the seaman in front of Captain Nemo, lifted him up with irresistible power. Captain Nemo uttered a cry and rushed out. We hurried after him.

What a scene! The unhappy man, seized by the tentacle, and attached to the suckers, was balanced in the air at the caprice of this enormous mollusc. He rattled in his throat, he was stifled, he cried, "Help! help!" These words, *spoken in French,* startled me! I had a fellow-countryman on board, perhaps several! That heartrending cry! I shall hear it all my life. The unfortunate man was lost. Who could rescue him from that powerful grip? However, Captain Nemo rushed to the poulp, and with one blow of the axe cut through one arm. His lieutenant struggled furiously against other monsters that crept along the flanks of the *Nautilus.* The crew fought with their axes. The Canadian, Conseil, and I, buried our weapons in the fleshy masses. A strong smell of musk penetrated the atmosphere. It was horrible!

For one instant, I thought the unhappy man, entangled with the poulp, would be torn from its powerful suction. Seven of the eight arms had been cut off. One only wriggled in the air, brandishing the victim like a feather. But just as

Captain Nemo and his lieutenant threw themselves on it, the animal ejected a stream of black liquid. We were blinded by it. When the cloud dispersed, the cuttle-fish had disappeared, and my unfortunate countryman with it. Ten or twelve poulps now invaded the deck and the sides of the *Nautilus*. We rolled pell-mell into the midst of this nest of serpents, that wriggled on the platform in waves of blood and ink. It seemed as though these slimy tentacles sprang up like the hydra's heads. Ned Land's harpoon, at each stroke, was plunged into the staring eyes of a cuttle-fish. But my bold companion was suddenly overturned by the tentacles of a monster he had not been able to avoid.

Ah! how my heart beat with emotion and horror! The formidable beak of a cuttle-fish was open over Ned Land. The unhappy man would be cut in two. I rushed to his aid. But Captain Nemo was ahead of me. His axe disappeared between the two enormous jaws, and, the Canadian, miraculously saved, got up and plunged his harpoon deep into the triple heart of the poulp.

"I owed myself this revenge!" said the Captain to the Canadian.

Ned bowed without replying. The combat had lasted a quarter of an hour. The monsters, vanquished and mutilated, left us at last, and disappeared under the waves. Captain Nemo, covered with blood, nearly exhausted, gazed upon the sea that had swallowed up one of his companions, and great tears gathered in his eyes.

Chapter 19
The Gulf Stream

None of us can ever forget that terrible scene of the 20th of April. I described it under the influence of violent emotion. Since then I have revised the account. I have read it to Conseil and to the Canadian. They found it accurate as to facts, but insufficient as to effect. To paint such pictures, one must have the pen of the most illustrious of our poets, Victor Hugo, of "The Toilers of the Deep."

I have said that Captain Nemo wept while watching the water. His grief was great. It was the second companion he had lost since our arrival on board, and what a death! That friend, crushed, stifled, bruised by the dreadful arms of a poulp, pounded by his iron jaws, would not rest with his comrades in the peaceful coral cemetery! In the midst of the struggle, the despairing cry uttered by the unfortunate man had torn my heart. The poor Frenchman, forgetting his conventional language, had taken to his own mother tongue, to utter a last appeal! Among the crew of the *Nautilus*, associated with the body and soul of the Captain, recoiling like him from all contact with men, I had a fellow countryman. Did he alone represent France in this mysterious association, evidently composed of individuals of diverse nationalities? It was one of these insoluble problems that rose up unceasingly in my mind!

Captain Nemo went to his room, and I saw him no more for some time. But that he was sad and irresolute I could tell from the ship, for he was its soul, and it received all his feelings. The *Nautilus* did not hold to its settled course; but floated about like a corpse at the will of the waves. It went at random. He could not tear himself away from the scene of the last struggle, from this sea that had devoured one of his men. Ten days passed thus. It was not till the 1st of May that the *Nautilus* resumed its northerly course, after having sighted the Bahamas at the mouth of the Bahama Channel. We were now following the current of the largest river in the sea, one that has its own shores, its fish and its natural temperatures. I mean, of course, the Gulf Stream, that same warm current, one of whose arms goes around the Sargasso Sea. It is actually a river, that flows freely in the middle of the Atlantic, its waters not mixing with those of the ocean. It is a salt river, saltier than the surrounding sea. Its mean depth is 1500 fathoms; its mean breadth ten miles. In certain places the current flows at the speed of two miles and a half an hour. The body of its waters is more considerable than that of all the rivers on the globe. It was on this ocean river that the *Nautilus* then sailed.

This current carried with it all kinds of living things. Argonauts, so common in the Mediterranean, were there in quantities. Of the gristly sort, the most remarkable were the turbot, whose slender tail forms nearly a third of its body, and who look like large lozenges twenty-five feet long; also, small sharks a yard long, with large heads, short rounded muzzles, pointed teeth in several rows, and bodies covered with scales. Among the bony fish I noticed some gray gobies, native to these waters; black giltheads, whose iris shone like fire; sirenes a yard long, with large snouts thickly set with little teeth, that uttered little cries; blue coryphaenes, in gold and silver; parrots, like the rainbows of the ocean, that could rival in color the most beautiful tropical birds; blennies with triangular heads; bluish rhombs destitute of scales; batrachoides covered with yellow transversal bands like a Greek; heaps of little gobies spotted with yellow; dipterodons with silvery heads and yellow tails; several specimens of salmon, mugilomores slender in shape, shining with a soft light that Lacepede consecrated to the devotion of his wife; and lastly, a beautiful fish, the American-knight, decorated with all the orders and ribbons, that frequents the shores of this great nation which esteems orders and ribbons so little.

I must add that, during the night, the phosphorescent waters of the Gulf Stream rivaled the electric power of our watch-light, especially in stormy weather, of which there was a great deal. May 8th, we were passing Cape Hatteras, at the latitude of North Carolina. The Gulf Stream there is seventy-five miles wide and 210 yards deep. The *Nautilus* still went at random. All supervision seemed abandoned. I thought that, under these circumstances, escape would be possible. Indeed, any inhabited shores offered an easy refuge. The sea was constantly ploughed by steamers that run between New York, or Boston, and the Gulf of Mexico, and covered day and night by little schooners and fishing smacks. We could hope to be picked up. It was a favorable opportunity, notwithstanding the thirty miles that lay between the *Nautilus* and the coasts of the United States. One unfortunate circumstance thwarted the Canadian's plans. The weather was very bad. We were nearing those shores where tempests are so frequent, that vicinity of waterspouts and cyclones actually engendered by the current of the Gulf Stream. To tempt the sea in a frail boat was certain destruction. Ned Land owned this himself. He fretted, seized with nostalgia that flight only could cure.

"Master," he said that day to me, "this must come to an end. I must make a clean breast of it. This Nemo is leaving land and going up to the north. But I declare to you, I have had enough of the South Pole, and I will not follow him to the North."

"What is to be done, Ned, since flight is out of the question now?"

"We must speak to the Captain," said he.

"You said nothing when we were in your native seas. I will speak, now we are in mine. When I think that before long the *Nautilus* will be near Nova Scotia, and that near Newfoundland is a large bay, and the St. Lawrence empties itself into that bay, and that the St. Lawrence is my river, the river of Quebec my native city—when I think of this, I feel furious, it makes my hair stand on end. Sir, I would rather throw myself into the sea! I will not stay here! I am stifled!"

The Canadian was evidently losing all patience. His vigorous nature could not stand this prolonged imprisonment. His face altered daily; his temper became more surly. I knew what he must suffer, for I was seized with nostalgia myself. Nearly seven months had passed without our having had any news from land. Captain Nemo's isolation, his altered spirits, ever since the fight with the poulps, his taciturnity, all made me view things in a different light.

"Well, sir?" said Ned, seeing I did not reply.

"Well, Ned! Do you wish me to ask Captain Nemo his intentions concerning us?"

"Yes, sir."

"Although he has already made them known?"

"Yes; I wish it settled finally. Speak for me, in my name only, if you like."

"But I so seldom meet him. He avoids me."

"That is all the more reason for you to go to see him."

I went to my room. From thence I meant to go to Captain Nemo's. It would not do to delay. I knocked at the door. No answer. I knocked again, then turned the handle. The door opened, I went in. The Captain was there. Bending over his work-table, he had not heard me. Resolved not to go without having spoken, I approached him. He raised his head quickly, frowned, and said roughly, "You here? What do you want?"

"To speak to you, Captain."

"But I am busy, sir; I am working. I leave you at liberty to work in privacy; cannot I be allowed the same?"

The reception was not encouraging; but I was determined to hear and answer everything.

"Sir," I said, coldly, "I have to speak to you on a matter that admits no delay."

"What is that, sir," he replied, ironically. "Have you discovered something that has escaped me, or has the sea delivered up any new secrets?"

We were at cross-purposes. But before I could reply, he showed me an open manuscript on his table, and said, in a more serious tone, "Here, M. Aronnax, is a manuscript written in several languages. It contains the sum of my studies of the sea. If it please God, it shall not perish with me. This manuscript, signed with my name, complete with the history of my life, will be shut up in a little box that cannot sink. The last survivor of all of us on board the *Nautilus* will throw this case into the sea, and it will go whither it is borne by the waves."

This man's name! His history written by himself! His mystery would then be revealed someday.

"Captain," I said, "I can approve of the idea

that makes you act thus. The result of your studies must not be lost. But the means you employ seem to me to be primitive. Who knows where the winds will carry this case, and into whose hands it will fall? Could you not use some other means? Could not you, or one of yours—"

"Never, sir!" he said, hastily interrupting me.

"But I, and my companions are ready to keep this manuscript in store; and, if you will set us at liberty—"

"At liberty?" said the Captain rising.

"Yes, sir; that is the subject on which I wish to question you. For seven months we have been here on board, and I ask you today, in the name of my companions, and in my own, if your intention is to keep us here always?"

"M. Aronnax, I will answer you today as I did seven months ago: Whoever enters the *Nautilus* must never quit it."

"You impose actual slavery on us!"

"Give it what name you please."

"But everywhere the slave has the right to regain his liberty."

"Who denies you this right? Have I ever tried to chain you with an oath?"

He looked at me with his arms crossed.

"Sir," I said, "to return a second time to this subject will be neither to your taste nor mine. But, as we have begun it, let us go through with it. I repeat, it is not only myself whom it concerns. Study is to me a relief, a diversion, a passion that could make me forget everything. Like you, I am willing to live obscure, in the frail hope of bequeathing one day, to future time, the result of my labors. But it is otherwise with Ned Land. Every man, worthy of the name, deserves some consideration. Have you thought that love of liberty, hatred of slavery, can give rise to schemes of revenge in a nature like the Canadian's; that he could think, attempt, and try—"

I was silenced; Captain Nemo rose.

"Whatever Ned Land thinks of, attempts, or tries, what does it matter to me? I did not seek him! It is not for my pleasure that I keep him on board! As for you, M. Aronnax, you are one of those who can understand everything, even silence. I have nothing more to say to you. Let this first time you have come to treat of this subject be the last. For a second time I will not listen to you."

I retired. Our situation was critical. I related my conversation to my two companions.

"We know now," said Ned, "that we can expect nothing from this man. The *Nautilus* is nearing Long Island. We will escape, whatever the weather may be."

But the sky became more and more threatening. Signs of a hurricane became manifest. The atmosphere was becoming white and misty. On the horizon fine streaks of cirrous clouds were succeeded by masses of cumuli. Other low clouds passed swiftly by. The swollen sea rose in huge billows. The birds disappeared, with the exception of the petrels, those friends of the storm. The barometer fell sharply, and indicated an extreme tension of the vapors. The mixture in the storm glass separated under the influence of the electricity that pervaded the atmosphere. The storm broke on the 18th of May, just as the *Nautilus* was floating off Long Island, some miles from the port of New York. I can describe this strife of the elements for, instead of fleeing to the depths of the sea, Captain Nemo, by an unaccountable caprice, braved it at the surface. The wind blew from the southwest at first. Captain Nemo, during the squalls, had taken his place on deck. He made himself fast, to prevent being washed overboard by the enormous waves. I had myself hoisted up, and made fast also, dividing my admiration between the tempest and this extraordinary man who was coping with it. The raging sea was swept by huge gusts of wind, which were picking up water from the waves.

The *Nautilus*, sometimes lying on its side, sometimes standing on end, rolled and pitched terribly. About five o'clock a torrent of rain fell, that lulled neither sea nor wind. The hurricane blew nearly forty leagues an hour. Under these conditions it overturns houses, breaks iron gates, displaces twenty-four pounders. However, the *Nautilus*, in the midst of the tempest, confirmed the words of a clever engineer, "There is no well-constructed hull that cannot defy the sea." This was not a resisting rock; it was a steel spindle, obedient and movable, without rigging or masts, that braved the fury of the sea with impunity. However, I watched these raging waves attentively. They measured fifteen feet in height, and were 150 to 175 yards long, and their speed of passage was thirty feet per second. Their bulk and power increased with the depth of the water. Such waves as these, at the Hebrides, have displaced a mass weighing 8400 lbs. The tempest of December 23rd, 1864, after destroying the town of Yeddo, in Japan, with waves like these, broke the same day on the shores of America. The intensity of the storm increased with the night. The barometer, as in 1860 at Reunion during a cyclone, fell seven-tenths by the close of day. I saw a large vessel on the horizon struggling painfully. She was trying to lie to under half steam, to keep up above the waves. It was probably one of the steamers of the line from New York to Liverpool, or Havre. It soon disappeared in the gloom. At ten o'clock in the evening the sky was on fire, streaked with vivid lightning. I could not bear the brightness of it, while the Captain, looking at it, seemed to envy the spirit of the tempest. A terrible noise filled the air, a complex noise, made up of the howls of the crushed waves, the roaring of the wind, and the claps of thunder. The wind veered suddenly to all points of the horizon. The cyclone, rising in the east, returned after passing by the north, west, and south, in the inverse course pursued by the circular storms of the southern hemisphere. Ah, that Gulf Stream! It deserves its name of the King of Tempests. It is that which causes those formidable cyclones, by the difference of temperature between its air and its currents. A shower of fire had succeeded the rain. The drops of water were changed to sharp spikes. One would have thought that Captain Nemo was courting a death worthy of himself, a death by lightning. As the *Nautilus*, pitching dreadfully, raised its steel spur in the air, it seemed to act as a conductor, and I saw long sparks burst from it. Crushed and without strength, I crawled to the panel, opened it, and descended to the saloon. The storm was then at its height. It was impossible to stand upright in the interior of the *Nautilus*. Captain Nemo came down about twelve. I heard the reservoirs filling by degrees, and the *Nautilus* sank slowly beneath the waves. Through the open windows in the saloon I saw large fish terrified, passing like phantoms in the water. Some were struck before my eyes. The *Nautilus* was still descending. I thought that at about eight fathoms we should find calm. But no! the upper layers were too violently agitated for that. We had to seek repose at more than twenty-five fathoms in the bowels of the deep. But there, what quiet, what silence, what peace! Who could have told that such a hurricane had been let loose on the surface of that ocean?

Chapter 20
From Latitude 47° 24'
Longitude 17° 28'

In consequence of the storm, we had been thrown eastward once more. All hope of escape on the shores of New York or the St. Lawrence had faded away. Poor Ned, in despair, had isolated himself like Captain Nemo. Conseil and I, however, never left each other. I said that the *Nautilus* had gone off to the east. I should have said (to be more exact) the northeast. For some days, it wandered first on the surface, and then beneath it, amid those fogs, so dreaded by sailors. What accidents are due to these thick fogs! How many ships go aground upon these reefs when the wind drowns the noise of the breaking of the waves! What collisions between vessels, in spite of their warning lights, whistles, and alarm bells! And the bottoms of these seas look like a field of battle where still lie all whom the ocean has conquered—some old and already encrusted, others fresh and reflecting from their iron bands and copper-plates the brilliancy of our lantern.

On the 15th of May we were at the extreme south of the Newfoundland Banks. These banks consist of alluvia, or large heaps of organic matter, brought either from the Equator by the Gulf Stream, or from the North Pole by the counter current of cold water which skirts the American coast. There also are heaped up those erratic blocks which are carried along by the broken ice; and close by, a vast charnel-house of molluscs or zoophytes, which perish here by millions. The depth of the sea is not great at Newfoundland—only a few hundred fathoms; but towards the south is a depression of 1500 fathoms. There the Gulf Stream widens. It loses some of its speed and some of its temperature, but it becomes a sea.

It was on the 17th of May, about 500 miles from Heart's Content, at a depth of more than 1400 fathoms, that I saw the electric cable lying on the bottom. Conseil, to whom I had not mentioned it, thought at first that it was a gigantic sea-serpent. But I undeceived the worthy fellow, and by way of consolation related several particulars regarding the laying of this cable. The first one was laid in the years 1857 and 1858; but, after transmitting about 400 telegrams, would not work any longer. In 1863, the engineers constructed another one, measuring 2000 miles in length, and weighing 4500 tons, which was embarked on the *Great Eastern*. This attempt also failed.

On the 25th of May the *Nautilus*, being at a depth of more than 1918 fathoms, was on the precise spot where the rupture occurred which ruined the enterprise. It was within 638 miles of the coast of Ireland; at half-past two in the afternoon, they discovered that communication with Europe had ceased. The electricians on board resolved to cut the cable before fishing it up, and at eleven o'clock at night they had recovered the damaged part. They made another point and spliced it, and it was once more submerged. But some days later it broke again, and in the depths of the ocean could not be recaptured. The Americans, however, were not discouraged. Cyrus Field, the bold promoter of the enterprise, in which he had sunk all his own fortune, started a new subscription, which was at once filled, and another cable was constructed on better principles. The bundles of conducting wires were each enveloped in gutta-percha, and protected by a wadding of hemp, contained in a metallic covering. The *Great Eastern* sailed on the 13th of July, 1866. The operation worked well. But one incident occurred. Several times in unrolling the cable they observed that nails had been recently forced into it, evidently with the motive of destroying it. Captain Anderson, the officers, and engineers, consulted together, and posted a notice that if the offender was surprised on board, he would, without further trial, be thrown into the sea. After that, the criminal attempt was never repeated.

On the 23rd of July the *Great Eastern* was not

more than 500 miles from Newfoundland, when they telegraphed the news from Ireland of the armistice concluded between Prussia and Austria after Sadowa. On the 27th, in the midst of heavy fogs, they reached the port of Heart's Content. The enterprise was successfully terminated; and as for its first message, young America addressed old Europe in these words of wisdom so rarely understood—"Glory to God in the highest, and on earth peace, goodwill towards men."

I did not expect to find an electric cable in its primitive state, such as it was on leaving the factory. The long serpent, covered with the remains of shells, bristling with foraminiferae, was encrusted with a strong coating which served as a protection against all boring molluscs. It lay quietly sheltered from the motions of the sea, and under a pressure favorable to the transmission of the electric spark which passes from Europe to America in .32 of a second. Doubtless this cable will last for a great length of time, for they find that the gutta-percha covering is improved by the seawater. Besides, on this level, so well chosen, the cable is never so deeply submerged as to cause it to break. The *Nautilus* followed it to the lowest depth, which was more than 2212 fathoms, and there it lay without any anchorage; and then we reached the spot where the accident had taken place in 1863. The bottom of the ocean there formed a valley about 100 miles broad, in which Mont Blanc might have been placed without its summit appearing above the waves. This valley is closed at the east by a perpendicular wall more than 2000 yards high. We arrived there on the 28th of May, and the *Nautilus* was then not more than 120 miles from Ireland.

Was Captain Nemo going to land on the British Isles? No. To my great surprise he made for the south, once more coming back towards European seas. In rounding the Emerald Isle, for one instant I caught sight of Cape Clear, and the light which guides the thousands of vessels leaving Glasgow or Liverpool. An important question then arose in my mind. Did the *Nautilus* dare entangle itself in the English Channel? Ned Land, who had reappeared since we had been nearing land, did not cease to question me. How could I answer? Captain Nemo remained invisible. After having shown the Canadian a glimpse of American shores, was he going to show me the coast of France?

But the *Nautilus* was still going southward. On the 30th of May, it passed in sight of Land's End, between the extreme end of England and the Scilly Isles, which were left to starboard. If he wished to enter the English Channel he must go straight to the east. He did not do so.

During the whole of the 31st of May, the *Nautilus* described a series of circles on the water, which greatly interested me. It seemed to be seeking a spot it had some trouble in finding. At noon, Captain Nemo himself came to work the ship's log. He spoke no word to me, but seemed gloomier than ever. What could sadden him thus? Was it his proximity to European shores? Had he some recollections of his abandoned country? If not, what did he feel? Remorse or regret? For a long while this thought haunted my mind, and I had a kind of presentiment that before long chance would betray the Captain's secrets.

The next day, the 1st of June, the *Nautilus* continued the same process. It was evidently seeking some particular spot in the ocean. Captain Nemo took the sun's altitude as he had done the day before. The sea was beautiful, the sky clear. About eight miles to the east, a large vessel could be discerned on the horizon. No flag fluttered from its mast, and I could not distinguish nationality. Some minutes before the sun passed the meridian, Captain Nemo took his sextant, and watched with great attention. The perfect quiet of the water greatly helped in the operation. The *Nautilus* was motionless; it neither rolled nor pitched.

I was on the deck when the altitude was taken, and the Captain pronounced these words—"It is here."

He turned and went below. Had he seen the vessel which was changing its course and seemed to be nearing us? I could not tell. I returned to the saloon. The panels closed, I heard the hissing of the air in the reservoirs. The *Nautilus* began to sink following a vertical line, for its screw communicated no motion to it. Some minutes later it stopped at a depth of more than 420 fathoms, resting on the bottom. The luminous ceiling was darkened, then the windows were opened, and through the glass I saw the sea brilliantly illuminated by the rays of our lantern for at least half a mile round us.

I looked to the port side, and saw nothing but an immensity of quiet waters. But to starboard, on the bottom appeared a large protuberance, which at once attracted my attention. One would have thought it a ruin buried under a coating of white shells, much resembling a covering of snow. Upon examining the mass attentively, I could recognize the ever thickening form of a vessel bare of its masts, which must have sunk long ago. It certainly belonged to times past. To be thus encrusted this wreck must already be able to count many years passed at the bottom of the ocean.

What was this vessel? Why did the *Nautilus* visit its tomb? Could it have been aught but a shipwreck which had drawn it underwater? I knew not what to think, when near me in a slow voice I heard Captain Nemo say—

"At one time this ship was called the *Marseillais*. It carried seventy-four guns, and was launched in 1762. In 1778, the 13th of August, commanded by La Poype-Vertrieux, it fought boldly against the *Preston*. In 1779, on the 4th of July, it was at the taking of Granada, with the squadron of Admiral Estaing. In 1781, on the 5th of September, it took part in the battle of Comte de Grasse, in Chesapeake Bay. In 1794, the French Republic changed its name. On the 16th of April, in the same year, it joined the squadron of Villaret Joyeuse, at Brest, being entrusted with the escort of a cargo of corn coming from America, under the command of Admiral Van Stabel. On the 11th and 12th Prairial of the second year, this squadron fell in with an English vessel. Sir, today is the 13th Prairial, the 1st of June 1868. It is now seventy-four years ago, day for day on this very spot, in latitude 47⁰ 24′, longitude 17⁰ 28′, that this vessel, after fighting heroically, losing its three masts, with water in its hold, and a third of its crew disabled, chose to sink with all hands aboard rather than surrender. Nailing its colors to the poop it disappeared under the waves to the cry of 'Long live the Republic!' ''

"The *Avenger!*" I exclaimed.

"Yes, sir, the *Avenger!* A good name!" muttered Captain Nemo, crossing his arms.

Chapter 21
A Hecatomb

His way of telling this unexpected tale, the history of this patriotic ship, told at first so coldly, then the emotion with which this strange man pronounced the last words, the name of the *Avenger*, the significance of which could not escape me, all impressed itself deeply on my mind. My eyes did not leave the Captain; who, with his hand stretched out to sea, was watching with a glowing eye the glorious wreck. Perhaps I was never to know who he was, whence he came, or where he was going, but I saw the man deeply moved, and separate from the scholar. It was no common misanthropy which had enclosed Captain Nemo and his companions within the *Nautilus*, but a hatred, either

414

monstrous or sublime, which time could never weaken. Did this hatred still seek for vengeance? The future would soon teach me that. But the *Nautilus* was rising slowly to the surface of the sea, and the *Avenger* disappeared by degrees from my sight. Soon a slight rolling told me that we were in the open air. At that moment a dull boom was heard. I looked at the Captain. He did not move.

"Captain?" said I.

He did not answer. I left him and went on deck. Conseil and the Canadian were already there.

"Where did that sound come from?" I asked.

"It was a gunshot," replied Ned Land.

I looked in the direction of the vessel I had already seen. It was nearing the *Nautilus*, and we could see that it was putting on steam. It was within six miles of us.

"What is that ship, Ned?"

"By her rigging, and the height of her lower masts," said the Canadian, "I will bet she is a ship of war. May she reach us; and, if necessary, sink this cursed *Nautilus*."

"Friend Ned," replied Conseil, "what harm can it do to the *Nautilus*? Can it attack beneath the waves? Can it cannonade us at the bottom of the sea?"

"Tell me, Ned," said I, "can you recognize what country she belongs to?"

The Canadian knitted his eyebrows, dropped his eyelids, and screwed up the corners of his eyes, and for a few moments fixed a piercing look upon the vessel.

"No, sir," he replied; "I cannot tell what nation she belongs to, for she shows no colors. But I can declare she is a man-of-war, for a long pennant flutters from her mainmast.''

For a quarter of an hour we watched the ship which was steaming towards us. I could not, however, believe that she could see the *Nautilus* from that distance; and still less, that she could recognize this submarine for what it was. Soon the Canadian informed me that she was a large armored two-decker ram. A thick black smoke was pouring from her two funnels. Her closely-furled sails were stopped to her yards. She hoisted no flag at her mizzen-peak. The distance prevented us from distinguishing the colors of her pennant, which floated like a thin ribbon. She advanced rapidly. If Captain Nemo allowed her to approach, there was a chance of salvation for us.

''Sir,'' said Ned Land, ''if that vessel passes within a mile of us I shall throw myself into the sea, and I should advise you to do the same.''

I did not reply to the Canadian's suggestion, but continued watching the ship. Whether English, French, American, or Russian, she would be sure to take us aboard if we could only reach her. Presently a white smoke burst from the forepart of the vessel. Some seconds later the water, stirred by the fall of an object, splashed the stern of the *Nautilus*, and shortly afterwards a loud explosion struck my ear.

''What! They are firing at us!'' I exclaimed.

''So please you, sir,'' said Ned. ''They have recognized the unicorn, and they are firing at us.''

''But,'' I exclaimed, ''surely they can see

that there are men aboard?"

"It is, perhaps, because of that," replied Ned Land, looking at me.

A whole flood of light burst upon my mind. Doubtless the admiralties knew now how much faith to put in the stories of the sea monster. On board the *Abraham Lincoln*, when the Canadian struck it with his harpoon, no doubt Commander Farragut had recognized in the supposed narwhal a submarine vessel, more dangerous than a supernatural cetacean. Yes, it must have been so; and on every sea they now were seeking this engine of destruction. Terrible indeed! If, as we supposed, Captain Nemo employed the *Nautilus* in works of vengeance. On the night when we were imprisoned in that cell, in the midst of the Indian Ocean, had he not attacked some vessel? The man buried in the coral cemetery, had he not been a victim to the shock caused by the *Nautilus?* Yes, I repeat it, it must be so. One part of the mysterious existence of Captain Nemo had been unveiled. And, if his identity had not been recognized, at least the nations united against him were no longer hunting a chimerical creature, but a man who had vowed a deadly hatred against them. All the formidable past rose before me. Instead of meeting friends on board the approaching ship, we could expect only pitiless enemies. But the shots rattled above us. Some struck the sea and ricocheted, then were lost. But none touched the *Nautilus*. The vessel was not more than three miles away. In spite of the cannonade, Captain Nemo did not appear on deck; but, if one of the projectiles struck the hull of the

Nautilus, it would be fatal. The Canadian then said, "Sir, we must do all we can to get out of this predicament. Let us signal them. They will, perhaps, understand that we are honest folk."

Ned Land took out his handkerchief, prepared to signal with it; but he had scarcely displayed it, when he was struck down by an iron hand, and in spite of his great strength, fell upon the deck.

"Fool!" exclaimed the Captain, "do you wish to be pierced by the spur of the *Nautilus* before it is hurled on this vessel?"

Captain Nemo was terrible to hear; he was still more terrible to see. His face was deadly pale, a spasm clutched his heart. For an instant it must have ceased to beat. His pupils were fearfully contracted. He did not *speak,* he *roared,* as, with his body thrown forward, he wrung the Canadian's shoulders. Then, turning to the ship of war, whose shot rained around him, he exclaimed, with a powerful voice, "Ah, ship of an accursed nation, you know who I am! I do not need your colors to know you! Look! And I will show you mine!"

And on the forepart of the deck Captain Nemo unfurled a black flag, similar to the one he had planted at the South Pole. At that moment a shot struck the shell of the *Nautilus* obliquely, without piercing it, and, rebounding near the Captain, was lost in the sea. He shrugged his shoulders; and addressing me, said shortly, "Go below, you and your companions, go below."

"Sir," I exclaimed, "are you going to attack this vessel?"

"Sir, I am going to sink it."

"You will not do that."

"I shall do it," he replied, coldly. "And I advise you not to judge me, sir. Fate has shown you what you ought not have seen. The attack has begun; go below."

"What is this vessel?"

"You do not know? Very well! So much the better! Its nationality, at least, will be a secret to you. Go below."

We could but obey. About fifteen of the sailors surrounded the Captain, looking at the vessel nearing them with implacable hatred. One could feel that the same desire of vengeance animated every soul. I went below at the moment another projectile struck the *Nautilus*, and I heard the Captain exclaim—

"Strike, mad vessel! Shower your useless shot! And then, you will not escape the spur of the *Nautilus*. But it is not here that you shall perish! I would not have your ruins mingle with those of the *Avenger*."

I reached my room. The Captain and his lieutenant had remained on the deck. The screw was set in motion, and the *Nautilus*, moving at top speed, was soon beyond the reach of the ship's guns. The pursuit continued, but Captain Nemo contented himself with keeping his distance.

About four in the afternoon, being no longer able to contain my impatience, I went to the main ladder. The panel was open, and I ventured onto the deck. The Captain was walking up and down with an agitated step, watching the ship, which was five or six miles to leeward.

He was hunting it as if it were a wild beast. Luring it eastward, he allowed it to pursue. But he did not attack. Perhaps he still hesitated? I wished to mediate once more. But I had scarcely spoken, when Captain Nemo imposed silence, saying—

"I am the law, and I am the judge! I am the oppressed, and there is the oppressor! Through him I have lost all that I loved, cherished, and venerated,—country, wife, children, father, and mother. All I saw perish! All that I hate is there! Say no more!"

I cast a last look at the man-of-war, which was putting on steam, and rejoined Ned and Conseil.

"We will fly!" I exclaimed.

"Good!" said Ned. "What is this vessel?"

"I do not know; but whatever it is, it will be sunk before night. In any case, it is better to perish with it, than be made accomplices in a vengeance, the justice of which we cannot judge."

"That is my opinion too," said Ned Land, coolly. "Let us wait for night."

Night arrived. Deep silence reigned on board. The compass showed that the *Nautilus* had not altered course. It was on the surface, rolling slightly. My companions and I resolved to escape when the vessel should be near enough either to hear us or to see us—for the moon, which would be full in two or three days, shone brightly. Once on board the ship, if we could not prevent the blow which threatened it, we could, at least we would, do all that circumstances would allow. Several times I thought the *Nautilus* was preparing for attack; but Captain Nemo still allowed his adversary to approach, and then fled once more before him.

Part of the night passed without any incident. We watched for our chance. We spoke little, we were too much moved. Ned Land would have thrown himself into the sea, but I forced him to wait. According to my idea, the *Nautilus* would attack the ship at her waterline, and then it would not only be possible, but easy to escape.

At three in the morning, full of uneasiness, I went on deck. Captain Nemo had not left it. He was standing at the forepart near his flag, which a slight breeze displayed above his head. He did not take his eyes from the vessel. The intensity of his look seemed to attract, and fascinate, and draw it onward more surely than if he had been towing it. The moon was passing the meridian. Jupiter was rising in the east. Amid this peaceful scene of nature, sky and ocean rivaled each other in tranquility, the sea offering to the orbs of night the finest mirror they could ever have in which to reflect their image. As I thought of the deep calm of these elements, compared with all those passions brooding within the *Nautilus*, I shuddered.

The vessel was within two miles of us. It was ever nearing that electric lantern, mysterious radiance, which spelled the presence of the *Nautilus*. I could see its green and red lights, and its white lantern hanging from the large foremast. A faint vibration quivered through its rigging, showing that the boilers were heated to the uttermost. Sparks and red ashes flew from the funnels, glittering like stars.

I remained thus until six in the morning, without Captain Nemo noticing me. The ship stood about a mile and a half away from us, and with the first dawn of day the firing began afresh. The moment could not be far off when, the *Nautilus* attacking its adversary, my companions and myself should forever leave this man. I was preparing to go below to call them, when the lieutenant came on deck, accompanied by several sailors. Captain Nemo either did not, or would not, see them. Some steps were taken which might be called the signal for action. They were very simple. The iron balustrade around the deck was lowered and the lantern and pilot cages were retracted within the hull until they were flush with the deck. The long surface of the steel cigar no longer offered a single point of resistance to impede its maneuvers. I returned to the saloon. The *Nautilus* still floated; then the windows were brightened by the red streaks of the rising sun, and this dreadful day of the 2nd of June had dawned.

At five o'clock the log showed that the speed of the *Nautilus* was slackening, and I knew that it was allowing the enemy to draw nearer. Besides, the reports of the guns were louder as was the sound of the projectiles, striking the water and being extinguished.

"My friends," said I, "the moment has come. One grasp of the hand, and may God protect us!"

Ned Land was resolute, Conseil calm, myself so nervous that I knew not how to contain myself. We went into the library; but the moment I opened the door leading to the main ladder, I heard the upper panel close sharply. The Canadian rushed to the stairs. A familiar hissing noise told me that the water was running into the reservoirs, and in a few minutes the *Nautilus* was several yards beneath the surface. I understood the maneuver. It was too late to act. The *Nautilus* did not intend to strike at the impenetrable armor, but below the waterline, where the metallic covering no longer protected the ship.

We were again imprisoned, unwilling witnesses of the dreadful drama that was preparing. We had scarcely time to reflect; taking refuge in my room, we looked at each other without speaking. A deep stupor had taken hold of my mind; thought seemed to stand still. I was in that painful state of expectation preceding a dreadful report. I waited, I listened, every sense was merged in that of hearing! The speed of the *Nautilus* was accelerated. It was preparing to rush. The whole ship trembled. Suddenly I screamed. I felt the shock, but it was comparatively light. I felt the penetrating power of the steel spur. I heard rattlings and scrapings. But the *Nautilus*, carried along by its propelling power, passed through the mass of the vessel, like a needle through sailcloth!

I could stand it no longer. Mad, out of my mind, I rushed from my room into the saloon. Captain Nemo was there, mute, gloomy, implacable. He was looking through the port panel. A large mass cast a shadow on the water;

and that he might miss nothing of her agony, the *Nautilus* was going down into the abyss with her. Ten yards from me I saw the open hull through which the water was rushing with the noise of thunder, then the double line of guns and the netting. The bridge was covered with black agitated shadows.

The water was rising. The poor creatures were crowding the ratlines, clinging to the masts struggling underwater. It was a human ant-heap overtaken by the sea. Paralyzed, stiffened with anguish, my hair standing on end, eyes wide open, panting, without breath, and without voice, I too was watching! An irresistible attraction glued me to the glass! Suddenly an explosion took place. The compressed air blew up her decks, as if the magazines had caught fire. Then the unfortunate ship sank more rapidly. Her topmast, laden with victims, appeared; then her spars, bending under the weight of men; and last of all, the top of her mainmast. Then the dark mass disappeared entirely, and with it the dead crew, drawn down by the strong eddy.

I turned to Captain Nemo. That terrible avenger, archangel of hatred, was still watching. When all was over, he turned to his room, opened the door, and went in. I followed him with my eyes. Beneath the pictures of his heroes, I saw the portrait of a woman still young, with two little children. Captain Nemo looked at them for some moments, stretched his arms towards them, and kneeling down, burst into deep sobs.

Chapter 22
The Last Words of Captain Nemo

The panels had closed on the dreadful vision, but light had not returned to the saloon; all was silence and darkness with the *Nautilus*. At wonderful speed, a hundred feet beneath the water, it was leaving this terrible place. Whither was it going? To the north or south? Where was the man flying to, after such dreadful revenge? I went back to my room, where Ned and Conseil had remained silent enough. I was totally horrified by Captain Nemo. Whatever he had suffered at the hands of these men, he had no right to punish thus. He had made me, if not an accomplice, at least a witness to his vengeance. At eleven the electric light reappeared. I went into the saloon. It was deserted. I consulted the different instruments. The *Nautilus* was flying northward at the rate of twenty-five miles an hour, now on the surface, and now thirty feet below it. Taking the bearings by the chart, I saw that we were passing the mouth of the English Channel and that our course was hurrying us towards the northern seas at a frightful speed. That night we crossed two hundred leagues of the Atlantic. The shadows fell, and the sea was covered with darkness until the rising of the moon. I went to my room, but could not sleep. I was troubled with dreadful nightmares. The scene of destruction was continually before my eyes. On such a day who could tell into what part of the North Atlantic basin the *Nautilus* might take us?—still going with unaccountable speed—again going through these northern fogs. Would it touch at Spitzbergen, or on the shores of Novaya Zemlya? Should we explore those unknown seas, the White Sea, the Sea of Kara, the Gulf of Obi, the Archipelago of Liarrov, or the unknown coast of Asia? I could not say. I could no longer estimate the passing of time. The clocks had been stopped on board. It seemed, as in polar countries, that night and day no longer followed their regular course. I felt myself being drawn into that strange region where the inflamed imagination of Edgar Allan Poe roamed at will. Like the fabulous Gordon Pym, at every moment I expected to see "That inhabitant of the earth thrown across the cataract which defends the approach to the pole." I estimated (though, perhaps I may be mistaken)—I estimated this adventurous course of the *Nautilus* to have lasted fifteen or twenty days. And I know not how much longer it might have lasted, had it not been for the catastrophe which ended this voyage. Of Captain Nemo I saw nothing whatever now, nor of his lieutenant. Not a man of the crew was visible for an instant. The *Nautilus* was almost always underwater. When we came to the surface to renew the air, the panels opened and shut mechanically. There were no more marks on the planisphere. I knew not where we were. And the Canadian, too, his strength and patience at an end, appeared no more. Conseil could not draw a word from him; and fearing that, in a dreadful fit of madness, he might kill himself, watched him with constant devotion. One morning (what date it was I could not say), I had fallen into a heavy sleep towards the early hours, a sleep both painfully uneasy and distressed when I suddenly awoke. Ned Land was leaning over me saying, in a low voice, "We are going to escape."

I sat up.

"When shall we go?" I asked.

"Tomorrow night. All inspection on board the *Nautilus* seems to have ceased. All appear to be stupefied. You will be ready, sir?"

"Yes; where are we?"

"In sight of land. I took the reckoning this morning in the fog—twenty miles to the east."

"What country is it?"

"I do not know; but whatever it is, we will take refuge there."

"Yes, Ned, yes. We will go tonight, even if the sea should swallow us up."

"The sea is bad, the wind violent, but twenty miles in that light boat of the *Nautilus* does not frighten me. Unknown to the crew, I have been able to procure food and some bottles of water."

"I will follow you."

"But," continued the Canadian, "if I am surprised, I will defend myself. I will force them to kill me."

"We will die together, friend Ned."

I had made up my mind to all. The Canadian left me. I reached the deck, on which I could support myself with difficulty against the shock of the waves. The sky was threatening but, since there was land in those thick brown shadows, we must fly. I returned to the saloon, fearing and yet hoping to see Captain Nemo, wishing and not wishing to see him. What could I say to him? Could I hide the involuntary horror with which he inspired me? No. It was better that I should not meet him face to face; better to forget him. And yet—. How long seemed that day, the last that I should pass in the *Nautilus*. I remained alone. Ned Land and Conseil avoided speaking, for fear of betraying themselves. At six I dined, but I was not hungry; I forced myself to eat in spite of my distaste, so that I might not weaken myself. At half-past six Ned Land came to my room, saying, "We shall not see each other again before our departure. At ten the moon will not have risen. We will take advantage of the darkness. Come to the boat; Conseil and I will wait for you."

The Canadian went out without giving me time to answer. Wishing to verify the course of the *Nautilus*, I went to the saloon. We were running N.N.E. at frightful speed and more than fifty yards deep. I cast a last look on those wonders of nature, on the riches of art heaped up in this museum, upon the unrivaled collection destined to perish at the bottom of the sea, along with him who had made it. I wished to fix an indelible impression of it in my memory. I remained an hour thus, bathed in the light of that luminous ceiling, and passing in review those treasures shining under their glass covers. Then I returned to my room.

I dressed in stout sea clothing. I collected my notes, arranging them carefully about me. My heart beat loudly. I could not control its pulsations. Certainly my trouble and agitation would have betrayed me to Captain Nemo's eyes. What was he doing at this moment? I listened at the door of his room. I heard steps. Captain Nemo was there. He had not gone to rest. At every moment I expected to see him appear, and ask me why I wished to leave. I was constantly on the alert. My imagination magnified everything. The vision became at last so poignant, that I asked myself if it would not be better to go to the Captain's room, see him face to face and brave him with look and gesture.

It was the inspiration of a madman. Fortunately, I resisted the desire and stretched myself on my bed to quiet my bodily agitation. My nerves were somewhat calmer, but in my excited brain I saw all over again my life on board the *Nautilus*; every incident either happy or unfortunate, which had happened since my disappearance from the *Abraham Lincoln*—the submarine hunt, the Torres Straits, the savages of Papua, the running ashore, the coral cemetery, the passage of Suez, the Island of Santorin, the Cretan diver, Vigo Bay, Atlantis, the iceberg, the south pole, the imprisonment in the ice, the fight among the poulps, the storm in the Gulf Stream, the *Avenger*, and the horrible scene of the vessel sunk with all her crew. All these events passed before my eyes like scenes in a drama. Then Captain Nemo seemed to grow enormously, his features to assume superhuman proportions. He was no longer my equal, but a man of the waters, the god of the sea.

It was then half-past nine. I held my head between my hands to keep it from bursting. I closed my eyes, I would not think any longer. There was another half hour to wait, another half hour of nightmare, which might drive me mad.

At that moment I heard the distant strains of the organ, a sad harmony to an undefinable melody, the wail of a soul longing to break these earthly bonds. I listened with every sense, scarcely breathing—plunged, like Captain Nemo, in that musical ecstasy, which was drawing him in spirit to the end of life.

Then a sudden thought terrified me. Captain Nemo had left his room. He was in the saloon, which I must cross in order to escape. There I should meet him for the last time. He would see me, perhaps speak to me. A gesture of his might destroy me, a single word chain me on board.

But ten was about to strike. The moment had come for me to leave my room, and join my companions.

I must not hesitate, even if Captain Nemo himself should rise before me. I opened my door carefully; and as it turned on its hinges, it seemed to me to make a dreadful noise. Perhaps it existed only in my imagination.

I crept along the dark alleyway of the *Nautilus*, stopping at each step to quiet the beating of my heart. I reached the door of the saloon, and opened it gently. It was plunged in profound darkness. The strains of the organ sounded faintly. Captain Nemo was there. He did not see me. In the full light I do not think he would have noticed me, so entirely was he absorbed in his ecstasy.

I crept along the carpet, avoiding the slightest sound which might betray my presence. I was at least five minutes reaching the door, at the opposite side that led into the library.

I opened it, when a sigh from Captain Nemo nailed me to the spot. I knew that he was rising. I could even see him, for the light from the library came through to the saloon. He came towards me silently, with his arms crossed, gliding like a specter rather than walking. His breast was swelling with sobs; and I heard him murmur these words (the last which ever struck my ears)—

"Almighty God! Enough! Enough!"

Was it a confession of remorse which thus escaped from this man's conscience?

In desperation I rushed through the library, climbed the ladder, and following the upper flight reached the boat. I crept through the opening, which had already admitted my two companions.

"Let us go! Let us go!" I exclaimed.

"Immediately!" replied the Canadian.

The orifice in the plates of the *Nautilus* was first closed, and fastened down by means of a false key, with which Ned Land had provided himself; the opening in the boat was also closed. The Canadian began to loosen the bolts which still held us to the submarine.

Suddenly a noise within was heard. Voices were calling to each other loudly. What was the matter? Had they discovered our flight? I felt Ned Land slipping a dagger into my hand.

"Yes," I murmured, "we know how to die!"

The Canadian had stopped in his work. But one word many times repeated, a dreadful word, revealed the cause of the excitement spreading through the *Nautilus*. It was not we the crew were concerned with.

"The maelstrom! the maelstrom!" they exclaimed.

The maelstrom! Could a more dreadful word in a more dreadful situation have sounded in our ears! We were then upon the dangerous coast of Norway. Was the *Nautilus* being drawn into this gulf at the moment our boat was going to leave its sides? We knew that at the tide the pent-up waters between the islands of Ferros and Lofoten rush with irresistible violence, forming a whirlpool from which no vessel ever escapes. From every point of the horizon enormous waves were meeting, forming a deep downdraft justly called the "Navel of the Ocean," whose power of attraction extends to a distance of twelve miles. There, not only ships, but whales are sacrificed, as well as white bears from the northern regions.

It was thither that the *Nautilus*, voluntarily or involuntarily, had been run by the Captain.

The *Nautilus* was describing a spiral, the circumference of which was lessening by degrees, and the boat, still fastened to its side, was carried along with giddy speed. I felt that sickly dizziness which comes with being endlessly whirled about.

We were filled with dread. Our horror was at its height, the blood had stopped, we were covered with cold sweat, like the death sweat of final agony! And what noise surrrounded our frail bark! What roars repeated miles away by the echo! What an uproar from the waters breaking on the sharp rocks at the bottom where the hardest bodies were crushed, and trees sucked down are split forth again "with all the fur rubbed off," according to the Norwegian phrase!

What a situation to be in! We rocked frightfully. The *Nautilus* defended itself like a human being. Its steel muscles cracked. Sometimes it seemed to stand upright, and we with it!

"We must hold on," said Ned, "and look after the bolts. We may still be saved if we stick to the *Nautilus*—"

He had not finished the words, when we heard a crashing noise, the bolts gave way, and the boat, torn from its groove, was hurled like a stone from a sling into the midst of the whirlpool.

My head struck on a piece of iron, and with the violent blow, I lost all consciousness.

Chapter 23
Conclusion

Thus ends the voyage under the seas. What passed during that night—how the boat escaped from the eddies of the maelstrom—how Ned Land, Conseil, and myself ever came out of the gulf, I cannot tell.

But when I returned to consciousness, I was lying in a fisherman's hut, on the Lofoten Isles. My two companions, safe and sound, were near me, holding my hands. We embraced each other heartily.

We could not plan on returning to France immediately. The means of communication between the north of Norway and the south are few. And I am therefore obliged to wait for the steamboat which runs from Cape North.

And among the worthy people who have so kindly welcomed us, I revise my record of these adventures once more. Not a fact has been omitted, not a detail exaggerated. It is a faithful narrative of this almost incredible expedition, through an element inaccessible to man, but to which Progress will one day open the way.

Shall I be believed? I do not know. And it matters little, after all. I now affirm only that I have a right to tell of these waters under which, in less than ten months, I traveled 20,000 leagues in that submarine tour of the world, which has revealed so many wonders.

But what happened to the *Nautilus*? Did it survive the violence of the maelstrom? Does Captain Nemo still live? And does he still pursue his frightful revenge throughout the oceans of the world? Or did he stop after that last hecatomb?

Will the waves one day carry to me that manuscript containing the history of his life? Shall I ever know his name? Will we learn from the nationality of the missing man-of-war the origin of Captain Nemo?

I hope so. And I also hope that his powerful ship has conquered the sea at its most terrible, and that the *Nautilus* has survived where so many other vessels have been lost! If it be so—if Captain Nemo still inhabits his adopted country, the ocean, may hatred be appeased in that savage heart! May the contemplation of so many wonders extinguish forever the spirit of vengeance! May the judge disappear, and the philosopher continue his peaceful exploration of the sea! If his destiny be strange, it is also sublime. Have I not understood it myself? Have I not lived ten months of this extraordinary life?

And to the question asked by Ecclesiastes 3000 years ago, ''That which is far off and exceeding deep, who can find it out?'' Two men alone of all now living have the right to give an answer—CAPTAIN NEMO and MYSELF.

About the author:
Jules Verne

Jules Verne has been called the father of science fiction. As a child growing up in Nantes, France, Verne enjoyed watching the ships on the river and began dreaming of wonderful voyages. It is said that he once tried unsuccessfully to run away in a ship, and promised his parents that all his future voyages would be imaginary.

The public's growing interest in science in the mid 1800s gave Verne an eager audience. His fantastic stories of travel and exploration were an immediate success. From 1870 to 1904, Verne published Journey to the Center of the Earth, Twenty Thousand Leagues Under the Sea, Master of the World, *and* Around the World in Eighty Days. *His stories opened up a whole new genre of literature, and inspired many great scientific achievements. Many of his books were made into popular motion pictures after his death in 1905.*